BLOOD
ON THE MOON

+The Obsidian Fate+

Courtney E. Smith

Year of the Book
135 Glen Avenue
Glen Rock, PA 17327

Print ISBN: 978-1-949150-50-6
Ebook ISBN: 978-1-949150-51-3

Cover design: Jay Aheer

DEDICATION

For my Mocha Goddess.

You know what you did.
You have my love and gratitude, always.

PROLOGUE

1483 – Northern Spain

The vicious rumble of a stormy sky jolted her awake. She groaned as pain pulsed through every corner of her mind. The sudden movement in response to the sky's threatening growls sent a wave of nausea straight through her system. She forced back the foul taste of bile and focused on her breathing. It wasn't long before the first cold stabs of rain pelted her skin and she began to shiver. Each little twitch of her body awakened a new level of pain that left her dizzy. She wondered if it were possible to feel more miserable. She tried to remain still until the throbbing eased. When the nausea mostly passed, she tentatively opened her eyes.

There was nothing but absolute, terrifying darkness. She blinked several times, refusing to face the overwhelming fear that surged through her. She could feel rain on her skin and the ground beneath her. She could hear the angry sky and the rustle of leaves as the wind pulled at tree branches. An entire world surrounded her, but she saw nothing of it. Blindness was a fate she was not ready to accept. She vigorously rubbed her eyes and willed her vision to return.

After several minutes of rallying courage, she tried again. When a blurry assortment of shapes and colors flooded her vision, she released a shaky breath. It would take time, but her sight would return. She was afraid to move, worried the darkness would swarm her vision again. But she could feel the power of the storm growing. She had to find shelter. The temperature was not bitterly cold, but the chilly rain made it impossible to control the trembles coursing through her body.

She squinted as a lone ray of sunlight broke through the dark clouds. It burned her eyes, but helped sharpen her vision. The ray quickly vanished, but its existence told her night had not yet fallen. It did little to comfort her.

She turned her head and began an inspection of her surroundings. Soft blades of grass tickled her cheek. She could almost make out the individual spears sprouting from the ground. Her hazy mind was captivated by the blurry drops of water that clung to them.

Buildings took shape in the distance. Some appeared to be homes while others looked more like shops or storage holdings. Most were dark and had signs over the doors in a language she couldn't read. The few with soft flickers of firelight in the windows made her all the more aware of the chill in the air. She hoped someone would be willing to share the warmth of their fire.

The sensation of muscle cramps motivated her to move. She stretched her body and gritted her teeth against the pain. In spite of the preparation, a whimper still escaped her lips as she sat up. She wondered how long she had been laying there. Her gaze lowered in search of clues, but all she found was her naked form. Annoyance sliced through the confusion. She brought her legs into her chest and wrapped her arms protectively around them. A fleeting thought crossed her mind and she began to check herself for injuries.

Her skin was alabaster bathed in moonlight. Bruises and cuts marred the perfection, but the wounds were minor. They appeared to be a day or two old, though she didn't believe she could have been laying on the ground for an entire day without anyone noticing. Strands of hair the color of ravens cascaded down her shoulders, a striking contrast to her skin. Lean and lined with powerful muscle, she continued to violently twitch from the cold. She hugged her legs tighter in an attempt to conserve body heat. It felt as though she'd been in an intense fight, but she had no memory of it.

Before she could dwell on the thought, lightning flashed and a shimmer on the ground caught her eye. Twin daggers rested neatly on the grass beside her. Their hilts were made of black metal with twisting strands of silver embedded within. The bottom of each hilt bore an intricately crafted head of a beautiful, but deadly-looking creature.

Curious, she recognized symbols of power. They read "Frozen" and "Shadow," though the runes made more sense if combined – The Frozen Shadow. It was possible the blades were named, which would only make them more powerful.

While tempting, caution bade her to dismiss the weapons. Items of obvious power were not to be tampered with unless the user understood everything about them. She found it odd to know that. Perhaps someone had taught her the lesson. She shrugged a slender shoulder and turned away from the weapons.

A tingling prick of power skittered across the back of her neck. She glanced over and her eyes widened in shock. The blades were now emitting tendrils of thick, black fog that slithered through the rain toward her. They stopped about a foot away, frozen in place as if awaiting instruction. She should be frightened, but was instead drawn to the energy, compelled. The space around her faded like the soft light of sunset. She no longer felt the chill of the rain, nor heard the rumbling of the sky. Her entire world became the twisting shadows and the power skittering across her skin.

Trancelike, she extended her hand toward the tendrils. The energy was hers. It whispered softly in her mind. It would answer her. All she had to do was command. She wanted to feel the power flow through her. Before she could stop herself, her lips formed the language of the runes and she made her call.

The tendrils immediately responded. Her fingertips entwined with the shadows. They swarmed up her arm, danced along her skin until they hit her elbow. Fascinated, she watched as her other arm rose of its own volition. The shadows extended across her body to wrap around her other arm. As they moved down, the temperature just above her skin drastically dropped. It slowed the quick, swirling movements of the airy darkness until it froze and encased her arms in black ice.

Strangely, it wasn't cold. It felt safe, comforting. It meant her no harm. The ice was protective. She didn't struggle with the weight. It was nothing but an extension of her body. Her lips curved in pleasure.

Movement distracted her from the display. She raised her gaze to find the blades hovering in the air just above her hands. They spilled shadowy tendrils around the rest of her body. A strong sense of ownership washed through her. The blades were hers. It was time she claimed them.

Her palms turned to the sky and the daggers sailed toward her until they were floating just above the ice. Shimmering with power, they began to shrink until they were small enough to rest on her slender arms. A rectangle of ice on each arm evaporated into pure shadows, exposing the pale skin beneath. The blades lowered into the provided spaces. She could feel their weight. The runic engravings began to grow black, and the swirling shadows were drawn back into the weapons. The ice around her arms became crystal clear. The daggers transformed into black fog and sank into her skin. Her body absorbed every last drop of power.

Her head fell back. The shivers that passed through her body were no longer from the cold. Power rushed in an intense combination of pleasure and pain. It filled her completely, and she loved it. But it was too much too fast. It rapidly grew beyond her ability to control. When she could no longer contain the mounting energy, she knew she had to release it or be consumed.

The building power erupted. Sharp spikes of ice exploded in a ring around her body. She jumped at the harsh sound of shattered glass and the heavy thud of impacted wood. The intensity of power was gone as quickly as it had come and she was left floundering.

Her mind slowly returned to reality. Her headache was gone. The soreness in her muscles became a dull echo. Her body was still bruised and cut, but she felt vigorous, confident, and keenly aware. She heard the impact of rain on saturated grass. She caught the scent of a variety of animals. Her vision was acute, catching minute details she had missed before. She sensed everything rustling within the shadows, even the smallest of insects.

She became aware of her arms once again. A strange tingling traveled along the skin. She looked down to find an image of a dagger on each arm. The marks were in full color. Intrigued, she ran a fingertip over one. Despite the new additions, her skin was soft and smooth, but after a moment of exploration, both images vanished and left behind nothing but pale flesh.

She shook her head in confusion. There had to be an explanation for the whole thing. Power lingered in the air, but the only physical evidence was the damage the ice shards had inflicted upon the village. As she looked over the town, guilt rushed through her. Some of the signs had been knocked down or destroyed. Several spikes had punctured building walls. She hoped no one had been on the other side.

She hadn't meant to cause harm. The power had felt so good, so strong. She hadn't realized it could become violent. She turned away from the village, overwhelmed with the sense that she should have known how to control it. But she couldn't remember how.

The thought gave her pause. The number of things she couldn't remember seemed to be growing quickly. Dread seeped into the pit of her stomach and she struggled to recall anything prior to waking up in the rain. Her name, age, birthplace, everything was a blank. She had no memory of a home or a family who might miss her. The more she concentrated, the more her thoughts unraveled. She couldn't come up with a single detail of her life.

She used her fingertips to check her head and face for signs of injuries she may have missed the first time. She found a scrape on her forehead and some tenderness beneath her right eye, but nothing serious enough to have affected her memory. Something else must have caused the lapse. Her lack of theories only increased her anxiety.

The rain started to fall harder. Survival was more important than things she could do nothing about in the moment. She pushed her concerns aside and focused on getting out of the weather. Looking back to the village, she hoped its citizens would be willing to help her. She stood and stretched her muscles once more. The stiffness remained but the pain was gone. She reached up and rubbed the back of her neck and encountered something metallic against her skin. Weary and in no mood for more surprises, she looked down at her chest.

A black pendant about two inches in diameter rested below her collar bones. It hung from a chain made of the same silvery metal as the daggers. Small, straight lines protruded from a solid, circular center. Each of those lines had even smaller bars extending out in different directions and angles. Embedded within that center was a large cerulean stone. It shimmered when the light caught. Its beautiful design reminded her of fractured ice.

Intrigued, she lifted the pendant from her chest to inspect it further. Markings were engraved on both sides, but they were too small to read with the naked eye. It looked exotic and valuable. She didn't want to part with it; like the daggers, it seemed to belong with her. But she understood she may have to barter for clothing, food, and shelter.

She unclasped the necklace and held it in her palm to admire its beauty. She ran her thumb across the stone. She regretted having to part with such a piece. Her gaze narrowed as small black dots began to form within the vibrant stone. They soon swallowed the entire stone. Shadows radiated around it. Within seconds, darkness encased the necklace and it vanished from her hand.

Dumbfounded, she searched around her feet, but the necklace was gone. A moment later, the same impression of energy that had caressed her arms earlier skittered across her throat. She trembled, unable to deny how wonderful it felt. Ripples of shadow swirled around her neck and the necklace appeared from them. It had taken its former position against her skin and the stone regained its sapphire hue.

Irritated with the strangeness of the events, she tried removing the necklace again. The process only repeated itself. Stubbornly, she made several more attempts before finally accepting she wouldn't be trading the necklace for anything after all.

Resigned, she turned and walked to the village. Most of the buildings were completely dark, but one large structure at the center was alive with music and laughter. She heard conversation from within but didn't recognize the language. She rubbed her arms and peered inside a window.

Men, women, and children were scattered at tables and booths in what appeared to be a tavern. A wiry man wiped down the bar at the back of the room next to a door where several women hurried in and out. They carried trays laden with food and drink. Three men played instruments she had never seen to the right of the bar while several others performed a complicated dance in the middle of the room. Everyone appeared to be happy and friendly. Hoping she would find aid, she walked to the door and pulled it open.

When the patrons turned to inspect the new arrival, all playful banter ceased. A tense and awkward silence filled the air. Before she could ask for assistance, she caught her reflection in a large mirror mounted on the wall behind the bar.

A profound, classic beauty defined her features. Her cheekbones were high and the curve of her jaw was soft. She towered over every woman in the tavern, and even some of the men. But it wasn't her height or beauty that captured their attention. It was her eyes. Pure obsidian orbs stared back at her. Her gaze had no pupils or iris; only an all-consuming darkness.

No one in the tavern looked like her. Skin tones were darker and hair came in a variety of tones and styles. But not one individual in the room matched the depth of her features or the nature of her eyes. She hoped it wouldn't matter. It was obvious she was hurt and in need of assistance, but the lingering silence left her with an increasing sensation of unease.

Some stared at her with terror. They cringed as though she was a hideous creature. Others seemed to shake with rage. A lone, young child stepped forward but before he could speak, a woman roughly grabbed his arm and pulled him protectively behind her. The men began to look at one another, an unspoken exchange passing between them. Something wasn't right. She had the sudden urge to flee. Power slid across her arms and she looked down to find the images of the daggers had returned to her skin.

Everyone watched the images materialize. It seemed to entice malice into the crowd. Suddenly, one of the men jumped up. He shouted and pointed a finger at her. When the rest of the men stood and began to advance, she fled. She could hear their shouts coalescing into a garbled, continuous pulse behind her. She risked a glance back. Several large, furry, four-legged creatures pursued. Their viciously sharp teeth dripped with saliva and terrible guttural sounds erupted from their throats. She cringed and ran faster.

Instinct took over as she sprinted toward the tree line. The creatures were fast and nipped at her heels. Terror surged and she pushed herself harder. She ducked under low branches and leapt over fallen logs with an unexpected grace. It didn't take her long to figure out she was much faster than both the men and the creatures. But sharp rocks dug into her bare feet and slowed her down. Scarlet samples of blood marked her trail on the forest floor.

After what felt like an eternity of aimless running, she glanced over her shoulder. She could no longer see the men or the creatures. The incessant barking had ceased, but she could still hear movement in the woods. She could feel her hunters within the shadows. Although she moved faster, they were not far behind. The beasts must have been bred to hunt, but since she was ignorant of the method they used to stalk, she had no idea how to lose them.

She needed to find a way. She knew in her heart they meant to kill her. She leaned against a tree to catch her breath and collect her thoughts. Panic clawed at her throat. Movement caught the corner of her eye. She whirled around just in time to put her arm up to protect her face. The full weight of one of the creatures slammed into her and knocked her flat. Intense pain shot up her arm as the beast sank its teeth into her skin. She fought back a scream as the animal shook its head, attempting to break her arm and get to her throat. Thankfully, her bones were stronger than the animal's jaws.

The weight of the beast was not a problem. She tried to fling it off, but it wouldn't release her. The sense of power slid over her unburdened arm and she felt the full weight of a dagger in her hand. She didn't hesitate or question.

She drove the blade into the creature repeatedly until she felt its jaws slacken. Fresh, hot blood poured across her body. She pulled her wounded arm free from the creature's jaws and shoved the animal off her, then rolled to her feet and crouched low to listen. The high-pitched yelps of the dying creature had to have alerted her pursuers. It wouldn't be long before they located her.

When she sensed nothing close, she stood up. Blood—a mixture of her own and the beast's—slid down her body in thick, scarlet streaks. Her ears twitched at the sound of water. Hoping to confuse the other animals she grabbed the corpse by the hind legs and threw it as far as she could in the opposite direction from which she intended to travel. She ran toward the water, a pale blur in the shade of the trees.

She stopped at the bank of a small river. Swimming across would be the best way to erase most of the blood from her skin, but doing so with a blade in hand wouldn't make the trip very easy. The current was fast. She might slice herself in the process.

The moment the thought crossed her mind, the dagger evaporated back into shadows and became nothing more than an image on her arm. The weapons must have some type of connection with her thoughts to sense her immediate needs. In no position to further ponder the idea, she waded out into the river and swam across.

She pulled herself onto the river bank and took a moment to gauge her injuries. The water had washed the blood from her body. She probed the new wound with her finger and found the teeth hadn't deeply penetrated her skin. She hoped the animal's bite wasn't venomous. Blood still oozed from the bite.

Loud shouts brought her attention back across the river. The men were about three hundred yards away from the edge. She jumped up and sprinted down the bank until she reached the end of the river. A waterfall poured into a crystal blue lake. The land around her cut off in a sharp cliff. There was no slope to the bottom in sight. The cliff went further than she could see on both sides.

With a frown, she leaned over the edge and looked for a way to climb down. There were little places for hand and foot holds, but they glistened from the spray of the waterfall. Trying to maneuver down the cliff face would be slow, dangerous work. The shouting behind her grew louder and she knew time was running out. She had to choose.

She could jump and possibly die on jagged rocks, or find the lake was only ankle deep. She could run along the cliff's edge, but she would eventually tire and the hunters outnumbered her. Their beasts could track her. Unless they knew of some secret way down, jumping appeared to give her the best chance to lose them. Preferring to leave her life to fate than to experience certain death, she gathered her courage and took several steadying breaths before taking a running leap off the cliff.

Time seemed to slow. The force of the waterfall beat roughly against her skin before she finally hit the lake. Pain exploded through her body, as though she'd shattered against stone. It was several moments before she realized she was fully submerged in water and had survived the fall.

The initial shock faded to a dull throb as she swam to the surface. The mist from the waterfall blocked her view of the top of the cliff, but she knew the hunters couldn't have made it to the edge yet. She had to get out of sight. She looked around for cover of any kind and saw an opening directly behind the waterfall. She quickly swam through and found herself in the mouth of a cave.

Encouraged, she swam further in until the water was shallow enough to stand. She descended deeper into the cave and, eventually, there was no water left. She could walk on rock. Completely swallowed by darkness, she could still see every detail of the cavern.

Exhausted and terrified, she collapsed against the wall. She could no longer hear the sounds of the hunters and their creatures, but the smallest of noises startled her. She didn't dare leave the safety of the cave. The cold stone against her back, her wet hair, and the adrenaline of her escape sent her body into violent tremors. She almost felt worse than when she had awakened.

She inspected the bite on her arm. The bleeding had clotted and the agonizing pain remained, but she noted no swelling or discoloration other than what typically came with a fresh wound. She put her hand over the bite and squeezed in an attempt to keep excess dirt out. The temperature around the wound dropped and small tendrils of shadows wrapped around her forearm. Uncertain, she pulled her hand away.

The shadows froze and formed the same black ice that had appeared in the village. A thin layer pressed against the wound with the perfect amount of pressure. She never felt a chill. Ice had formed the perfect bandage.

With the injury surprisingly addressed, she pulled her knees against her chest and rubbed her arms in an attempt to find warmth. She replayed the day's events and tried to make sense of the confusing puzzle. The only reason she could find for the villager's violent reaction was her different appearance. She hadn't threatened them in any way. She could find no logical reason for their hatred. She decided to avoid their kind in the future.

That brought her focus back to herself. She was obviously capable of using ice and shadow energies, but the conscious control of the power eluded her. It gave her exactly what she needed without actively thinking about it, but the accidental damage to the village proved it needed to be restrained. She spent hours scouring her brain for any memory that would help her manipulate the energies, or for some blip of the life she had before waking. Everything was blank. At least her mind no longer felt fuzzy when she attempted to search, but the absence of answers frustrated her. Emotionally and physically drained, she laid down on the unforgiving stone and closed her eyes. Sleep overtook her within minutes.

She dreamed of war. Torn, tattered bodies littered the ground around her. She was covered in blood. Pieces of flesh and bone clung to her armor. The daggers in her hands dripped gore onto her boots. She looked around. Both the fallen and those still fighting looked like her. While they carried a certain darkness about them, their enemies seemed to be made of light. She knew she was supposed to lead them, but their objective eluded her.

The dream changed and she found herself in a great white and golden hall. Shackled to the floor at the foot of a man in ivory armor who shimmered with the same light of the enemy, she knew him, but could not recall a name or any specifics. She only knew he was important. He gazed down at her and spoke, but the words were jumbled. He seemed to know she was afraid and transformed into the massive form of the beast that had chased her in the woods. She screamed and fought her chains, but the last things she saw were the massive, sharp teeth of his gaping maw before he swallowed her whole.

She awoke with a start. Her heart raced. The taste of fear was bitter at the back of her throat. It had just been a nightmare. She struggled to recall the details, but they faded with each passing moment. She pounded her fist against the floor in anger and frustration. The skin on her knuckles broke and blood slowly began to seep through. She didn't understand why she couldn't remember anything that seemed important. She pushed herself up to sit against the wall. Her muscles were stiff from overuse and sleeping on stone.

She raised her gaze to the various rock formations in the cave and pondered her situation. It was becoming painfully obvious she wouldn't be able to retrieve her memory through sheer force of will. If a way presented itself, she would take advantage, but she refused to dwell on the memory lapse any longer. She shouldn't be the type of woman who lived in perpetual fear. In fact, she found herself irritated with the emotion. She refused to be defined by it. A new seed formed in her mind. It took root as she scrutinized her potential future. She would no longer let outside events control her reaction, or her direction. From that moment on, she would choose who she would be and how she would spend the rest of her life. She deserved much better living conditions than a damp, dirty cave.

She stood and walked toward the entrance until she was forced to swim. When the first ray of light touched her eyes, she winced and slowed her movements to a languid pace, giving her eyes time to adjust. She swam through the waterfall and out into the center of the lake. The storm had passed and she was left alone in the woods. A clean slate, a new life in a world she knew nothing about. The possibilities were endless. She could have anything she wanted. All she had to do was learn. Food and clothing were good places to start. She swam to the water's edge and strode into the forest, abandoning her fear and doubt in the silent cave.

CHAPTER ONE

2020, New York City

Lightning surged across the black sky, illuminating the angry clouds that hid the midnight moon. The thunder was so violent it shook the ground. Rain poured in waves driven horizontal by the force of the wind. But the display of Nature's fury wasn't enough to extinguish the vibrant life of New York City. People continued on in spite of the weather. They ran from buildings to taxies or buses with suitcases or bags futilely held over their heads. Nature was nothing more than an aggravating inconvenience.

But at least one entity within city limits had taken a moment to appreciate the power that pulsed above. Sitting on a Ducati at a stoplight in Times Square, Alexis Montral looked up at the unforgiving sky. While she had no direct connection with the energies of the storm, she tried never to ignore power or beauty when it presented itself. She wouldn't have taken the bike if she had known the storm was coming, but Alexis was already out in it. She let herself enjoy the challenge.

Alexis sensed the stoplight's change and resumed her crouched position over the bike. The sensual purr of its engine heightened to a growl as she throttled the Ducati through Manhattan. Her body shifted and leaned to maneuver through traffic. She took several side streets to keep the time spent on slick roads at a minimum, then made a sharp right and pulled into the safety of a parking garage. Slipping a plain, white plastic card from her jacket pocket, she pressed it to a reader on the ticket machine. The gate opened and Alexis pulled into the first reserved spot.

She pushed the kickstand down and let the bike's weight rest before silencing the engine. She swung her leg off the bike and took a quick moment to stretch her muscles. Alexis was tall, clearing six feet even without the aid of the black, calf-high riding boots that adorned her feet. Tight leather pants accentuated her lithe lower body. A black leather jacket matched the pants, but concealed her upper body.

After a quick glance at her surroundings, Alexis pulled her hand free of a Kevlar glove and ran her fingertips gently over the seat of the bike. Dark shadows spilled out of her hand in waves, contrasting with her alabaster skin. They encased the Ducati in a smoky haze. A moment later, the shadows vanished and left the bike appearing as though nothing had happened.

Alexis smiled behind the visor of her helmet. There were never any attempts at theft on her bike. The thin layer of energy coating it was enough to strike irrational fear into the heart of the average human, and it provided a clear warning to those more sensitive to power and wards.

As she slipped her glove back on, a warm energy gently pushed at the edge of her shielding. Alexis looked over her shoulder to see a man leaning against one of the concrete pillars that supported the garage. His arms were folded across his chest and he watched her intently. He was attractive, taller than her, with high cheekbones and a strong chin. A worn leather coat stretched across broad shoulders. His narrow hips filled out fitted black jeans. He hadn't been there moments before.

Hot energy simmered around him like a bomb on the verge of explosion. He was powerful, but the amount of energy that poured off him told Alexis he was mostly wild. His level of control was small and undisciplined. Alexis nodded politely to acknowledge his presence and express her wish to remain peaceful. Then, she turned her back to him and stepped out into the rain.

Alexis walked two blocks. Her pace slowed as she was forced to weave through lines of people rushing to find shelter from the rain. She stopped at a building with a single blue neon sign displaying the word "Power." Two large, well-built bouncers in matching black shirts and pants stood at the entrance, protected by the club's canopy. They both nodded in greeting and the one on the left opened the door for her.

Alexis stepped into the club. Fast-paced electronic dance music flowed from the adjacent room. The slight coat check woman smiled softly and waved. An estimate of 5'2" was generous. Alexis was sure she weighed only a hundred pounds soaking wet. Her hair was a deep crimson and her skin was pale, though a much softer shade than Alexis'. Observant, emerald eyes gave her a haunted quality. Her shoulders were always tense, as if bracing for a blow. Alexis figured she actually was, subconsciously at least.

Makeup hid the scars around her right eye and along her jaw, but Alexis knew they were there. She was pretty, but lacked the confidence to let other people see it. Her ex-husband had beaten out any light that had once been inside her. Only time would tell if she could take back what was stolen. Alexis had a soft, protective spot for her.

"Terrible night for a ride," the woman said. Her voice rang with a thick Scottish accent, though barely loud enough for Alexis to hear over the music.

Alexis reached up and opened the visor on her helmet. She closed her eyes and pulled a pair of stylish, but dense sunglasses from her face through the visor. After removing the helmet, she immediately covered her eyes with frames that rested tightly against her ocular bones. They had been custom-designed to prevent light from entering.

"I know, Liz. It started after I was already on the road."

Liz took the helmet from her and lowered her gaze. "If you'll give me a minute, I'll put this away and get you a towel."

Alexis nodded. "Much appreciated, thank you."

When her shy employee vanished, Alexis slipped out of her gloves and jacket. Liz soon returned with a small, black towel. She and Alexis made a trade and Alexis began to dry her pants.

"You're always so thoughtful. How are things?" Alexis asked.

"I... I've been thinking, maybe, about getting a puppy," Liz replied carefully.

Alexis raised a curious eyebrow as she finished drying. She had chosen a plum, fitted long-sleeve shirt. The V at the neck was deep, but tasteful. A combination of leather and silk gave her the look of elegance with a sharp edge, and the black, snowflake pendant still rested in full view against her chest. She never had found a way to take it off.

"What did your therapist say?"

"She thought a puppy would be a good addition, since I've been supporting myself for a while now." Liz peeked uncertainly up at Alexis.

"Then you should get one. Have you given any thought to a breed?" Alexis asked as she returned the towel.

"Back home I had a black Labrador. I think I might want one again."

Alexis smiled. "That sounds like a good idea. I'm proud of you."

"But..." Liz replied. Her gaze fell to the floor and she fidgeted with the towel nervously. "It's just... your building. It doesn't allow pets. I could move..." Her voice trailed away with her confidence.

Alexis understood what it had taken Liz to ask. Once upon a time, the malicious voices in her head would have told her she didn't deserve a puppy. Liz had grown a great deal during her time at Power. Alexis wasn't going to crush the hope in the woman's eyes. It came so infrequently.

"There are exceptions for service and therapy animals. Your case will fall under those rules. You may certainly have a puppy, Liz."

"Really? You don't mind? You've done so much for me already."

"I've done nothing but give you opportunities. You had to have the courage to seize them."

Even though her cheeks flushed crimson, Liz's face was alive with excitement. It suited her better than the lost, defeated look she wore most days.

"Thank you so much!"

Alexis pulled a fifty-dollar bill from her back pocket for a tip. "Don't thank me. You've more than earned it."

Alexis nodded and left Liz to tend to other customers escaping the rain.

The club was packed with glistening bodies that moved together to the strong, steady beat. The main hall had two floors illuminated by an array of colored neon laser lights that hung discreetly from the ceiling. A bar ran along the wall opposite the entrance where three bartenders kept thirsty patrons happy. A black spiral staircase in the back left corner led to the second floor.

Alexis scanned the dance floor and spotted several circulating bouncers keeping a close eye on the more inebriated customers. The right wall opened to a lounge-style room that catered to more conservative, quiet guests. That room was typically Alexis' chosen space. As she wove a path through the crowd, beckoning gestures and lusty stares followed. Alexis wasn't interested. She had seen and sampled their type more times than she could count. A quick fix had lost its appeal long ago.

She made her way into the lounge and headed straight to the bar. Alexis took a stool and leaned her elbows on the dark wood.

The bartender was a spunky blonde who couldn't have been more than twenty-five. She was already pouring a glass of the establishment's best scotch. She set it down in front of Alexis with a smile. "Hey there, gorgeous. How are you doing?"

Her voice was peppy and friendly with a southern drawl that made her stand out from the New York masses. But her upbeat attitude didn't quite hide the exhaustion in her eyes. Alexis knew she was also a full-time law student. She had to work hard to pay tuition. Alexis respected the young woman all the more for it.

"I'm well, Candice. How are classes?"

"Well, I'm not failing any of them and my professors know who I am. That's a start," Candice answered.

Alexis brought the scotch to her lips but paused as a familiar sizzle of power fluttered into the room. Alexis had suspected he would follow her. The bartender smiled over Alexis' shoulder at the newcomer. When Candice laughed and shook her head, Alexis raised an eyebrow at her.

"Don't look now, but a new guy's scoping you out pretty hard. And he's definitely not a troll. How come the new ones always go straight for you?"

Alexis set her glass down on the bar and smiled. "They don't know any better."

"Ain't that the truth."

Alexis chuckled and nodded. "A bit of advice from someone many years your elder. Being hard is always better than being soft."

Candice smirked and picked up a wet, clean glass to wipe it down. "I call your bluff, ma'am. You're no more than thirty, I bet. Five years is not 'many'."

Alexis grinned teasingly. "I'm still not telling. You have a couple behind you."

Candice looked over her shoulder and spotted the two leaning against the bar. She turned back to Alexis and shrugged with mock impatience. "I'm going to get it out of you one day. You just wait."

Alexis smirked as the bartender went to the other customers. She sipped her scotch and waited for the man from the garage. It was only a matter of time. Hunters were nothing if not predictable.

Her glass was half empty when he finally eased onto the stool next to her. His jacket was gone. A black button-up shirt covered his torso. Alexis just smiled.

Candice returned with a friendly smile and an encouraging tone. "Name your poison, sugar."

His voice was deep and carried no accent to hint at a background other than American. "Rum and coke, please."

"You're easy to please. Comin' right up," Candice replied.

Reaching for a glass, Candice glanced at Alexis, who nodded once to answer the bartender's unspoken question. Candice mixed the man's drink and set it down on the bar in front of him.

"How much do I owe you?" he asked as he reached into the pocket of his jeans.

"Oh, don't worry about it, honey. It's been taken care of," Candice replied with a wink. She refilled Alexis' glass before she left to see to other patrons.

The man looked down at the glass on the bar, but made no move to drink. "I don't need your tainted charity."

Alexis laughed. "You could just say thank you. You watched her mix it. The only poison in it is alcohol."

The man seemed to consider her for a moment before he picked up the glass and sampled the husky flavor. "Do you buy every man who sits beside you a drink?"

Alexis swirled the amber liquid in her own idly. "Only if they're interesting. Do you stalk every woman you see in a parking garage?"

A lopsided grin amplified his rugged features. "Only if they're interesting." But the grin fell away as his expression sobered. "I know what you are."

Alexis shifted in her seat to face him. She tilted her head to one side and ran a finger around the rim of her glass. "Naturally. If a hunter can't recognize his prey, he dies. But this isn't a discussion for the bar."

Alexis rose from her stool and walked to an empty booth in the back corner. She heard his footsteps behind her. His presence was heavy in the air. She gave him a small bit of credit. His power was more potent than most witches she encountered. But he either flaunted that power or could not control it. Neither was worthy of genuine respect.

She slid her body into the booth and set her glass on the table. Alexis gestured to the seat across from her and a teasing smile touched her lips. "Of course, you could sit by me. I don't bite unless you ask nicely."

He stared at her for a moment before choosing the seat opposite her. "You're awfully cocky. That's twice tonight you've turned your back to me knowing I'm a demon hunter. You're either stupid or you have a death wish."

His attitude amused her and she let it show. Alexis relaxed against the back of the booth tauntingly. He was strong, but she would beat him in the unlikely event of a public fight. She wouldn't even need her power.

"You mistake confidence for cockiness. It might do you good to consider why I wouldn't fear you."

He didn't appear amused. "I'm not some clumsy chump who thinks just because he has a little power, he can gallivant across the world and save humanity. I've faced your kind many times before and lived to tell the tale."

Alexis believed him. His only mistake had been to make her aware of his intent. She had no doubt he had faced horrors, but that didn't make him prepared for her power and skill. A smart player never flaunted her full hand.

"That sounds like a threat," she answered in a voice smooth as silk.

"It is, if your intent is to take someone home and drain them dry," he replied. He watched her expression carefully.

Alexis couldn't help herself. She laughed, loud and full. When Alexis finally settled, she grinned at him. "Your assumptions are adorable. I'll take it as a compliment that you find me attractive enough to be a succubus."

Confused by her reaction, the hunter's eyebrows raised. But it wasn't long before confusion turned to annoyance. "Shit stinks, no matter what kind it is."

"Well, aren't you a charmer?" Alexis answered before she finished her drink. Her gaze met his. Experience told Alexis he felt the weight of it, despite his inability to see beyond her reflective lenses. "Know this, little hunter: there are creatures out there who mean more harm to your precious humanity than I ever will. I suggest you focus your talents on them. If you decide to act on your subtle threat, you will find yourself face down in a gutter with just enough consciousness left to feel that other filth come and feed on your carcass."

He snickered into his glass. "Threatening me now, are you?"

Alexis picked up her glass and slid out of the booth. "I prefer to remain unseen, but if you force my hand, I will not hesitate." She paused for a moment to let the message sink in. "Don't come looking for me again."

Alexis turned and walked to the bar. She left her glass and another fifty-dollar tip. She was just outside the lounge when his hand encircled her wrist. A spark of power shot up her arm and she had to fight the urge to yank away. Instead, she let him pull her close. Her back pressed against his chest and his other arm wrapped around her waist.

He whispered softly in her ear, "Dance with me."

She chuckled and whispered back, "I try not to dance with people who want to kill me. It's just poor taste."

With the close contact, her shielding pressed against his. Their energies began to mingle without her lowering her defense. The ease with which the connection had gotten under her skin was unsettling. She felt him stiffen and knew it surprised him, too.

His power glided across her skin and blended with hers in ways she had never experienced. Her body wanted to shiver, but she refused to give him the satisfaction. Yet she couldn't deny the rush, the pleasure. His energy was hot and chaotic. It shouldn't have been able to complement the cold, dark nature of hers. But it did. The blend of power had the potential to increase the energy in them both. Alexis was intrigued, but not enough to drop her defense and willingly share.

"And I don't dance with demons. But you'll say yes anyway," he replied. His voice was just a bit breathless.

She turned her head to look over her shoulder at him. "What makes you think that?"

He laughed in her ear. "For the same reason I asked you. Curiosity."

Alexis took a moment to consider his request. It was risky. He was still dangerous. It was possible he was arrogant enough to make a public attempt on her life. The hunter didn't appear stupid, but the man was foolish enough to think he had the right to touch her without permission. In addition, the link between them existed despite her attempts to block it. The connection was tempting.

Alexis decided to play his game, but on her terms. Reaching a hand up to clasp the one he set at her waist, she took a step forward. His other hand fell from her wrist. She led him into the darkness of the dance floor.

Alexis found open space in the back corner away from the main crowd. Fewer people would be caught in the crossfire if the hunter attacked. It also gave them the illusion of privacy. Alexis put her back to a wall and turned to him. Her arms slid around his neck as his hands found her waist. When their bodies pressed together, they found the rhythm of the music and began to move.

His power washed over Alexis in waves. It heated her skin and sent tingles down her spine. She wanted more of it, more of him. The connection between them grew and pulsed. Alexis had to make a concentrated effort to keep her shielding intact and her own energy at bay. She had never felt anything quite as potent or naturally persistent as the link between them. Then she felt him shudder and her lips curved in a knowing smile.

"I think you're trying to seduce me," the hunter said. His breath caressed her ear and sent a jolt of unwanted sensation through her system. Her body's reaction to him complicated things. Her mind hadn't decided what to do with him.

She looked up and laughter escaped her. "Really? I'm certain it's the other way around."

His face went carefully blank and he raised a questioning eyebrow. A subtle tension passed through his muscles. Alexis knew she had him.

"You follow me into the club. We have a civilized conversation where we threaten each other over cocktails. Then, after I blatantly dismiss you, you ask me to dance. You are hoping this strange anomaly between us is enough for me to take you home." When the hunter remained silent, Alexis continued, "I can think of three reasons for your actions. You want to kill me when we get there and free any victims I keep chained in my basement. Or you want to learn where I live for future reference so you can come back and kill me later. Or just maybe you aren't as smart as I gave you credit for… and you actually want in my pants."

Aiden stiffened and their fluid movements came to a slow stop.

Alexis let her tone harden. "None of those options suit me, so I'll tell it to you straight. You are not that attractive and your power isn't that tempting."

"Brutal honesty is rare for a demon," the hunter replied carefully.

It was time for Alexis to go. Any further conversation wouldn't change her decision, or the evening's outcome. Alexis wasn't in the mood to commit murder.

She looked over his shoulder and let concern flush her features. Predictably, his gaze followed. With his attention diverted, Alexis let her energy consume her body and she faded into the darkness, becoming incorporeal, one with the shadows. Alexis scanned the crowd to make sure no one had seen her disappear. The hunter's body had hidden her well. No one seemed disturbed.

She watched as he turned back when he no longer felt her body against his. Puzzled, the hunter turned and scanned the crowd. He spun back around and muttered, "Fuck." Frustration carved his face and he found his way back to the lounge bar. As a creature of shadows, Alexis could move within any darkness. Where there was none, she could create it. Luckily, the club was only dimly lit.

Alexis followed the hunter and watched as he sat at the bar. Candice made her way over. A sympathetic smile marked her features. "She get away from you, honey?"

"So it would seem," he scowled.

Candice mixed another rum and coke. "Don't feel bad, sweetie. Everyone chases her. I ain't seen one yet fast enough to catch her." She set the drink in front of him. "This one's on the house."

Alexis nodded to herself as she watched Candice leave the hunter to stare down his glass. She traveled through the shadows into the privacy of her office, where she let her body return to its corporeal form. Then she exited and locked the door behind her, making her way back to the coat check.

Alexis bade Liz goodnight before stepping out into the rain. As she walked the blocks back to the garage, she wondered whether she hoped to see the hunter again. In the past months, she had grown bored. A challenge could be just what she needed. The way her power responded to his was certainly interesting. On the other hand, if she saw him again, he would likely be hunting her. If he was smart, he would bring friends.

That wouldn't leave her much choice but to kill him.

And his team.

Alexis decided to hope he stayed away. His death would be a vast waste of potential.

CHAPTER TWO

A jerk in his body woke him. The sheets were ropes around his body and drenched in cold sweat. He looked straight up, but hazel eyes didn't see the bedroom ceiling. His mind was still caught in the cobwebs of his dreams. Her smile teased him. The scent of her skin clung to his. He felt her body in his hands and echoes of her power swirled around the edges of his awareness.

When the dreams began to fade, he became aware of a dull, throbbing pain in the back of his skull. An incessant ringing only made the headache worse. He groaned and rubbed some of the grit from his eyes. The persistent tone soon chased away the lingering remnants of his nightmares.

"Fuck. What is that?" he grumbled.

He turned in the direction of the sound and found his phone vibrating across the bedside table. It took him a moment to realize the ringtone was his partner's number. He reached across the table. Weak fingers fumbled with the touch screen lock. He just barely made the call before his phone automatically sent it to voicemail.

"Thompson," he mumbled.

"Jesus Christ, Aiden! I've been trying to get hold of you for a fucking hour. You better be bleeding out in a hospital somewhere." Carley's voice slammed through the phone like a freight train.

Aiden winced and pulled the phone from his ear to rub away the pain. He could still hear his partner's voice, so Aiden hesitantly brought the phone back. "Ow, jeez. Tone it down a bit, Jameson. What time is it?"

"Six-twelve, asshole. What happened to you?"

"I had a late night," he replied.

Aiden opened his eyes a bit more when he realized he wasn't late for work. He didn't have to be there until eight-thirty. He sat up and his mind focused through the haze.

"Why are you calling, Carley?" he asked.

"Because I just had this really vivid sex dream about you and wanted to tell you all about it," she replied, her voice laced with harsh sarcasm.

21

"Aw, don't tease me like that. We both know you like your dicks made of black silicone."

"How cute. You made a strap-on joke. Now, I know you're aren't lying in a cesspool of your own vomit. Get your punk ass out of bed and get down here. Now. There's a body," Carley replied. She rattled off an address in Manhattan and hung up before he could reply.

It wasn't the first time she had hung up on him. Carley was a blunt woman. He recognized the sharpness in her tone. If Carley was that irritated, his Captain would be worse. He needed to get moving. Aiden jotted the address down in the notepad on his phone.

His room was a mess. He had no idea where his pillows were and his comforter was a waterfall of navy that spilled over the side of the bed. His clothing from the night before had been strewn around the floor, along with clothing from previous days that never made the hamper.

Aiden had stayed at the club long after the demon vanished. If she frequented the club enough to have a tab and for the staff to be familiar with her, then he would see her there again. He planned on going back and needed to be prepared.

He'd had a few drinks while memorizing the club's interior. Exits and doors were of particular interest. The club had a large storage room and at least two offices hidden out of customers' normal view. Aiden noted how many bouncers were present at any given time and the patrol patterns they followed. Next time, the demon wouldn't slip away so easily. But all his reconnaissance meant he hadn't fallen into bed until two-thirty in the morning.

Once Aiden finally slept, the demon had invaded his dreams. They spoke at length. They laughed. He enjoyed her company. She was intelligent and engaging. Her mind kept Aiden on his toes. Her body was strong. He had felt the lean muscle. She wasn't fragile. The power within him wouldn't harm her. Aiden's attraction was no surprise, even if it did conflict with his instinct and training.

But the dreams turned dark. Once the demon gained his trust, she changed. She became the twisted creature that hungered beneath her polished exterior. There was no forgiveness in her, no mercy. All that was left was her appetite for blood, pain, and chaos. The demon was ravenous and Aiden's attraction had given her the opening she needed. She fed from him and left him with gruesome images of exposed wounds and severed limbs. Phantom pain still echoed in his body. The nightmares persisted throughout the night and Aiden had gotten little actual rest.

The vivid imagery and detail made Aiden question the dream's origin. It was possible the demon could touch minds. She may have entered his and given him nightmares. If that was the case, she had bypassed Aiden's defenses with an ease no other demon had been able to duplicate. It made her even more dangerous than previously thought.

Aiden had hunted demons for eighteen years. He made his first kill when he was fourteen. Never had he come across one with the amount of power he sensed from her. This demon possessed a level of sophistication Aiden had only read about in the ancient chronicles of his clan. She was also one of the extremely rare demons that could pass for human. If she could enter Aiden's mind that easily, she had to die. No questions. No uncertainties. No mistakes.

Aiden wasn't under the delusion it would be simple. Her power still lingered on his skin. It was unique, and the way it mixed with his own had given Aiden a rush he never felt before. Dangerously compelling. Aiden wanted to feel it again, and that was one of the many factors that concerned him. He had never been so tempted by a target. If it was just her power he was up against, he might try to slay her alone. But the allure convinced him he would need assistance.

Aiden shook his head. The demon was a challenge for another time. A crime scene awaited. He lifted his arms above his head and stretched the muscles across his chest and back. Aiden packed two hundred and thirty pounds of solid muscle on a 6'5" frame. The creatures he hunted were stronger and faster than him. His magic was powerful, but his body and reflexes were still human. He needed every advantage he could get to survive. Fitness was the difference between life and death.

Aiden untangled himself from the sheets and stumbled into the bathroom. He flipped the light switch and instantly regretted it. Bright light stung his eyes. He rubbed them a bit and then forced himself to suck it up and keep moving.

He moved to the tub and set the water to frigid. Aiden didn't technically have time for a shower, but he needed to be awake and alert. Crime scenes were always dangerous, but the ones his unit dealt with were a step beyond normal homicide. A few minutes under cold water would help. Aiden stripped off his boxers and threw them into the overflowing hamper. He made a mental note to do laundry before he ran out of clean underwear.

Aiden glanced at the running water with apprehension. Cold showers were not his idea of fun, but he bit the bullet and jumped in. Water poured over his skin and washed away the evidence of the night before. It wasn't long before he began to shiver. Drowsy muscles finally awoke and he lingered only long enough for his mind to sharpen. Aiden shut off the water and jumped out to dry himself.

He moved to the sink and ran a hand over five o'clock shadow. Aiden would have to shave later. He brushed his teeth before walking stark naked back into his bedroom.

His apartment wasn't big. Aiden had one bedroom, one bathroom, and a kitchen that opened to a small living room. He lived light and didn't burden himself with unnecessary or useless possessions. If Aiden ever needed to run, he didn't want to leave a trail.

It didn't matter that Aiden protected the general public. If he was identified, he would suffer the same fate as every other creature who didn't fall under the category of "entirely human." His service as a federal officer would earn him a lifetime stay in a research prison instead of execution.

It wasn't much of a consolation prize.

No one knew what actually happened in the prisons. The government stated it was looking to "cure" the "diseased." It didn't matter that most of them were a separate species entirely. Those who went into the prisons never came back out. Aiden didn't agree with it, but he did believe in protecting the innocent. It's why he became a cop, despite personal risk. He could put away those who gave the magical community a bad name while keeping the innocents out of prison. It also meant he could hunt a substantial portion of the demons he encountered legally and with more resources.

Aiden dressed in black slacks and a plain, white dress shirt. He slid a leather belt through the belt loops and knotted a black tie around his throat. Dress shoes were a waste for field work. He went straight for a pair of black sneakers. They were less expensive to replace if they happened to get ruined at a crime scene. No one would ever accuse him of being fashionably sensible. Aiden slipped his wallet into his back pocket and his badge inside his coat. He picked his standard issue side arm up from his dresser and attached the holster to his belt. It was the only gun Aiden kept out of the large weapon safe beside his bed. He grabbed his phone and walked to the bathroom. A glance in the mirror told him he was presentable. He checked to make sure he wasn't forgetting anything before making his way to the living room.

Aiden picked up his keys from the corner of his desk and walked out. He secured both the lock and the deadbolt. Magical wards protected his apartment, so he rarely worried about intruders. The deadbolt was more of a trained habit than any actual protection. He jogged down four flights of stairs and pushed through the front door of his building.

The autumn air sent a breeze against any exposed skin. To most, it would have been cold. But the nature of Aiden's power was hot and it warmed him from within. He could call fire and air. Aiden was not a conjurer, so he couldn't produce something from nothing, but he could manipulate them if they were present.

Aiden paused a moment and looked to the morning sky. It was still dark, but a thick cloud cover lingered over the city. The previous night's storm still stirred. It would be back in full force by the end of the day. The power pulled at him, tempted him to open himself and let the energy flow.

He looked away and jogged down the street where his Honda was parked. It wasn't the time to answer a call of power. Aiden had to shut that side of himself down completely to avoid detection at his job. It had taken time and practice to be able to trick the computer sensors. The last thing Aiden needed before going to a crime scene was a boost. He opened the driver's side door and slipped inside.

In the city that never slept, there was always traffic. It took Aiden forty-five minutes to get to the address Carley had given him. Skyline Publishing was a large business building with an underground garage. Uniformed officers surrounded the entrance, along with vehicles for the medical examiner and crime scene technicians. Aiden pulled up to the yellow tape and a uniform stepped to him. He rolled down his window and displayed his badge.

"Detective Thompson, FDPC."

The cop looked young. Aiden bet he was fresh from the academy. There was a hint of excitement and hopefulness in his eyes. All of that would die out when the kid got his first glimpse of the kind of bodies the unit dealt with. The Federal Department of Paranormal Containment was called in for crimes committed by non-humans. The scenes were always horrific. Someday soon, the officer would have his first look into the face of darkness and decide if his sanity could take looking into the abyss day in and day out.

"Yes, sir. Detective Jameson is already inside. If you'll park in the open space down the street, you'll be able to go straight down into the garage. I'm sure you'll see everyone down there," the uniform said as he gestured to the parking space.

"Thanks," Aiden replied and rolled up the window to park in the designated spot.

He killed the engine and stepped out, locking the door behind him. Aiden made his way to the entrance of the underground garage where several officers were stationed to ensure no unauthorized personnel made it down. He flashed his badge and slipped between them.

As he descended, Aiden could feel a thick layer of power covering the entire level. He shivered as it latched onto his skin. It pressed against him in viscous folds, as if he were neck deep in a pool of tar. The pure potency of the energy almost choked him. Aiden was forced to bring some of his own power to the surface to shield himself. The energy tasted demonic and he found it unsettling to encounter evidence of two extremely powerful demons in less than twenty-four hours.

Beneath the heavy weight of power was a very subtle, weak hum of energy. It was a challenge to distinguish it from the thick pool, but there was a distinct difference in tone. Someone had warded the garage, but the ward wasn't strong enough to keep the oppressive energy out. Either the person responsible for creating the ward wasn't powerful or the ward itself hadn't been designed to keep magic out.

Aiden's instincts flared to life as he scanned the path to the scene. Not a single drop of blood. Even the technicians who scurried around the surrounding area were squeaky clean. Killings committed by demons were never neat. In fact, they were hard to stomach. It was as if demons enjoyed seeing how big a mess they could make from any creature unlucky enough to cross their path. Demons didn't discriminate. Aiden hadn't seen the full scene yet, but something wasn't right.

The majority of people were concentrated in the back right corner. Aiden recognized most of them, but there was always a new person or two running around. He was surprised to see his Captain. Devant's presence on the scene so early meant the case had already gotten the attention of the offices in Washington. It only made the red tape thicker.

Aiden scanned the crowd for his partner. At 5'3", Carley often got lost in the sea of people. When he couldn't put eyes on her, Aiden switched his focus and listened instead. It wasn't long before he heard her voice. Carley may have been small, but her presence towered over lesser beings.

Carley Jameson had short, brunette locks she often styled to accent her sharp features. Despite her stature, she was strong. Her ability to best most of the men in the unit was a testament to both grit and intelligence. Carley's victories never made her arrogant. Aiden knew Carley was aware of her limitations.

Aiden followed the sound of her voice. A wall of people blocked his view, so he stepped forward and pushed through. His eyes widened when he saw what was on the other side. His stomach tensed and lurched once before his mind shut his body down. Aiden went cold. The body ceased to be a person, but pieces to a puzzle, the key to finding his prey. If he thought of the body as an individual, he would lose whatever was left from his dinner in the nearest trash can.

Carley was crouched beside the most oddly positioned set of limbs he had ever seen. Douglas Reed, the medical examiner, was with her. He gestured to different things across the scene. Aiden took the time to study it for himself. It was always better to get his own ideas before he let someone else's opinion filter in. He often knew more than they did and there were things he needed to keep to himself to protect potential innocents, like whoever had warded the garage.

Human arms and legs had been severed from a torso. They appeared male, given the musculature and hair. The extremities had been cut cleanly. No tattered edges or marks for teeth or claws marred the limbs. It looked to be the work of a very sharp blade.

Each limb had been bent and broken in a way that left them entirely straight. The ankle bones had been crushed so the feet pointed dramatically. The knees were bent backward to take the curve out of them. The legs were arranged vertically with one foot pointing north and the other south. The arms mirrored the state of the legs, though one faced east and the other west. Eight fingers had been removed from the hands and broken in a similar nature to the limbs. Each limb had two fingers resting perpendicular to the limbs at opposing angles. All of the severed parts formed a circle, like a clock or compass. In the middle was a perfect crimson sphere about the size of a basketball.

Aiden bet the sphere had been formed from all the blood in the body. The limbs were extremely pale and the severed ends showed no signs of oozing. The sphere explained why there was no blood across the rest of the garage. Something had completely drained the body before taking the time to disfigure and position the limbs. It also explained the nature of the power crawling over him. Blood manipulation was rare and frightening. It meant the killer could end a life with even the smallest cut.

The rest of the body wasn't in the immediate area of the limbs, so he looked around the remainder of the scene. The leftover pieces were piled in the corner, shredded. Small bits of fat and sinew were mixed with larger pieces of bone and organs the monster hadn't had time to destroy. There was no distinguishable head, no chunks of flesh large enough to be labeled properly. It was a pile of ground meat and there wasn't a mortician in the world who could put it back together.

Something caught Aiden's eye and he shifted his gaze to the wall immediately behind the arrangement of limbs. His eyes narrowed instantly and a twinge of cold fear stabbed his gut. A message written in strange, complex runes painted the gray concrete crimson. The writing was done in blood, though the blood was in the same crystallized form as the sphere. There were no running trails. The only reason Aiden was certain was the magic in the air.

It was the language that interested him most. Aiden had only ever seen it once and, even then, it had only been two runes. It wasn't something a man forgot. The message confirmed his belief the killer was demonic. There were five entire lines of text displayed on the wall. The murderer was talking to someone. Lesser demons were like beasts. They fed and killed randomly, mindlessly. They had an appetite for chaos and destruction. It made them difficult to track because there was no pattern to their attacks, but they always left a trail and could typically be baited.

The demon responsible for this scene was vastly more powerful. It wasn't clear if he was being controlled by a summoner, but he was intelligent and capable of communication. Aiden had only come across two that displayed that level of intelligence. He tilted his head and corrected himself. *Three.* The demon from the previous night fell into the category. Aiden sighed. The day promised to be long. He turned his attention back to his partner and began to listen to what she was saying.

"So, what could have enough strength to break bone this precisely? It's fucking meticulous. The strength and control to splinter bone but not completely snap it is almost inconceivable," Carley said.

Douglas Reed was in his early fifties. His hair was neatly clipped and there was a substantial amount of gray mixed in with brown. He was a shorter man with a thin, wiry frame that matched his hollow features. Large glasses rested on his pointy nose. While Reed lacked the physical prowess to pursue suspects, he was completely brilliant and crucial in the background.

His voice was a bit shaky when he spoke. "Most diseased individuals have the strength to do this. A vampire or were-animal, for example, would have the strength to break almost all known metals. The control, however, is another matter."

Carley shook her head. Her sharp and stormy eyes swept across the scene. "A vampire wouldn't have left the blood behind, and I'm fairly certain they can't manipulate it in this fashion. I've never seen it, at least. A were-animal would have eaten that mess," she gestured to the chunks behind her. "My gut says it's a demon, but we can't say for sure without Aiden and a transient field detector. He's the demon expert. This isn't a typical scene a demon would leave."

"Perhaps the security videos will help. When I get back to the lab, I'll look in the database and compile a list of potential creatures for you," Reed replied as he pushed his glasses further up his nose.

"Carley's right. It's demonic," Aiden finally said.

Carley looked up immediately and narrowed her gaze. "It's about fucking time. Did you get stuck in the toilet or something?"

"Save it, Jameson. You don't get yours until I get mine," Captain Devant said as he stepped through the crowd. "I'm more interested in what Detective Thompson thinks he knows. After all, he did get more beauty sleep than the rest of us." His disapproving gaze slammed into Aiden.

Carley's expression sobered and she stood up with the coroner. They both took a step back to provide Aiden with the room to maneuver around the scene.

"What did this was no garden variety diseased psycho," Aiden said. He flashed Carley the cocky, teasing smile he saved just to irritate her.

"If that's the best you got, I swear, I'm going to kick you in the balls," Carley answered. She made sure to plaster a sweet and innocent expression across her features.

Aiden gave her credit. Not many could pull off the face when they were elbow deep in chopped up bits of human flesh.

Devant's voice sliced between them like a knife. It was cold, demanding, and it brought silence to the entire garage. "Enough. I don't have time for this bullshit. If you both were not so damned good at your jobs, I'd have kicked your asses to the curb long ago. I'm out of patience with you, Thompson. You have two minutes to spit out a viable theory."

Aiden cleared his throat and began to walk around the body as he cautiously replied, "Way to put me on the spot, Captain."

Devant's expression didn't change. "That's what you get for being late. Again."

Aiden studied Devant for a moment. He was a hard, but fair man. As tall as Aiden, thirty years of crime scene experience had taken their toll. His midsection had grown a little soft and there was a strain in his cerulean eyes. Aiden knew people higher up in the chain of command were putting pressure on him. That was enough to make anyone cranky.

He hurried to his thoughts on the scene. "I agree with Carley. It's demonic."

Carley stepped forward and her gray eyes found Aiden's. "Demons work like a combination of zombies and starved were-animals. Minimal thought process. They kill to eat or to fill the need for destruction. This is clearly deliberate."

"And yet, you still identified it correctly," Aiden said. "All the basic elements of a demonic killing are here. There are just some wild cards. Lesser demons run around like rabid dogs. They accidentally find their way to our plane through holes left by unskilled summoners. What did this was not lesser. The higher up the demonic food chain you are, the smarter and stronger you have to be. You have to be powerful enough to ignore the call of a summoner, though there are some capable of calling high demons."

"So, you're saying this isn't a demonic animal, but an individual person?" Carley asked.

"A summoner could have done this, in which case we would be looking for a person and not the demon, yes. But it is also possible that a higher demon came here for his or her own reasons. Regardless, someone is talking to somebody. The demon set this up. The message on the wall makes this scene entirely unique."

A very obese and greasy man raised his chubby hand. Those unfortunate enough to be standing next to him caught a slight stench of body odor. "Detective, I'm Gary Finch, the language expert for the department. I've seen and translated most forms of written language the diseased use to communicate, but I've never come across anything like that."

Aiden nodded once in confirmation. "That's because this particular language is almost never seen and what uses it is not a diseased individual as we think of it. A demon is not diseased. They are a separate race. The runes on the wall are a rare gem. The only reason I even recognize them is because I've seen them before. Only two words that went alongside a particularly violent crime. What we have here is five lines of written demonic text."

"If they have a language, why wouldn't they use it more?" Devant asked.

"Demons have no reason to leave messages. The lesser ones are incapable of it and the more powerful ones know better. Either a summoner forced this demon or there is something more to this scene. It's very hard to say for sure since I can't read the language."

Carley seemed to think on his words. Aiden folded his arms across his chest and watched her mind work. She was pale. He could see her fight the same sickness that had bile in the back of his throat. While it was mostly forgivable for rookies to vomit at paranormal scenes, provided it wasn't on evidence, Carley would never have the luxury. She was a very attractive woman who didn't hide she was gay. She had to be better than the rest to survive in her career path, let alone succeed. Aiden respected her all the more for it.

"Do you know of anyone who can translate it? Our department linguist has already stated he's useless," Carley asked.

Aiden stiffened. He did know of someone who might be able to decrypt the message, but he refused to let the rest of the FDPC near the man. The retired hunter had done too much. He was haunted and stopped trying to hide it several years ago. The FDPC would squeeze every last drop of information from him, even if that would finish driving him insane. Aiden had no intention of subjecting a veteran to that.

"I do not. Maybe we will get lucky with the database. Perhaps others across the country have encountered it," he replied.

"Alright. That will mostly be a dead end, I suspect. Let's look back at the body," Carley said. "What we have is a higher demon that is as intelligent as a human. He takes the pieces he needs from the body to make a message to someone. Why shred the rest? Is he knowledgeable enough to know we won't be able to get much evidence from that pile of slop back there?"

"I think he is smart enough to know destroying a body in that fashion would make him more difficult to trace, but I doubt that was his primary motivation. Demons have a savage nature. The need to cause pain and chaos burns in them like a vampire's thirst. If there is no other victim, they have no problem turning on each other. Their strength or intelligence does not matter. The need is the same. They all succumb to it eventually. This body was shredded to sate that need."

Carley fell silent for a moment and returned her gaze to the arrangement on the floor. She tilted her head curiously and looked back up to the writing on the wall. "Could the body parts here also be a symbol?"

Aiden hadn't thought of that. He stepped back to get a better view of the limbs. Though they didn't have the same shapes or lines of the runes drawn on the wall, Aiden couldn't deny the body seemed to assume a symbolic tone. He raised an eyebrow and shrugged.

"It could, yeah. A representation of something, perhaps. Or, it could be ritualistic."

"If it was a ritual, there would still be traces of energy here. A transient field detector should pick it up. I've been asking for that damned thing for an hour," Carley said.

The detector would help. It measured the tetrabind waves in the air, which were a byproduct of magic use. However, Aiden wasn't sure he wanted to encourage the haste of the technician and the machine. He was using magic to shield himself. While he used shielding to pass through the machine for cleanings often, the machine could pick him up if he was careless.

The scanner might also pick up the wards in the garage. Since Aiden wasn't sure whether the person responsible for those wards had anything to do with the murder, he was loathe to bring in a machine that couldn't distinguish between harmful and helpful types of energy. Aiden weighed the danger to himself and a caster he did not know against the need to find the demon.

"It should, yes. I was just wondering why it wasn't already down here. We might be able to learn what type of energy he uses and track him by it." Aiden planned on staying as far away from the machine as he could get.

Captain Devant came up behind Aiden and slapped him harshly across the shoulder. "A workable theory, Thompson. But it doesn't excuse you from being chronically late. Fix your damned alarm clock."

"Thank you, Captain. I'll be sure to."

Aiden felt the weight of his partner's gaze on him and shifted his attention to her. Carley gave him a look Aiden recognized. It was the one she got when she sank her teeth into something and wouldn't let go. It made him want to squirm. Carley always seemed to know when he was holding something back. It was unnerving.

Aiden hoped she continued to keep her nose out of his business. Carley was like his sister, but that would change the moment she acted on whatever thoughts were running through her mind. Aiden would never hurt her, but he wouldn't offer himself over to research, either. He flashed his most charming smile in hopes of disarming her. It seemed to work. Carley grinned back at him and the calculating gaze disappeared. Aiden was safe, for the moment.

The subtle sound of vibration touched Aiden's ears and his head snapped in that direction. It was a trained reaction. His gaze landed on the breast pocket of his Captain's coat just as Devant reached in to pull out the phone. He pressed it to his ear and nodded once, as if the person on the other end could see him.

"I'm sending Thompson and Jameson up to you." Devant ended the call and looked to Carley and Aiden. "The owner of both the building and the business is here. If you two are finished, I'll have the squad start breaking it down."

Aiden nodded once. "I've seen enough to get started, but I'll need the complete scene file immediately. That includes all images taken, not just some of them. I don't care if there are twenty flash drives full of shit. I need everything."

Devant nodded in acknowledgment. "There will be no bureaucratic bullshit on this one, Aiden. Brass wants this fucker put down ASAP. Something tells me this isn't going to be a single occurrence."

"No. It won't be, and it's going to take us too many bodies to figure it out. Jameson, are you done?" Aiden asked.

"Yeah, I'm done. I've been staring at it longer than you, asshole," Carley replied.

Aiden smirked and they walked halfway up to the entrance to wait for the owner. With the media outside, they wouldn't be able to converse out in the open. The rest of the building was still being secured. Being in the garage and out of sight would have to suffice for the interview.

The distinct sound of high heels echoed through the garage. It was a fast, professional pace.

Carley closed her eyes and a large, predatory grin curved her lips. "That, my friend, is the sound of Manolo Blahniks. It's utterly feminine and insanely sensual. You should take a moment to savor it."

Aiden grinned. "You're such a player."

Aiden knew Carley was trying to lighten the mood and steer their thoughts away from what they had just seen. She made him smile, even when they both knew they were not done looking at death for the day. But Aiden's entertainment was short-lived as a familiar power skimmed across his shields.

"No fucking way," he whispered to himself.

Flanked by two uniformed officers was the demon from his dreams. In heels.

CHAPTER THREE

Aiden first noted the demon had changed fashion. A black A-line skirt accented her form without flaunting. A cerulean blouse stood out against a tailored black jacket. Her dark tresses were down and straight, and the sunglasses she wore had different frames. The repetitive use of reflective lenses told him her eyes were not human. Aiden was sure she had well-practiced excuses for why she never removed the glasses.

Even in lace instead of leather, the demon was striking. But her presence wasn't a coincidence. A demonic killing in a different demon's territory was curious, though the fact that she had territory at all was strange.

"You must be the owner. I'm Detective Jameson," Carley said as she offered her hand.

"Alexis Montral. It's a pleasure, Detective, circumstances notwithstanding." Alexis smiled as she took Jameson's hand.

"This is my partner, Detective Thompson."

Aiden could sense the moment their eyes connected. He knew she recognized him, but no surprise registered in her expression. It seemed she planned to pretend they had never met, which suited him. But she did study him intently and offered her hand.

Aiden took it without hesitation and was grateful his tight shielding kept her power at bay. The last thing he needed was another accidental connection.

"Do you know who the victim is, Detectives?" Alexis asked.

"How would you know there is a victim?" Carley asked. She watched Montral's expression as she reached into her pocket and pulled out a small pen and notebook.

Aiden knew the answer. The wards placed in the garage were hers. When he focused on them, he could sense her subtle touch. But he was interested in her answer, so he remained silent.

Alexis flashed the smile of a woman used to being in charge. Aiden caught a flicker of heat in his partner's gaze. There and gone in less than a moment.

Aiden couldn't blame her when his own gut twisted. Montral was not the average beautiful woman.

"Well, Detective, all of the personnel you have down here and the lengths you have gone to block traffic outside would lead anyone to believe there is a victim. However, my security company contacted me after they called you. I actually received their call before yours. I will gladly submit my phone records," Alexis replied. She pulled something that looked more like a small computer than a smartphone from her pocket. Despite the ever-growing power of technology, Aiden still didn't recognize the brand.

"We appreciate it, ma'am. We have not identified the body," Carley said.

"Perhaps I can help you with that. I have both night maintenance and security on staff. I can pull employee lists and time clock reports. Perhaps someone didn't clock out or in. If it's not any of my people, you'll at least have a list of those who had my authorization to be in the building." Alexis began typing as if she knew they wouldn't refuse.

"You can access all that from your phone?" Carley asked, studying the device in Montral's hands.

Alexis paused and looked up at Carley, amused. "I can access anything I wish from my phone. It's a prototype and the operating system was designed to interface directly with my business networks."

Alexis pulled a small flash drive from her jacket pocket and inserted it into the bottom of the phone. After a brief moment, she pulled it back out and offered it to Jameson.

"Here is the information."

Carley accepted the drive and slipped it in her pocket. "This will help, thank you."

"Where were you last night, Ms. Montral?" Aiden asked. He kept his tone as flat as possible.

"I'm a busy woman, Detective. What time are you interested in?" Alexis asked. The calm, professional serenity never faltered.

There was something about the subtle hint of teasing beneath her crisp demeanor. She was baiting him. Aiden was in no mood for games. But it occurred to him he didn't know the time of death. He looked to Jameson, but found no help in her blank expression. The state of the body must have given the medical examiner difficulty. Aiden wondered if Alexis knew the time of death. Her wards should have told her, but the weakness of them was peculiar.

Either she wasn't as powerful as he believed, or the killer had put up some kind of interference.

He'd bet on the latter.

"All night, if you please," Aiden replied.

"I left my central office here around seven. I drove straight from there to Le Bernardin for a business dinner with Lydia Cardone. She is the CEO of my company Miracore. She handles the software and hardware needs of my businesses. I arrived around seven-thirty and left around nine forty-five. I went home alone to shower and change. I arrived around ten-fifteen and left around eleven. From there, I drove to a club called Power. Arrived around eleven-thirty and stayed for about an hour. I went straight home alone and went to bed. I'm sure personnel at each establishment will verify my presence, but I can do nothing about the times I was home alone. I don't live with anyone and I'm doubtful my personal security records will hold much weight, considering I have full access to them. Am I a suspect?"

"Not yet, Ms. Montral, but I would like the security records, regardless," Carley answered.

Aiden glanced at Carley. He had wanted to keep the pressure on Montral. He knew she didn't commit the murder; the power in the air wasn't hers. A public kill in her own garage seemed below her intelligence, but Aiden was sure she was involved in some fashion.

Montral played human very well. No one would believe she was physically capable of producing such a crime scene—which was why Carley had already ruled her out. The logic behind his partner's assumption didn't make him any less annoyed. He wanted Montral to feel a little heat.

"It's not sunny down here, or outside. Is there a reason you're wearing sunglasses?" he asked.

"A medical condition, Detective. I have albinism. The color of my eyes disturbs most people and I'm exceedingly sensitive to the light. Unfortunately, sunglasses are a mandatory accessory to my attire. I fail to see what that has to do with the matter at hand."

Aiden was about to reply when a loud noise, followed by several curses echoed through the garage. Both he and Carley looked back toward the scene. People were rushing to it.

"Damn it," Carley muttered before she glanced at Aiden.

He sighed and they both jogged back to the scene.

The staff cleared a path for them. When Aiden's gaze searched for what had changed, he immediately noticed a large diamond-shaped crack in the center of the blood sphere. Douglas Reed was crouched over the ball shaking his head in disbelief.

Carley's sharp, accusatory tongue voiced his own thoughts perfectly. "What the hell did you do to my evidence?"

Used to Jameson's rash tones, Reed calmly answered, "I was attempting to get preliminary measurements for the internal content of the sphere. It would have made a bit less work for me in the lab. It cracked before I could even touch it."

Aiden felt the caress of Montral's power at his back and swore under his breath. He couldn't believe the two uniforms were careless enough to allow a civilian access to the scene. He turned to escort her away, but the look on her face stopped him. She stared at the message on the wall with an intensity that sent chills down his spine. To the average eye, Montral was frozen in shock or fear. Aiden wasn't fooled. She was surprised and could read the message. But he couldn't openly ask her about it, so he stepped in front of her to block the view.

"You shouldn't be here, Ms. Montral. Where are the officers who escorted you?" he said softly. Her attention returned to him and he watched a small shiver pass through her.

"They went running with you. Move your team away, Thompson," she whispered.

It was then he noticed the pressure that had been constantly plaguing him was gone. All that remained was the quiet pulse of Montral's wards. Aiden glanced at his partner and found Carley's eyes wide. He turned back to the sphere to see a column of red light splinter out from the crack. He knew Alexis was right.

"Get back! Everyone, get back now!" he yelled, but he was too late.

More splinters rained down from the crack and Aiden had just enough time to run to Reed and shield him before the sphere exploded. The force felt like a thousand knives ripping into his back. Sticky crimson fluid splattered across the garage and coated everyone within the vicinity. He could feel the warmth of blood as it oozed down the back of his neck. He looked up to the wall in time to see the message turn to liquid and drip until there was nothing left but streaks.

Officers ran in different directions, taking turns emptying their stomachs in metal trash cans strategically placed around the garage. When Reed shifted a bit, Aiden looked down to make sure the man was still okay. When he appeared fine, Aiden realized they hadn't been thrown by the force of the explosion. He wondered if he had just felt what remained of the power dissipating.

"You okay?" he asked.

When Reed merely nodded, Aiden turned to find Carley. She was shielding one of the newer technicians. She stood up and a haunted look moved across her face when she looked down at herself. He recognized the battle within her because he was fighting it himself. He wouldn't puke if she didn't. He was relieved when she immediately tried to lighten the mood.

"Great. Now the dry cleaners will think I've completely lost my shit. They already believe I'm a serial killer with a badge."

"There isn't a cleaner in the world who can save your outfit, Detective," Alexis said. The disgust in her voice caused them both to look at her.

Alexis was soaked. As she removed her jacket, blood dripped off the tips of her raven tresses and tainted the soft blue of her shirt. She should be alarmed something powerful enough to create and destroy the sphere was challenging her. But she stood poised and stared bitterly down at her ruined Armani. He had a feeling the disgust on her face was for the benefit of his peers.

"How did you even get here?" Carley asked.

"Jameson! Thompson! Get your asses over here now!"

Aiden cringed at the fury in Devant's voice. He looked at Carley to see if she wanted to be first in line, but she was still studying Montral. In that moment, Aiden knew Carley suspected Montral was more than she appeared. He couldn't decide if he was relieved or scared. Jameson had good instincts and followed them like a hound, but if she sniffed too close, the demon might take action to protect herself.

To distract her, Aiden punched Carley's shoulder lightly. "Come on, half pint. The boss is barking."

Carley glanced over her shoulder at Devant before looking back at Aiden. "After you. He'll drag the first one of us he sees through barbed wire. I've dealt with it all morning. It's your turn."

Aiden sighed. Fair was fair. He turned to Devant and walked forward, meeting the Captain's eyes. Stress poured off the man in waves. Aiden knew he was doing his best not to take it out on others, but an exploding crime scene may have pushed the limits of his patience.

"Captain," Aiden said.

"What the fuck just happened?!" Devant demanded.

"I'm not entirely sure," Aiden replied.

It wasn't a complete lie. He didn't know how Montral's power may have affected the scene. He also didn't fully understand the nature of the killer's power. But he did know and understand more about the scene than he was willing to say.

The look in Devant's eyes told Aiden the man knew he was holding back. Devant may have gone a little soft in the middle from age and time behind a desk, but his mind was still razor sharp. Aiden didn't want to press his luck. He now had two demons to hunt, but he could only use police resources for one. He had to be careful about what information he fed the Captain.

"You don't know?" Devant asked as he took a step closer. "Why don't I believe you?"

"I'm not sure, Captain, but I'm not lying. I have a weak theory, but I can't give you a solid run-down of the events here," Aiden answered.

"Then cough it up, smart ass. A theory is better than nothing and I don't have all fucking day."

"All I've got is that there was a residual energy holding the sphere together. It's possible that energy wasn't sustainable and it faded, causing the sphere to explode. But I would think, if that were the case, the sphere would have just melted or slowly fallen apart. The other possibility is something triggered the residual energy and caused it to explode. If that's the case, it's more likely the killer planned it. Given the intelligence of our target, that's a viable possibility."

"I find it difficult to believe something small enough to slip past our perimeter detectors could trigger something this big," Carley chimed in.

"Is it possible this thing set a trap for us?" Devant asked.

"It's either the loss of power that was holding the scene together, a trap, or a demon's idea of a joke. I mean, we're all covered in blood, but I didn't notice anyone injured," Aiden replied.

Devant's face was flat but his voice was a borderline growl. "A joke... A demon with a sense of humor? That's fucking brilliant."

"I don't know what else it could be, Captain. If it were a trap, you'd think he would've set it to cause more damage. I wish I knew a method to determine what actually happened. We will have to go in expecting something similar in the future."

"I hate to be a distraction to your squad, Captain. However, I am covered in your evidence and to say the experience is unsettling is a gross understatement. What would you have me do?"

All three officers turned to look at Alexis. A ring of blood now surrounded her expensive shoes from where it had dripped off her clothing. Her arms were folded across her chest with one hand protruding to the side to suspend her drenched jacket in her fingertips. It was clear she was doing her best to touch nothing.

"You're holding up remarkably well for a woman who has never been around bloody murders, Ms. Montral."

"Tell me, Detective Jameson, why is it you have not succumbed to the panic several of your fellow officers have? If you say it's from experience, I will call you a liar. I'm fairly certain no amount of experience prepares one for something of this nature," Alexis replied in an infuriatingly reasonable tone.

Aiden watched Carley's suspicious expression change to surprise. He knew Montral's insight had just scored her points. It also deflected the probe into the possibility that she had seen plenty of death before. Montral played the game very well.

"Because I'm a girl playing with the boys and I have to be better," Carley answered.

"Precisely. Would it help any of you solve this crime if I fell into hysterics and added my bodily fluids to this scene?" Alexis asked.

"No," Devant answered before Carley had the chance.

"That victim could have been an employee or a client of mine. Whatever did this is frightening and needs to be stopped. Now, can we get back to my original question?"

Aiden sighed. "She does have a point, Captain. We can't have everyone strip and walk outside naked. We'll be tracking the scene all over the place no matter what we do."

Devant sighed and ran a hand through his short, graying hair. He suddenly looked tired. "I swear, I'm going to fire the two that let you get this far, Ms. Montral. Hopefully, there will not be a next time, but I must tell you not to approach a crime scene again. As you can see, they are dangerous."

"I assure you, Captain, I've learned my lesson."

"Alright. There isn't much we can do in the field. The lab is going to hate us, but anyone at the scene is going to have to stop by to be cleaned. That includes you, Ms. Montral. I'm afraid we are going to have to confiscate your suit."

"I am not worried about the loss of clothing. I keep a travel bag in my car. I have offices all over the country."

Aiden did not like the idea of going into the lab for a cleaning. The only thing he had going for him was they would just be gathering evidence and not looking to pick out a suspect. Montral would not be so lucky.

The lab had equipment used to determine who could produce magic and who could not. It was useful in narrowing down suspects, but Aiden knew the equipment was flawed. Just because an individual had magic didn't mean they were guilty. All too often, the detectors were used as a measure of guilt. The individual with the highest tetrabind readings was often pinned with the crime. In addition, anyone identified with any level of magic was sent to the research facilities, whether they were assigned blame or not.

It was no question Montral would produce massive amounts of tetrabind waves. If the technicians did scan her, she would be blamed for a crime she didn't commit. Aiden was certain she had committed other crimes in the past, but it would not solve the current problem. Alexis hadn't committed the murder in the garage. Arresting her for it would only leave the killer at large to murder again. While Aiden wanted Montral off the streets, the timing wasn't right. Given her reaction to the message on the wall, the killer was talking to her.

"Very good, then," Devant said. "We will have officers get the bag for you so it stays clean. We appreciate your cooperation."

"Of course," Alexis replied.

"Jameson, have the crew take a new set of pictures and video for the scene in its current condition," Devant ordered. "After that, bag the evidence, clean the scene and have everyone report to the lab. Anyone who was hit by the explosion rides in a lab truck. Thompson, get Montral an evidence bag for her coat and find some uniforms to transport her to the precinct." Then the captain turned to take care of his own tasks.

"If you'll follow me," Aiden said. He led the way to one of the abandoned equipment cases the technicians had placed around the scene.

The constant click of her heels let Aiden knew she followed. He crouched down and opened the case to pull a large, clear plastic bag from inside. He stood and offered it to Alexis as his eyes scanned the garage. The crew scurried around the scene, following orders Jameson barked out. He and Montral were as alone as they would get.

"The amount of questions I have for you is astronomical," Aiden said quietly, "but since I don't have the time and I doubt you'll answer, I'll keep this simple. Stay the fuck out of my mind."

Montral raised an eyebrow as she reached out to accept the bags. She slid her jacket inside one before looking back at Aiden. The knowing smile that touched her lips only irritated him.

"If these questions refer to the case at hand and didn't involve records or any of your co-workers, you might be surprised at what I'd be willing to answer. As for the rest, I assume you must be speaking of the dreams last night. You believe they were my doing?" She paused for a moment, as if to consider the possibility. "Interesting."

Doubt suddenly moved through Aiden's mind. Her answer was unexpected. It seemed she not only knew about the dreams, but felt there was more to them than he thought. Aiden didn't like the idea that she was one or two steps ahead of him.

"If you weren't responsible, then who was?" he demanded.

Her laughter slid across his skin. Aiden wanted to shudder, to close his eyes and lose himself in it. To make matters worse, he knew she wasn't using magic against him. Alexis hadn't the night before, either. In fact, he knew she was shielding as tightly as he was. He refused to let himself be swayed. Her charm and personality were only skin deep, tools she used to trap victims.

"That's the million dollar question, little hunter. I'm a woman of many talents, but the ability to enter the mind and manipulate dreams is not among them. I should be the one warning you to keep your dreams to yourself. Before you go accusing others, perhaps you should take a closer look at yourself. I will find my own 'uniform' to take me to your lab. Go back and play with your friends, Detective. If you can call people who would kill you if they knew what you truly are friends."

Alexis turned her back on Aiden and headed for the front of the garage. Her shoes left a trail of small crimson dots out of the slaughterhouse. He knew the image would resonate through his mind whenever he thought of her.

Aiden wanted to follow. He had more questions now than before the brief conversation. Alexis implied he had sent his dreams to her. But he didn't have that ability. At least, he thought he didn't. It had never occurred to him to try. To make himself feel better, he rationalized that even if he had invaded her mind, he had witnessed her dreams instead of his own.

Jameson came up beside him and watched him observe Alexis' departure. He glanced over to see her studying him again.

"Come on, Carley. Let's get our asses to the lab. The sooner that's done, the better. Maybe we'll even manage a less painful shower later," Aiden said casually. He wanted to ignore the topic of Montral for as long as possible.

"Your offer is sweet, Aiden, but your ass is way too hairy for me. You really should consider wax. I'd rather shower with the gorgeous thing that just walked out." She flashed him a playful smile.

Aiden couldn't help the smile that touched his own lips. "Fuck you. My ass is not hairy."

Carley smirked as they both walked toward the entrance, following the bloody path Montral had left for them.

CHAPTER FOUR

Alexis didn't make it halfway out of the garage before she was flanked by three officers and someone with a badge indicating he was part of the forensics team. The officers formed a circle around her. While they would claim it was for her protection, Alexis knew it was to keep her from wandering. Allowing a civilian to slip onto a crime scene was negligence. She had no doubt the Captain wanted to keep the mistake from getting to the public.

Alexis couldn't believe the demon hunter from the previous evening was an FDPC detective. While she vaguely understood the correlation, the fact remained Detective Thompson was a witch. The formation of the FDPC had been a reaction to the fear humans developed from the realization they had never been on top of the food chain. The unit didn't deal in justice. They dealt in genocide. Alexis immediately thought less of Aiden for his chosen involvement.

Following Aiden to the murder scene had cast a shroud of suspicion over Alexis she would have to contend with for the duration of the case. She had caught a tiny glimpse of the message on the wall during the interview and the sheer shock had her desperately wanting a closer look. Alexis had never seen the writing before outside of the names of her daggers. But had she known the blood sphere would erupt, she never would have gotten close. Surprise and curiosity had earned her an FDPC inspection, a fate she had hoped to never face.

Paranormal crimes attracted the media like flies. Alexis had passed a sea of reporters and photographers to get to the garage. Most of the crew shared her bloody state. It would be difficult to get the entire team out without leaking a few details.

As she walked with the officers in silence, Alexis put thoughts of the crime scene aside. For the next twelve hours, her sole focus had to be passing through the inspection undetected. If the FPDC identified her as one of the magical, they would either try to capture or kill her. And she had no intention of spending the rest of her life being dissected alive.

Alexis had done her research and had centuries of experience hiding in human society. In the modern world, it was all about looking human on paper.

Science was favored in matters like health and crime. In conversation, physical characteristics could be lied about and were often overlooked because of the diverse evolution of human subcultures. Passing medical tests was substantially more difficult and expensive. Alexis had paid a great deal of money for a background that explained her oddities and could stand up to scrutiny. The time had come to see if her efforts paid off.

At the very least, Alexis would have to face a physical cleaning, a scan by FDPC energy machines, and a DNA test. The challenge in the cleaning would be keeping her sunglasses. She could lie about her pale skin, but there was nothing she could say that would validate completely black eyes. Eye tattoos had become an interesting possibility, but so few humans took the risk to get them. Alexis would have to rely solely on wits and charm.

The energy scan would take more magical finesse. Fortunately for her, the killer had saturated the garage in his power. Everyone on the scene was swimming in it, and it clung to Alexis like tar. She worked to reign in her power and bury it beneath the killer's signature.

Unfortunately, the level of her power rivaled her opponent's. To compensate, Alexis began to apply layer upon layer of shielding. But even shields generated energy. Without knowing what threshold the machines could detect, Alexis was left with making herself as small as possible. It was no easy task.

The DNA test concerned her most. Cleverness and skill couldn't change her DNA, but perhaps the results could be altered. All she needed was a great deal of money and her phone. The former was much less challenging than the latter.

Her phone had thus far escaped the blood splatter by being inside her shirt pocket beneath her jacket, but her hands were coated. If she touched her phone with bloody hands, the police would want to confiscate it. None of Alexis' efforts would matter if she didn't get a message to her hacker before the DNA test was done. Her mind raced as they turned toward a side exit instead of the main entrance. She thought of asking for gloves, but in order to access the private network she needed for her less legal activities, her phone required fingerprints. Alexis paused her thoughts when the officers around her stopped.

There were technicians setting up a station of some kind by the side exit. Alexis understood. It would keep the media away as much as possible. But she didn't know what to make of the team by the door.

One of them stepped up and escorted her to a large, white basin. "May I see your hands, please?"

Alexis knew better than to refuse. She extended her hands out. "Sure, but why?"

"If all of us walk out of here with bloody fingers, the city will be painted red. Media is already a problem. The Captain doesn't want to give them a trail to follow."

Alexis was momentarily dumbfounded by her luck.

The technician looked over her hands and said, "Unfortunately, your watch and your bracelet have blood on them. They will have to go into evidence."

Alexis didn't mind. They could take as much jewelry as they wanted if it meant her hands would be clean. "Of course. Take whatever you need."

The moment the words left her lips, a sliver of fear crept through her. Alexis had forgotten there was one item the police couldn't have—not because Alexis wouldn't offer it—but because she literally couldn't take it off. The pendant around her throat could expose her just as quickly as her eyes.

Alexis was grateful the technician was preoccupied with her hands. The realization had likely shown on her face.

The pendant was hidden beneath her blouse, but the chain still extended up around her neck. Most of the splatter had hit her back and her side, but since there wasn't a mirror in sight, Alexis was forced to accept she would have to be patient and worry about the pendant when the time came.

The water was cold and the brush wasn't exactly pleasant as the technician scrubbed her hands and cleaned under her nails, but it wasn't long before he offered her a towel and moved on to the other officers. When they finished, Alexis handed back the towel and the five of them approached an officer guarding the exit. He opened the door and looked out before waving them through.

Alexis kept the quick pace of the other officers and they slipped out the door and directly into the back of a van. The guard from the garage closed the van doors. Alexis took a seat on a bench and tried not to lean against the side of the vehicle. There were no windows for her to gauge time or direction.

Alexis looked at each officer and pondered how to proceed. If she expected her hacker to give her a miracle, she needed to give him time to work. But she couldn't exactly pull out her phone and pretend to browse social media. She turned to the officer who appeared to be in charge.

"Excuse me. I was wondering if it would be okay to send a message out to my managers for this building. It would help both your unit and my staff if they were given some instruction on how to handle questions and curious employees."

The officer studied her for long enough Alexis worried. When he finally did reply, his tone was skeptical. "Alright, but I'd like to read any messages before you send them."

"Of course. I'll send it to just my secretary. He's knowledgeable enough to distribute information as needed," Alexis replied.

She pulled her phone from her pocket and was happy to see it free of blood. She unlocked the screen and pressed her thumbs against opposite corners of the display. The screen itself read her thumbprints and pulled up a security interface for her hidden network. Alexis had five seconds and one attempt to enter the correct password or the phone would shut down. She entered the code with a practiced ease.

When the network unlocked, Alexis pulled up her encrypted messages with contacts she couldn't publicly be associated with. She selected her hacker and sent him a brief message outlining her needs, the urgency of the matter, and the promise of payment before midnight. He wouldn't like the job because it was risky, but greed was one of the few human traits that could continuously be relied upon.

Alexis closed her private network and pulled up her email to draft a longer message to her secretary. She sent instructions for all non-management personnel and cleaning crews to be sent home for the day. The managers were to help the police in any way they could before going home themselves. Alexis promised to be in contact as much as she could, but she expected to be busy at the precinct for the rest of the day.

Alexis offered her phone to the officer when she finished. He took it from her and read through the message before handing it back. "That's alright. You can send it out, but don't delete it when you're done."

"Alright. I'll move it to its own folder and keep any other correspondence regarding the matter there," Alexis replied as she accepted the phone.

She hit the send button and locked the phone before slipping it back in her pocket. Alexis wanted to sigh with relief, but the game had only just begun. Hacking the FDPC system was no small task. Her contact was the best Alexis had ever known, but she didn't doubt the job would tax his abilities. There wasn't anything more Alexis could do about it. She put it in the back of her mind.

She spent the rest of the long ride building layers of shielding. Alexis had spent a great deal of time studying and practicing the art. It was an invaluable tool against magical predators, and anyone with power could learn it. In her corporal form, Alexis was too strong to hide from other magical creatures, despite shielding, so she avoided known, marked territory with only one or two exceptions. However, when she shadowmelded, her power dispersed through the darkness and she became substantially harder to detect. Alexis didn't think shadowmelding would prove productive in her current circumstance. She could only hope the machines were less sensitive than beings in the magical community.

When the van finally stopped, Alexis tensed. Her heart rate elevated, but she kept her expression calm and collected. She had a role to play.

The back doors opened to a team of people in white scrubs and lab coats. From her limited view, Alexis believed they were in an enclosed garage.

"Alright, I need everyone to exit single file starting with the civilian," a man called out.

Alexis got up and slowly stepped out. Two women immediately came to her. One smiled while the other retrieved the evidence bag with her belongings.

"Hi. I'm Lindsey and that's Steph. We are the techs assigned to take care of you today. You're Alexis, right? Alexis Montral?"

"That's correct," she replied.

"Perfect. I'm sorry you got caught in the crossfire. We're going to get you all cleaned up. Follow me, please."

Alexis nodded and followed the technician down a short hallway and into a room painted blindingly white. The lighting was fluorescent and harsh. The back corner of the room was done completely in tile. The drain in the middle of the floor and the variety of hoses with nozzles looked nowhere near as appealing as a standard shower. Plastic suits and other equipment hung from one of the tiled walls.

Adjacent to the tile was a small series of lockers and a bench. A few of the lockers had been left open, displaying towels and neat stacks of clothing.

The most intimidating feature was the large glass cylinder in the center of the room. It extended from floor to ceiling, though there were steel plates built into each end. Alexis imagined they were there to keep whatever was trapped inside from getting out by tearing through the ceiling. The outside of the glass was covered in rails with camera-like lenses attached to them. The cylinder itself was only wide enough to compensate a moderately obese individual.

"It's kind of scary looking, I know. But it's not so bad, I promise," Lindsey said as she turned to face Alexis.

"What is it?" Alexis asked, purposefully inflecting both curiosity and fear in her voice.

"Similar to an MRI scan at the hospital, only this one looks at magical energy, not anatomy. Crime scenes like the one you were on are sometimes volatile, as you were unfortunate enough to find out. The scanner just helps us make sure you didn't pick up anything too nasty," Lindsey replied.

It was also to make sure *she* wasn't anything too nasty. But Alexis kept her thoughts to herself. "What happens if I did pick up something bad?"

"We have a facility nearby that can help you. Don't worry. You're going to be alright. We'll take good care of you. Why don't you follow me and we'll get you cleaned up? That can't be very comfortable," Steph said from behind Alexis.

Roughly translated, Steph's reassuring words actually meant there would be a reinforced jail cell waiting for her if something showed up on the scan.

Alexis knew better than to be distracted by a future that hadn't happened yet. She nodded and followed Steph to the tiled corner. Alexis mentally reviewed the details of her background. She hadn't had to use them often, since the majority of her human interactions were business-related. Alexis excelled at separating business from private life. But those little details would matter to the technicians. They could make all the difference.

"It's not very pleasant, no. I'm happy my clothing got hit with most of it," Alexis said softly.

"Are you allergic to latex? We have gloves that are latex free if it's an issue," Lindsey said.

"As far as I'm aware, no," Alexis answered.

"How about shampoos or lotions?" Steph asked.

"I don't recall ever having a reaction to either."

"Great. Unfortunately, these soaps are not very gentle on the skin. They're meant to pretty much kill everything," Steph said apologetically.

"I figured that might be the case. It's alright," Alexis replied.

Both Lindsey and Steph walked to the far wall where the rows of equipment hung. Each technician stepped into a clear, plastic suit that zipped all the way up to their throats. Each pulled on a helmet with a curved face shield that tucked under their chins. They finished the outfit with a set of sterile gloves. Lindsey carried a bucket to Alexis while Steph walked to the hoses behind her.

"This part gets a little awkward. We have to strip you down entirely. Do you have a particular attachment to those clothes? It's not very likely we'll be able to get the blood stains out without damaging them. Cutting them would be safer for you," Lindsey said.

"Clothing is replaceable, provided I don't have to walk home naked. I've no doubt the media has somehow caught a picture of me in this state. No need to provide them with nude photos, too," Alexis replied.

"The media are assholes, for sure. But when you're as pretty as you are, any publicity is good publicity, right? We do have clothes for you, though," Lindsey said as she reached into the bucket for rescue shears and a rubber band.

Alexis laughed and let just a hint of bitterness slip through. "You're kind for saying so, but I'm well aware of the shade of my skin, among other things."

"Pale skin doesn't make you any less pretty. I'm going to tie your hair up so it doesn't get caught in the shears or drip more blood, even though I bet most of it is dry by now," Lindsey said as she stepped behind Alexis and began to gather her hair into a bun.

Alexis sighed softly. "You're right, I know. But for a long time, I didn't. Some days are still better than others."

"Well, don't worry. We aren't going to make fun of you here," Lindsey replied just before Alexis felt the cold edge of steel against the back of her neck, "Try to stay still as I cut these off."

"Wait, my phone is in my front pocket. Can you grab it? I don't want it to break if it falls," Alexis said.

"I got it," Steph replied as she slipped around Alexis to snag it.

"Thank you."

She stiffened as clothing quickly began to litter the floor. Alexis wasn't modest, but if she wanted to pass as insecure about the differences in her body, she needed to play the part. The room wasn't cold, but she shivered anyway. She lowered her head and let embarrassment creep across her features. It wasn't long until she was completely naked in front of two strangers.

"That's a really beautiful necklace," Lindsey commented.

Alexis internally braced for impact. She looked down at her chest and casually lifted a finger to toy with the pendant.

"My mother gave it to me when I was young. It was meant to be a reminder," Alexis replied quietly.

"Of what?" Lindsey asked with what Alexis assumed was trained curiosity.

"I have Oculocutaneous Albinism. My hair's natural color is so blonde it's almost white. I never did like it. I've been dying it since I was a teenager. My skin is very pale and my eyes tend to frighten people. They don't have the same color as everyone else's. I'm extremely sensitive to light," Alexis replied bitterly.

"What does that have to do with the necklace?" Lindsey wondered.

"When I was a child, the other kids used to call me names like 'Vampire' or 'Blood Sucker.' I've no doubt the media will elevate it to 'Blood Queen' or something now. Anyway, whenever I'd look in the mirror and cry, my mother would come behind me and tell me I was as beautiful as winter's first snowfall. She eventually gave me the nickname 'Snow'."

"And so she gave you a snowflake pendant to wear," Lindsey said with a sympathetic tilt of her head.

Alexis nodded quietly and kept her expression melancholy. She continued to spin the pendant absently in her fingertips. Beautiful lies often spared more lives than ugly truths. If Alexis could convince Lindsey and Steph she was human, they might not have to die.

"Well, I'd hate for you to have to part with it, but you might if it got blood on it," Lindsey said.

"I'd really rather not, if at all possible. The rest of my jewelry has no value. You could keep it and I wouldn't care. But this necklace is different. I don't remember the last time I took it off and it's one of the few things helping me stay together right now. This day has been like reliving the past and the necklace helps remind me that I persevere," Alexis replied softly.

"How about I take a look while it's still on you? If I don't see anything, it can be cleaned with you. Otherwise, I'll have to take it off so we can sterilize it. If that happens, you could wait here until it's done. It takes about three hours or so," Lindsey offered.

Alexis nodded. "Alright. I understand if you have to take it. I just don't want to part with it if I don't have to."

Lindsey stepped in close and began her inspection. Not even the chain escaped her careful eye. "Forgive my curiosity, but why is this like reliving the past?"

Alexis let hints of pain flash across her face. "I'm actually adopted. My biological father was abusive, to say the least. I'd rather not talk about it."

Lindsey nodded. "I'm sorry to hear that. Do people still call you 'Snow'?"

"Not so much anymore. My mother passed away a few years ago. It was her name for me. My actual name is better for business. There is a formality to it that board rooms identify with."

"So, you're a business woman, huh?" Lindsey asked.

"I am. I'm good at it."

"Sometimes, I wish I had interest in business. But I'm really good at crime stuff. Your necklace looks good. I'm going to have to take your glasses, though. They do have splatter on them," Lindsey said as she reached for Alexis' face.

Alexis didn't have time to be grateful they were not going to try to take the pendant. She jumped out of the frying pan and into the volcano. Instinctually, she moved her head out of reach.

"May I have my back-up pair of glasses from the bag with my things in it?"

"Why? I told you we wouldn't criticize you for being a little different, especially when you have a genetic disease," Lindsey replied with a raised eyebrow.

Alexis shook her head. "When I said I was light sensitive, it was a gross understatement. The headaches are crippling. The harsh lighting in this room will put me on the floor in minutes if you take them from me. I feel I've been very cooperative today and I don't mean to cause problems, but all of this is humiliating enough. I don't want to be in pain, too."

"You said the glasses are in your bag?" Steph asked.

"Yes," Alexis answered nervously.

"I'll go look for them. If they're blood free, we will give them to you when we are done cleaning. Water is going to splash everywhere, anyway. You can just keep your eyes closed. Does that sound fair?" Steph asked.

Alexis stalled a moment and then sighed. "Alright, if it's the best you can do."

She folded her hands in front of her and fidgeted. She kept her head bowed and her weight shifting from side to side. She wasn't genuinely nervous. In reality, there were only two outcomes, and she was equipped to handle either.

As she continued to fidget, Lindsey put a gloved hand on her shoulder comfortingly. "It's going to be alright. I promise. You're doing great."

Alexis bit her bottom lip. "I'm sorry. I don't mean to be unruly. I never imagined it would be like this when I got the call this morning."

"You're holding your own really well. Trust me. We've seen worse," Lindsey replied.

"I found the glasses. They're okay. The bag kept them safe. I'll keep them close so you can have them as soon as we're done," Steph said.

Alexis let out a sigh of relief. "Thank you. I hope you don't mind helping me move around. Fluorescent lighting is nasty. It's usually bright enough to get past eyelids."

"That's no problem. I'm going to take the glasses now," Lindsey said.

Alexis squeezed her eyes tightly shut and winced as she felt the glasses leave her face. Lindsey took her arm and guided her to a chair. Alexis made her steps clumsy and she sat down awkwardly. It wouldn't be good to let the techs know she could move well without sight. Luck and lies had gotten her as far as she was. She couldn't afford carelessness.

"Alright," Steph said. "Tilt your head back and get ready. This won't be the most enjoyable shower you've ever had, for sure."

When Alexis complied, the assault began. She was certain she would have no hair left by the time they were done. The shampoo smelled of alcohol and other unfamiliar antiseptics. It burned her scalp. She didn't have to fake the flinches and winces, though she did exaggerate. She had a higher pain tolerance than most humans but she didn't want it to show.

Neither Lindsey nor Steph took the time to apologize. When they finished with her hair, they stood Alexis up and sprayed her down with streams of uncomfortably hot water that were strong enough to noticeably sting. It was followed by a scrubbing so thorough Alexis pondered if the two of them owed her dinner.

It felt like an eternity before the water was shut off and they wrapped her in a towel. Someone slipped a pair of glasses on her face. Alexis peeked with one eye to make sure they were actually her glasses before opening them the rest of the way. Steph and Lindsey had moved to the wall to strip out of their protective gear.

"I feel like I was just scrubbed with sandpaper," Alexis said miserably.

"That was the hardest part. The rest is a cake walk. Come here so we can get you some clothes," Lindsey said.

With her glasses secured, Alexis followed the technician with ease. She needed the clothing as soon as possible. Any marks she received from the scrubbing would disappear soon, fast enough to draw attention.

Lindsey opened one of the lockers and began to look through its contents. "I bet you're a small in the waist, but there's no way the pants will be long enough. A medium with a small shirt will probably be okay."

"I'm not really in a position to be picky. I'm grateful for whatever you have," Alexis replied.

Lindsey passed Alexis a stack of folded clothes as Steph walked to the scanner. There was a small desk not far from the cylinder. A computer rested upon it. Steph began to boot up the machine while Alexis dressed. Lindsey left her to help Steph.

The pants were blue military fatigues and too big, but not big enough to fall off without a belt. She was also given a plain, white tank top and a blue tee-shirt to go over it. A pair of cheap, black sandals sufficed for footwear.

Noise and movement drew her eye to the glass cylinder. The lenses were moving along the rails in circles around the glass. They abruptly stopped and a door in the glass opened.

"Alright. A scan is next. It's quick and painless. All you have to do is step in and stand still," Lindsey said with a smile.

"Sounds easy enough," Alexis replied, though there was nothing easy about it.

She doubled her efforts in shielding. While she didn't hesitate to step inside, she paid close attention to the mechanics of the door as it closed behind her. It had an air-tight seal. The glass was likely bullet proof and designed for the containment of powerful creatures. If the scan was positive, Lindsey and Steph would try to lock her inside. Alexis was certain the FDPC had never captured a creature as powerful as she, otherwise the cylinder wouldn't be made of glass.

Escaping through shadowmelding would be difficult and time consuming because of the seal on the door. It wasn't impossible, but it wouldn't be Alexis' first choice. Breaking the glass would be much more efficient, which Alexis was confident she could do through pure power or freezing it first. She had yet to meet a form of glass she could not shatter.

The lenses around the glass began to move. Alexis stood still with her hands at her sides. She watched the expressions that crossed Lindsey and Steph's faces. If they detected her, Alexis would have to drop some of her shielding to escape. She didn't want the FDPC knowing magical beings could hide their energy levels. It would be disastrous to the community, and even humanity itself. She would have to completely destroy the entire scanning machine as well as the computer that was collecting data.

Suddenly, the machines stopped and the door opened. Alexis stepped out immediately. She didn't want to be under the machine's scrutiny any longer than necessary. Lindsey came up to her with a cotton swab on a plastic stick and a specimen tube.

"So, there is good news and bad news."

Still on guard, Alexis wasn't quite sure how to respond. "Alright."

"The bad news is you do have some energy from the scene clinging to you. The good news is that's not uncommon when you've been exposed to such high levels. Pretty much everyone who comes through here today will have it. Most don't notice any adverse effects though and it wears off in a few days. However, if you start having horrific nightmares, notice changes in your thought patterns, or strange and unexplainable things start happening around you, come back here immediately. We will put you under observational care until the energy wears off."

Alexis knew none of those reactions would occur in her. She even pondered how often they occurred in humans. Humanity walked around in the thick of magic every day and didn't know it. "So, I'm okay?"

Lindsey smiled. "Yes. You check out just fine. The last thing we need is a DNA sample so we can account for any traces you might have left at the scene."

Knowing she had done all that was possible Alexis could only smile. "Certainly."

"Just open your mouth so I can take a quick swab of your cheek. Then you'll be all done," Lindsey said.

Alexis opened her mouth and Lindsey did just that before sliding the swab into the tube. "Great. I'm going to stay behind and log the data. Steph will take you to the front desk. Thank you so much for your cooperation," Lindsey said.

"Thank you for your kindness and understanding," Alexis replied.

"We appreciate it. Most times, we get disgruntled employees or rowdy suspects. It was a nice change. Try to enjoy the rest of your day," Lindsey said before turning back toward the desk.

"If you'll follow me, please," Steph said from behind her.

Alexis turned and followed Steph out of the room. She let out a silent breath of relief. Blind luck, cleverness, and magical finesse had gotten her through unscathed. The DNA test was still a concern, but she wouldn't know more until the evening or morning hours. She would have to go straight home and prepare for both outcomes. No matter what some in the magical community thought, humans were dangerous and not to be underestimated. They had strength in numbers and technology. Alexis' life and current identity were still intact. For the moment.

More dire was the need to find the individual stupid enough to murder on her property... and ensure he never had the opportunity to do it again.

CHAPTER FIVE

Carley pushed through the double doors that led to the FDPC central offices, rubbing a towel through damp, brunette tresses. A cleaning from the lab was never fun. Technologists sprayed people down in places they just shouldn't be sprayed. Her skin was still red and raw, but Carley was definitely clean. The blue military fatigues and matching FDPC tee-shirt were not exactly fashionable, but she could walk on the street without getting horrified stares. Massive blood stains were still out of style.

She collapsed into her chair and propped her feet up on her desk. As she finished drying her hair, she looked across the room and watched Alexis Montral gather her belongings from the front desk. Montral had been given the same blue outfit that Carley sported. She had thought much of Montral's charisma and appeal would fade when she wasn't in expensive, tailored clothing. Being wrong was both annoying and intriguing.

Though she was too far away to hear the conversation, Carley watched the body language of both Montral and the desk officer. He didn't stiffen or glare the way he often did when visitors were rude, and Montral's smiles were polite. The conversation went smoothly and, once all her things were accounted for, Montral was escorted out by a uniform. Carley tossed the towel on the desk and stared after her, deep in thought.

"What do you think of that one?"

Carley looked over her shoulder to find Aiden staring down at her. He walked around to his desk and sank in his chair.

"About Montral?" Carley asked.

Aiden nodded. "Yeah."

Carley took a moment to put her thoughts in order. "Well, she didn't hinder us in any way. She didn't throw a tantrum or toss her corporate executive title around. I haven't looked into her background yet, but given her expensive taste in clothes and cars, I bet she's loaded. So far, she hasn't used her financial status to be rude or threatening. She answered all of our questions and helped where she could. On the surface, she's everything we want from someone in her position."

"There is a 'but' in that tone," Captain Devant said as he approached the desks and leaned a hip against Carley's.

Carley looked up at Devant and nodded once in greeting. "But she strolled onto our crime scene as if she has been on hundreds of them before. Part of that might just be cockiness and her being accustomed to doing whatever she pleases, but then you toss in her iron clad composure throughout this whole thing. I don't care who you are. You don't hold your breakfast if it's your first time seeing a body like the one she saw. She should have been tossing her cookies with the rest of the newbies. That woman has seen violent death before."

"I was thinking something similar," Devant replied. "Do either of you think she's diseased? Her skin is as pale as a vampire's, but we watched her walk in daylight."

Carley's features twisted in thought. "The tetrabind detectors didn't pick up anything other than the energy we all were exposed to from the scene. You talked to the techs, right Aiden? What were their impressions?"

Aiden leaned back in his chair and shrugged. "They said she was cooperative and polite. When asked for a DNA sample, she gave it freely. The only thing they had trouble with was her sunglasses. She refused to give them up until a back-up pair was retrieved from her bag. She claims she has albinism and her eyes are painfully sensitive to light. If DNA confirms that, it would explain both her skin and her eyes. DNA would also reveal if she is non-magically diseased. Vampirism, lycanthropy, and other similar conditions show up in DNA."

"I've also noticed when we come across diseased individuals who have not lost their sanity or committed a crime, they fear us. They're nervous, hesitant, and generally unhelpful. I can't say Montral was any of those, but she is definitely off in a different way," Carley added.

"How would you proceed, Thompson?" Devant asked. His tone had a mild curiosity in it.

Carley studied Aiden closely. Everyone in the unit knew his knowledge of demons was superior to anyone in the state, but he was also proficient in other species. Carley had always found it strange, considering all officers were given the same training.

Aiden sometimes knew things she couldn't find in the FDPC research archives. She often asked where he learned them, but he always casually blew her off. Whatever he hid never interfered with the case, so Carley had always let it go.

"Even if the tests clear her, it doesn't explain her composure at the crime scene. That being said, if we know she isn't capable of committing the murder, we shouldn't spend too much time on her. Our job is to stop a demon. If something about her comes up fishy and it's outside our scope, we can always pass her on to the appropriate department later," Aiden said.

"How long until we know the results of her test?" the Captain asked.

"The techs said the earliest would be late this evening. They sent her sample in first, but even without having to outsource our testing, it still takes hours to process. I told them to call me as soon as they know," Aiden replied.

"Alright," Devant said. "In the meantime, we still have a victim to identify, evidence to organize, and a background to look into. I want the evidence ready for display and the 3-D projector by the end of the day. If you can get a name for our victim, all the better. That's on you, Thompson. Jameson, I want a report on Montral on my desk before you leave. Be thorough. I want to know where her parents bought her diapers. Get moving. We're burning daylight." He pushed off Carley's desk and disappeared into his office.

Aiden waited until Devant's door was closed before he sighed. "Slave driver."

Carley smirked as she turned on her computer. "Stop pretending you don't want to be balls deep in details. You turn into an obsessive freak every time you don't like how the evidence is organized. Besides, it's not like we weren't going to do the work, anyway."

Aiden countered her smirk with one of his own. "Maybe I'd rather be balls deep in Montral's background."

Carley didn't doubt it. She looked across the table at him. Something had bothered her since they first met Montral in the garage. "You mean balls deep in the woman herself. What was up with you this morning? For a second, you looked surprised to see her, almost like you knew her."

"You're going to laugh at me, but I dated someone once a long time ago. Montral looks a lot like her, only she has super pale skin. The relationship didn't end well. When I thought it was Jennifer walking down, I almost had a heart attack," Aiden replied with a sheepish half smile.

Carley was fairly certain it was a lie. He didn't hold eye contact. He glanced up and down at her, which was consistent with shame or embarrassment. But when he did fleetingly meet her gaze, it wasn't fear of ridicule Carley saw. It was calculation. Aiden was judging her response. His expression could fool someone less observant, but part of her job was seeing the truth. She had seen the look in Aiden's eye before. Every time she thought Aiden wasn't telling the whole story, his gaze took on that cold tone.

Whenever Carley caught a glimpse of that particular gaze, she and Aiden were usually discussing an inconsequential but curious detail. Aiden was a good man and a great cop so she had never seen the use of calling him out when the topic wasn't crucial to the case.

But the lie about Alexis Montral made her more than curious. If Aiden knew her, he shouldn't lie about it. His insight would help them figure out what to do with her. Once again, with nothing solid to back her suspicions, Carley just smiled and rolled her eyes.

"Please. No one as hot as Montral would ever glance at your ugly mug."

"You're a terrible judge of male beauty. Even if I wasn't a superior specimen, my wit and charming personality win them over every time," Aiden replied. The hardness in his eyes melted and his usual arrogant confidence broke through.

"Right. That's why you haven't been laid in a year. When you're done organizing, make sure you upload to the shared drives. You have this dumb habit of hogging it all to yourself."

"It's not dumb. I just get a little hyper focused. I enter the zone, you know?"

"Aiden's zone of irresponsible forgetfulness," Carley replied sarcastically. When he glared at her, she blew him a kiss and turned her attention to her computer. She had a pretty lady to stalk.

Carley started with Montral's taxes. The Internal Revenue Service knew more about the average citizen than the person knew about himself. Luckily for her, the President and Congress deemed the paranormal threat to humanity large enough to grant the FDPC freedoms many other agencies would give their entire budget to have. It was a bit disturbing, but made digging substantially easier. Carley pulled up the tax database and ran a search for Montral. Given her financial status, she wasn't difficult to find.

Even knowing Montral was wealthy ahead of time didn't stop Carley's jaw from dropping when she saw the actual numbers. Much of her monetary value was tied into her businesses, of which there were so many Carley had to print off a list, but the woman's personal accounts were still substantial. Carley was surprised Montral's name wasn't more notorious. There were not many billionaires in the world. There were even fewer female ones. Montral had done a fantastic job at keeping her name out of the media.

Carley printed off another list containing all the buildings and properties with Montral's name attached. It was possible the murder had been random, but Carley had an aching suspicion it wasn't. A carefully arranged body and a message usually led to some kind of personal motive. She just hoped if the killer did have a vendetta, he would stick to Montral's holdings in New York. Crossing state lines brought red tape and politics no one wanted to deal with.

As time ticked by, Carley found nothing in the vast tax documents. Montral paid on time and in full. The I.R.S. watched her because of the sheer volume of funds she represented, but the results of several audits had revealed nothing suspicious. Carley was mildly surprised. In her experience, the rich wanted to stay rich. They spent time and effort on the best ways to avoid paying the government.

Carley moved onto the Motor Vehicle Administration and brought up Montral's driving record. As she predicted, it was peppered with speeding tickets. While large in number, none of the citations were for reckless driving or driving under the influence. Each ticket had been paid without court appearances. Montral had a lead foot and a total disregard for posted speed limits, but so did almost every driver in New York. She merely possessed cars capable of breaking sound barriers.

Carley printed off a list of all Montral's registered vehicles, searched separately for insurance information on each and called the company for more details. Each car had full coverage. Carley found it interesting Alexis had taken out no life insurance policies. She set the new list in her rapidly growing pile.

Montral's criminal and legal records were next. Carley found no arrests or convictions. Montral's businesses had been sued a few times, but that wasn't entirely uncommon in the corporate world. There was always a disgruntled customer or offended competitor looking for money. Carley did, however, spot two red flags. Montral's name was attached to a twenty-eight-year-old serial murderer and a four-year-old domestic assault. Instantly intrigued, Carley navigated through security portals and cracked the murder file. As she read through the information, her heart began to soften and she wished she hadn't been right about Montral's association with death.

Alexis Montral had been born Alexis Sutherland, daughter of a serial murderer. He had slaughtered her mother and at least six other women in her presence. According to the lead detective on the case, the maniac had been frustrated with the lack of medical treatment for his daughter's skin condition. So, he tried to cure her by bathing her in fresh blood. The man was killed in the attempt to capture, and Alexis had become a ward of the state until she was adopted at age eight. Carley grimaced as she scanned the old photographs.

"Holy fuck," she muttered.

Aiden looked up at her. "Hmm?"

"I just found out how our billionaire is able to handle being covered in blood," Carley responded, unable to tear her gaze from the monitor.

When she didn't elaborate right away, Aiden turned his chair to face Carley completely. "Well, are you going to keep me waiting in suspense? Spill the beans, man."

"Her father was a fucking psycho. He didn't like that she was albino, so he killed women to drain their blood into a bathtub. He made her bathe in it."

Aiden's gaze narrowed suspiciously. "Traumatized children rarely grow up to be well adjusted members of society. I would think having that history would make her more susceptible to a breakdown, not less."

Carley considered the thought for a moment while she dug into state adoption records. "Some kids are tough. Alexis was adopted less than a year later. Since she was in the system, she had insurance for therapy. Maybe she got lucky and the Montrals were good people. I'm still digging. Her name was also attached to a much more recent case. I'm pulling it up now."

"I just don't trust all the extraordinary things about her. I mean, how many people do you know who have fucking albinism? How many of those people are billionaires?" Aiden pondered.

"I know. I've been looking for signs of forgery, but I'm not seeing anything. If everything I find stays along these lines and her DNA test is as she states, I'm inclined to consider protection for her. You once told me violence and trauma can leave marks that attract predators like demons. Her father's murders occurred before the FDPC was established. We're only twenty years old. Maybe he was subjecting her to some kind of magic ritual."

Aiden was silent for a long time, obviously unhappy with his thoughts. "That's possible. However, if she isn't the one the killer is after, I don't want to draw needless attention to her. The killer is highly intelligent. Making her seem important could put her in harm's way. This won't be a typical demonic cleansing, anyway."

Carley tilted her head. "How so?"

"For starters, he's too powerful for us to be looking for a summoner. I haven't seen any signs of one as I've gone through the evidence, either. The intelligent ones don't emerge very often. It's so rare I haven't encountered any before. I've read stories about them, though."

"What did those stories tell you?" Carley asked.

"Higher demons are humanoid and immensely powerful with magic. They're capable of complex thought and manipulation. They have enhanced speed, strength, and agility. Their healing and regenerative abilities are unknown, but it is said their skin is difficult to penetrate with standard weaponry."

"I've only encountered a non-feral demon once, but it was controlled by a summoner. It spoke some broken English, but it didn't write. To be fair, we didn't give it a chance to. The summoner was killed in combat and our bad-ass priest destroyed the demon. Do you think holy items would help with the skin penetration?" Carley asked.

"Out of maybe four stories I've gotten my hands on, I think only one resulted in a kill. I do believe holy items were implemented, so having priests on hand definitely wouldn't hurt us. This won't be a casualty-free hunt, and given that all we really have is a body and an energy signature, there will be more victims," Aiden answered with a frown.

Carley sighed as she returned her attention to her computer. "The Captain isn't going to like that, but I won't lie. I was over here thinking the same thing. Montral's second case is a domestic assault she witnessed. She owns a club called Power downtown. Apparently, the husband of an employee came. He verbally and physically assaulted that employee. Montral made the call to the police herself. Nothing special. "

Aiden nodded. "Alright. Keep digging until you find those diapers, I guess. I'm almost done here, but I'm still looking for a known symbol that matches how the body was arranged."

"It doesn't look like any symbol I've encountered, but that might be because it's made from body parts. Maybe try drawing the shape as lines instead of limbs," Carley suggested.

Aiden raised an eyebrow. "That's not a bad idea."

As he scrambled through the mess on his desk for fresh paper, Carley focused on Montral. She spent the rest of the afternoon sorting through adoption records, college transcripts, and following career paths. Montral had gotten a scholarship to New York University's MBA program, followed by an apprenticeship at an upscale company, which earned her a solid management position. Her career had shot through the roof from there and she branched out on her own. Carley assembled her report and stood up to stretch before walking around to Aiden's desk. She peered over his shoulder.

"What are you looking at?" she asked.

"Surveillance footage. Looks like something out of a horror movie."

Carley hadn't seen the video. The crime scene was haunting enough. She had no desire to witness the construction, but unfortunately it was her job to make sense of nightmares. She sucked it up and watched the video on Aiden's screen.

Instantly, the sickness Carley felt all morning churned in her stomach. Thankfully, the victim didn't suffer. His head was cut off in one clean, unexpected swipe. Blood magically siphoned from his body in a long, scarlet arch. When the victim's body fell to the ground, the blood compressed into the solid sphere. The sophistication of the magic was both haunting and strangely beautiful.

The body was then sliced as efficiently as vegetables in a professional kitchen. Bones were snapped, limbs contorted. The worst part wasn't the slaughter, or even the speed at which it happened. What terrified Carley was the killer didn't appear once on the footage.

"Why didn't the cameras capture him? Cameras have filmed demons before," Carley said.

"I don't know. I've already passed it down to our video guys. They'll look for tampering. I really hope someone managed to edit it," Aiden replied. He sounded as concerned as she was.

Carley folded her arms and frowned. "I've seen spells that could hide someone from sight before."

"Yes, but usually those spells shatter if you touch something. I suppose it's possible he had a skilled witch weave him a sophisticated spell, but I don't like it. I'm going to have to go digging through the illusionary magic archives tonight. There were no witnesses and the victim was dead before he knew what happened. It's impossible to tell if the killer was only invisible to the cameras."

"Did you ever find the victim's name?"

"Yeah. They found the remains of a wallet underneath the mass of scraps. Part of a driver's license—Tyler Feit. He was on Montral's employee list. Evening cleaning crew," Aiden answered.

"An attack of opportunity, then? He got killed because it was time to empty trash cans in the garage?"

"That's what I'm leaning toward, though you'll have to run his background to rule out involvement with the diseased population. We should also check to see if Montral knew him personally. We need to talk to his family tonight," Aiden replied.

"Alright. I think you and I are going to have a date night. Let me drop off this report and we'll go talk to the family, followed by takeout and bunking down to finish up research."

"Whose place?" Aiden asked.

"Mine. Yours is a dirty cesspit," Carley answered immediately.

Aiden grinned. "You buying dinner, then?"

Carley rolled her eyes. "Fuck you. You showed up late and didn't even have the common courtesy to bring doughnuts."

"How does being late always equate to me buying dinner?" Aiden asked with a pout.

"Maybe next time you'll answer your stupid phone on the first try instead of, like, the tenth. Stop your pouting. I'll get dessert. I have a feeling it's going to be a long, sugar-fueled night."

Carley took her report to Devant's office. As she slapped it on his desk, she noted his gaze was locked on Aiden through the window. The Captain hadn't earned his position by kissing ass. Perhaps she wasn't the only one who noted Aiden's periodic strange behavior.

When Devant merely raised eyebrows at her, she slipped out of the office and found Aiden waiting. Carley nodded and stopped by her desk for her phone, wallet, and keys before leaving the precinct with him.

As they fought over the toppings for a pizza, Carley pondered Devant. She knew she shouldn't be surprised the Captain noticed the subtleties in Aiden's behavior, but he had never mentioned it to her before. Despite her own suspicions, a wave of protectiveness washed through her. Carley hoped whatever Aiden was hiding didn't end up destroying his career, or his life.

CHAPTER SIX

Alexis polished off her third cup of coffee as the last of the morning's meetings ended. The brew had long gone cold, but she craved its bitter flavor. It matched the tone of her day. The murder had unleashed a slew of issues regarding security, employee safety, and staffing. Given Alexis didn't have many associates capable of handling themselves, it was likely the killer would continue to target her businesses. Those issues needed to be addressed for all her New York companies.

Humans were ill-prepared to deal with an attack from the magical community. Her security was already more than reasonable, but she couldn't bring up the possibilities of empowered wards or magical traps without revealing her nature. The options left were costly and even her board members were unconvinced those measures could stop another attack by the creature. She wouldn't have minded the cost, but it made no sense to spend money on something she knew would be ineffective. They had settled on increased awareness of the situation for all security personnel and a temporary increase in security staff. The meetings had gone into the afternoon and ended with no satisfaction for anyone.

As her staff filed out of the board room, Alexis powered off her tablet and headed back to her office, closing the door behind her. She smiled when lunch already waited on her desk. Her secretary was exceptional at his job. Alexis made it a point to be in the office an hour early, and Mark Harrison often arrived at the same time. He worked hard, anticipated her needs, and was well-liked by the other staff. He more than earned his keep and Alexis always made sure his paycheck reflected it.

She sat down at her desk and picked up her phone to dial Mark's extension. He answered immediately.

"Hey there. Lunch okay?"

"It looks great, thanks. Where did you find it?" Alexis asked.

"This little shop about two blocks up. Their salads are amazing. I figured you wouldn't want to run out. It's got blackened fish with this sweet chipotle dressing they make by hand."

"I'm sure I'll love it. Do you mind holding my calls for thirty minutes?"

"I can do that. *Bon appetit*," Mark replied and hung up.

With thirty minutes to herself, Alexis put away thoughts of work and used the desk computer to open her private network. The encrypted server had been designed by one of the best and most discreet information technology specialists in the world. His hacking skills were also invaluable, as yesterday's events had proven. The police hadn't raided her home during the evening.

Alexis spent the night at home to avoid suspicion, but she had sent several tactful messages in hopes of picking up any information the magical community might have about the murder. She took a bite of her salad and frowned at the screen. The replies in her inbox spoke of nothing more than different factions being intrigued but cautious of someone bold enough to brazenly kill in view of human citizens.

This murder wasn't an accident by a weak youngling or the lost sanity of a Master. The death had been methodical, planned, and public. Having seen the scene herself, Alexis couldn't disagree with the magical community's assessment. She erased the messages and took another bite of her salad.

She wasn't surprised her sources had come up dry, but it was irritating nonetheless. In order to maintain anonymity, her contacts had to be few and far between. Though they were good, her sources could only really bring her gossip. There was a very fine line between having a life free of power games and still having an ear on the streets.

The only productive message had been from the hacker. The results of her DNA test for the FDPC had been altered to include albinism and exclude anything that would have the police looking closer. *One less thing to worry about.* She opened a separate window on the network and released the rest of his payment.

Alexis pulled up the security footage of the crime scene next. The videos had been copied to her network before the FDPC confiscated the originals. She'd pored over them the night before and one particular detail stuck in her mind. She skipped ahead on one of the tapes until the bloody message appeared on the wall. Pausing the frame, she leaned back in her chair with her bottled water.

The message unsettled her, but not for the reasons most would think. Alexis didn't fear the killer, nor did she fear the power he wielded. What shook her was that she could read the exotic message as fluently as she read English. Over hundreds of years, she had learned many of the different languages used around the world. Only once had she come across text like the kind from this crime scene. She shouldn't be able to understand it, yet she did.

And she could think of only one reason why.

Alexis had come to accept there was a portion of her memory she would never get back. But there were a few innate things from her past she still had access to. The first was her magical abilities. It had taken time to relearn how to use them, but the learning had come easily. Second, her body could move through a fight with almost no real thought. While she learned new techniques over the course of time, it didn't change the fact that she already possessed a vast knowledge of warfare. Alexis could only assume the language had been learned in whatever life she had prior to her arrival in Europe. The killer was someone from her past then—a past she had long abandoned hope of understanding.

Though she was happy with her current existence, the killer had awakened her desire to know the truth. Every day the case remained open, the risk of the authorities discovering Alexis' magical race grew. Her current life and many of the resources she had acquired would be lost if she did not find the killer.

It hadn't even been twenty-four hours and Alexis was already sick of the FDPC. Officers were currently in her building questioning employees and looking through work spaces. She knew it wouldn't be long before her office was searched and she was questioned further. With a sigh, she took a screenshot of the message and saved it in the folder she had created for the case, along with a translation:

For ages, the seven Seekers sought
Throughout the whole of light and dark.
But man's jungle obstructs their sight,
Leaving the lost alone to fight.
I see you.

Though most of the message made little sense to Alexis, it confirmed her theory that the killer was from her past.

Alexis had encountered demons before. More beast like, they walked on four legs and lacked signs of sentient-level intelligence. Warlocks could summon demons that were smarter, but not by much. Some could walk on two legs, but others didn't have any legs at all. Regardless, none had humanoid shapes like hers, and no warlock had ever been able to take control of Alexis.

Several had met their deaths making the attempt.

Based on that evidence, Alexis had never been genuinely convinced she was actually demonic. After all, it had been the humans who labeled her as such. But other species had tossed her in the category, too, so she had come to accept it. The murder and the message pushed any lingering doubts from her mind. The unfortunate event proved there were others like her.

Despite the new conviction of her demonic heritage, Alexis still had nothing in common with her brethren save for physical characteristics. She had no lusts for death or destruction. She found no joy in evil acts, though that wasn't to say she wasn't capable of them. Alexis served herself. She could kill ruthlessly and without guilt if the situation demanded. The morals of man rarely factored into her decisions.

But Alexis did none of those things without logical reason and a need for self-preservation. She would never create the type of scene found in the garage. It reeked of poor taste. A being capable of such forethought and execution should know better, despite any hatred they had for humans.

Even if she learned about her history, Alexis would not find a home among demons.

The message itself hinted the 'Seekers' didn't know Alexis was different. They were looking for someone she had once been, not the person she was now. Modern human cities were often called concrete jungles and different types of metal had been known to interfere with scrying and magical discernment. Yet, there were countless years when Alexis didn't live with humans at all. It couldn't just be New York keeping demonic eyes from seeing her, especially if they had been searching for ages.

Alexis shook her head. The message brought up more questions than answers. There didn't appear to be any instruction or demands. The killer left her with a mess, but gave no clues as to what she was supposed to do about it. Alexis sighed and looked down at her half-eaten lunch. She was suddenly no longer hungry.

She scrolled through the video for even a slight glimpse of the killer. Though she had seen the footage several times already, Alexis hoped fresh eyes would reveal something she'd missed.

She wasn't so lucky. The victim's death had been recorded in explicit detail, but it was as if he had been slaughtered by a ghost. She tilted her head and supposed she should consider the idea of a spirit. Perhaps not a ghost, but maybe the killer wasn't in their corporal realm. Maybe he was in between her world and somewhere else, which was why the cameras couldn't see him.

While Alexis wouldn't toss the theory out, something didn't feel right about it. Too many pieces didn't add up. Her wards should have sensed the intruder much sooner than they did. Either the killer actively disrupted them—which Alexis also should have felt—or something deeper was going on.

A knock on the door brought her out of her thoughts and she hid her server from the computer screen.

"Come in."

Mark peeked his head through the door. "Ready to put your nose back on the grindstone?"

Alexis glanced at the clock. Thirty minutes had come and gone. "I guess I am. Thanks."

"Oh, don't thank me yet. The phones have been backed up all day. I'm about to unlock the virtual flood gates."

Alexis locked her server away and flashed Mark a smile. "Good thing I'm a strong swimmer."

"Thank the higher powers or the rest of us would be fucked."

* * *

It was eight o'clock before Alexis finally left the office. She had sent a text alerting Liz, but there was no doubt the food was cold by now. Her Aston Martin hugged the Manhattan streets to an apartment building five blocks from Power. Traffic was lighter with the later hour, but at forty-five minutes, the trip still couldn't be called convenient. She pulled into a reserved spot across the street from the entrance.

It was rare her weekly dinner with Liz actually fit into her schedule, but Alexis always jumbled things to make it work. She never knew what compulsion had encouraged her to pick up that particular stray. When Power opened two years ago, Liz had quietly stepped into her office to apply for a bartending position. She had been qualified, but Alexis had immediately caught signs of abuse. Liz shied away from eye contact and wasn't talkative enough, neither of which sold drinks. Alexis also noticed hints of bruising beneath clothing far too big for her.

When denied the job, Liz had only nodded and asked if there were any other available opportunities. Intrigued by the little show of courage, Alexis had offered her the coat check position.

Liz accepted despite lower pay. So, Alexis sat back to watch for a few weeks. Liz was never late and often stayed after her shift to help clean though it wasn't in her job description.

But the club bouncers had to repeatedly throw out her harassing husband, and they walked her home to the shelter each night. Once it had gotten so violent, Alexis had been forced to intervene. It was bad for business.

That same night, Alexis visited Liz in the hospital. The defeat and resignation in Liz's eyes was evident. She believed Alexis had come to fire her. Instead, Alexis had offered her a deal. She could keep her job, earn a raise if she divorced her husband and took advantage of the shelter's therapy programs, and have reduced rent in an apartment with controlled access Alexis owned. Liz agreed and had been flourishing ever since. She had slowly crept into a hidden corner of Alexis' affections.

Alexis stepped out of the car, locked the doors and started crossing the street. She almost paused when a trickle of power grazed the edge of her awareness, but it wouldn't do to let the detective know she was aware of his presence. Alexis had expected the hunter to follow her, but thought he would do a better job hiding it. Since Aiden was no direct threat and she wasn't looking to pursue anything illegal that evening, he could sit in the cold and waste his time while she enjoyed a quiet, warm dinner inside.

She finished crossing the street and smiled at the doorman as she approached. "Good evening, Edward."

The doorman was older with well-kept but graying hair and a kind smile. "Late night at the office, Ms. Montral?"

Alexis nodded and stepped inside. "Much to my regret. Don't forget to stay inside here if that wind gets too chilly."

"We vets are made of tougher stuff than a little wind."

"You vets have already done your duty. Don't let stubbornness make you cold and slow," Alexis replied teasingly.

As she walked through the second set of double doors, she caught the smile that tugged Edward's lips in the reflection of the glass doors. The building manager had done well proposing to hire homeless veterans for security positions. Most had adjusted well and were fantastic employees, according to their performance reports.

Liz's apartment was on the sixth floor. The elevator ride was quick. Alexis stepped out into the hallway and walked to the last door on the left. It didn't take long for Liz to answer, but she smiled when she heard Liz pause to look through the peep hole before opening the door.

"Long day?" Liz asked.

Alexis walked inside and draped her thigh-length pea coat over the back of the couch.

"Yes. I had some meetings this morning that pushed my day back several hours."

Liz came into the living room and offered Alexis a mug of steaming tea. "Did they have anything to do with that murder on the news? I know you have an office in that building."

Alexis took the mug and let the smile fade from her face. "Sadly, yes. New security and procedures had to be discussed and implemented."

Liz gestured to the TV. "The news said the FDPC is investigating. That means whatever did it wasn't human."

Alexis raised an eyebrow as she took a sip of tea. "The creature hasn't been caught or killed yet. Employee safety is a top priority for me, but I feel any security personnel not trained by the FDPC are unequipped to deal with something like this. I want you to be careful, too. Keep your pepper spray and your phone with you always, and don't walk alone."

"If you don't think trained security staff could handle this thing, what good is a can of mace going to do?"

"You never know what might save your life."

Liz chuckled softly and shook her head. "Are you going to follow your own advice?"

Alexis smirked. "Don't worry too much about me. I'm rich, and as unfair as it is, it makes me a higher priority. I've no doubt law enforcement will soon deem it appropriate to have a little boy in blue follow me around."

"Much to your annoyance, I'm sure. I doubt he'll be able to keep up with you. Are you hungry? I can reheat the soup."

"I only finished half my lunch and then drowned in work."

"Alright. It won't take me long. Make yourself at home."

Liz disappeared into the kitchen and Alexis turned to the living room. The walls were a soft cream color and displayed a fair amount of artwork. The canvases were mostly landscapes, but every now and then there was a powerful abstract piece and several that depicted people.

Art was one of the few worlds Alexis didn't keep an eye on, despite its potential for profit. But she did have a cultured taste and enough education to know what lined the walls would sell in a gallery.

The room itself was filled with second hand, but well cared for furniture. There was a couch, a reclining chair with an afghan piled in it, and a love seat. Books covered a pretty wooden coffee table. Small pictures of the family Liz left in Scotland littered side tables. She didn't speak of them often and Alexis didn't pry. She sensed some type of painful rift.

Alexis walked around the couch to sit and noticed something new. A trail of animal toys carried her gaze to a dog bed in the corner where a small black puppy snored quietly. Alexis had no love for dogs.

The dog's presence surprised her, though she realized it shouldn't have. Liz rarely asked for things, and when she did, it was planned long in advance. With no desire to engage the animal, Alexis leaned back against the couch and let the puppy sleep.

Liz stepped into the living room carrying a tray loaded with bowls of broccoli cheese soup and slices of bread Alexis knew had been made from scratch. She set the tray on the coffee table and fell into the couch beside Alexis.

"You move fast," Alexis said.

"Huh?" Liz asked curiously.

Alexis pointed to the puppy and Liz grinned.

"Isn't she so adorable? Someone dropped an entire box of puppies off at the pound. You know I volunteer there. Since you, my therapist, and the building manager said it was okay, the pound let me take one home."

"I thought puppies were wild and energetic. She's looking pretty lazy to me," Alexis commented as she reached for a bowl.

"They are. I just wore her out today. We went to the pet store and the dog park and a training class. She plopped down on that bed right after she stuffed her face about an hour ago. It's really cute when she starts dreaming."

Alexis smiled at the happiness in Liz's voice. "You're entirely smitten."

Liz looked down bashfully. "I know. How bad is that? I've not had her two days, even."

Alexis laughed before taking a sip of soup. "It's good that she makes you happy. What did you name her?"

"Hope. She melts my heart every time I look at her."

"Speaking of melting hearts, how is therapy going?"

"It sucks. But I'm doing better at standing up for myself. The other day, some woman tried to bully me for my seat on the subway. Maybe I have a sign that says 'I'm a wimp' on my back or something. Anyway, I didn't give it to her. Was really hard, though."

Alexis let her gaze shift from the soup to Liz. "There is a difference between kindness and letting yourself get walked on. You get stronger every day. You just have to let yourself see it."

"Even the smallest confrontations make me want to hide in the corner."

"But you don't anymore," Alexis said softly.

"Sometimes I still do," Liz said, circling her spoon in what remained of her soup.

"And sometimes running is the right thing. You stand up more than you run. That's progress. Don't be so hard on yourself."

Liz nodded quietly and Alexis fought back a sigh. She looked to the art-covered walls. There was a new painting hidden among the many landscapes. It was of a woman looking out a window with her hand pressed longingly against the glass. A beautiful but lonely piece.

Liz noticed her gaze. "I finished that one last week."

"It's good," Alexis said casually.

"It's how I was feeling, like there is this whole world out there I can see but can't touch."

"You'd have to step outside the window to touch."

"I know. Maybe one day I'll stop feeling like he's right behind me." Liz sighed softly. "Speaking of being followed, Candice says you ditched another boy from the club the other night. What was wrong with this one?"

Alexis laughed. Any details about the demon hunter that found their way to her ear were useful. "So, we're going to discuss my love life now, huh?"

"She said he moped at the bar for hours, completely ignoring the other women gawking at him," Liz replied as she finished her soup.

Alexis contemplated how Liz would react to the truth. Dating someone whose primary purpose in life was to kill you was a recipe for dead bodies. Liz had faced enough challenges and Alexis didn't want to endanger her further. "He just wasn't for me."

"But why? I trust Candice when she says he had good manners and was attractive. He tipped her well. Maybe you're self-conscious because you have albinism? I mean... you shouldn't be. You're... you're really pretty. It's just, I thought, maybe, maybe you might be nervous," Liz stammered, her cheeks flushing ten shades of crimson.

Alexis laughed and shook her head. "No. He's just pushy, Liz. He wants to run the show, regardless of whether or not I want to let him."

"So, you like to take the lead in relationships?"

Alexis raised an eyebrow. "I can follow a leader, if they lead properly. So why are you and Candice suddenly so interested in my tastes?"

Liz smiled innocently. "I'm just curious."

"You're a bad liar."

Liz looked down at Hope. "You're young, beautiful, smart, and successful. But you're always alone. Do you like it that way?"

"I do, yes. I find company when I want it. I will tell you that if you and Candice are trying to fix me up, you'll fail miserably."

"You never know," Liz said sheepishly.

"There will be no convincing you it's a waste of time, will there?"

Surprise flashed on Liz's features. "You'll give up so easily?"

Alexis grinned. "One of the keys to business is knowing which battles are worth fighting. It's much easier for me to let the two of you exhaust yourselves and see the folly of your ways on your own. I should get going. Thanks for waiting for me."

Liz took Alexis' bowl and set it on the coffee table with hers as they stood. "I didn't mind. I'm just sorry for the reason you had to stay late."

Alexis slipped into her coat and they walked to the door. "Remember what I said. Be safe and smart until this mess is over."

Liz nodded once.

Alexis walked out but waited until she heard both the dead bolt and the chain slide into place. They would do little against the predator that roamed the streets, but she couldn't easily ward Liz's apartment. The killer seemed proficient in slipping past wards, anyway.

Alexis made her way out and across the street. She was about to get into her car when a pulse of power gave her pause. She raised her gaze and slowly scanned the street. Alexis reached out into the shadows and located Detective Thompson in an alley a block down with two other beings of power.

It was one thing for Aiden to hunt alone. It was quite another to bring friends.

Irritation and anger washed through her as she walked the block to the alley. Alexis turned down it, and once hidden from the main street, she let her body dissolve and become the darkness itself. Shadow melding was nearly as effective as invisibility.

Alexis traveled through the darkness until she came across Thompson. She was surprised to see the two additional men were not demon hunters, but werewolves. Even in human form, there was no mistaking the way they moved. They had him backed into a wall. It had temporarily escaped Alexis' mind Liz's building was in wolf territory. It was habit for her to shield her presence after several years of visiting.

"A witch does not belong in our territory," the man on the left snarled. "Your kind have been warned before. Our generosity ends here."

"I belong to no coven, so I've not heard your warnings. Like I said, I'm a demon hunter and I've tracked a very powerful one to this neighborhood," Aiden replied. Alexis could hear the irritation in his voice.

"There are no demons here. The alpha wouldn't tolerate their kind, either. Even if there was, you didn't get his permission to hunt. He doesn't like rude, uninvited guests."

Aiden narrowed his gaze and Alexis watched as he discreetly reached into his pocket. As tempted as she was to leave him to his fate, Aiden's job title had her contemplating saving him. The last thing she needed was the FDPC finding the body of the lead investigator on her case. She had enough trouble.

With an internal sigh, Alexis sent a wave of power down the alley that carried enough weight for the wolves to know they were more than outmatched. Instantly they looked in her direction, so she let the shape of her body reform, but nothing else.

A faceless, obsidian figure forged of shadows, she whispered, "Your alpha does not see all that goes on under his nose. I will gladly take care of this hunter for you, but if you are still here in five seconds, I will take care of you, too."

The men glanced at Aiden and then each other before taking off down the alley, moving at the speed known for were-animals.

Alexis traced their movements until they were fifteen blocks away. They had given in surprisingly fast. Alexis surrounded Aiden in full darkness and let her body reform, so close they almost touched. She wasn't a fan of his nearness, but sight would be blocked by the fog with increased distance.

Aiden's power rubbed against hers and the overwhelming temptation to let his energy meld into hers reminded her why she shouldn't have let him live.

"I had that handled just fine."

"So I saw. You were doing a fantastic job," Alexis replied sarcastically.

Aiden's fists clenched at his sides. Alexis remembered he had something in his left hand, but she stayed where she was. There was no point in letting him know she knew.

"Why save me? Unless you're not really saving me?"

"As tempting as it was to leave you, you are an even larger problem to me as a corpse. The FDPC wouldn't take kindly to the murder of one of their own. Besides, you still have work to do. Following me won't get you anywhere."

Aiden raised an eyebrow. "Maybe I was trying to protect you."

Alexis sighed and folded her arms across her chest. "Please don't waste my time and your breath on lies. Whether you acknowledge it or not, we want the same thing."

Aiden studied her with an intensity that made her acutely aware of how close his body was to hers. Her pulse picked up and her stomach tightened. The annoyance evaporated from his face. His left hand came up and a lighter sparked a flame. Her darkness swallowed most of the light, but enough remained to illuminate her face. His right hand came toward her cheek, but Alexis caught his wrist before he even got half the distance. Heat shot through her skin and tangled with her shadow energy as it traveled up her arm. She had to yank her own power before it progressed farther than his elbow.

Alexis shivered. So did Aiden.

"What are you doing?" Alexis asked.

"I wanted to see your eyes. It's hard when you hide behind glasses," Aiden replied. He didn't fight her hold on his wrist.

"You can't see much of anything right now."

"Hence the light. Would you let me see?"

Alexis found it strange that she wanted to trust him. A little physical contact shouldn't change her perspective. A minute ago, she'd have left him to die. Now, she wanted him to believe she wasn't like the demon who left the mess in her garage. But rationality always prevailed. She hadn't forgotten he could use that small flame to try and kill her. Alexis released his arm and stepped out of reach.

"No," she replied softly.

He let his hand fall to his side. "Scared I'll see through you?"

Alexis shook her head. "I don't fear you."

When Aiden started to reply, Alexis took another step back and cut him off. "There are no other wolves in the area for the moment. Don't follow me out too closely. The doorman at the apartment building is very good. He notices things. As it is, the next time I'm there, he'll question me."

Alexis let the shroud of darkness fall and the subtle lights from the streets filtered in. Aiden put the lighter back into his pocket while Alexis turned and headed for the street, peeling his power off her as she went.

"Wait," Aiden said as he pushed off the wall to follow.

Without looking back, Alexis sent a wave of shadow energy at him and kept walking. It wasn't an attack, as the energy just washed around him like water, but it accomplished her goal. He skidded to a stop.

"Just do your job, little hunter. Remember, following me will not lead you to the killer. If I knew who did it, they would be dead already."

Alexis was pleased when she made it to her car and he still hadn't left the alley. She brought the engine to life, and shot out of the neighborhood. Her fingertips still tingled from touching his skin. Her body's reaction made no more sense now than it had the first time she'd encountered him. Aiden Thompson was several different kinds of trouble she did not want.

CHAPTER SEVEN

The flash of a digital camera went off in Aiden's peripheral vision. He wasn't startled. They were a constant in his life and couldn't distract from the crime scene before him.

"It's been four days. I expected to see this sooner," Carley said from beside him.

Aiden sighed and folded his arms over his chest as he took in the body. The call had come in mid-morning. He and Carley had been onsite for forty-five minutes and the scene was still less than two and a half hours old. The killer had made his move during some of the busiest hours of human society.

"I thought we would, too. Our killer definitely has a purpose. He wants something and he's got enough balls to communicate with blood in daylight," Aiden replied.

They stood shoulder to shoulder just outside an elevator. Even with the doors locked in the open position, the elevator entrance was small and didn't offer much room to view the carnage inside. The officers who responded first to the scene had shut down the elevator and evacuated the whole third floor. It was standard procedure when the crime was suspected to be paranormal.

"Killings by demons happen at all times, so I'm not sure this is much of a stretch," Carley replied with a curious tone.

"True, beasts rarely care about time and would have slaughtered the whole building. This demon is intelligent. Brave and patient enough to wait for opportunities. Singularly focused."

"Patient for a demon, maybe, but he still killed again because he didn't get what he wanted the first time." Carley paused. "Or he's getting what he wants by taunting us. This message is different."

Aiden nodded. "Not having even the smallest bit of that language is becoming increasingly frustrating. It's a huge fucking handicap."

Aiden's gaze slowly traveled around the inside of the elevator. Much like the first scene, there was no splatter. The blood had been solidified into a large crescent moon and used as paint for the five-line message, as well as hundreds of tiny crescent moons that peppered the four small walls. Aiden knew technicians were spelunking in the elevator shaft in search of blood traces, but he didn't think they would find any. The killer had used it all to make his point.

There was an intact body, which Aiden attributed to the elevator's speed. A cleanly severed head was tucked into a corner. Aiden suspected it was the cause of death, as opposed to the victim's other injuries. The medical examiner hadn't reported to them yet.

The victim's hair was long, blonde, and free of blood, despite how messy normal decapitations would be. Her makeup hadn't smeared. Even in death, her beauty had been captured in time. There was nothing quite as haunting as a severed head.

Though the victim's skirt was hiked up, Aiden had seen no signs of sexual abuse. Lace underwear remained untouched. The skirt had merely gotten in the killer's way. Both legs were flayed open from hip to knee. The quadriceps had been removed entirely and used to suspend the body from the ceiling through a crescent-shaped hole the killer carved in the chest.

Dissected muscle was also used to hang the solidified blood crescent around what was left of the victim's neck. Bits of meat and bone cut from the victim laid in a pile in another corner. All in all, the small amount of chopped human tissue made the scene less gruesome than the first, but equally disturbing. The killer had made the victim look like a toy doll with detachable parts.

Aiden's stomach lurched and his skin itched beneath the weight of the killer's power. None of it was pleasant the second time around.

"I think we should assume this demon is armed. Every cut is precise and clean. I've never seen a demon carry a weapon, but these injuries were not made by any kind of claws I've seen. Reed confirmed the first scene wasn't done by claws or teeth, either," Carley noted.

"Given his talent for blood manipulation, I'd guess it's a large ritual blade or a sword, though the latter would be hard to use in this small space," Aiden replied thoughtfully. The possibility of armed demons was a frightening thought. It made Aiden wonder if Alexis used weapons.

Carley accepted a note given to her by a passing technician. "It seems her name was Teresa Bates. Real estate agent for Pristine Living Realtors who specialized in condos. The techs lifted a business card from inside her jacket."

"I don't think her job mattered. I think being alone in the elevator sealed her fate," Aiden replied.

Carley's gaze narrowed. "We know he can remove himself from sight, but not how. Are you thinking he sat in the elevator and rode until the right opportunity came?"

"I think so, yeah. Minus the holes he made in the ceiling to hang the body, the elevator isn't damaged. He didn't force his way in here."

"Could he still be in the building waiting to pick off other people or cause more 'accidental' deaths?"

Aiden glanced at the techs photographing the scene. Their already pale faces turned ghostly. Aiden hadn't thought of Carley's proposal because he hadn't sensed any demons since his arrival. While the elevator and the surrounding area were soaked in the killer's power, there was nothing new or more potent radiating in the vicinity. The energy weighing on Aiden was dispersed and slowly fading. A demon as powerful as the suspect wouldn't be able to easily hide from him, especially after using so much power to commit a murder.

The demon wasn't there... but he could come up with no logical reason why the killer couldn't be.

"Well, he didn't hang around the first scene. We brought the detectors in after the explosion to be sure. The killer wants something very specific. Mass murder doesn't fit his profile. That being said, he is still a demon. It might be a good idea to send a scanning team to sweep the building," Aiden replied.

Carley pulled her phone from her jacket pocket and walked away to make the call. Aiden slipped on a pair of latex gloves and stepped into the elevator for a closer look at the body. The killer had, thus far, not tortured his victims. He killed his prey efficiently and never gave the opportunity to fight back. There was a professional tone to both crimes. This demon was an assassin.

Aiden searched the gaping hole in the victim's chest. He ran his fingers along the inside of the wound, vainly attempting to ignore it was raw, human flesh. There were no claw or bite impressions. He saw no runes and felt no marks of power. The killer had left the clothing on, so much of the victim's body was still covered. Aiden would have to wait for Douglas' report.

He sighed and switched his train of thought. The killer was talking to Alexis Montral, but Aiden didn't sense any of her power in the building. He hadn't checked the list of properties Alexis owned before arriving at the scene, but he was willing to bet his paycheck that this was one of them. Aiden wondered what criteria Alexis used to determine which buildings got wards and which did not.

He'd believed Alexis when she said she had no love for the demon, but her inability to find and end him herself made no sense. If Alexis could read the messages—and Aiden was confident she could—she should easily be able to communicate with the killer. There were pieces to her puzzle Aiden was missing.

Though if he was honest with himself, he didn't even know how many pieces Alexis' puzzle had.

"The Captain is sending a team discreetly through the building. What are you looking for?" Carley asked from behind him.

Aiden stripped off the gloves and put them into an evidence bag. "I was hoping to get lucky with a rune or a mark of some kind. There might still be one under her clothing, but I doubt it. The medical examiner will have to let us know."

Carley gestured to the blood crescent around the victim's neck. "Then I suggest you step back. Given what happened last time, we should probably let the techs box that up."

Aiden didn't think twice. He moved quickly out of the elevator. He couldn't remember the last time he had gotten away from a crime scene clean. He really didn't want to waste the rest of the afternoon in the lab. As soon as he stepped out, Aiden nodded to the technicians who had been waiting for him and Carley to finish. They flooded the elevator and began dismantling the scene.

"Thanks," Aiden said to Carley.

"*Psh*. That was for me. We drove my car here. The last thing I need is a permanent blood stain of your ass in my passenger seat," Carley replied before she frowned. "I don't think we learned anything new here."

"About the killer? No, I don't think so, either. But maybe we don't need to know everything about him to catch him. Maybe we should focus on what he wants. Do you know if Alexis Montral owns this building?"

Carley smiled. "I wondered that, too. I checked after I got off the phone with the Captain. She does own the building… *and* the real estate company our victim worked for. The other businesses in this building rent from her."

"So, the victim is another one of her employees," Aiden replied.

Carley nodded. "Yeah. She's involved somehow. It can't be coincidence. With her background and the scans, I think she might be the target. The only solid thing that links the scenes is her, besides the fact that we know it's the same killer."

Aiden still wasn't entirely sure Alexis was a target. He supposed she could be, if she and the killer were battling over territory. But Aiden had put his ear to the gossip of the magical community. There was no word of Alexis at all. It was as if she didn't exist to them. So Alexis technically had no territory to defend.

She must have something the killer needed or wanted. That led Aiden to believe the killer wasn't threatening Alexis' life.

"We can't rule out the victims are related just yet, but my gut is following yours," Aiden said.

"We should put her under protection."

"The killer hasn't moved against her, yet," Aiden said skeptically.

"No, but his direct moves look like that," Carley said as she pointed to the elevator. "It only takes seconds for this guy to make killing blows. Alexis wouldn't survive his direct approach."

Aiden sighed. It was very likely Alexis Montral would survive, though at the moment, Aiden wasn't sure which demon he preferred to come out on top.

This killer slaughtered humans just to send messages. Once his intentions were discovered, he would become predictable and that would make him possible to hunt. His magic, however, was terrifying and had limitless potentially deadly uses.

Alexis had committed no crime that Aiden was aware of, though he didn't doubt she was guilty of something. She flourished in human society, meaning she had an advanced level of self-control and manipulation. Alexis was bold and wildly unpredictable. Aiden possessed no clear vision of her motivations yet either, nor did he have a full understanding of her magic. Despite the way his personal emotions became clouded around her, he found himself hoping the killer would defeat Alexis. It was even possible he would stop slaughtering humans once Alexis was dead or the killer got what he came for.

None of that helped Aiden explain why putting a detail of officers around Alexis was unwise. While it was tempting to have someone watching her twenty-four hours a day, Aiden genuinely believed the officers would lose their lives needlessly.

He also couldn't out Alexis as a demon now. She had managed to fool the tetrabind detectors. No one would believe him. It also irritated Aiden she had somehow managed to alter the DNA results. He was stuck. Carley wasn't going to like his opinion.

"I understand why you are going down that line of thought, but I'm not sure it would do Montral any good," Aiden said carefully.

Carley folded her arms across her chest and narrowed her gaze. Her tone dropped below freezing. Aiden almost winced.

"And just what makes you think that?" she asked.

Aiden met the controlled fury in her bright emerald eyes. "Just hear me out. Given what we already know about the killer, I don't think it's possible for three or four body guards to terminate him. None of the victims have seen him coming. To kill this demon, we will need a large team, a rock-solid plan, and equipment that guard details couldn't carry by hand. Our officers will just die right along with her."

"So, you're saying we shouldn't waste the lives of officers trained for just this type of situation in order to keep a potential victim from dying," Carley said flatly.

"I'm saying it'll be more than one innocent body we find. You know it's true. The extra protection might even entice the demon. He could say, 'Look at all the juicy meat she's offering me'," Aiden replied.

"I can't justify leaving a known potential victim without protection. Our guys signed up to protect the civilian population. They knew the risks when they joined. No one is assigned here. You choose to come. That's why we're always understaffed. Montral is one of the people who needs our protection."

Aiden knew he wasn't going to change Carley's mind. He admired and agreed with her position under normal circumstances, but there was nothing normal about Alexis Montral.

"Let's present our points of view to the Captain and let him decide," Aiden said.

The frown on Carley's face deepened. "It's bullshit, Aiden, and you know it."

Aiden lowered his head and sighed. He refused to relent. "We are going to have to agree to disagree on this one. I don't want to see any more people die unnecessarily."

The scowl on Carley's face was almost painful. He would feel the same in her position. She was a good cop and a good woman. Aiden knew he would have to tread lightly for the rest of the case. Carley had stayed out of his business for years. She trusted him, but Aiden wasn't sure how far that trust stretched. She nodded over Aiden's shoulder toward the elevator.

"What else did you see in there? I saw a lot of crescent moons that might be symbolic when tied to the body at the first scene. I'm also wondering why the killer is targeting employees rather than people close to her," Carley said.

"Those infected with lycanthropy are ruled by the moon, but a full one. Not a crescent. Maybe the symbols build on each other somehow. We might get lucky in the database. I would say employees are plentiful and easier to access,"

Aiden replied, allowing Carley to drop the previous topic. He didn't want to discuss it further, either.

"But based off the argument you just used, the killer is capable of taking any target he chooses. Picking off someone alone at home is substantially easier than the fiasco he pulled in that elevator. I'm wondering if he's targeting what Alexis genuinely values. Her family is already dead, so he's targeting her next love. Her business," Carley said.

Aiden thought about the theory. He had no idea what a demon would find valuable and precious. They were creatures of death, destruction, and pain. Alexis was unknown to the magical community. If she had friends or associates there, they had done an amazing job of keeping themselves hidden and her name out of the gossip. Aiden had a hard time believing Alexis had human friends. They would ask too many questions.

"That's a very viable theory," Aiden replied.

"Montral has to be made aware of our suspicions, at the very least. I do want to bring our opinions in front of the Captain, mostly because yours is shitty. But Montral might be able to help us predict the killer's next strike."

Unfortunately, Carley's argument was valid. It was possible Alexis would share information about her businesses. The only question was whether or not she would lie.

"Agreed. The Captain can make the choice there, too," Aiden said.

Carley's phone rang and she pulled it from her pocket and showed him the screen. An image of Devant filled it. "Speak of the devil."

Aiden watched the expression on her face as Carley listened. Devant was as brief as always. Carley ended the call without saying a word. Her gaze rose to meet Aiden's.

"Two devils in one day. Montral is downstairs in the lobby."

"Routinely punctual," Aiden noted.

"I'm having trouble deciding if it's useful, suspicious, annoying, or all three," Carley replied and slipped her phone back in her pocket.

"It's also potentially dangerous. Did Devant say whether the team finished the sweep?" Aiden asked.

"Fuck! No, he didn't. We need to stick to her like white on rice."

"We would have to do that, anyway. She has an adventuring spirit. The department can't afford a repeat performance of the first scene," Aiden said flatly.

"Truth. Let's go find the Captain and greet the princess," Carley said.

Aiden raised an eyebrow. "Why is she suddenly a princess?"

Carley sighed. "I'm tired and she's tall and gorgeous and flawless and has enough money to be a damned princess."

Aiden laughed and held the door to the stairs open for her. "Just remember you left your shining armor back at the station."

When Carley smirked, Aiden followed her down the stairwell. In truth, he wasn't averse to talking with Alexis again. The strange connection between them was troublesome and never far from his mind. It clouded his judgment when he was around her, but Aiden felt the more they interacted, the easier it would become to control his responses.

As certain as Aiden was about her true nature, there were still far too many unknowns. The more information he could gather, the easier it would be to hunt her. It would also give his clan more knowledge about her race.

It could save the lives of future demon hunters.

Chapter Eight

Irritation pulsed just beneath the surface as Alexis sat on a bench in the lobby of Pristine Living Realtors. She hated being kept waiting, especially when she was pressed for time. She understood crime scenes were complicated and the FDPC needed to decide what information they wanted from her, but she was annoyed nonetheless.

The core of her irritation stemmed from the inability to see the scene in person. Since she couldn't go upstairs without causing irreparable problems, it was almost pointless for her to be there at all. She had gotten lucky with the first murder. Alexis would be forced to rely on surveillance footage for the second. She already had a copy of it on her private server. She just wanted to answer the FDPC's questions and leave.

After twenty minutes surrounded by a pack of eight armed and armored guards, Alexis wasn't sure if they were for her protection or if Aiden had found something to implicate her as a threat. The officers faced away from her with their automatic weapons pointed toward the ground, but since she wasn't resisting, the stance of the guards meant very little. If she'd learned anything during her time with humans, their logic was rarely linear. For a species that craved order, they were incredibly skilled at creating their own chaos.

The mere existence of the guards was frustrating. It was as if the killer didn't know involving the police made it harder for her to understand what he was trying to say. Alexis spent her nights scouring the city for traces of his power. The fact that he had managed to kill a second time before she found him grated on her. Four nights of effort had brought her nothing.

Regardless, she didn't want the FDPC to catch wind of her foul mood. She needed her composure to slide into the role she was expected to play, and losing her temper would be a sign of immaturity. She was skilled at making her displeasure known in other ways.

Alexis checked her watch and fought back a sigh. She'd seen Aiden and his partner step out from the stairwell ten minutes ago. They'd disappeared into the security office down the main hallway. She was curious about their discussion and could easily listen by tapping into the shadows in the room but would have to flex power to do so. Alexis had already encased herself in heavy shielding on the drive over. A second trip to the lab was not on her agenda.

Another ten minutes passed before the two detectives and their Captain emerged from the room. Detective Jameson was noticeably angry. Her body was wrought with tension.

During Alexis' brief encounters with the FDPC, she had only spotted a handful of women in the field or the lab. She wasn't certain if it was because the FDPC had gender limits, or if females just didn't apply for the positions. Either way, Alexis had more appreciation for Jameson because of it. Humans were notoriously cruel to their women.

Aiden didn't seem particularly happy either, though his expression was more apologetic. Whatever discussion or argument was had in the security office had been won by him and he wasn't proud of it. It made Alexis all the more curious, but there was no way to broach the topic without raising suspicion. The Captain parted ways with them at the stairwell and she rose as the detectives crossed the lobby to greet her. Four of the guards stepped out of the way, but they didn't go far.

"Good morning, Detectives. I'm sorry to see you again under these circumstances," Alexis said.

"We're sorry, too. We were hoping you could help answer some things for us," Jameson replied.

"Of course," Alexis said.

"Let's start with where you've been this morning. You're still not a suspect at this point, but we want to be able to account for your whereabouts," Aiden said.

Alexis shifted her attention to the demon hunter. He was studying her closely, but that was nothing new. The apologetic look on his face had shifted into stern silence.

"I woke up at five this morning for fitness. I have a gym at home so I don't need to travel. I showered and was out of the house by six-thirty. By seven-twenty, I was at Skyline. You guys still have the garage blocked off, so I had to park two blocks down. I've been at the office until I got the call from my security company. I handled everything I could over the phone before heading here."

"Do you do most of your business out of that office?" Carley asked.

"Yes, actually. The whole building is utilized by several of my companies. It has large rooms for meetings and is in a relatively central location."

"What about this building? Do you come here often?" Aiden asked.

"Not as frequently. Real estate is a constantly fluctuating field. My manager requires my approval before he buys or sells anything of substantial value, so I visit occasionally."

"Do you know Teresa Bates?" asked Aiden.

"Yes. I hired her personally. She deals with the more residential aspects of the company. Is she okay?" Alexis replied. The worry in her voice was real, despite knowing they wouldn't have asked if Teresa was still alive.

"I'm afraid not. She's dead," Carley said with a sympathetic softness.

Alexis let her shoulders slump and her gaze lower. Sadness that was only partially fake overtook her expression. Teresa had been a talented woman and a valuable asset. "Did she suffer?"

"From first observations, it doesn't appear so. We won't be able to determine the exact nature of her death until the medical examiner is finished. Did you work with Ms. Bates often?" Aiden questioned.

"I wouldn't say often. I had meetings with her once every three or four months to discuss problems and progress. If we were both busy, the conversations would happen over the phone. She was good at her job. I was completely confident in leaving her alone to do it."

"What about the first victim? Tyler Feit? Did you know him at all?" Carley asked.

Alexis raised an eyebrow. She was beginning to see where the line of questioning was going. "I did not. He was hired by the maintenance manager for Skyline. Is there a reason my association with them is important?"

Carley and Aiden glanced at each other before Carley spoke up. "We think the killer might be targeting you."

Alexis let waves of emotions she didn't feel wash over her body language. She had already known. In fact, she was sure she knew more about it than the FDPC. But it wouldn't do to let Aiden's partner catch hints of that knowledge. While he surely suspected the killer was after her, Carley would still be under the impression Alexis was human. She needed that belief to persevere.

Alexis paused the casual movements of her body and let the stillness of fear make her muscles rigid. Confusion and worry masked her face. "Do you know why?"

"You tell us," Aiden replied coldly.

Alexis had expected such a response from him, but it was interesting the statement brought the anger in Carley's eyes to life. The detective held her tongue, though. Even when angry, Carley would back Aiden. Loyalty and the wisdom to hear answers to questions she didn't like were why Carley had rank.

Alexis didn't have to lie. She would certainly fluff the facts if she had to, but the truth was entirely suitable for this question. "I really have no idea, Detectives. My money is tied up in my corporation and a rock-solid will. I live a quiet, boring life, really. Sometimes I go out, but it's never to any place dangerous or questionable—excursions and travel with business associates—but that's about it."

"Alright. What we've seen in these scenes is highly unusual for the type of creature we're hunting," Carley said. "This creature is immensely dangerous, Ms. Montral. If you do have something or someone you are protecting, now's the time to give it up. Your life is worth more."

"I am not, and would not, protect someone who would do this. Why would I jeopardize my own business? Despite the fact that I will miss Teresa as a person, she will be difficult to replace. Her death makes my business suffer in more ways than just the loss of an employee," Alexis said.

Aiden sighed and nodded.

Alexis ran her fingers through her hair nervously. "So, what do I do?"

"Do you have any friends or family you are close with?" he asked.

Alexis shook her head. She never had family, and her few friends were more than capable of protecting themselves. She didn't see them publicly or frequently, and Alexis wouldn't give them up to the FDPC.

"Not really. My parents are dead, and I have no siblings. I don't have much time for a social life," she said.

"Is there no one at all? Not even a significant other you keep tucked in your back pocket?" Carley asked with skepticism.

"Unfortunately, I have found as soon as people discover how much money I have, my value as a person diminishes. Because of that, the people I am closest to are the ones I work with, which is what you've been building to all along, I suppose," Alexis replied sadly.

Aiden nodded. "Greed is a powerful motivator for many, but I don't think it is this killer's motivation. He kicked it up a notch with this murder."

"What do you mean?"

"The first victim was someone you didn't know. The second was someone you spent regular, if infrequent, intervals of time with. He's been watching you and paying attention. I believe the next victim will be someone even closer to you. Can you think of anyone who might fit that pattern? Anyone you care about more than the others?" Aiden asked.

"There are a lot of people I interact with daily. My secretary and his assistants come to mind first. My entire managerial staff. That's already more than thirty people," Alexis replied with worry in her tone.

"We will need you to think hard on it and give us a list. All of them are potential victims," Carley said.

"How do I protect my staff? How do I protect myself? I saw what was done to the first victim."

Aiden looked to Carley. When she only folded her arms across her chest, he sighed. Evidence of discontent between them continued to mount. Alexis didn't envy Aiden his position. He knew things about the scene his partner did not. Apparently, he found the knowledge too risky to share.

Assuming Carley had a keen eye, she picked up on any oddities in Aiden's behavior that might be caused by the information he didn't share. The case was potentially as dangerous for him as it was for Alexis.

"The type of creature we suspect is very powerful," Aiden said.

Alexis frowned. "You've told me that several times now. I assure you, I am sufficiently frightened. I will take the necessary steps to ensure the safety of my team. But I can't do that unless you tell me how."

Aiden's gaze grew hot. Alexis felt a hint of heat from his power before it was snuffed out. She wanted to chastise him for letting anger trigger his power, but she decided to be grateful he'd maintained some level of control. Neither one of them needed the annoying connection between them to flare. It was always better for Aiden to be angry rather than her. It gave Alexis leverage. He was irritated because he knew she was aware there was nothing she could do to protect her employees within the realm of human security. She'd forced him to own up to his shortcomings.

"There isn't much you can do, I'm afraid. He's an expert stalker and takes his victims by surprise. Both times now, he has killed when his victims were alone. I wouldn't go anywhere by myself. Tell your staff to do the same. Just going to the bathroom or taking a shower is enough time for him to get the job done," Aiden replied flatly.

Alexis shivered and rubbed her arms. "Okay. So, travel in packs. Would sending my staff away on vacation make a difference?"

"As much as I want to say yes, I don't think it would. The killer would just move down the ladder or speed up whatever plan he has and directly assault you.

You would only be playing a shell game with people's lives," Aiden replied with a frown of his own.

"That's a very bleak prognosis," Alexis said quietly.

"We know. We promise to do everything we can to stop this guy before he gets any further," Carley said sympathetically.

"I'm sure you're doing everything you can, Detectives. Is there anything else you need from me, or can I go back to my office to brief my people?"

Carley looked to Aiden. He shook his head and Carley turned back to Alexis. "I think that's it for now. Some of our guys will escort you to your office. You have our number if you can think of anything else."

Alexis nodded solemnly. "Thank you."

With no reason to stay, Alexis sighed and left the lobby with four officers in tow. They silently escorted her to her vehicle. Once she left, two new police cars pulled into traffic behind her. Though she kept an eye on them, Alexis didn't watch too closely. She knew their intentions. She synced her phone to the wireless in her car and made a call to Mark to task him with setting up a conference call for every New York manager. He didn't question her but hurried off the phone.

There was nothing her staff could do to protect themselves using human methods. The killer had all her same physical attributes and obvious training. Even humans experienced in terminating magical creatures wouldn't last much longer than corporate executives.

Providing her staff with all the details would only cause panic. However, Alexis had to tell them something. Aiden's idea wasn't a bad one. There was a level of safety in numbers that was worth a try.

Alexis pulled into the same garage she had parked in earlier that morning. The police vehicles blocked several cars behind hers and four new officers escorted her all the way to Mark's desk. Alexis couldn't fault them for doing their job, but they drew unwanted attention. Rumors had already begun.

She turned and smiled softly. "Thank you, gentlemen. I'll be here for most of the day."

"You're welcome, ma'am. Just remember what Detective Thompson said. This thing is no joke. Stay in groups and watch out for each other," an officer replied.

"I'll spread the word, for sure. Thank you, again."

Each of the four nodded to her and made their way to the main elevator. Alexis sighed and folded her arms across her chest as she leaned a hip against Mark's desk.

"Escorted by four boys in blue. Must be a record for you," Mark said with a smile that didn't quite meet his eyes.

Alexis chuckled lightly because she knew he was trying to make her laugh. "None of them offered to strip for me. Quite the disappointment."

Mark laughed before he leaned back in his chair. His expression sobered. "Do you know who it was?"

Alexis met his gaze. "Teresa Bates."

Mark's eyes widened. "Oh fuck."

"Yeah," Alexis replied as she looked at her shoes.

"Do the cops have any clue?"

Alexis shrugged. "I don't think the FDPC works like most police departments. I think they know what type of thing is doing this but finding and killing it is another matter entirely. Were you able to get the call set up?"

"It's scheduled to start in fifteen minutes. I wanted to give you some time to settle. I know none of this is easy," Mark said.

"It isn't, no. But the meeting needs to happen. The police gave me some information about safety that needs to be distributed. Please cancel any upcoming meetings that require me to go out of town or that bring others into New York," Alexis replied.

"Why?"

"The police asked that I stay available to help them. I'll explain the rest in the meeting, but it will suffice to say we don't need to bring more people into the city right now. So, clear my schedule of everything that isn't New York based for a month. Switch it to telecommunication if you have to," Alexis said.

"I'll get working on that, and put the call through to your office when it's time," Mark replied.

"Thanks."

Alexis gave him a half smile before she pushed off his desk and passed through the wooden double doors behind him. She didn't always lock herself in, but the rest of the day following the conference call wouldn't be work related. Alexis kicked off her heels and sat down to formulate the notes she wanted to cover during the call.

The meeting was brief, and conversation ended without disagreement. No one liked the situation, but there was nothing anyone could do about it. Precautions would be implemented. Alexis pushed her notes aside and pulled up her private server on her desktop. The surveillance video of the murder was waiting for her. She pressed play and watched with cold objectiveness. Once again, the killer never appeared on camera. Alexis would have to put more thought into why that could be, but for the moment, she gave her full attention to the scene in front of her. The killer had planned ahead and never hesitated. The killing blow had come the moment the elevator doors closed behind Teresa.

Her head was instantly severed. Alexis tilted her own as she watched the killer's skill with both magic and a blade she couldn't see. Even as he carved and strung the body, Teresa's blood swirled around the elevator. It solidified as it painted the walls in crescent moons. The shape he chose was another point to ponder, since it didn't seem to match the shape in the first murder at all. Nor did it relate to her power. She had a hard time believing his energy was driven by the moon in any of its phases.

Alexis could fight physically and use her power at the same time, so it didn't surprise her that the killer could, too. But it did give her a gauge of his aptitude for dual combat. Not all magic users could do multiple things at once and do them well. The killer's speed and precision never faltered. Each slice was done in a single, efficient stroke. He didn't waste movements. He promised to be one of the few true challenges in combat Alexis had faced in years.

Alexis frowned with annoyance when the video ended. The camera wasn't mobile and there was only one in each elevator. Her view of the message on the back wall wasn't suitable. She could only see the tail end of one or two letters. Alexis leaned back in her chair and tapped her fingers on her desk. Without the message, the scene didn't tell her anything new. There were new angles to consider, but none of them gave her a direct link to her prey. It was just another dead body drawing the FDPC closer to her.

There was something deeper brewing, but Alexis had no idea what it could be. The FDPC had done a good job of keeping her from the scene and would continue to do so for any crime scene in the future. The frustration burned beneath her skin. She needed that message.

Her train of thought brought her back to Aiden. Both she and the hunter had information the other wanted. While an alliance was the obvious option, Alexis wasn't in a hurry to align herself with someone who made the destruction of her race his sole purpose in life. Aiden wasn't alone in his hatred. Demon hunters came in clans. But the killer wasn't going to stop until she answered him somehow. Murder had a funny way of forcing hands.

Aiden was either still at the crime scene or he had moved on to the FDPC precinct. Neither location was suitable for a visit, nor was it wise to see him when the sun was high in the sky. His power was ruled by heat, while hers was strongest in the dark. Alexis knew better than to think she could control the fire in him, but she could guide his actions if she used enough potent, well-placed fuel.

With a plan of action slowly formulating, Alexis sent a message to Mark informing him she would be leaving early. New York's magical community was full of all kinds of interesting gossip. Whispers in the dark were her expertise, and there was darkness all over the city despite the burning sun. If she got lucky, she would hear something that would render her need for the hunter—and the trouble he would bring—obsolete.

But Alexis wasn't a woman to count on luck. She spent the remainder of the afternoon looking through her cards to stack her deck accordingly.

Chapter Nine

Carley sat at her desk in the precinct and stared blankly at the computer. Her pen tapped against her thigh at a merciless pace. Instead of the typical quick flash and casual fade, her anger had only grown throughout the day. Working into the night usually didn't bother her, but her mood was foul enough the smallest details pressed her last nerve. Co-workers chose to interact only if they had information she needed. While she wasn't blatantly rude, her frustration was obvious.

The medical examiner's report was displayed on her screen. As with the first body, the examiner confirmed the cause of death as decapitation. It was likely all other injuries had occurred post-mortem, though it was difficult to say for certain since the killer extracted the victim's blood. This absence of blood minimized evidence of clotting and flow. There were no bite or claw marks, nor symbols of power of any kind. The report provided nothing she hadn't determined herself at the scene. Carley flexed her jaw and the pace of her tapping pen increased.

An officer passed and quietly set a file on the corner of her desk. She mumbled her thanks and even managed to take the folder without snatching. It was a report containing the field data collected by the lab. The tetrabind readings matched the first scene in wavelength, waveform, and amplitude, which eliminated the possibility of a copy-cat.

The numbers quantifying the energy at both scenes were the highest Carley had ever seen. She had scoured the research databases for similar data, but the instances were rare and typically involved whole covens of witches combining power. There were less than five cases where tetrabind readings from a singular entity were as high as this killer's. Only two of those resulted in terminations. The rest were unsolved. It was both fascinating and frightening.

Carley sighed and set the lab report on her desk and closed the medical examiner's file. Both were academically intriguing, but neither gave her clues to locate or kill the demon. They only promised the termination would be messy.

That train of thought led her to Alexis Montral. Carley still struggled with Devant's decision. Her day had been filled with the delivery of bad news and interviewing distraught family members. If Montral died now, Carley wanted to be able to tell anyone left behind that the FDPC had done their very best. Devant's decision would rob her of that ability and went against everything she joined the force for. Disgust churned in her stomach.

Her gaze found Aiden across their joined desks. He was neck deep in a computer search for a connection between the two symbols the killer had carved. Concentration lined his face, but he checked his phone constantly. Carley wanted to know who he was talking to and why, but believed he would lie if questioned. That notion only added fuel to her steadily growing fire.

The root of her anger stemmed from confusion. Carley didn't understand why he'd changed his stance on protection for potential victims. Every other case they had worked together with similar circumstances, his views had matched hers. Most times, the protection saved lives. The power of this killer shouldn't play a factor in civilian defense. The only fathomable reason for such a change of heart was knowledge. Aiden knew something about the killer he wasn't sharing.

Whether he knew it or not, his dislike for Alexis Montral was evident. His strange behavior had begun the moment she stepped foot onto the first crime scene. He'd pressed her harder than any cooperative informant they had encountered in the past. Montral handled the pressure elegantly, which only seemed to irritate Aiden more.

Carley conceded Montral's background was strange. Not many had such an intimate relationship with death. But she'd been a child and a victim, not a criminal. The nature of her father's killings certainly hinted at ritualistic magic, but Montral's DNA and lab exam were negative. Carley found no logical reason for Aiden's opinion, but his behavior only solidified a connection between her and the killer.

Devant's decision meant the only way to protect the target was to stop the killer. So Carley put aside her displeasure and pulled up the long personnel list Montral emailed earlier. If Devant hadn't approved protection for a billionaire, he certainly wouldn't approve it for the lesser minions. Regardless, the New York division of the FDPC didn't have the staff. A request for assistance would have to be sent to Washington, D.C. They were notoriously slow and carried unrealistic expectations.

Yet, to lay a trap for the demon, the FDPC needed to watch his prey. Demons didn't hide from daylight or hunt in packs. Typical methods of finding the diseased didn't apply. Carley didn't believe they would find his resting place through sheer detective prowess. There just wasn't enough evidence to follow. There had to be a way to watch the people on the list without spreading FDPC forces too thin.

As Carley browsed the information, an idea formed in her mind. She grabbed her notepad and flipped to a fresh page. The case file had a list of properties owned by Montral. She began to reference the names on the list to the different properties on record.

Montral was thorough. She'd included where each listed individual worked, their job title, and their usual business hours. It allowed Carley to group employees by buildings. Once she had accounted for everyone, she prioritized the buildings by the number of potential targets. The FPDC couldn't watch every property, but she might be able to convince the Captain to set small teams equipped with tetrabind scanners in statistically high-target zones.

"The computer techs finished with the surveillance video," Aiden said.

Carley looked up. Frustration lined his tone, but she had no sympathy. The only response she gave was to grab her notepad and walk around to his desk. She folded her arms as he pressed play.

The video was just as disturbing as the footage from the first scene. Carley was relieved she had forgotten about dinner. The brutality had been committed in under forty seconds, according to the time stamp on the screen. The killer had barely finished stringing up the body with the victim's own dissected muscle when the elevator doors opened to the male witness. The killer could have easily taken his life, too, but didn't. All activity from the killer stopped with the witness.

"Our boy can wield magic and cut people up at the same time."

Carley looked over her shoulder to see Devant staring at Aiden's computer screen. She stepped aside to include him in the discussion. His expression and gaze were hollow. In that moment, she realized Devant was tired of looking at death. She didn't know how long the man held the position, or what he had done prior, but she did know he was away from his desk more than behind it.

While she empathized, Carley was still angry. He should be haunted by the victim's death. Montral stood to share a similar fate.

"He seems strangely efficient at it, yes," Carley replied. "He displayed that skill in the first scene, too."

"It makes him even more deadly," Aiden said. "He didn't leave a demonic mess this time. He is capable of controlling the urge when he wants to."

"I was just noting that he left the witness alive when he could have easily silenced him to buy more time," Carley commented.

"I find that strange, too," Aiden said. "I guess he finished what he came to do, but it speaks volumes about his self-control."

"The more I see of him, the more I get the impression he is some demonic assassin. Outside of the gruesome nature, these killings are almost professional," Carley observed.

"They are very professional," Aiden agreed, "but that doesn't really help us. It's not like there are schools that train demons for us to raid."

"No, but it makes his methods more predictable," Carley countered. "Instead of hunting a rabid dog, we hunt a terrorist. Knowing his patterns will help us during the termination."

"Speaking of termination," Devant interrupted, "any ideas on how we go about killing this thing yet? I know there were general ideas, but have we seen enough for a solid plan?"

"Combat priests, dense iron bullets, iron shackles that can be fired from trap cannons, holy water, fire… and luck," Aiden said bleakly.

"We can get teams set up with equipment on constant standby. The weasels in Washington have been breathing down my neck for an intact carcass. They want it for the labs," Devant said with a frown.

Aiden's face dropped with disbelief. "You've got to be fucking kidding me, Captain. With all due respect, that's dangerous. I understand the knowledge it could bring, but at what cost?"

"I agree here," Carley said. "We don't know what will even define death to a demon this powerful. Say we bring back an intact corpse. What happens if he gets off the table and slaughters everyone in the lab?"

Devant sighed. "I know. I'm not going to sacrifice the lives of my people and civilians for the book worms. I told them I would try. I never said how hard. Given your suggestions so far, my plan is to have the head severed, the heart blown out with lead, the body burned in holy fire, and the ashes drenched in holy water."

Aiden grinned. "I knew there was a reason I liked you, Captain."

Devant grunted. "We have to find the bastard first."

"I've been working on that. Since the two of you are assholes and don't want to put a detail on the person we think is the primary target, I came up with a different approach," Carley said.

"Drop it, Jameson. The decision is made. None of us are happy about it, but if this demon is as powerful as the evidence suggests, we'll need every last man to shut him down. I don't want to hear any more jabs from you," Devant replied sharply.

"I don't see how we'll be able to find where this demon sleeps if he can make himself vanish from sight. As much as it sucks, to catch him, we're going to have to watch his prey somehow. Otherwise, we're nothing more than body counters," Carley replied as she fearlessly met the Captain's annoyed gaze.

"You want to set up surveillance teams," Devant said.

"Montral sent the list we asked for," Carley replied. "I referenced it to our list of properties and came up with a few buildings the demon might find most tempting. We can ignore all her other properties. Small task forces equipped with tetrabind scanners might be able to catch a hint of the killer as he enters a building. It obviously still requires man power and will leave huge gaps in target coverage, but it's less risky to our forces."

Devant folded his arms across his chest and glanced at Aiden. "What do you think?"

Carley set her jaw as Aiden thought about it. She wouldn't allow him to impede the investigation any longer and she was angry enough to be petty. The FDPC couldn't afford to just sit and wait for bodies to pile up. If he went against her idea, she planned to call him out on whatever he was withholding.

"I think it's a long shot, but it might be the best we have. We can set termination teams in central areas where they could cover more than one building if a surveillance team puts out a call. We could also monitor Montral's movements that way, at least when she's working," Aiden finally said.

Carley almost sighed with relief. Aiden's agreement didn't make up for his earlier actions, but it made her more inclined to discuss things with him privately.

"Agreed. Hand over the list and I'll get the teams mobilized. Any word on the messages?" Devant asked.

"Nothing of value. The linguist analyzing it identified words that were used repeatedly in one or both messages, but he says those words are likely conjunctions. He can't do more without better data," Aiden said as Carley tore the list from her notepad.

"Another dead end," Devant noted. "At least the language will be a consolation prize for the Washington boys."

Aiden's phone vibrated on his desk. Carley watched as his eyes widened when he read the number. He quickly excused himself and stepped out into the hallway. Carley's gaze narrowed.

"An interesting time for a personal phone call," Devant observed quietly.

"Very interesting, indeed," she replied with a frown.

"Get him straightened up. I don't like worrying about good cops," Devant said quietly before disappearing back into his office.

Carley frowned. He wanted her to fix the problem before he had to step in. She didn't want to see Aiden's career end any more than the Captain.

With a sigh, she returned to her desk and watched her partner through the windows. He paced back and forth as he spoke. She couldn't make herself believe he was compromised. Though his behavior and logic for the case were atypical, he hadn't lost control of his temper or his enthusiasm for finding the killer. He had yet to cross any real lines, though he was coming too close for comfort. Crooked officers existed in all divisions of law enforcement and they gave good cops bad names. At least the diseased often had no control over their actions. They were driven by unimaginable impulses and hungers. Humans made choices and Carley didn't want to believe Aiden had become something worse than the diseased.

She shook her head and looked down at the notes on her desk. She couldn't think of a single reason to hide information. There was no one to protect. Everyone involved in the case was a stranger. But then a memory flashed through her mind and her eyes widened. Aiden had recognized Montral at the first crime scene. When she asked him about it later, he fed her a story. Yet, because he was her partner, Carley had believed him.

As the realization sank in, her chest began to burn. She drew in a breath, and tried not to let her mind jump to unjustified conclusions. She had no proof, and despite current circumstances, she did trust her partner. But she knew, without a doubt, Aiden already knew Montral.

Carley needed to discover the connection. The information might not help catch the killer, but it would give her peace of mind. Aiden was a good person. Moments of life and death always revealed the truth of a person, and they had shared many of those moments. She witnessed his compassion for both victims and those who lost themselves to disease time and again. There had to be a logical reason Aiden would lie for someone he otherwise appeared to dislike.

Carley was still contemplating the theory when Aiden returned and began to gather his belongings. She raised an eyebrow at him. "Did you finally succumb and pay for a date?"

Aiden paused and looked at her from across the desks. Something flashed in his eyes Carley couldn't quite read. "There is nothing more you or I can do tonight. I'm going home. You should, too."

The shock from his reply froze Carley temporarily, but she recovered and tossed her pen and notepad on her desk before moving to sit on his. She waited until Aiden's gaze locked with hers and then lowered her voice for only him. "What's going on, Aiden? You know you can trust me. I've got your back. I always have. Who was on the phone?"

Aiden instantly looked away, frustration etched into his features. He jammed his phone and his wallet into his pockets and grabbed the jacket off the back of his chair.

"Nothing's wrong. I'm allowed to be in as shitty of a mood as you. We've been spinning our wheels here all day and I'm sick of it. I'm going home to a beer and my bed."

He didn't give Carley a chance to answer. He turned his back and walked out the door. The power of his reaction overtook her. Though she knew his frustration wasn't with her directly, Aiden was her friend and his refusal of her help stung. He had also lied to her face.

Her temper reignited. If friendship and compassion hadn't worked, perhaps a good verbal beating would do the trick. She hopped off his desk and grabbed her own coat before rushing after him. The full power of the storm brewed within her and she planned to rain down hard on whatever game was endangering her friend's career.

CHAPTER TEN

Alexis watched the doors of the FDPC precinct from an alley across the street. The sun had fallen and artificial lights from the city took its place. Rush hour had passed, but the streets were still filled with people enjoying the precious freedom the evening offered. Every now and then, a pedestrian would glance down her alley, but none saw her. She was one with the shadows, her body nothing but darkness. It was almost as good as true invisibility.

She'd come earlier in the afternoon with hopes of catching either or both detectives. Her sources had run dry and she wanted to see if the police had any more luck than her. Both of their vehicles were in the parking lot and hadn't moved since her arrival. Aiden and Carley were either using different cars or they hadn't left the precinct in hours. Alexis was patient, but she would be irritated if she'd wasted a night staring at the chipping paint on the station's doors.

Sneaking into the building was an option. She could be the shadows in every room with no one physically able to see a difference. If it were any other place, Alexis wouldn't have hesitated. But the FDPC held too many unknowns. She'd barely made it past the sensors in the laboratory undetected. If Aiden didn't sense her presence, one of the machines might. Being identified as non-human in a room full of police wasn't on her agenda.

Her patience was finally rewarded when Aiden shoved his way through the double doors. He made no attempt to hide his irritation. Carley was fast on his heels and grabbed his arm. They argued and the topic of discussion piqued Alexis' interest. They were outside and Alexis didn't mind if Aiden sensed her there. She had more room to move. She tapped into the shadows around the pair to listen.

"Dammit, Aiden! Share. I know you're not a glory hound. You want this monster gone as much as I do, but you're acting like a jackass. I don't understand why."

"Share what? I'm exhausted, and my head is killing me. We've chased our tails for twelve hours. Being tired and frustrated won't help."

"Oh, so one phone call after a crap-tastic day and you suddenly turn into Cinder-fucking-rella? You're drowning in so much shit your lungs are brown!" Carley said, exasperated.

"If I had a damned lead, I'd tell you. You know that. The call was from a concerned friend. I missed..." Aiden trailed off and glanced around his surroundings.

Alexis knew he sensed her. That he could do so in her least tangible form was irritating but nothing could be done about how her power reacted with his and she wanted to hear the rest. Aiden's expression seemed to alarm Carley. She put a hand on his shoulder and her tone softened.

"What is it? Talk to me. Please."

Carley's touch snapped Aiden back to the conversation. "Let it go. I was supposed to have dinner with a friend and forgot. He reminded me of what can happen if you stretch yourself too thin. I'm going home. You should, too."

Aiden yanked his shoulder out from under Carley's hand and stalked to his car. Alexis focused on Carley's face, interested in what kind of person the detective was. Hurt blossomed across her features and her gaze lowered. But it didn't stay that way for more than a moment. Her head snapped up, pain replaced with determination. She sprinted to her car and took off after him.

Amused, Alexis followed one detective as she followed the other. In shadow form, Alexis moved faster than any man-made vehicle. She didn't have to worry about running into other cars or pedestrians. She matched the pace the detectives drove easily.

Aiden pulled into a parking space in front of an apartment building. Carley managed to find street parking two blocks down. Alexis watched as he jogged up the stairs to a door and glanced over his shoulder for a quick sweep of the street. There was no indication he saw Carley. Alexis wasn't sure how he could have missed her, but he quickly disappeared inside the building.

Alexis returned her attention to the female detective. Contrary to Aiden, she was entirely focused. It was clear she didn't believe the story Aiden had fed her. He had a lead he didn't want to share at work. Alexis sympathized, given the difficulty of his position, but he'd done a poor job of lying and now his partner was sniffing on his heels. Carley struck her as a loyal individual, so she was curious to see what was powerful enough to motivate the woman to invade Aiden's privacy.

Twenty minutes later, he reappeared in fitted jeans and his leather jacket. The coat didn't drape perfectly over his body, a slight bulge visible beneath his left shoulder. It wouldn't be obvious to a bystander, but a trained eye could see the detective was armed. Wherever he was going must be dangerous enough for him to want a gun but not enough to carry heavy equipment.

Aiden jogged to his car and drove off without a glance. Carley waited an appropriate amount of time before she followed. She was a good tail. Her instincts were solid and she had training, but she was far from invisible. Aiden should have seen her. Either he wasn't as good as Alexis believed or whatever was on his mind was clouding his awareness. Alexis bet on the latter. Hunters often forgot they could become prey.

He drove out to Brooklyn and navigated through several back streets before parking a few blocks down from a club called Dark Heart. Carley switched her lights off early and parked two blocks behind him. Alexis remained in the shadows and stayed in an alley between Aiden and the club. It gave her a clear view of both detectives.

Dark Heart was a safehouse for the non-human community, a place where socializing could happen without prying eyes. Unfortunately, it wasn't an upstanding establishment. No Master or high-ranking individual would be caught there. It catered to the squalid desires of the lowest trash in the community, but it was a good place to go for information or rumors.

Aiden was either fishing or meeting someone. If the former, there was nothing to catch. At best, he would hear intangible rumors about her and nothing he didn't already know about the demon they both hunted. Alexis had a source check the club already. If he was meeting someone, she was interested in who and the topic of conversation.

Aiden got out of his car and walked toward the club. He paused in front of her alley. He perused the darkness thoroughly. Again, he sensed her. She knew he saw nothing but empty shadows. Years of experience and training forged her confidence. Her energy was dispersed through every shadow in the vicinity. It made her feel like nothing more than a whisper in the wind. She stared back at him and waited. After several long moments, he sighed and shook his head.

"She's got you chasing ghosts, man," he mumbled before moving on.

Alexis smirked then looked back to Carley. The woman had left her car and followed Aiden on foot. Alexis sighed inwardly at her persistence. It made her a good cop, but such behavior often led to trouble.

When Carley stopped walking and leaned against a building, Alexis turned her attention back to Aiden. He was speaking with the club's bouncer. She recognized the doorman as a vampire named Militar, notorious in the community for the rare ability to sense the nature of power in anyone he touched.

It wasn't easy to trick him. Militar was a full-fledged Adult of Belladona Le'Roe's bloodline, overkill for the simple task of bouncing. But his abilities were ideal for maintaining the public invisibility of Dark Heart's patrons. It also meant the club had Le'Roe's backing, even if she never went there.

Militar and Aiden shook hands and the door mysteriously opened. Militar stepped to the side and Aiden disappeared into the club. With him gone, Alexis looked back to Carley. Aiden could handle himself. Carley was another matter.

Her determined expression left Alexis with no doubt she would attempt to follow. There was no fear in her. To Carley, Dark Heart was a nondescript club in the bad side of Brooklyn. To get in she would have to get past Militar. He only gave passage to those who had power. Alexis knew Carley possessed a little. She'd felt small hints of it during their interactions.

But it would be in the detective's best interest for Militar to deny her. She had no knowledge of the rules or customs in the community. With no viable power to defend herself, Carley would either end up accidentally insulting someone… or as a snack. She'd die in a fight. Neither option was pleasant. Alexis was curious to see how she handled Militar, so she tapped into the shadows to listen and pondered whether she should care about the detective's fate.

* * *

Carley watched Aiden disappear into the club. She'd never heard of Dark Heart. From the outside, the club looked trashy. The bouncer made her think otherwise. He was about 5'10" and around 175 pounds, dressed in perfectly tailored black slacks and a short-sleeve button up shirt with the top three buttons undone.

He looked like a cover boy for a fashion magazine. A punch from her grandmother would knock him out and it put her on edge. He shouldn't be the sole bouncer at a club in Brooklyn. She had learned to be cautious when the pieces of a puzzle didn't make a picture.

Carley took the time to pull her hair down, untuck her shirt, and pull the zipper of her coat halfway down. She needed to look less like a cop and more like a woman. When she did approach the bouncer, she made sure there was a cocky smile on her lips and a flirty expression in her eyes.

Her gut twitched when she got her first solid look. Something about him wasn't right. His skin was sickly pale and his hair was such a light shade of blond it bordered on white. But she wouldn't put him over the age of thirty. When he smiled, there was a flash of elongated canines and Carley had to fight to keep from gasping. He was diseased, and of the vampiric variety.

Ice cold fear slid through her, but she clamped onto her resolve like a life jacket and forced herself to maintain the playful expression. She hadn't been prepared to face vampires. She only had her gun. If there was an altercation, the gun would slow them down. Nothing more. Carley knew she should walk away, but the thought of Aiden alone inside gnawed on her conscience.

The vampire's voice carried a distinct French accent. "Haven't seen you here before, Miss. Is tonight your first at Dark Heart?"

His voice was liquid sex. Carley wanted him to slide that foreign tongue over every inch of her skin. She almost stepped forward to let him do just that before she caught herself. Never in her life had she wanted a man's tongue anywhere near her body. He was using vampiric influence, a kind she had never felt before. But the realization didn't change the desire. She barely contained her reaction.

Her previous encounters with people suffering from vampirism involved holy water, stakes, and lots of bad language. Crosses and other religious symbols only worked if the holder had true faith, as odd and unscientific as it was. So they were of no use to her. She believed there could be a higher power, but she wasn't quite sure what it was… and either way she questioned the extent of its benevolence. However, holy water seemed to work for anyone. Her kit was fully stocked with vials of it and conveniently in her locker at the precinct.

Carley had never held a civil conversation with a vampire. They either went down swinging or were terminated during the day where they slept. It was rumored they could smell fear. Carley was certain she must reek of it, along with the lust he seemed to be evoking within her. Yet there wasn't much she could do but hope she was able to keep a straight face and lie through her teeth.

"It is. I've gotten a job offer, so I'm thinking about moving here. I thought I'd see what the night life has to offer. A friend recommended this place, but I'm a hard sell. Think Dark Heart has what it takes?" Carley asked.

His smile grew, and she couldn't deny his beauty. There was no difference between the way her body heated for him and the way it heated for a woman. She was grateful she was gay, certain it was the only reason she'd seen through the vampire's power.

"New York has much to offer beautiful, curious women. However, this club is the flavor of the few. To enjoy its wares, you must pass a test. Are you willing to try?"

Carley had no idea what kind of club required a test for entry. New York was always about the dollar sign. Aiden had shaken the vampire's hand before entering, and she refused to believe he was oblivious to what the bouncer was.

She didn't want the man to touch her, mostly because every inch of her body screamed for him. Carley worried she would lose herself in his influence. She had to fight the powerful instinct to flee. She couldn't abandon Aiden. Even if she didn't understand the reasoning behind his actions, he was still her partner. There would be trouble. Every time she ignored her instincts, there was trouble.

"I'm always up for a challenge."

The bouncer laughed softly, and the sound wrapped around her like a warm blanket. "The test is simple, belle. Place your hand in mine."

Carley refused to hesitate. She slipped a hand from her pocket and offered it to him. "Are we going to arm wrestle? We could make a bet."

He laughed again. "As entertaining as that would be, I'm afraid this is much simpler."

The vampire's hand appeared above hers. She hadn't seen him move. Carley felt the cold sweat of terror sink into her bones. She knew young vampires could block a human's vision and sense of time, but the older ones didn't need mind tricks. They were that fast. She wondered which the bouncer was, but quickly decided it didn't matter. She was screwed either way.

He slid his hand slowly over hers. His skin was cold. Even knowing the vampire's flesh was dead, it felt amazing. While the weight of the lust he pushed on Carley was constantly growing, it didn't spike to an uncontrollable level with skin contact. Carley considered herself fortunate but knew luck wouldn't hold her forever.

The vampire turned her hand over in his and tilted his head to study her palm. Carley felt a strange tingling sensation shoot up her arm and filter through her body. She couldn't stop herself from shivering. It wasn't exactly unpleasant, but she felt violated. She wanted to yank her hand away.

The bouncer smiled and raised his gaze to hers. Carley caught a flash of violet before she looked away. She didn't care whether he knew or not. She had never seen a human resist a vampire's call if eye contact was made. His smile only widened.

He brought her hand to his lips and pressed a chaste kiss to her knuckles. "Welcome to Dark Heart, Miss. I'm sure we can provide everything you're looking for."

The door behind him opened and Carley itched to turn back. Instead, she flashed Militar a knowing smile and thanked him. As she descended into the darkness, she couldn't help but feel she had entered a chess match and managed to make herself the unwitting, sacrificial pawn.

* * *

Alexis sighed as she watched Carley disappear into the club. Her inexperience was painfully obvious. She may have fooled a Child, but Militar was an Adult and had passed her knowing what little power she had wouldn't protect her. Alexis weighed the consequences. Aiden wouldn't be in a position to help unless he wanted to blow his cover.

Dark Heart was beneath Alexis. She had never wanted anything to do with underground politics. If she aided Carley, she would lose the anonymity of being just a rumor in the night. Alexis wasn't certain a cop was worth the level of disruption in her life.

On the other hand, the last thing Alexis needed was one, maybe two, dead police officers associated with her. She'd already saved Aiden once for similar reasons. Carley seemed good at her job and Alexis didn't entirely despise her. With a silent sigh, she resigned herself to interfering.

Militar was a substantial guard for the door, but he wasn't without weakness. Physical contact was required to sense power. She didn't plan on letting him get that far. She could slip around him without ever being seen.

Alexis kept her shadow form, careful to lock her shields firmly in place. She moved to the club and glided around Militar to slip through the small space between the door and the ground.

She followed the sound of heavy metal music down a dark hallway until she came to an open doorway. One look around reminded her of why she stayed away. The club was one rectangular room. Each corner had a large, reinforced steel cage housing a fully shifted werewolf. Drool spilled over their massive jaws as they paced the blood-stained floor.

The wolves were emaciated. Sharp, angled bones protruded through matted fur. Savage hunger pulsed in their eyes as they watched the club patrons. Starving a lycanthrope was easy. They had one of the fastest metabolisms on the planet.

Without consistent nutrition, the wolves had lost themselves to hunger. Alexis wasn't certain they would ever be able to shift back into human form again.

The space between the two cages along the right wall had been boarded up to create a room with an open doorway in the middle. Erotic noises and the scent of raw sex spilled from it. The sexual energy of nymphs hung heavily in the air.

The back and left walls were lined with couches and chairs. Several vampires were sprawled out among them, fangs deep in the flesh of their victims. Some of the humans appeared sated, their faces slack with pleasure. Others were not so lucky. Pain and fear were evident in their eyes as they felt their life force drained away. Some were screaming, but the sounds fell on deaf ears, buried beneath the roaring music.

A circular bar made of black steel stood in the middle of the room. Deep crimson fluorescent lighting lined the edges, casting a blood-like glow along the black stools wrapped around the bar. Above it, mimicking the circular style, was another wall of steel lined in red lighting. Racks of glasses hung upside down within easy reach of the bartender.

Small metallic bird cages hung from the top portion of the bar, spread out between the glass racks. Pixies danced nude within them. Iron collars were painfully clamped around their tiny throats. Pixies were small creatures, no taller than Alexis' forearm. But what they lacked in size, they made up for in power. They were crafty, intelligent creatures that could easily dispatch beings ten times their size. Capturing one took immense skill. They never left the forest willingly. It was unfortunate many saw pixie hunting as sport and there was a black market trade.

Metal of any kind weakened their power. If the collars were on long enough, their necks would scar. Alexis doubted the owners of the club ever removed them. Eventually, the dancing pixies would die, used as nothing more but visual pleasure and status symbols.

The remaining space in the club was left for dancing. The mixture of power was chaotic. Alexis understood how the taste of so many different energies could entice the young, but she knew better. The superficial sampling that occurred there was substantially less enjoyable than a true, deep blending of power.

Dark Heart was a cesspool. Alexis felt dirty for even entering. It was vulgar, and it smelled of cheap sex, blood, and wet dog. It wasn't an establishment she would support, even if she was well known in the community. There were better ways to run a safehouse.

Her presence had gone unnoticed. The patrons were bottom feeders. It was a place they came to feel strong without the presence of their Masters.

The warmth of Aiden's power drew her attention to a table in the back. He wasn't hiding his strength. It let others know he wasn't worth tasting. He was having a discussion with an older, burly man. The stranger's arms and legs were muscled and scarred, but his stomach was large and soft. A bushel of white, matted hair buried his face in gritty strands. Alexis never understood why men let their facial hair get that atrocious. The man was filthy, but he had a hard look about him. His eyes scanned the club with experience. Alexis bet he was a retired hunter.

As much as she was interested in his conversation, Aiden could take care of himself. She scanned the rest of the club and found Carley at the bar, deathly pale. She gave the girl some credit. Carley hid her shock well. But more than half the creatures in the club could smell fear. Jameson might have been a tough-as-nails homicide detective in her world, but her experience didn't give her an edge in Dark Heart. She was afraid and there wasn't a predator in the club who didn't know it.

* * *

Carley threw back a shot of straight vodka. She shouldn't drink but she needed something to settle her system. She was aware she didn't fit in and could easily become one of the victims on the couches.

She couldn't even look at them. Watching their suffering while knowing she was powerless to stop it was too much. Carley was outnumbered and would die along with them if she tried. But the knowledge wouldn't stop their screams from haunting her dreams at night.

She kept her attention mostly on Aiden. He was speaking with an old man Carley didn't recognize. She suspected he was a source, but he wasn't in any of the FDPC files she had seen. Aiden confirmed her theory when he pulled a crumpled piece of paper from his pocket and handed it over.

The man's eyes widened and he snatched the paper for a closer look. She wondered what could put shock on the face of a man who frequented a club like Dark Heart. She also wondered if Aiden's friend had seen the inside of a bathroom in the past five years.

She raised her empty glass to silently order another. The bartender was tall and his bare chest flaunted enough lean muscle to take down a tank. Golden rings were threaded through his nipples and black leather hugged narrow hips.

Shaggy brown hair fell across his amber eyes, but it wasn't their color that caught Carley's attention. The pupils were vertical and expanded horizontally with the changing light. He had to be a lycanthrope. Carley was willing to bet every last cent of her paycheck his beast was a large cat.

He sauntered over, showing off a body Carley had no interest in. He gave her a condescending look, which irritated her. Usually, she wouldn't tolerate it, but losing her temper in this club could get her killed. She knew the importance of respect on any playing field. Her brain and her low tolerance for ineptitude earned her respect at the office, but Carley wasn't at the precinct where anger was motivational. Yet, she still needed to establish some form of presence before something decided she looked tasty. It wasn't going to be easy. Sitting on a stool, Carley's eyes only made it to the bartender's nipples. Instead of explosive anger, she tried chilly irritation.

"I'm paying for a shot of vodka, not condescension. Do you want my money or not?"

His look changed to curiosity as he pulled the bottle from beneath the bar and poured her another. The deep Creole in his voice surprised her. "Ya break a man's pride, love. Most find my smirk appealing."

"Your pride isn't my problem," Carley replied as she raised the glass to her lips.

She almost paused when her stomach churned so violently she had to fight to keep from doubling over. It took everything she had to finish the shot and hold her expression. Not even a moment later, a sharp shiver moved down her spine. She didn't have to turn around to know three people had caged her into the bar.

She refused to face them with fear. Anger always felt better. When the bartender looked down at her with amusement, she ordered another shot with her middle finger.

"Whoa, Michael. We've got a live one here," a raspy voice teased from behind.

"I like 'em fiery. Dey brighten da night. But I'm thinkin' ya should leave this one to her business. Fire don' come from nothin', man," the bartender replied as he tipped the bottle into Carley's glass.

"Spicy food is worth the risk," the man behind her said.

Carley let her anger show in her gaze as she picked up her glass and spun to face what was likely her death. She knocked the shot back and slammed the empty glass upside down on the bar. She let her gaze roam over the men who surrounded her. She was no match for three vampires. Even if she had come prepared, three was two more than anyone should take on alone. Their grins were savage. Carley looked over each of her aggressors and mentally prepared for a fight. She kept her gun hand free, subtly shifted her stance, and released the leash on her sarcasm.

"Well, look what we have here. You guys might be the ugliest three fucking stooges I've ever seen," Carley said. She braced for impact.

* * *

Alexis watched as the female detective spun on her stool and tossed back a third shot. Either she could hold her liquor well or her adrenaline was high enough she didn't feel the effects. She hoped Carley could get out on her own. The chances were slim, but she wasn't stupid. Alexis didn't want to show herself if she didn't have to.

But the evening wasn't destined to go in her favor. The vampire in front of Carley slapped the detective across the face. Carley tilted back in her stool but managed to stay upright. A fresh scratch blossomed on her cheekbone just below the eye. She took it well, even glared at the vampire as the caged wolves caught the scent of her blood and shifted their hungry gazes. The strike was enough to convince Alexis the vampires were not going to relent. She needed to act before it got worse.

Alexis sent her words to the shadows in Carley's ears, a whisper no one else could hear. "Don't stop looking at the man in front of you. Only you can hear me. You're in the kind of trouble your partner can't save you from without compromising himself and his source. I can, but it will require your trust and full cooperation. Put your left hand in your pocket if you agree."

Carley said something that made the bartender laugh. The vampire didn't seem to think it was amusing and snarled at her. But not even a heartbeat later, Carley noticeably stiffened, shock washing through her expression. The rise and fall of her chest paused enough to make the vampire before her raise an eyebrow. Yet, she still casually slipped her left hand into her pocket. It was all Alexis needed.

She condensed her shadowy form into a thick, black fog that took the shape of her physical body. As the fog grew denser, several dancers stopped to stare. The effect seemed to cascade and it wasn't long before the dance floor was motionless.

The fog faded completely and revealed Alexis' true form. She hadn't anticipated being visible that night and wasn't dressed in the attire she would have preferred. Presentation was always half the battle. Fortunately, there wasn't anything in her wardrobe that didn't suit her.

Dark blue jeans hugged her hips. A fitted white tee-shirt was covered by an unzipped black leather riding jacket. Her pendant stood out against the plain cotton. Raven tresses were pulled back in a ponytail, allowing the luminescence of her pale skin to shine. She had chosen sleek, silver reflective lenses for her eyes. Even when not in her best, Alexis knew she made an impression. Only the nymphs had her beat. No one could compete with them except the fey.

The club fell silent, apart from the cries of ecstasy in the adjourning room. The song ended and the DJ was too preoccupied to start another. Alexis moved forward. Her step was light enough that her calf-high leather boots made no noise on the dance floor. Patrons parted, bunching to either side as she slid confidently through. The reaction was unanticipated, but it would help her bully a few vampires.

Alexis resisted the urge to shake her head as the vampire that struck Carley noticed her. He snatched the detective and used her as a shield. His chest pressed to her back as his left hand encircled her waist. His right clamped around Carley's throat. Alexis found the act cowardly, but she'd expected nothing less from a vampiric Child who faced a stronger adversary. Alexis came to a stop two feet from the pair.

The vampire eyed Alexis from across Carley's shoulder. His voice rumbled, as if he had injured his vocal cords before he died. "Well, well, well. So, the rumors are true. A higher demon walks the streets of our fair city. If you're thinking I share, fuck off. I saw her first."

Alexis let her lips curve in an amused but patronizing smile. She ignored the vampire entirely, knowing it would irritate him. Carley hid her confusion well, though it haunted the edges of her eyes. Alexis hoped the detective was capable of quick adaptation.

"Why do I always find you in these cesspools, pet? You know better," Alexis said. She kept her tone relaxed but firm.

There was a brief flash of understanding in Carley's eyes before she quickly lowered them to the floor. Her expression was contrite and her voice shook lightly with fear.

"My apologies, ma'am. I was only curious."

"Curiosity is one of your best and worst attributes. You have forced me to come fetch you," Alexis replied. She stepped forward and placed a finger beneath Carley's chin. She pulled up with enough force to raise Carley's gaze.

The vampire holding her twitched uncertainly. "Hey! Get your grubby fucking paws off my food!"

Alexis continued to ignore him and was pleased when Carley did the same. She played along and plastered a deeply apologetic look on her face. It was genuine enough that Alexis wondered if she could cry on demand.

"Yes, ma'am. I'm sorry. I didn't mean to inconvenience you."

The relaxed tone of Alexis' voice turned cold and uncaring. "But you have, and you will pay for it later."

Carley winced then gasped when Alexis took a firm hold of her chin. Alexis turned the detective's head sharply to the side to inspect the injury. The cut was at least three inches long and several trails of blood marked Carley's cheek. Alexis finally gave the vampire some attention. The annoyance in his gaze was almost tangible.

She raised her voice for the whole club and switched to a professional tone. "You are holding my property, Child. Release her. Now."

"This meat has no tag, demon. It's mine for the taking," he hissed and ran his tongue across one of the crimson trails on Carley's cheek.

The hard part had come. Alexis hadn't marked Carley. She had no real authority or claim to the detective. The trick would be to get the vampire to think she did. Power left traces on everything it came in contact with. The stronger the power and the longer the contact, the greater the trace would be. Alexis hoped the few physical connections she had with Carley recently were enough to fool a young vampire. She had never marked anyone before, so no one knew what her mark felt like. If Alexis couldn't convince him, violence would be the only answer.

Alexis let her tone drop low and dangerous. "You felt my tag. Don't presume to lie to me."

The two men flanking the leader began to look nervous. They either believed her or they sensed enough of her power they didn't want to risk crossing her. Alexis didn't care which. With any luck, they would keep the leader from doing anything to provoke further confrontation. The leader regarded her with calculation, but it wasn't long before his lips curled in a sneer.

"Alright, bitch. It was faint, like you hadn't touched this sweet little piece in months. So, I said 'fuck it'."

Typically, Alexis despised ignorance, but there were times when it worked in her favor. The Child had given her exactly what she needed. But he didn't fear her yet, and she could only take so many steps without offending all of House Le'Roe. It was one of the largest vampiric houses in the world. Alexis was in no hurry to make enemies unnecessarily.

"My tags are designed to keep my property out of the detectable range of human authorities. You sensed a tag and ignored it. Thus, you have committed theft. I am well within my rights to take back what was stolen from me. If you offer no more trouble, I'll take my payment and forget to pay a visit to your Elder."

Uncertainty clouded the young vampire's eyes, but he dropped his gaze to Carley and Alexis knew any reasonable thought would fade. Children were weak and prone to impulsive attacks. It was why most Elders sheltered them. The vampire leaned into Carley's cheek and drew in a deep breath laced with her scent. Alexis knew he wasn't going to give her up without a stronger threat.

"You are full of shit. You don't even know who my Elder is," he countered. Hunger gave him a confidence his friends didn't share.

The man on the right finally spoke up and put his hand on the leader's shoulder. "Shawn, a quick snack isn't worth Mother's anger. Take her deal, man."

Shawn growled, and his friend snatched his hand away. "Shut the fuck up, Eric. This bitch doesn't get to show up for the first time and act like she owns the place. She's not even strong enough to leave a solid mark on her pet!"

"Do not mistake finesse for weakness, Child. I am powerful enough to slip past Militar undetected. Powerful enough to watch your entire exchange with my pet without anyone in this room feeling the kiss of my power." She let anger and impatience drip through her tone. "I could destroy you before you begin to squeeze the girl's throat. The only reason I haven't is respect for Belladona Le'Roe. Are you so arrogant to believe I don't know what goes on in my own city?"

Surprise blossomed on Shawn's features. Alexis always made it a point to discreetly listen to what went on in the gifted community. Though she didn't dive deep into politics, she was always aware of the major players. It was good to know who had the potential to be dangerous to her. It allowed Alexis to be prepared for moments like her current situation.

The scent of fear finally began to pour off him. His voice was barely above a whisper. "Militar doesn't know you're here?"

"No. Shall I alert him? He is one of your Adults, after all. I'm sure he would sort out this mess. Perhaps I'll acquire an invitation to dine with Lady Le'Roe. I'll be sure to request your heart as the main course."

"Take her," Shawn said and shoved Carley forward.

Alexis immediately held out her hand and Carley didn't hesitate. Alexis stepped defensively in front of her and positioned herself within arm's reach of the vampire. She was several inches taller than him, which made establishing a dominant presence easier. Alexis had to make an example without taking more than what was stolen from her. She didn't need someone else giving them trouble, but also knew Shawn had left her with no choice but to meet with Le'Roe. Alexis didn't want to come to such a meeting with offenses of her own.

She struck without warning. Though he wasn't human, he was still the youngest form of a vampire. Alexis didn't need much strength or speed to send him flying. His head snapped to the side and he fell into his comrades. The three stumbled into the bar and the stools threw off their balance. They ended up in a heap on the floor. The only reactionary movement from the club came from the bartender. He reached out to keep several glasses from falling to the floor.

Alexis gave the three a moment to untangle before she reached down and twisted her fist in Shawn's shirt. She hauled him effortlessly to his feet and slammed his back into the bar. He grunted with the force of the impact as she grabbed his chin and roughly turned his head to the side. The gash she had left with her nail was identical to Carley's.

Alexis leaned in close but didn't hide her words from the rest of the club. "If you ever steal from me again, I will rip your chest open and let you watch as I tear your heart from you. One ligament at a time. Have I made myself perfectly clear?"

She kept her grip on his jaw tight to force him to answer without moving his head.

"Yes," he replied.

Dissatisfied, Alexis squeezed his jaw hard enough to make him whimper. "Yes what, Child?"

The bitterness and fear were evident in his acknowledgment of her position. "Yes, my lady."

Alexis nodded once and leaned in to run her tongue along a single trail of blood that dripped from the gash on his cheek. The older the vampire, the faster wounds healed. An Adult wouldn't have even bled. Children, on the other hand, healed only a touch faster than humans and were almost as fragile.

Having taken from the vampire what he presumably stole from her, Alexis abruptly released him. He collapsed to his knees and rotated his jaw. She turned her back to him and zoned in on Carley. Alexis gave the vampire no further acknowledgment.

What she needed to do would shatter any boundaries she had with the female detective. While she enjoyed the dark and rough sides of sex, she did not enjoy force. She had to return the blood to Carley, and the club needed to believe she belonged to her. Their smooth departure and Carley's future safety depended on it. Not everyone in the club was as foolish as the Child. So, despite knowing her actions would be unwelcomed, Alexis didn't hesitate. She stepped forward and slipped an arm around Carley's waist. The fingers of her other hand threaded through Carley's tresses and she pulled her head back.

Alexis advanced quickly and set her lips firmly against Carley's. She slowed down after and let Carley set the tone. If she had to force a kiss, Alexis could at least give her the freedom to set the pace.

Carley surprised her when she slipped her arms around Alexis' shoulders and dove headfirst into the kiss. She pressed her body against Alexis' and parted her lips. Alexis felt greed take over and answered it with her own. Her fingertips tightened in Carley's hair and the kiss became a war of teeth and tongues. There was a fierce heat in Carley and Alexis couldn't deny her body's reaction. Her skin was alive and hungry. She hadn't expected to be more than mildly attracted to the woman. The strength of her response caught her off guard.

A small portion of her power opened and reached into Carley. Alexis felt the power inside Carley twitch in response. She vaguely remembered the detective had likely never shared power with anyone. But their energies merged before Alexis could yank hers back. She heard Carley gasp and then moan quietly. Guilt surged through Alexis and she pulled her power back sharply, shattering the small connection.

Carley sagged a bit against her. The heat and magic of the moment was lost, and the taste of blood saturated the kiss. Alexis was glad her face hid Carley's when her nose wrinkled with disgust. All creatures had a different taste. It took time for vampires to lose their human aspects. Shawn's blood was a combination of the human, coppery flavor and something akin to sour milk. Alexis didn't blame Carley for finding it offensive. She did, too.

When she determined Carley had enough, Alexis slowly pulled back. Need lingered between them as she gazed into Carley's upturned face. While her expression was for the crowd, there had been too much promise in the kiss for it to be a total lie. She didn't think Carley's face was completely fake, either. She was grateful the detective acted as well as she did police work.

Alexis slid a fingertip down Carley's cheek and continued the path along the soft curve of her throat. The pulse was fast and hard. When Alexis spoke, her voice was firm but as soft as her caress. "It's time to go, pet. You're not to come here again. It's beneath you. Understood?"

Carley nodded. Her heated expression turned contrite. "Yes, ma'am. I'm sorry."

Alexis nodded once and let her finger fall from Carley's throat. She took her hand and stepped to the side. Walking to the exit, she forced Carley to keep up with her long strides. She knew Aiden would follow them. The hunter wouldn't leave his partner in the arms of a monster, especially when it was his fault she was there.

Alexis guided Carley effortlessly through the dark hall, her vision flawless. The door to the city opened automatically when they approached. Militar turned and his eyes widened at the sight of Alexis with Carley. He recovered quickly and began to speak, but she raised a hand to silence him, brushing past with Carley in tow. She didn't miss the annoyance in his gaze.

"Relax, Militar. I've only come to fetch my property. You may tell Lady Le'Roe that Alexis Montral is requesting an audience regarding theft of property. You really should keep your offensive Children on a tighter leash. She has one night to consider my request. I will return tomorrow for her answer."

Militar studied them carefully. There was more curiosity in his gaze than Alexis wanted. When he didn't answer, Alexis let out an impatient sigh. "Is there a problem?"

Militar shook his head, as if her voice had broken his train of thought. "No. My apologies, Lady Montral. If our Children committed theft and offended you, I'm sure our Elder will graciously accept the pleasure of your company. I will be here tomorrow with an answer."

"Until tomorrow evening, then, son of House Le'Roe," Alexis answered.

She turned and walked back to the alley she'd claimed earlier in the evening. Her pace was quick enough Carley had to move at a light jog to keep up. Once they were deep enough in the alley, Alexis called a shield of shadows around them. She blocked the light from the street but allowed the shallow moonlight so Carley could see. Their words would be lost in the darkness. She added a temporary fear ward for good measure then released Carley's hand. "My apologies for the crude treatment. It was necessary for a smooth exit. We would have met violence otherwise. You can speak freely. I've ensured no one will hear us."

Carley pulled away, put several feet of distance between them, and let out a shaky sigh. Whether it was relief or impatience, Alexis couldn't say. The detective was entitled to both. Unsure of what else she could say, Alexis folded her arms across her chest and waited.

Carley looked back the way they had come. Shadows blocked her view of the street. Worry seeped into her expression and she ran her fingertips through her hair. She sighed again and looked back to Alexis.

"Is that vampire blood going to infect me?" Carley asked.

"Surely your research has shown you it takes more than a little blood."

"Yeah, but research has been wrong before."

"What you ingested tonight won't harm you," Alexis assured.

Carley sighed. "Alright. If that's your definition of crude treatment, I'd prefer it to being a vampire's chew toy. I'm grateful you saved my ass, but I just can't leave Aiden. He could get killed just as easily."

"Don't worry, Detective. You partner is more than capable of taking care of himself. He'll follow us on his own. I imagine you're rather confused. I suggest we get moving. It isn't safe. Not everything should be explained here."

"No shit, Sherlock." Her gaze turned sharp and suspicious. "Why do you think that about Aiden? His training is the same as mine, and where the hell are we going?" Carley asked.

"I think it because it's true. I assure you, he'll be fine. As for where, I was thinking my apartment. I believe it's time the three of us laid our cards on the table. Don't you?"

"Yeah. You can start by telling me what the fuck that place was and, more importantly, whether you're really a demon."

Alexis ignored the first for the moment and simply said, "Yes."

"Are you inviting me back to your place so you can kill me instead?" Carley asked, an uneasiness and fear evident in her gaze.

"What do you think?" Alexis asked carefully.

She felt Carley's penetrating gaze move over her and she didn't hide from it. If Carley refused to believe she meant no harm, Alexis would have to start the process of changing her life early. The idea was distasteful. She was oddly attached to what she'd built in New York and didn't want to have to leave before it was time. The thought alone should have her packing. Attachment always brought trouble. Instead, she stood waiting for an answer from a cop she shouldn't trust.

The silence between them stretched on for several minutes before Carley finally spoke. "No, I don't think you're going to kill me. I can't really explain why and that makes me nervous as shit. But if you really meant me harm, you would have just let the vampire have me."

Alexis sighed with relief and slipped off her coat. She offered it to Carley. "That's fair. Take this."

Alexis smiled as the direction of Carley's gaze dropped to her body. It took a moment for Carley to realize she was staring. She yanked her gaze back up to Alexis' face. The flush in Carley's cheeks was rather enjoyable.

"Why? Designer clothing doesn't exactly fit my budget. But still."

"Take it and I'll show you," Alexis replied.

Skeptical, Carley took the coat and slipped it on. The sleeves extended past her wrists and the length ended just below her hips. It was obviously too big, but Alexis wasn't looking for the perfect fit. The leather would offer Carley protection.

"This doesn't look nearly as good on me as it does on you," Carley observed.

"That's because it wasn't made to fit you. It will do the job."

"Which is?"

Alexis smiled before she turned her back to Carley and focused. The spell she called took finesse. She ran her hand through the air at waist height. Shadows poured from her arm and formed the shape of a large mass. She concentrated on the image in her mind and the shadows slowly brought her Ducati into reality. Alexis turned to find Carley gaping at her.

"Holy fuck," Carley said.

"I didn't drive here and I can't take you with me when I change forms. The bike is how we'll have to travel," Alexis said as she judged Carley's reaction.

"I didn't even know shadows could do that. You can just pull anything out of them?"

Alexis shrugged and turned back to the bike to gather the gloves and helmet. She handed them to Carley.

"Shadows and darkness are one and the same. I am a creature of them. However, I'm not a conjurer. I can't make things appear out of thin air. I can only call something I've infused with my power. There are not many objects I've taken the time to do so. It's a painstaking and exhausting process."

Carley took the helmet and gloves before she glanced around Alexis at the bike. "No protection for you?"

Alexis smirked. "Your concern is touching, but my body can take significantly more damage than yours. I didn't just risk myself to save your skin only to paint the street with it on the very, very slim chance I wreck the bike."

Emerald eyes narrowed, and the irritation was plain on Carley's face. "Fuck you, Montral. I'm not amused. And don't think I forgot about the questions you evaded."

Alexis nodded as Carley slammed the helmet on and pulled gloves over her hands. "I'll answer everything I can at my apartment."

Alexis threw her leg over the bike and straddled the engine. She nodded over her shoulder at the seat behind her. Carley walked over, but before she could hop on, Alexis grabbed the front of her coat. Carley pushed the visor up. Alexis knew she shouldn't tease. The woman had a long night ahead of her, but the indignation that covered the nervousness was more than Alexis could resist. So, she stayed silent until Carley threw her hands up in exasperation.

"Fucking what now?"

"My keys are in your right pocket," Alexis replied calmly. She did her best to mask her amusement, but from the look on Carley's face, she wasn't successful.

"Oh. Right." She fished around in the pocket before producing the key.

Alexis held out her hand and Carley slammed it in her palm none too gently. She climbed on the back of the bike and slipped her arms around Alexis' waist and hugged her close. Alexis glanced back at her.

"I drive fast, so hold tight and lean when I lean."

Alexis slapped Carley's visor down before the detective could respond, and brought the engine to life. She dropped the shadow veil and shot out into the street. Alexis tried to ignore the way Carley's body fit against hers. She had enough problems. The last thing she needed was to find herself attracted to both the hunter and the cop.

CHAPTER ELEVEN

A quick sigh of relief left Carley's lips as Alexis brought the bike to a stop in front of a massive metal gate surrounding an apartment building. Carley sat up to stretch tense muscles in her lower back. She'd ridden motorcycles before, but nothing like the Ducati. The ride was exhilarating but she had lots to learn before she would feel comfortable.

The apartment building was huge. Alexis didn't seem like the type who wanted to live close to others. Carley had expected a mansion out in the suburbs. She had seen Alexis' address in the case records, but it hadn't included an apartment number. She found it odd and made a mental note to cross reference the building's address with the one the department had on file.

Carley jumped when a professional, female voice sounded over the hum of the bike. Her attention instantly shifted to a monitor beside them. She pushed the visor on the helmet up to get a better view.

"Good evening. Visiting or resident?"

"Resident," Alexis answered.

"Voice frequency accepted. Good evening, Ms. Montral. An entry code and physical verification are required."

"Hello, Terry," Alexis answered.

Alexis pressed her bare palm to the blank screen. It briefly flashed blue as Alexis rattled off a series of letters and numbers too long for Carley to remember.

"Verification accepted. Welcome home, Alexis," the computer said.

The gate opened, and the bike's engine revved. Carley slammed the visor down and tightened her grip around Alexis' slender waist. The bike passed the gate and down through a large, steel garage door which closed behind them. Alexis pulled into the first free space in a row of parked motorcycles.

Carley sat up and pulled the helmet off her head. Her gaze scanned the contents of the garage. It was filled with bikes and cars with names she was relatively certain she couldn't pronounce.

"Holy shit, Montral. Do you own the top one percent of this country's wealth?"

"Close," Alexis replied as she stepped off the bike.

"I was being sarcastic." She handed Alexis the helmet and the gloves.

"And I was not." Alexis set the helmet on a rack holding several others and slipped the gloves into her back pocket and brushed past on her way to the elevator.

Carley raised an eyebrow and slid her hands into the jacket pockets before she followed. The shock of Alexis' demonic heritage was still raw in her system, yet even knowing, she couldn't keep her gaze from roaming over the woman's lithe frame. Carley didn't know what to think. Demons didn't save lives, they took them. But Alexis had, and she was even helpful to the investigation, though now it was obvious she hadn't told the whole truth. Carley had yet to meet a diseased individual who came forward willingly.

When the elevator doors opened, Alexis gestured for her to go first. Carley stepped to the back and leaned against it. She studied her hostess who followed, and the doors closed behind them. She knew she should be afraid, but she couldn't shake the feeling Montral meant no harm. Yet, it was still unnerving being in a tight, enclosed space with a demon.

Carley jumped when the same voice from the gate filled the elevator. "Where can I take you?"

"Manual input, Terry," Alexis replied.

"Certainly."

A silver panel to the left of the doors slid open and revealed a small, blue screen. A keypad appeared, and Alexis entered a series of numbers. Carley gave up trying to keep up with the speed of those fingertips. The screen soon turned black and the silver panel closed. The elevator began to move.

"Is this entire place run by a computer?" Carley asked.

Alexis glanced over her shoulder. "Terry is a prototype artificial intelligence. She assists me in many things, including home security. She's a closely guarded project."

"Why would you put something experimental in your home? A.I. is one of those creepy things that could go wrong in so many ways."

"Because she works. On top of that, I have very demanding needs. Programs are often made or broken depending on whether they can keep up with me. Terry has been with me for a while now."

"What makes these needs of yours any different from someone else's?"

"As you get to know me, I'm sure you'll see," Alexis replied.

"I don't think I'm going to be able to get the chance. You must know I have to report you," Carley said carefully.

"You don't have to do anything you don't want to, Detective. But I'm aware of your integrity and hoping that our conversation tonight will persuade you otherwise."

"And if it doesn't?"

Alexis turned to face Carley. Their eyes met, and Carley found herself wondering what was behind the glasses. She now understood it had nothing to do with albinism. The look on Montral's face was blank, but that was just as telling as an expression. Alexis felt threatened enough to hide her reaction.

"Then I will be forced to make changes I didn't want to make for years."

Confused, Carley raised an eyebrow. But before she could ask for clarification, the elevator doors parted, and Alexis stepped out into a large living room.

"Welcome to my home."

Carley nodded once and followed. The lighting was automatic and low. The dark wood furniture looked both classic and comfortable. What surprised her was the number of books. Shelves lined every wall in sight. There was a fireplace and a bar, but it was clear the living room was built to be a comfortable reading nook.

"Terry, would you light the fireplace, please?" Alexis asked.

"My pleasure," Terry replied.

Carley wasn't sure where the voice came from. There were no speakers in sight.

The stone fireplace came to life with small, flickering flames. It only added to the sense of comfort. Carley could easily get lost for hours in the stories on the walls.

"Make yourself at home. I stink of the club. I'm going to change. I'll only be a moment," Alexis stated before turning to disappear down the only hallway that led from the room.

Carley immediately took the opportunity to be nosy. The bar was well stocked with top-shelf labels and finger food, but nothing out of the ordinary. She slowly walked around the bookshelves and browsed titles. Everything from modern fiction to first edition historical novels to erotica could be found. Overall, it told her nothing other than Alexis enjoyed reading.

She sighed and looked out the glass doors leading to a balcony. The gorgeous view of Manhattan meant they were on one of the higher floors. It occurred to her Alexis had kept her from knowing any information regarding her location inside the building. In hopes of getting a general idea of the floor number, Carley stepped closer to the glass.

When she was two yards away, an irrational fear seized her chest. Her feet stopped moving. There was nothing to be afraid of in the room and she didn't fear heights. The terror was irrational, but undeniably potent. Carley backed away from the doors and narrowed her gaze. The intensity receded with each step. The only explanation was magic.

She forced herself to step closer again and fought the fear as it came. It wasn't easy. By the time she was a foot away, she was so terrified her hands shook. She wanted to touch the doors, but the overwhelming horror left her fighting just to stand still.

"It's called a 'ward.' You must have encountered them before."

Carley let out a small yelp of surprise. She turned to find Alexis leaning a shoulder against a bookshelf, a small, plastic case tucked under her arm. She'd changed into a fitted emerald cashmere sweater and a pair of faded blue jeans. Her hair was down around her shoulders and her feet were bare. Carley wasn't sure if her racing heart was from fear or attraction. She stepped away from the doors and folded her arms across her chest.

"I thought wards were for protection against energies, like barriers. How could it influence someone who has none?"

Alexis studied her for a moment before pushing off the wall and gesturing to the couch. "The word 'barrier' has a fluid definition. Come and sit so I can tend to your cheek."

The demon moved with a grace Carley both admired and envied. She continued to struggle with the knowledge of Alexis' heritage. It made no sense. She displayed none of the behavioral traits of demons. Carley would even say Alexis was kind. A few hours ago, violence wouldn't have been a trait listed in Alexis' profile. The display at the club proved otherwise, yet it was still in defense of another. Nothing about the situation added up and it left Carley on edge. She sighed and sat on the wide and inviting couch.

"It's going to be a long night if you avoid all my questions."

Alexis set the first aid kit on the coffee table and pushed it closer to the couch. She sat on the table directly in front of Carley and began to look through the kit's contents.

"I consider your health a higher priority. If you will lean forward for me, please."

Carley raised an eyebrow. "Did you just manage to politely call me impatient?"

A soft smile touched Alexis' lips as she pulled on a pair of gloves. She opened a small cleansing pad and looked back at Carley. "I would never."

Carley couldn't help but laugh. "Bullshit."

Alexis' smile turned into a smirk. "Perhaps. But it's true. Come here."

Carley shrugged and slid forward on the couch. "No one is perfect."

"I didn't say it was a bad thing. This might sting."

As Alexis gently ran the pad over the cut on her face, Carley wondered how much experience this demon had in treating human wounds. Her touch was efficient but thorough. It did sting, but Carley didn't mind. The situation gave her a closer look at Alexis' face, which made the minor pain worth it. The urge to dig deeper into the woman was strong. It was rare her mind conflicted with her gut. Carley needed to know more before she could pass judgment.

"Do you sweet talk all women like that?"

Alexis chuckled as she slipped the blood-stained pad back into its wrapper. She pulled out a cotton swab and applied antibacterial cream to the tip before returning her attention to Carley's wound.

"I'm rather selective. You should feel lucky."

"For tonight, call me Carley. I mean, you saved my ass, slipped me some pretty intense tongue, and took me home with you. That's practically a date."

Alexis gathered up the trash and stared intently as she removed her gloves. Carley leaned back into the couch and didn't shy away from the intensity. Her hesitancy was understandable. The FDPC didn't take chances with demons. Most of them slaughtered humans. The annoying, moral part of her mind reminded her that one shouldn't be judged solely on the actions of many.

"Alright. Alexis is also fine. I'm sorry to say I've no gifts for healing. The cut is as clean as it's going to get. I can put some steri-strips on it, but I think it'll be okay without them. I do think you may get a black eye, though," Alexis finally replied.

"Honestly, I don't even really feel it right now," Carley admitted.

"I imagine you're in a bit of shock. I'm sure you've seen your fair share of horrific scenes, but it's different when you're the victim. I'll get you an ice pack, anyway."

Alexis took the trash to the bar. Carley glanced over her shoulder at the double doors leading to the balcony. She searched the frame and the wall for marks or other physical signs of a ward but found none. She looked back to find

Alexis sitting on the coffee table with an offered ice pack. She pressed it to her cheek. The biting cold made her wince and sent goosebumps down her neck.

"So, about that ward…"

"Tenacious, aren't you? Just because a human can't manipulate magic doesn't mean they can't be affected by it. You've encountered them daily and not known it. They can be as subtle as suggesting to your mind that it's better to go right instead of left. You wouldn't think anything of it. The right is just the better path. Such wards are often used to hide the gifted from humans. Invisible barriers."

"Is that why you have a ward? To hide?"

"I have many wards to protect my home from both humans and non-humans. There are humans who are just as dangerous as the beings you hunt. The ward will frighten those without magic away and warns others the property is spoken for."

Given her display of magic and strength in the club, Carley doubted Alexis had much to fear from humans… or anything else for that matter. "I really don't believe you fear humans enough to put up a ward."

"Well, first I'll say you highly underestimate humans. I respect their cleverness and ingenuity. They're far from helpless and can be just as brutal as anything in the magical community. But you're right. I don't fear them. I do have a distaste for creating scenes, though, that would draw the attention of someone like you. Fights of any kind never end with rainbows and flowers."

Carley folded her arms across her chest. "I suppose I can understand, if your goal is to live a quiet life. Is that what you want?"

"It is," Alexis replied simply.

"Then why do you even need the ward? You hide among humans flawlessly. I had suspicions at first, but you somehow managed to pass the lab exam, and I want to know more about that later. Nothing more than a few speeding tickets on your record. You pay your taxes. Your employees have nothing but praise for you. Why would a human come knocking at your door looking for trouble? How would they even know?"

Alexis shrugged. "There are those who hunt me because of my race alone. They don't carry your badge and are better trained than you. There are no laws to protect me from them. If I killed one in self-defense and did a poor job disposing of the body, you and your department would come for me. Even tonight, you threatened me with death when the only thing about our relationship that changed is that you know I'm a demon. I won't hesitate to protect myself from thieves, hunters, and anyone else who wishes me harm. I keep wards because they're a simple and harmless way of ensuring safety."

Carley narrowed her gaze. "I said I would report you. I didn't say anything about killing."

"Please, Carley. Don't be naive. We both know a report is a death sentence."

She couldn't say Alexis was wrong. The mere fact she existed made Carley wonder just how many innocent people had been put to death. The thought didn't sit well. She hadn't become an officer for vengeful reasons. She wanted to make a difference, to protect people. It never occurred to her some diseased were harmless. The FDPC considered all diseased a threat. Guilt started to prod her heart.

Yet she also knew higher-ranking demons were capable of manipulation. Carley felt a sudden, powerful urge to know how genuine Alexis was. She must be a good actor to move so perfectly around humans. Perhaps she was still acting.

"Can you take off your sunglasses, please? I think it's obvious you don't wear them because you're an albino."

Alexis stiffened. "My eyes scare people."

"Honestly, I don't give a fuck. If you want me to have sympathy for your situation, I need to see you, Alexis. The real you."

She was silent for so long Carley wasn't certain she would give in. But she finally reached up and slowly removed the lenses. When their eyes met, Carley drew in a slow breath. They were, indeed, frightening, but they were also beautiful. Soft rays of light reflected off deep wells of pure darkness. If Carley didn't know better, she would have thought she was gazing into the night sky.

Those eyes were alien, but Carley couldn't deny they suited Alexis. Despite their unsettling nature, emotion still existed in the inky darkness. They were confident but guarded, without malice. Carley understood the expression. She had worn it herself often, proud of who she was in the face of those who hated her for it.

"I can see why you use the glasses. There's no way contacts could hide that."

"No. Have you seen what you are looking for?" Alexis asked.

Carley smirked. "Now who's the impatient one?"

When Alexis didn't smile back, she ensured their gazes stayed locked. Alexis didn't waver, but it was clear she wasn't comfortable. Carley was alright with that. It was good to see the demon rattled.

There was a lot Carley didn't understand, but she didn't believe the woman was a danger to her or others. The moment she made that conscious decision, tension in her body melted away. She wasn't quite sure why, but she felt better.

"I believe you. I even think I understand why you would ward your home. When you kissed me at the club, it felt like something inside me exploded. Not like an orgasm, but close. I don't know how to describe it, other than I could feel you flowing through my veins. Is that how it works with you? Are you a succubus or something?" Carley asked. She didn't need to fight her own impulses as well as some kind of magical lust.

Alexis sighed and broke eye contact. She slipped her sunglasses back on and walked to the bar. She pulled two glasses from a cabinet. "What kind of wine do you like?"

"Please don't evade this question," Carley replied. "It wasn't easy to ask."

"I'm not evading. It gave me the desire to drink. Red or white?"

Curious, Carley let the ice pack fall from her eye. It was past numb, anyway. "Red."

Alexis nodded and selected a bottle from a rack then walked back to sit on the couch beside Carley. She poured a glass for each and settled back casually.

"I must apologize. What I did is considered very rude when not invited. I shared power with you. What you felt was your own power answering the call of mine, and I am deeply sorry for the intrusion."

For a moment, Carley's mind went blank. She was certain she had misunderstood.

"I'm sorry, but did you just say *my* power mixed with yours?"

"That is correct."

"I'm human. I don't have power. I'm not diseased," Carley replied.

"What you call diseased, I call gifted. To have power isn't shameful. But I'm not mistaken," Alexis said before she took a slow sip of wine.

"How? How do you know that for sure?" Carley asked as dread sank into the pit of her stomach.

"Three reasons. First, if you had no power, it would have felt like a normal kiss. Nothing more. Second, I've felt it in you before. I just didn't think it was enough to pass Militar's test, and certainly not enough to react with mine," Alexis replied.

"Militar?" Carley asked.

"My third reason. Militar is the vampire you met at the door. There are only two ways into Dark Heart, Carley. You are either gifted or food. And food comes in through the back," Alexis said.

"How could he know that I have power?" Carley asked.

"Militar has the ability to sense the nature of power in others. He influences the minds of humans and sends them away if they try to enter from the street," Alexis said. "He verifies the power of the gifted and grants them access. Simply put, there is no way you could have entered Dark Heart through the front door if you had no power."

Carley sat frozen and wide-eyed, trying to process the information. It wasn't until her lungs burned that she snapped out of her stupor and drew in much needed oxygen. She chased the breath with the entire glass of wine and Alexis topped it off.

It couldn't be true. While she had been around her fair share of preternatural murders, as well as apprehensions and terminations, Carley was fortunate enough to never have sustained an infectious injury. She hadn't been the victim of a curse or other type of magical attack.

All her apprehensions and terminations had gone by the book. The only way she could have power was if she had been born with it. But if that was the case, she would have been identified early and sent to an institution. Diseased people didn't grow up with normal lives. They hurt people, even if it was accidental.

Carley shook her head in denial, her voice shaky. "I would have been detected by now."

Alexis calmly refilled her glass. "Not necessarily. I passed your lab's tests. It's possible to trick them, or for them to miss things. The power within you is untapped. You didn't know you had it, so you never made an effort to use it. It's more than possible for you to be under the range of detection."

The color drained from Carley's skin and she shivered. She didn't want to believe it. She wasn't like the monsters. She wasn't perfect, but she was a good person. Her heart wouldn't stop thudding in her ears, so she raised a shaky hand and took another long drink of wine.

Alexis' expression softened. "Power doesn't equate to evil. While I admit to being entirely self-serving, I don't go around preying on humans. You didn't do terrible things four hours ago. Having the knowledge you are different isn't going to turn you into something awful."

Carley chuckled but there was no humor in it. "You sound like you're trying to comfort me after having told me I have a S.T.D or something."

Alexis smirked. "Yes and no. Your life will certainly change, depending on what you want to do with the information. But having power won't make you sick or kill you. It's not a death sentence. There are many out there like you."

Carley wasn't sure what to think anymore. Her brain had reached its overload point. Suddenly, exhaustion saturated her system.

"Excuse me, Alexis," Terry cut in. "There is a visitor at the gate. He seems a little... volatile. Shall I bring him on screen?"

"Yes, please."

Alexis looked up at the ceiling and a panel opened. A twenty-four-inch touch screen lowered from the opening. Alexis leaned forward and tapped it once. Aiden's face filled the monitor. Carley raised an eyebrow. The anger in his eyes was almost frightening.

"Where is she, Montral? Release her. Now. I won't ask twice," he said.

Alexis merely smiled at him and settled back against the couch. "Well now, little hunter. You're rather rude. I save both your partner and your cover and you have the audacity to come to my home and make demands?"

"Damn it, Montral. This isn't a game. I'll call for back-up. Nothing will keep me out of this building. You'll have to do better than a stupid gate."

Carley watched Alexis' expression flatten. Her tone grew hard and cold. "No, Detective. It's not a game. If you believe a gate is all that protects my home, you truly are a fool. An entire legion of your friends won't get in if I don't desire it. If you want to play, you'll follow my rules. Have I made myself clear?"

The anger in Aiden's eyes only grew. Carley didn't understand. Alexis had saved her. She hadn't done anything wrong. Carley understood Aiden might be frightened for her, but she had never seen his anger uncontrolled. Carley found herself supporting Alexis' caution.

"Fine. Your way, demon," Aiden said through clenched teeth.

"The computer will pass you through the gate. You will park in the first available slot. Any and all weapons are to be left in your car. There is an elevator at the end of the garage. It will bring you to us. Don't bother trying to fool my security system. You will not be brought up unless you are unarmed. I would also check your attitude at the door. I have no patience for ignorance tonight," Alexis replied before she reached forward and tapped the screen. Aiden's face disappeared and the monitor was pulled back through the opening in the ceiling.

"Keep a close eye on him, Terry," Alexis said.

"Of course."

Alexis was a mystery Carley didn't think she would be solving in the near future. It was fortunate she liked puzzles.

"Why is he so pissed at you?"

Alexis turned to look at her. "He believes you hopped out of the frying pan and into the freezer. He has known I'm demonic since the beginning."

"If Aiden knew, then he has also seen you don't display the same traits as most demons. His anger is illogical. I understand concern, but he's flat out pissed. Why did you call him 'little hunter'?"

"He's one of the people I told you about earlier. A demon hunter. He just happens to carry a badge, which I find shocking considering he's also a witch. I'm hoping his anger only stems from concern for your safety."

Carley tilted her head. "Aiden is a witch? He has power, too?"

"He knew of Dark Heart and got in effortlessly, did he not?"

Carley narrowed her gaze. "That might explain why he didn't immediately report you, along with lots of other things. As it is, you being demonic changes my perspective on the murder scene."

"I'm hoping that's something we all find agreement on. We have the same goal. I want the killer stopped as much as you."

Carley nodded. Aiden had loads of explaining to do. But, it could wait if they got Alexis to answer their questions about the scene. She could be the key to catching the murderer.

Before Carley's thoughts could go any further, the elevator doors opened, and Aiden stepped into the room. His gaze instantly found hers.

Slowly, she leaned forward and set the ice pack on top of the first aid kit. She wanted him to see she had been treated with kindness. He studied her closely for several moments before his glare shifted to Alexis. Aiden's expression was guarded, but the anger seemed to shift to confusion.

Alexis gestured toward the empty chair adjacent to the couch. Her tone was cool and professional, a quality Carley was coming to expect from her. "Welcome to my home, Detective. There is much we should discuss."

CHAPTER TWELVE

The elevator ride was nothing short of an eternity. Aiden had no idea how Carley had gotten into Dark Heart, but the result was disastrous. While Alexis had proven to be unique, she was still unpredictable, dangerous, and untrustworthy. Carley didn't carry her mark. While the ruse had worked, the magical community now believed Carley belonged to the demon. There was nothing beneficial about that.

Aiden's hands itched from knowing he was unarmed. He hadn't been able to slip even the lighter past Alexis. The voice in the elevator made him go back twice before allowing him access. He felt naked. Given her cool response to his temper, Aiden hoped Alexis would remain civil, but there was no way to know for certain.

On the other hand, Aiden was looking forward to seeing the inside of Alexis' living space. It was a rare opportunity to learn about the building's strengths and weaknesses. Any information gained would be useful if Aiden needed to break in later.

The elevator was clearly unreliable. There were not buttons for floors and something else governed its movements. When the doors finally opened, Aiden refocused on getting himself and Carley out alive.

He stepped out and scanned the room slowly. Alexis was clearly fond of books. The room was an upscale, small library. There was one open doorway across from him that likely led to the other rooms on the floor. The only window was a large glass wall to his left that appeared to open to a balcony. He detected a ward protecting it. A small bar was tucked in the corner to his right and expensive furniture was scattered throughout the room. But what captured his attention was the fireplace and Alexis' proximity. The flames in the hearth were real, and Alexis was in a chair adjacent to them. Some of his tension eased.

Aiden had a weapon, after all.

He shifted his attention to Carley. A bruise was forming around her eye, but the cut on her cheekbone was clean. Carley looked at ease with a glass of wine on a comfortable couch. While everything appeared to be alright, Aiden couldn't help but maintain a sense of distrust. His failure to notice Carley following him had been an unforgiveable mistake. He didn't want to make another.

Alexis gestured to the chair across from her and poured a glass of wine. He crossed the room and accepted the drink. As he sat, habit had him sniffing the wine for anything suspicious. It earned him an annoyed sigh.

"If I wanted you dead, Detective, I've a million more efficient methods. I could even have left you to the wolves with clean hands," she said coolly.

Aiden shrugged. "Old habits die hard. Besides, poisons can do more than just kill. They can alter mental states or carry spells."

"Neither of which are detectable by scent in today's times. Both Carley and I drink from the same bottle. Search her for spells or influence if you want. I've also not forgotten the nature of your power, little hunter. The fire in the hearth burns as a gesture of good faith, which you've given me no reason to offer. You could stand to be less condescending."

Aiden fought back a sigh of his own. It annoyed him that she knew his gift. Her gesture would make him less inclined to use it. Alexis was always one frustrating step ahead. He sampled the wine and had to admit it was good.

"What's so important about the fire?" Carley asked.

Even with just a glance, Aiden could see the anger, hurt, and confusion etched in Carley's face. The time for lies had passed. "I have the ability to manipulate fire and wind. Though I wasn't allowed to bring weapons, I could use the fire as one."

"What the fuck, Aiden? Alexis admits to being a demon and tells me you're a demon-hunting witch. How is that even possible? How could you pass the FDPC exams if you're able to control fire and wind?"

"Well-trained magic users can trick machines. It isn't easy and it's risky, but it's doable in an emergency. Both Alexis and I managed to beat them at the lab," Aiden replied.

"That doesn't explain how I don't get caught. I'm not trained at all. I didn't even know I had power until tonight," Carley replied.

Aiden's train of thought froze. Carley didn't have power. He would have sensed it. "What are you talking about?"

"Come now, little hunter," Alexis cooed. "How do you think she got past Militar? Her charming personality?"

"He could have let her in to be a dick," Aiden said. "Maybe he read her mind and saw she was a cop and sent her in to die."

"Even Militar knows admitting an officer risks the entire club," Alexis countered. "He sensed her power and let her in, though he is still a dick because he was aware of her vulnerability. The reason your machines don't detect her is because her power is buried and dormant."

"So, this supposed power of mine is too low to detect?" Carley asked. "Is that what you're saying?"

"Indeed. You have to look hard in a manner your machines are not capable of yet. There has been a great deal of power swirling around the crime scenes. I noticed Carley at the first scene while sampling the energy around me," Alexis answered.

"I never thought to pay closer attention because you're a cop," Aiden admitted.

Carley sighed and shook her head before looking to Aiden. "Why would you join the force if you're a witch? If even a hint of it got out, you'd be arrested on the spot."

"Joining the force had its risks, but it also gave me access to significantly more tools and resources to hunt demons," Aiden replied. He didn't mention he was also able to keep some heat off his own clan. He regularly gave them early warnings of police involvement whenever he could.

"But we don't just destroy demons. We hunt the diseased, no matter the form, including witches," Carley replied.

"I know," Aiden said. "Seven out of ten times, we take a dangerous creature off the streets—things both humanity and the magical community don't want roaming free. Most of the factions don't like the exposure a renegade brings. There is a delicate balance just beneath the human eye. Leaders don't want to disturb it, so they abandon the troublemakers to their own fates."

Carley was silent for a moment. "What do you mean, seven out of ten?"

"He means the other thirty percent are innocents," Alexis said. "Magical beings who did nothing wrong but are arrested or killed purely by association or discovery. People like you, Carley."

Aiden scowled but Alexis was right. He wasn't fond of the percentage, but there was only so much he could do. He warned them away when he had the opportunity, but it was rare for him to be able to offer it without compromising himself. As of yet, humanity had no group advocating for the magical community. Fear mongering kept the media and society hateful. To show any sympathy would draw suspicion. Aiden watched the reality sink into Carley and inwardly winced. She was a good person and a good cop. Unjustly harming innocents would never sit well with her.

Carley narrowed her gaze. "Are there many who go through life not knowing they have power?"

"I wouldn't say many, but they do exist," Aiden replied.

"You're caught in the crossfire, Carley. While you're an officer actively involved in this case, had tonight not happened, you would have remained safely ignorant of your power. The base of my accusation against Le'Roe's Child was a lie. Your face is known now. It won't take long for someone to discover you're unmarked. It leaves you exceedingly vulnerable," Alexis said.

"What do you mean?" Carley asked.

"I can protect her," Aiden interjected.

Aiden hoped he sounded more confident than he felt. Le'Roe was notoriously greedy, short-tempered, and fond of beauty. Alexis was a prize Le'Roe would covet. Carley could easily become a pawn in a deadly game. She needed hunter training.

"Yes," Alexis replied, "because you've done such a fantastic job at that thus far."

Anger blossomed in Aiden's chest but before he could reply, Carley's annoyed voice erupted. "Protect me from what? I'm a trained officer of the FDPC, for fuck's sake."

"While you are better prepared than the average citizen, tonight proved your training is insufficient. What if Militar had attacked you? Do you think you could kill him without the aid of daylight? Your training focused on your ability to work in a unit with tools you don't own for hunts that are planned well in advance. You had none of those tonight and you failed," Alexis said bluntly.

A scowl twisted Carley's features. "I'll concede all of that, but I don't plan on accidentally walking into another den in the near future."

"That's not what I'm concerned about. House Le'Roe is powerful and their Elder will likely take offense at my actions, call my bluff. To try and weaken me, she could send several Adults to assassinate or capture you. Honestly, capture is worse. In the Elder's care, it will be quickly discovered you are unmarked. Le'Roe would take you for her own to prove she is stronger and smarter than me. If that happens, she will likely change you into a human servant."

Carley's already pale features blanched. Aiden wanted to shield her, but hiding the truth was just as dangerous. Everything between himself and Carley would change. There was nothing he could do to protect her from emotional blows. Aiden was angry with himself for being so careless.

"I refuse to become one of those things. I've read the research and have killed some. They're mindless blood bags. Even when the Elder that created them dies, they don't recover. The body lives but the mind is gone. They can't even feed themselves. I'd rather die," Carley said.

"Unfortunately, Le'Roe wouldn't give you a choice. You're not strong enough to tell her no," Aiden said.

"So, what do I do? I won't be a sitting duck. I won't go out without a fight," Carley replied, the determination in her voice unwavering.

"You train with me. We get rid of one apartment and bunk together. We start the process of making you a hunter," Aiden answered.

"Training takes time," Alexis stated, "and skills learned on the fly are unreliable. We don't have the luxury of time. If I wouldn't let you die to werewolves, I won't let her die to vampires. There is another option."

Aiden immediately understood. He shook his head vehemently as fear and desperation chilled his skin. "No. That is not an option. Period."

"It is not your decision to make, little hunter. It's not your ass in the hot seat."

"Stop talking like I'm not sitting right here. Put all the cards on the table. I have a right to know," Carley said as frustration crept into her tone.

Aiden drained his glass and set it on the table. He pushed out of his chair and walked behind the couch to pace. Every fiber of his being was alert and vibrating. He needed to protect her, but he wasn't sure how. She had no idea how her decisions would impact the rest of her life. The consequences of Alexis' proposal were not worth the protection it brought.

"I could actually mark you," Alexis said carefully. "Anyone thinking about touching you would have to fear answering to me."

"How would that help?" Carley asked. "You just said being associated with you is what would get me killed."

"While that is true, if they come at you and sense the real mark, they might think twice. If you're captured, the Elder won't be able to claim you magically. The mark would also allow me to sense when and where you're in danger. I can move substantially faster than Aiden. Plus, you would gain some of my endurance, which would make you harder to kill. Those are all things you won't get from simple training."

"But you would be bound to a demon for the rest of your life, Carley. The only way to reverse a mark is death," Aiden said. "If she dies, so do you. It's her demonic energy that would make you harder to kill. You'd be infected with it. Even having power of your own, you are pure. Alexis' power would taint and possibly corrupt you." He rounded the couch to look down at Carley. "You'd be nothing more than a possession."

He had to make her see the mark wasn't worth it. He was willing to admit there was much more to Alexis than the usual demon, but she still shouldn't be trusted.

Carley studied Aiden for a moment before looking to Alexis. "Is that true?"

Alexis nodded once. "To an extent, yes. You would be bound to me for life and my power would exist in you. My death would mean yours, but I assure you, I'm very difficult to kill. However, Aiden's views are clouded by his own prejudice. 'Infect' is a negative term for the sharing of power. He also presumes I treat people like objects."

"No, you think even less of people," Aiden interjected. "Your money and material things hold more value to you."

Alexis ignored him and continued to focus on Carley. "I happen to take very good care of what belongs to me."

"Carley, please trust me when I say being bound to a demon—even one as unique as Alexis—is a really bad idea. I can protect you while you train. You don't need her. Don't make a decision that will follow you for the rest of your life."

Alexis sighed. "The fact that Aiden is still alive to chat is a demonstration of his skill as a hunter and I have felt his power. He isn't weak. But he's not invulnerable or as strong as me, which is a large contributing factor to his fear. Both options have pros and cons. How you choose to protect yourself will be up to you. I suggest you don't make the decision now. You're in some level of shock, probably a little drunk, and there is still more to discuss."

Aiden folded his arms across his chest and sat next to Carley. As much as he wanted to, if he pushed too hard, Carley might make the wrong decision. "She's right. It's probably best to hold the topic for now."

When Carley only nodded her agreement, Aiden looked to Alexis. "Why were you following us?"

"My sources have run dry. I was hoping to learn something new from you. I keep telling you that we want the same thing. We all look at the problem with different views and resources. If we worked together, perhaps we could make a picture and keep another from dying. However, anything you learned from me would have to be kept off your records," Alexis answered.

"What could you give us that we don't already have?" Carley asked skeptically.

"Knowledge of the magic, my history, and message translation," Alexis replied. "I got to see the first scene, but you guys did a good job sealing the second. If I could see it, maybe I could find something in the text that would shed some light for us all."

"So, you're telling me you actually want to team up with two cops?" Aiden said dubiously.

"*Want*, no. But necessary? Yes. We have a better chance of killing this demon if we work together," Alexis said. "None of us wants another body and I don't want more of your colleagues knocking at my door. The two of you are unique in that you have somewhat flexible minds. The rest of your department is not so understanding."

Aiden leaned back and studied Alexis. Though he didn't trust her, he did believe she wanted to kill the individual responsible. If nothing else she said was true, Alexis was a business woman. And murder was bad for business. Her ability to translate the messages alone made an agreement worth it. Her magical abilities could also be advantageous against the killer if the circumstances were right, and he would learn more about her in the process.

"Alright. I'm in. The information you provide won't enter the station," Aiden said.

"I'm not going to turn down help, either," Carley added.

"Does that mean you've changed your mind about turning me in, Detective Jameson?" Alexis asked carefully.

Aiden raised an eyebrow and looked at Carley. She must have threatened Alexis, though he supposed it shouldn't have surprised him. He watched her struggle with the decision. He believed Alexis wasn't responsible for the murders, but while she was likely guilty of a million other things, he had no proof. As far as this case was concerned, Alexis was one of the innocent thirty percent.

Carley finally sighed and shook her head. "I'm not going to turn you in. But my mind could easily change if I find evidence suggesting you're dangerous to the population."

Aiden caught a flicker of relief in Alexis' features. Usually, her mask was flawless. Carley's answer must have mattered to her. Being turned into the FDPC would be a hassle, but Aiden didn't think Alexis would ever see the inside of a holding cell. She had enough resources and power to disappear, even if it was at a cost she'd rather not incur. He wondered what else was at stake to make Alexis worry over a cop's decision.

"I'm glad to hear that," Alexis replied. "I suggest we meet tomorrow evening to discuss the case. We've all had a long night. We'll see things more clearly with fresh eyes."

Aiden pulled a piece of paper from his pocket. "Agreed, but could you look at these now? Knowing what the messages mean could determine how we proceed at the office tomorrow."

Carley raised an eyebrow. "Is that why you went to the club? You were trying to find someone to translate?"

"Yes. I wasn't lying when I said this text is extremely rare. An old teacher of mine offered to take a look. But he didn't know enough, and shit hit the fan before we could finish."

"You asshole! This whole mess could have been avoided if you'd just told me," Carley said with a glare.

"Come on. I couldn't explain the source, where I was going, or why you couldn't come with me. Don't give me that look. We both know you would have fought to come," Aiden shot back.

Carley continued to glare for a moment before she pulled a notebook and pen from her jacket pocket. She turned to Alexis. "Well, can you translate them, then?"

Alexis nodded and accepted the paper from Aiden. "Yes. The first I've known for a while.

For ages, the seven seekers sought
Throughout the whole of light and dark.
But man's jungle obstructs their sight
Leaving the lost alone to fight.
I see you.
The second says:
Grains of sand fall in single file,
Eroding rock and reason all the while.
Has blatant neglect been paid in blood?
Or did the desert actually swallow the flood?
Do you know me?"

Alexis took her phone from her pocket and snapped a picture of the paper before she handed it back to Aiden. Carley scribbled down the translations into her notebook.

"Do they mean anything to you?" Carley asked.

"I've had time to process the first. I have my theories. I'll need some time with the second. I have no instant answers for you presently, though. The killer is talking to me, but I don't know him."

"He seems to think otherwise," Aiden said as he watched Alexis closely.

Much to Aiden's annoyance, Alexis didn't flinch. "Yes. However, the explanation for that is lengthy and better left for tomorrow. I've said countless times before, if I knew who he was, he would be dead already. I stand to lose a fair bit from this game he's playing. I have no reason to protect him."

"You're talking about money and material things. You don't particularly care about the loss of human life," Carley said.

Alexis tilted her head and looked at Carley. "I am talking about time and resources, yes. My companies are all set up to exist as their own entities. There is written documentation already in place for it. I only have to send it out. But if I am forced to leave this name behind prematurely, I will not only lose years of work and all the profits I have earned, but also what I have invested to create it. That may seem materialistic to you, and in a sense it is, but my lifespan is substantially longer than yours."

"What does that have to do with it?" Carley asked.

"Do you think I passed the FDPC DNA test by luck? I had to pay a very skilled individual to hack your system and alter my results. Good work is not free. The senseless loss of life is regrettable, even sad. I certainly don't agree, but I'll freely admit I'm not a noble creature. I care more about my existence than corpses on the ground."

Her response intrigued Aiden. She hadn't lied to maintain her image. He imagined Alexis trusted him about as much as he trusted her, but for the moment, she was an ally.

"I suppose I can respect that point of view. Most humans even think that way. Doesn't mean I have to like it," Carley replied.

"Self-preservation is a drive all creatures possess. It may not be noble or charitable, but that's irrelevant. All that is required to make this work is respect," Alexis answered.

"Through the investigation, yes. But what about after?" Aiden asked.

Alexis took a last sip of wine and set her glass on the table. "A hard question for all of us, so let's be frank. I worry that the two of you will turn me in. You worry I'll kill you. It's a circular problem with only one very difficult, unreliable solution. Trust."

"That's not very reassuring," Carley replied.

Alexis shrugged. "I convinced you to change your mind tonight."

"We all know what's at risk. We are agreed for now, yes?" Aiden asked.

When Alexis and Carley nodded, Aiden checked his watch. "It's almost two in the morning. We should go."

"I offer the both of you my home. It's safer here than either of your apartments. I'll even allow you your weapons," Alexis said as she rose to gather the empty bottle and the glasses.

Aiden was flummoxed. He wanted to take Carley away long enough to convince her not to accept the mark. But he couldn't deny this building was significantly more fortified than his apartment. It wasn't close enough to dawn for vampire activity to minimize. He glanced at Carley and saw his logic mirrored in her face. Access to his weapons made the offer more appealing.

"I take it you have plenty of guest rooms," Carley said teasingly.

Alexis smirked and walked to the bar. "All you have to do is take the elevator. Terry will guide you to your rooms."

Aiden looked at Alexis. "Terry?"

"The crazy-advanced artificial intelligence that runs the building," Carley answered.

Aiden caught the sarcasm, but beneath it was disbelief and a touch of fear. Artificial intelligence research was highly regulated. Alexis' reach must extend beyond anything he had imagined.

"I thought that was a computer-generated speaker in the elevator," Aiden said skeptically.

Alexis glanced up at both of them while she cleaned glasses. "It's actually a 'she.' Just because she's artificial doesn't mean she can't decide what she is."

Aiden had a hard time believing A.I. existed at all, let alone being chastised about artificial gender. "How do you even have A.I.? Research in that field has so many regulations you couldn't read them all in a month," he asked, flabbergasted.

Alexis dried the glasses and moved to the front of the bar. "Illegal research is alive and thriving."

Aiden ran his fingers through his hair. "You have to know artificial intelligence is dangerous."

Alexis lifted her shoulder in a shrug. "Human beings have the ability to destroy this planet one hundred times over. Terry exists and—much like me—she hasn't taken over and slaughtered all of mankind."

Aiden narrowed his gaze. "I could argue it's only a matter of time."

Though Aiden couldn't see behind the lenses, he could tell Alexis rolled her eyes.

"I've been on this world for hundreds of years and never once have I felt the inclination to wipe out the human race… even when they get on my last nerve."

Carley interjected quietly, "Terry is extraordinary but still illegal."

Terry spoke for the first time during the discussion. "Thank you for thinking I am special, Detective Jameson. Typically, I hide and stay quiet when strangers are here. Had it not been revealed, neither one of you would have known I exist. I may not have a body like yours, but I enjoy my life. I do not want to be erased."

Aiden suddenly felt the weight of the evening's events. Artificial intelligence had just spoken to him and he found himself sympathizing. "Alright, alright. We'll stay."

Alexis nodded. "Terry will guide you to your rooms. Rest well."

With that, she pushed off the bar and disappeared down the hallway. Aiden frowned after her. He sighed, shook his head, and refocused on his partner. "Are you alright?"

"No, I'm not fucking alright," Carley replied as she leaned forward and put her head in her hands.

Guilt stabbed him through the chest. "I'm sorry, Carley."

"You should be. I knew you were lying… and so did the Captain. I have so many questions, I don't even know where to begin. Or whether you would even tell me the truth. Do you have any idea how much it sucks not to be sure you can trust your partner?"

Aiden winced. He'd never once sensed the power in Carley and felt it would be rude to try after what she'd just gone through. Militar's morals were questionable at best and Aiden couldn't change the past. Carley was his responsibility now. He had to keep her safe until she could protect herself.

"All the things I lied about were to keep me out of a cell. Now that you know what I am, I have no reason to hide. You can trust me more than Alexis Montral, Carley. I have your back and I can teach you what I know."

Carley raised her head to study him. The sadness in her expression made his gut twist. "I'm not sure I believe you. I've seen sides of you tonight I didn't know existed. But I'm too tired and too tipsy to get into it. I just want to go to sleep and wake up from this nightmare. I'm going to follow Terry down the rabbit hole."

Carley stood up and walked to the elevator. The doors opened when she got there.

Aiden was fast on her heels and they stepped into the elevator together. The doors closed on their own. "Let me guide you," he said. "I've lived down the rabbit hole my whole life."

Carley glanced up at him and her lips curved with just a hint of a smile. "At least now I know why you're always late. I'm going to buy you a fuzzy tail and bunny ears to wear at the office for a month."

Aiden groaned and brought a hand to his heart. "The torture you put me through, Red Queen. Those cute lab chicks will have even more reason to stare at my ass."

Carley's wicked smile was its own reward. "Just for that, I'm going to make them pink."

CHAPTER THIRTEEN

The room was dark when Carley awoke. Her head throbbed, and her eyes were gritty. Fading nightmares skittered around the outskirts of her consciousness. When the fear subsided, she realized she was vastly too comfortable to be in her own bed. However, her sleepy mind pushed the thought away. There wasn't anything wrong with being comfortable.

She groaned in protest as her mind slowly began to come alive instead of drifting back into peaceful oblivion. Much to her annoyance, the awareness she wasn't in her own bed shoved back into her thoughts.

Her eyes snapped open. Instinct and training suppressed the panic and fear. Slowly and gently, Carley slid her hand around the bedsheets. Once she determined she was alone, she checked herself for injuries. Only her head gave her trouble. It was a bit unnerving to realize the clothes she wore also did not belong to her.

When her eyes adjusted, she looked around. The light of the city snuck through small spaces in the blinds and left thin streaks around the room. Her entire apartment could fit in the bedroom alone, not counting the additional square footage of the private bathroom and walk-in closet.

Carley rubbed her eyes and tried to recall the events of the previous hours. Fuzzy images of vampires and blood came first but were soon overpowered by the all-too-real taste of Alexis' lips. Carley whimpered and pulled the covers over her head. She was mortifyingly safe in one of Montral's guest rooms.

After a few moments, she sighed and accepted that denial and hiding beneath fantastic sheets wouldn't erase the previous night's events. She threw the covers back and looked at the clock on the bedside table. Small fluorescent numbers read five in the morning. She sat up slowly and leaned back against the headboard. The throbbing soon turned to mallets banging inside her skull, and she couldn't silence her wince. After several shots of vodka and almost dying, wine hadn't been the best decision. Three hours of sleep was nowhere near sufficient.

She remembered tossing and turning. With her head aching and her thoughts scattered, she knew she was awake for the day. If her dreams kept the same theme, she didn't want to go back to sleep anyway.

Carley ran her fingers through her hair and gently massaged her scalp as she tried to figure out what to do next. Her life had completely changed in less than twenty-four hours. She was *diseased*, one of the very people she had spent her career hunting. Worse, she believed she had been born that way.

Research theorized those born with power could not be treated. In the hours before sleep finally came, Carley had searched for a flaw in Alexis' logic, for even the smallest error to cast a shadow of doubt. When she found none, she felt the entire foundation she'd built her life on crack.

Carley rolled her shoulders and rubbed her stiff neck. Her body was exhausted, but her mind jumped with questions she wasn't sure she wanted the answers to. Beneath all the confusion and anger, she was terrified. She felt alone. While she thought of Aiden as a brother, he had hidden who he really was from her. Carley understood why, but she wasn't sure she could completely trust him anymore.

It was as if the man Carley knew was a mask. Now that she saw the real Aiden, she wasn't sure what to make of him. He made no attempt to hide his blind hatred of Alexis. Carley now realized the woman was a demon, but she was unlike anything they had ever encountered. That had to count for something.

Granted, Alexis had also hidden what she was. Carley couldn't blame her, either. The policy on demons was kill-on-sight. Coming clean was a death wish. But that didn't change the fact Alexis' mask was just as big as Aiden's.

Though she had known Aiden longer, Carley wasn't certain the answers she would get from him would be unbiased. She hadn't become a cop so she could spread ignorance and hate. She wanted to help the sick and save the public from the ones who were too far gone. Carley wanted facts and to learn more about the world Alexis and Aiden lived in.

Carley didn't doubt Alexis had her own agenda, but she was a respected and successful business woman who didn't appear to waste her valuable time with death and destruction. As odd as it sounded, Carley felt she would get the straight truth from the demon rather than Aiden.

She wondered if Alexis would be awake at five, or if she even slept at all. Alexis had said if Carley needed anything, she only had to ask the computer. It felt weird talking to an inanimate object, especially one that wasn't visible. But her own curiosity was greater than the feeling of stupidity.

"Uh, Terry?"

"Good morning, Detective Jameson. Is there something I can help you with?" the crisp, feminine voice replied.

"I was wondering if Alexis was awake," Carley said as she fought the urge to fidget.

"She is. In anticipation of your restless night, she instructed me to alert her if you wish to see her. She is currently on the fitness floor. Would you like me to guide you there?"

Carley raised an eyebrow and wished she had something to make eye contact with. "Anticipated? Have both of you been watching me the whole night?"

"Ms. Montral has not. She has a great deal of respect for privacy. I am fairly certain she noticed your discomfort during last night's discussion. As for me, I am in charge of your protection and Ms. Montral's protection from you. I am sure you understand," Terry replied.

Carley did, but it unnerved her just the same. She could have sworn she detected amusement in the computer's tone, but that was absurd. Computers didn't have *tones*. At least, that's what Carley told herself.

Montral's building was more technologically advanced than anything she had ever come in contact with. Even the computer division of the FDPC and the top hospitals in the area were not as well equipped. Carley had heard rumors of several companies fooling around with artificial intelligence, but as far as she knew, they were still debating the topic. It made Terry's existence a little frightening.

"That's creepy," Carley mumbled as she began to untangle herself from the twisted sheets.

"Perhaps, but at least I am not an underpaid, perverted security guard who gets his jollies from watching guests through cameras. I promise not to stare at you in the shower."

Carley laughed before she could help herself. "I appreciate it. Can you tell me how to get to the fitness floor?"

"When you are ready, go to the elevator at the end of the hall to your right. I will take you to her."

"Thanks," Carley said as she slid out of bed.

"It is my pleasure, Detective Jameson."

Carley smiled as she walked into the bathroom. She wasn't awake enough to get ready for work, but she also wasn't about to speak with Alexis looking like something that crawled out of a gutter. Alexis was gorgeous and Carley still had her pride.

She flicked the bathroom lights on. It was pristinely clean with white tile floors and black marble countertops. Two sinks with silver faucets were built into the marble and the entire wall behind them was mirrored. There was a linen closet filled with plush, matching towels. A full shower stall with a black curtain was tucked into the corner. A Jacuzzi tub large enough for four people rested against the opposite wall. The soft floor mats matched the shower curtain. Her body longed for the tub, but she chose the shower to save time.

Carley took a towel from the closet and set it on the counter before she stripped out of her bra and panties. She then paused.

"Terry, where are my clothes?"

"They are currently dry cleaning. Ms. Montral believed you and Mr. Thompson would enjoy clean clothing to spend the day in and did not think either of you would accept apparel from her collection."

"I don't think I want to know how they got into dry cleaning. So, I'm stuck with pajama pants for now?"

"The closet in the bedroom is stocked with a variety of sizes," Terry replied.

"Really?" Carley asked, intrigued.

"Ms. Montral does not often entertain, but surprise guests come every now and then. Sometimes fresh clothing is required."

Carley raised an eyebrow before she chuckled and shook her head. "Is that so? I bet those are interesting stories."

"Is yours not interesting, Detective Jameson?" Terry asked.

Now there was definite sarcasm in the computer's tone and Carley couldn't help but smirk. "Fair enough."

She hopped in the shower. The water was warm and helped relax tight muscles. The day promised to be long. She rushed through the shower, afraid she'd never leave if she lingered. After toweling dry, she ran a brush through damp hair and picked up her underwear.

Carley moved into the walk-in closet and the light automatically turned on. She found a simple pair of jeans and a sweatshirt. On a shoe rack were sandals that suited her needs. She walked out and took one last glance in the mirror above the chest of drawers. Not her best, but at least her butt looked good. That was all that really mattered.

She walked into the hall and found the elevator. The doors opened automatically when she got there and it moved on its own. There was still no display to tell her what floor she was on, no way to orient herself. If Terry broke, she'd never escape the maze. It made her wonder what Alexis did when Terry needed maintenance.

The elevator doors opened and Carley stepped off. Terry hadn't been kidding when she said "fitness floor." The entire level was nothing but open space, with the exception of an enclosed indoor pool and locker rooms along the right wall. There was a track that ran around the border. Inside was a variety of cardio machines, free weights, benches, and tumbling mats. Speakers and projectors hung from the ceiling.

Carley knew what it was to be rich. She had grown up on a huge estate in southern California, but Alexis' property made her father's house look like a small summer home.

She began to wonder if Alexis aged like vampires. There was a scientific debate whether vampires were immortal or just aged too slowly for human detection. Regardless, Alexis had spoken of her need for wealth because of her lifespan. Carley made a mental note to ask later.

Terry's voice poured over the speakers and brought her back to focus. "Phase four complete. Confirmation to proceed to phase five?"

"Confirmed," Alexis replied.

Curious, Carley walked toward the middle of the gym. She found Alexis on a large mat in a combat stance. Attached to her bare hands and feet were odd looking circular pads containing small electrodes. The skin-tight pants and shirt she wore had smaller versions of the pads sewn into the black fabric. A small bead or two of sweat dripped off her chin.

The projectors on the ceiling came to life and Carley's eyes widened as she realized they were holographic. The FDPC used similar ones to help reconstruct crime scenes, visualize potential scenarios, and theorize what an unknown creature might look like based on empirical evidence collected from a scene. They were operated by highly specialized technicians who had extensive training in programming. Even then, holographic projectors took time to prepare and, frequently, couldn't adjust for more than a few variables.

She had never seen a more advanced use for the projectors. These images were not static. Carley counted twenty holographic thugs surrounding Alexis. The pads on her body turned neon green and the thugs attacked.

Carley watched Alexis with a combination of awe, jealousy, and a new-found respect for the demon's skills. Alexis handled all twenty thugs with a stunning skill in martial arts. There was no magic being used. Alexis employed pure physical prowess to systematically take out the thugs one by one. Worse, she made it look easy.

Alexis ducked under a punch and drove her fist into her attacker's stomach, her body already prepared for the next attack. While she dealt with two attackers at her front, a new thug came up behind her, outside her visual field, and slammed a bat down across her back. The green sensors on her back flared red and the projectors froze.

"Phase five failed. Opponent seven landed a successful upper back strike. Detective Jameson is here. Shall I terminate this morning's session?" Terry asked.

Alexis stood up straight. Annoyance painted her features. "Yes. This session can be terminated early."

Carley stepped forward as Alexis walked to the edge of the mat and picked up a towel. "So, is this how you make all that money? Hire yourself out as a professional assassin?"

Alexis raised an eyebrow. "Being proficient in self-defense doesn't make one a murderer."

"Could have fooled me. Why did the projectors stop after one hit? You could have still easily won the fight."

"The goal of the program is to increase the number of opponents I can defeat without being hit."

"So, having magic, durability, and whatever the fuck else you have up your sleeve isn't enough? You also have to train in crazy martial arts?"

Alexis tilted her head. "Power doesn't make you immune. What brings you here?"

Carley sighed. "Restless. Questions?"

"I'm headed back to my room for a shower. Walk with me."

Carley nodded once and followed to the elevator. "Is this world, for a lack of a better word, always like last night?"

"In what sense?"

"The high level of violence and games. You can't tell me you weren't tap dancing with that vampire."

"There are politics everywhere, territories and customs. It's a bit like living in a jungle. You must be strong enough to protect yourself, wise enough to trick and evade, or ally yourself with others who are willing to protect you."

"People are okay with living in a constant state of fear?" Carley asked.

Alexis held the elevator doors for Carley and they traveled to the main floor. "I didn't say it was all bad. The jungle is as beautiful as it is deadly. Most are content and safe within their groups. It's unfortunate your knowledge of this world is crime scenes and Dark Heart. They're an ugly side of the community."

"So, there is better and worse than what I saw?"

"Correct," Alexis answered.

They walked the path to Alexis' room in silence. Carley had a hard time believing the community of unnatural and diseased reflected her own. She couldn't picture a person infected with lycanthropy having a white picket fence and two point five children. They ate flesh and killed each other in dominance battles.

Alexis opened the door to her bedroom. Carley pushed her thoughts aside for a moment to study the room. There was much to learn about a person from how they kept their personal space.

Cream-colored carpet and dark cherry furniture greeted them. The curtains, linen, and furniture pillows were different combinations of black, red, and silver. A beautiful, king-sized, four-poster bed was the centerpiece. A desk with a computer monitor, a couch, several small tables, a chest of drawers and several mirrors filled the space well. Adorning the walls were some of the most detailed landscape paintings Carley had ever seen. One stood out, depicting a clearing in a beautiful forest. The open space was occupied by a massive, strangely black tower. Carley promised to get a better look later.

On several tables there were books with bookmarks in random locations. Jewelry boxes and small trinkets rested on the chest of drawers. The room was elegant, tasteful without being gaudy. Most importantly, it was comfortable.

"Have a seat wherever you like. I have time before I have to get ready for work."

Carley moved to the couch and took a seat. "What path in the jungle have you taken?"

"Before last night, there were only a select few who knew I even existed," Alexis answered, coming to sit down next to her.

"Why? You're obviously powerful. You're not prey."

"No, but I like my privacy and the freedom of no obligations."

"And now?"

"Now I must play politics. I'll have to show my strength and demonstrate I'm more than capable of protecting myself… and what's mine."

Carley lowered her head and closed her eyes. She had to swallow a lump in her throat before she could speak. "Can I survive in this world?"

Alexis shook her head. "While you're more knowledgeable and experienced than the average human, it isn't enough. Your power is completely untrained. Perhaps, if you were associated with someone much weaker than me, no one would pay you any interest."

"Your help seems like quite the double-edged sword."

"You're not wrong, but you survived the night. Without my help, you wouldn't have."

"Can Aiden help me?"

Alexis lifted a shoulder in a shrug. "He's more powerful than he knows. He's also street wise and maneuvers well between both societies, but he isn't without flaws."

"So I am seeing. I would like your perspective," Carley said.

"Aiden has unexplored talent of his own. I doubt he ever takes the time to look closely within. He seems to focus only on the outside and that limits his potential and ability to teach you self-exploration."

"Alright. What else?"

"He's an elemental witch. You are not. I can't say for certain he has the capability of guiding you. He's also a demon hunter. Aiden doesn't try to just survive. He goes out looking for trouble."

"Correct me if I'm wrong, but you're not a witch either. What makes you think you can teach me?"

"Centuries of experience honing my own power and interacting with others of varying gifts have given me a fair bit of perspective. When you outgrow me, I have more contacts you can learn from."

Carley sighed and rubbed her eyes. "I'm not sure I even want to learn."

Alexis' expression softened. "Power doesn't make you sick or evil, merely different. You're not the type to hide because you're different."

"Think you know me well enough to know that?" Carley demanded.

"I don't presume to know you at all," Alexis replied calmly, "but I've been where you are. I know what it is to be thrust into a world you don't understand. I know what it is to have no control over the power you possess. Remember, you came to me for answers."

Carley sighed and ran her fingers through her hair. "I'm sorry. I'm just exhausted and don't know what to make of all this shit."

"Forgiven. My skin is thick."

Carley leaned back in the couch and studied Alexis closely. "You said last night you could protect me through some kind of mark."

"It's not a physical mark. In essence, a little of my power would meld with yours and an intimate connection would form between us. We would be aware of each other's physical well-being, no matter the distance between us. If I pressed deeply enough and I allowed you to see into me, we would be able to sense each other's emotions, even speak telepathically. But I would be marking you, so I will have more potential control over you than you would have over me."

"What if I marked you?"

"Not everyone is capable of doing it. While the limits of your power have not been tested, it takes time to master," Alexis replied.

"Are there risks beyond you having a stupidly large influence over my life?"

Alexis nodded. "If not done with a skilled touch, the connection could grow too deep too quickly. It could pull us both in and we would be lost in the mixture of power. We wouldn't be able to tell where you left off and I began. We would forget about our bodies. Anyone who looked at us would think we had fallen into comas. Unless you were put on life support, you'd eventually die of starvation. I would then spend the rest of my time searching the magic for you until someone finally killed my body. I've never felt the need to test beyond two weeks how long I could go without food."

"Is it a life-long connection? Can we break it once all this is over?"

"The success rate of intentional breaks is low. Accidental breaks seem to have higher chances, but still not something to seek out."

"Have you ever given anyone a mark before?"

Alexis sighed and got up. She walked to the one window in the room and said nothing for a long time.

Carley didn't doubt Alexis could cast the mark safely, nor did she fear the possibility of failure. Dying in a blissful mental haze sounded a great deal better than being torn to pieces for food or slowly tortured to death.

However, she didn't want to be bound to someone for the rest of her life for the wrong reasons. Carley didn't want to be bound to anyone at all… but needed to live long enough to learn to survive on her own.

Alexis finally turned to face her and took off her sunglasses. The obsidian eyes caught her off guard. They were beautifully terrifying but Carley met them head on.

"I've never chosen to mark someone. My responsibility has been almost completely to myself, and I like it that way. Placing a mark is taking on someone's life. Many out there won't see it that way, but I don't see you as property."

Carley inwardly sighed with relief. If Alexis had said anything less genuine, Carley would have declined the offer. Alexis viewed a mark as a burden, not a prize. While Carley had no desire to become a burden to anyone, it was better than being considered a possession that could be used whenever and for whatever reason. Even having made her decision, Carley needed to press a little harder to fully satisfy herself.

"In other words, you don't want the burden of caring about what happens to someone other than yourself. You only care about your own happiness and well-being."

To her credit, Alexis didn't hesitate or bat an eyelash. "Yes."

"Then why are you offering to mark me? I mean, I'm grateful you wouldn't treat me like an object, but I will only chain you and your way of life."

"The magical society in this city believes you are mine. If they find out otherwise, I'll appear weak and come under fire from every predatory group that would love to get their hands on anything of value in this building and whatever else I own. Then they would either try to kill or enslave me. That is a great deal of bodies I would have to dispose of."

"I could see how that would be problematic," Carley said dryly.

Alexis continued, "It is also possible that I would fall to pure numbers. Unlikely, but possible. Either way, your FDPC would start to take notice, which brings me to my next reason."

Carley raised an eyebrow.

"I do not need to be associated with a dead or missing FDPC detective. The very fact that I am forced to deal with the FDPC is dangerous enough. A dead cop is more than enough reason to take a closer look at me."

"That's entirely fair," Carley said.

"You're a good cop. This stalker of mine has done an annoyingly good job of evading both of us. You need me as much as I need you. If you disappear or die, they'll replace you with someone less intelligent, less open minded, and more fanatical in his or her beliefs about the black and white of this world. No one needs that."

"Look at you, sweet talker."

"It's the truth. I don't utterly loathe you. My involvement in your life after this case is negotiable. While we will always be linked and drawn to one another, it doesn't mean we have to stay in constant touch. If one is in danger, the other will know."

"How?"

"You'll feel it. After you have been trained to control your power, we only have to see each other if one is threatened."

Carley thought about Alexis' words. "At least you find the idea of marking me as shitty as I do."

"Nothing about this situation is ideal."

"Ain't that the truth."

Alexis sighed and nodded. "Your involvement with the FDPC makes this just as dangerous for me as it is for you."

"I sort of get why you would fear us, but not entirely. We are trying to help people."

"One day, when this is all over, I will both explain and show you why. For now, I will just tell you that most people in your organization are not as honest and open minded as you. Nor is justice or helping the sick their true motive."

Carley felt a stone form in the pit of her stomach. "I'll let that go, but only because I've had about as much as I can take. I accept your offer. How does this work, then?"

"I'll be doing the work. For a brief moment, you'll feel like you are drowning in me. The weight of my power will seem unbearably heavy, especially since you've never been truly aware of yours."

"Sounds pleasant," Carley replied skeptically.

"Before you so hastily agree, you must be aware of one other thing. You have unconsciously put up barriers around your power, binding it essentially. When I mark you, they will be torn down. Your power will be free. You will need instruction to keep yourself in control and to keep from being noticed by your co-workers. I won't mark you if you don't agree to instruction. I don't care if you learn from me or another, but that person has to be credible."

"I get it," Carley said. "Being noticed by my co-workers is bad. I probably know that better than you."

"You agree to instruction, then?" Alexis asked.

Carley nodded. "I can learn from you until I need something more."

Alexis nodded and offered her hand. "Alright."

Butterflies chased away the stone and it took all of Carley's nerve to keep her hand steady.

Alexis looked up and held Carley's gaze. "There is no going back. Are you sure?"

Carley felt her heart race and she blew out a breath. "Just fucking do it, already. I don't want to lose my nerve."

"You will never lose your nerve, Carley. Wrap your hand around my wrist as I wrap mine around yours," Alexis said quietly.

As soon as Carley returned the grip, small tendrils of shadow poured out of Alexis' fingertips. The tendrils swirled around their joined hands until their arms were completely hidden from sight. Carley gasped and fought the urge to yank her hand away. The shadows were intimidating but right when she was about to wonder why it didn't hurt, she felt Alexis's power pour into her.

Carley's eyes closed as darkness filled her to the brim. Waves of fluid obsidian slammed through her mind, burying her alive. She couldn't breathe. She fought to shove back, but Alexis was too strong.

The terror of suffocation burned in her chest. An eternity passed and just when Carley thought she would die from the pressure, something inside her broke. In an instant, she could breathe. The shadows no longer choked but embraced. In less than a heartbeat, Carley understood the wispy nature of darkness. The shadows felt like home.

Alexis' heartbeat pulsed through her body. Carley felt the light fatigue from the workout. She could feel her need for breakfast. It was unnerving and comforting at the same time. She opened her eyes and looked down at their joined hands. The shadows were gone. Alexis' grip was still gentle, but Carley had squeezed Alexis' wrist so tightly there were half-moon indentations. Carley released the hand and collapsed against the couch.

"Holy shit," she said, breathing heavily.

Carley tried to adjust to feeling Alexis' life pulse within her. She looked down at her wrist and found it was as flawless as it had been before the mark. The only difference was now she couldn't stop herself from shaking. She swallowed and took a deep breath, letting it out slowly. "Is it always this intense?"

Alexis got up and moved to sit on the bed to put some distance between them. "Better?"

Carley nodded. "Yes. So, it's proportionate to the distance between us?"

"No amount of distance will ever be enough to silence the sensation entirely. I could be around the world and you'll still feel me. You can follow that feeling to find me. We can't hide from each other now."

"Fuck. I have to be able to work with this constantly in my head," Carley realized.

"Yes, and you will have to learn quickly. Your power may not show itself for a little while. If you start to have strange and intense dreams, hear other people's thoughts, or have anything odd happen around you, you must come to me. I don't care if you are in the middle of a case. Do you understand? This isn't a game or a trivial warning. If your power overtakes you while working, people will notice," Alexis said.

Carley nodded. "I start to see or do weird shit, I come to you. Got it."

Alexis nodded in return. "Good. Now, it's time for me to get ready for work. I suggest you go take another shower. Today, work on giving even the smallest of tasks your full attention. It will help you practice pushing the sensation to the back of your mind. Terry will guide you back to your room, unless you wish me to."

Carley shook her head and stood up. She took a moment to make sure she was steady. "No, I think you should stay right where you are."

"It will get better. I promise," Alexis said.

Carley nodded and walked to the door. A thought crossed her mind and caused her to look back at the other woman. "Is it this intense for you, too?"

Alexis smirked. "Yes. I'm just more practiced at handling magical connections."

Carley turned her back without answering and walked out. The door closed silently behind her. As she walked down the hallway and the distance between them grew, Carley began to feel more like herself.

She grinned at the realization that she had a gorgeous, rich woman bound to her for life. The humor of it struck her and she laughed. She hadn't even had to buy a ring.

CHAPTER FOURTEEN

Alexis slowly inhaled the rich aroma of French roast coffee. She brought the mug to her lips and took her first sip as she looked out over the city. The dawn's first light trickled through the window and crept along her hands. The day was already long and the sun was just rising. She took some time to enjoy the drink and the simple silence of her kitchen.

Exhaustion skittered through the depths of her body. The mark had proven to be more difficult than anticipated. Carley's power had been locked behind a series of complicated walls resistant to blunt force. They were old, but well-constructed. Something other than Carley had built them, and in order for Alexis to place her mark, they had to be destroyed.

Alexis had to search for subtle cracks in these mental walls to seep into. Once inside, she flooded them with her power until those cracks grew large enough that the walls crumbled. She then had to flush out the foreign influence before she could bind Carley's power to hers. Alexis hadn't prepared to spend that much energy, a minor issue but irritating just the same. Alexis had no doubt the experience had been just as difficult for Carley.

She took another sip and let her thoughts drift. She wasn't capable of constructing new walls to contain Carley's power. Typically, she wouldn't have considered it, but given Carley's chosen path in life and her reaction to learning she had power at all, Alexis believed the walls might have been beneficial. It was likely they were forged very early in Carley's childhood.

Usually, powerful individuals grew up learning how to control and manipulate what was inside them. They had years to master it. Carley would not have that opportunity. In the very near future, the full extent of her power would wash over her like a tidal wave. The depth of power within the detective was surprising.

While the issue of Carley's emerging power was no laughing matter, a much darker problem lurked in the shadows. Someone had feared what Carley would become enough to construct a magical prison. Those walls had been built too well for their destruction to go unnoticed. Someone would now come looking for Carley. It might not be soon, but eventually, someone would come.

Alexis shivered. Carley's heartbeat pulsed through her, faster than her own. The two rhythms were out of sync. Alexis didn't care for the constant reminder she was directly responsible for another's life. She had been, and still was, a protective influence on several, but nothing on the scale of a mark. There had always been an escape route. But there was no escaping Carley.

Ultimately, any problem of Carley's would become Alexis'. The detective would have to be told about the prison she had spent her life in—but not until the case was solved. The unknown demon needed to be removed from the streets first. It threatened Alexis' life in New York, which also meant it threatened Carley's. If Alexis had to disappear, Carley would have to come with her. For the moment, she needed Carley focused on her job, and that was going to be challenging enough without the mark and the expression of her power. Carley would be angry with her later for withholding the information, but Alexis couldn't risk it when there was a larger threat looming.

Terry's voice pulled Alexis from her thoughts. "Good morning, Alexis. The two detectives have just met in the hallway. I thought you might like to see."

"Always so thoughtful. Thank you. Sound isn't necessary, though. I think I'll savor these last few precious moments of quiet."

"They will be brief, indeed," Terry replied.

Alexis turned her attention to the flat screen on the wall at the far side of the kitchen. She leaned a hip against the counter and took a last sip of coffee as she watched the conversation between Aiden and Carley. It escalated quickly.

"He will ask you where I am. Tell him," Alexis said calmly.

"The probability of his aggression turning to violence is high," Terry warned.

"I know. Lead him here anyway. If you can, make it so he gets here before Carley," Alexis replied casually.

"I will do my best. Try not to destroy the furniture. I have grown attached to this set. It is very aesthetically pleasing."

Alexis laughed as she watched Aiden turn and sprint to the elevator. He drew his gun on the way. She shook her head and set her mug on the counter, debating whether to rethink her permission to allow him weapons. She removed her watch and the simple, yet elegant sapphire bracelet and set them neatly beside the mug. She walked to the open doorway of the kitchen, put her back to the wall beside it, and waited.

It wasn't long before she heard the elevator and felt his heated power flood the hall. Alexis let her own energy evenly fill the kitchen to make sure he knew she was there, but left him unable to pinpoint where she was standing. Aiden's pace slowed as he approached the kitchen. His footsteps were about as quiet as a human could manage, but she still heard them clearly. He had the movements of a professional, but that's what made him predictable.

Aiden's gun appeared through the doorway first. The moment she saw it, Alexis slammed her hand down on his wrist. She kept the weapon pointed safely toward the ground. The moment her skin touched his, heat twisted up her arm and entwined itself with her power. Alexis shivered, even as she yanked him into the kitchen and swung her free arm into his chest with enough force to knock him off his feet. Aiden's back hit the floor with a solid thud.

Once she got him down and coughing to get his wind back, Alexis pulled a chair from the nearby table and slammed it down over him. The legs of the chair hit the floor on either side of his head and under his shoulders. She held the chair down, caging his body, while she pulled his gun arm straight and drove the heel of her stiletto into the soft tissue inside his elbow. He cried out, but stubbornly refused to release the weapon. With her power dancing with his, her entire body alive and vibrating, Alexis didn't have much patience. She continued to add pressure until Aiden grunted and finally dropped the gun.

She released his wrist to pick up the weapon, breaking the physical connection between them. The magical connection was harder. Her power didn't want to let go. Fire spun with darkness throughout her body. It left goosebumps on her skin and danced the line of pleasured pain. As always, she craved more.

But more wasn't an option. She ripped her power away from his and turned her back to walk to the counter. It was worse than pulling teeth. When she was finally free, she felt holes in her energy where Aiden's had been. With practiced motions, she pulled the magazine from the gun and emptied the round from the chamber before taking a deep, silent breath.

Alexis worked to settle her system, even out her power, and establish shielding. She knew Aiden would try to touch her again and since she planned on allowing it, she needed protection.

It was easy to forget what had erupted between them until it was shoved in her face. Their energies connected so quickly it was difficult to prepare. The echoes of Aiden lingered in her body. It felt so good it was aggravating. Having just marked Carley, she was more vulnerable to magical connections. She solidified her shielding and counted the seconds it took for Aiden to recover.

Alexis got to five before she heard him move. Another two passed before she felt his hand wrap roughly around her arm. The fabric of her shirt helped, but she still felt his heat push against her shields. She didn't fight when he yanked her around and slammed her back into the refrigerator. Aiden pressed his body to hers and pinned her with his weight. His free hand wrapped around her throat and squeezed threateningly.

Alexis was grateful for her defense. It made it easier to hold her composure and smile into the fury of his eyes.

"You selfish, manipulative bitch," Aiden said, leaning his face into hers. "This is someone's life you are fucking with. Break the mark. It's still fresh. It won't kill her. Break it or I swear, I'll do it myself by killing you where you stand."

Her smile only widened. "No."

He growled and tightened his grip on her throat, slamming her back against the refrigerator hard enough to make it shake.

"I'm not fucking around!"

Aiden's power pressed harder against her as his anger grew. Alexis had to actively fight the urge to let her power mingle with his.

"Neither am I."

"This isn't a game."

"No, it isn't. Someone must protect her and you're woefully inadequate. This little temper tantrum you're throwing only adds weight to my point."

Alexis watched guilt form behind the fury in his eyes. She understood but held no sympathy. Aiden had made careless mistakes and all three of them were suffering for it.

"You're using her as a means to an end. She isn't a toy or one of your countless possessions," Aiden said.

"No one is more aware of that than me. I can feel her life, Aiden. It's true I will do whatever it takes to see this case closed, but I forced nothing on her. I showed her options, one of which was not taking my mark. I never removed her freedom of choice. She came to me," Alexis replied calmly.

"You filled her head with manipulative lies."

"I told her the frank, hard truth."

"There are other options."

"Like what?" Alexis countered "The moment anyone takes a closer look at her, or you, they will learn you're FDPC detectives. Both of you will have targets on your backs. No one likes rats that turn on their own people. You'll barely be able to keep yourself alive, let alone Carley. Marking her gives her my protection and makes me seem both crazy and brilliant for having an ear within the police. Your identity will remain secure. You're just her partner."

She needed Aiden to think past his anger. It was foolish to hope for him to see past his prejudice, but Alexis wished just the same. Every argument needed to be countered.

"You don't have her best intentions at heart. You can't. You're not capable of it," Aiden said, almost more to himself than her.

"I have nothing to gain by marking a federal officer who has gone through life with no idea she has power," Alexis said. "In fact, it weakens me. Believe what you want. It's done."

Aiden studied Alexis closely, and she didn't shy away from his scrutiny. He reached up to carefully pull the sunglasses from her face. With the mark she had given Carley, Aiden was going to become a part of her life, too. She wanted him to believe she would protect his partner.

Aiden didn't flinch at the darkness in her eyes, nor did his expression turn to disgust. She let him see her resolve, her determination, her sincerity. It wasn't long before the heat of anger in Aiden's gaze shifted. For a heartbeat, the tension in the air wasn't from conflict, and in that moment, she drowned in the fire of his eyes.

But the moment was short lived. Alexis was okay with him witnessing her confidence. She was not okay with him reaching beyond that. Without breaking eye contact, Alexis locked down her personal reactions. Her gaze grew hard and blank. Aiden tilted his head and eased the pressure on her throat.

"I want to believe you won't hurt her," he said quietly.

"Why is that so hard?"

"Because you're a demon."

"Has my behavior given you reason to believe I am anything like my kin?"

"All demons are the same. You're just smarter, more powerful. You're capable of complex manipulation," Aiden said.

"Is that the mantra you repeat to yourself every time you find yourself wanting me?"

Aiden was silent as he leaned into her. He came so close she could feel the brush of his lips when his grip on her throat tightened again. "Your façade is almost flawless, Alexis. Almost. Whatever this power is between us, it affects you, too. For a split second, I saw it in your face. I felt it. I'm not the only one who wants what I shouldn't have."

Alexis raised an intrigued eyebrow. She didn't bother denying it. Instead, she tilted her head just slightly, enough to cut the already small distance between them in half. Her lips briefly touched his.

"Have I finally left you speechless?" he whispered with an almost cocky smile.

"Not quite. Look left, Aiden."

She pulled her head back as he looked over his shoulder in time to see a set of knuckles slam into his cheekbone. Aiden grunted and released her before stumbling backward.

Alexis smirked and straightened the collar of her shirt as Carley's furious voice filled the kitchen, "You fucking asshole. What the hell did you think you were doing?"

"Ow! For fuck's sake!" Aiden brought his hand to his eye to check for blood.

"It seems your lessons on viewing the larger picture will be painful ones," Alexis said as she smoothed the wrinkles from her shirt and stepped away from the refrigerator. Aiden sneered at her.

"Did you really think racing up here and man-handling Alexis would get you your way?" Carley demanded. "What the hell is wrong with you?"

"You don't understand the level of shit you've gotten yourself into," Aiden retorted. "You don't want to be magically bound to anyone, especially not her. She's dangerous."

"Apparently, so are you. So is walking out on the street every day," Carley said furiously. "I'm a grown woman and I make my own choices. Don't make me get on my fucking feminist soapbox."

Amused, Alexis listened to the banter before the phone in her pocket vibrated. She pulled it out to see a message from her secretary. She was going to be late. Alexis slid the phone back into her pocket.

"Enough, both of you. We've all had a long, exhausting night with a full day's work ahead. This demon won't wait for us to settle petty arguments. Aiden, try to see the mark as a business arrangement. Carley wants to live and I need her to do her job. Carley, Aiden is a demon hunter. I imagine he has seen and killed enough of my kind to have plenty of reason for his blind hatred. So cut him some slack. That being said…" Alexis trailed off as she moved to the counter.

She loaded the spare round into the magazine and slid it back into the gun. Alexis stepped to Aiden and offered him the weapon.

"If you ever run through my home with a firearm live and ready to fire when it is not an emergency again, I'm going to toss you out on your ass and you won't be back. Understood?"

Aiden studied her for a moment before reaching out to accept the gun. He offered Alexis her sunglasses in return. "Understood."

Alexis took the glasses and slid them on her face. "Good. If we can't be friends, we can at least be allies until this is over."

"I said I was on board last night," Aiden replied as Alexis went back to the counter to slide her jewelry over her wrists.

"You have a funny way of showing it," Carley commented.

"It's not my fault you made a rash and stupid decision," Aiden snapped back. "The window to correct it is very, very small."

Alexis rolled her eyes and walked to the door. "Fantastic. The two best detectives the FDPC has to offer are squabbling children. Figure out whatever mess you have between you and get to work. There is coffee in the pot. Mugs are in the cabinet above it. I'll be in touch to discuss when I'm available to meet. Terry will show you out."

With that, Alexis left them. She had made her moves and her intent known. The rest was up to them.

CHAPTER FIFTEEN

There were times Alexis preferred the quiet solitude of her office at Power. While there were employees cleaning, stocking, and preparing for the evening's business, the noise never came close to the constant interruptions she experienced at Skyline. She could get the same amount of work done in half the time.

After the past evening, Alexis needed silence. Work had backed up while she dealt with the FDPC and ensuring the families of her deceased employees received all the proper benefits. She spent the morning whittling down her massive backlog.

A soft knock on her door pulled her attention away from a transcript of a meeting earlier in the week. Annoyance flared, but her irritation quickly faded when she recognized the pattern of the knock.

"Come in."

Liz pushed through the door, arms loaded with something that smelled delicious. Alexis' stomach grumbled in response. It seemed she had worked straight into lunch. The urge to continue despite hunger was strong, but she wasn't going to reject a spontaneous visit from Liz. The woman never did anything without asking first.

"Need help with that?" Alexis asked.

Liz smiled as she used her foot to close the door behind her. "I've got it. I used to be a waitress, you know."

Liz set several bags and a tray loaded with travel mugs of tea on Alexis' desk.

"Don't pine for the person you were. Celebrate the person you are," Alexis said as she helped pull containers of soup from one of the bags.

"Change isn't always for the better," Liz replied.

"While that is true, different doesn't always mean bad. You didn't change for the worse."

Liz freed a small loaf of bread from one bag and pulled cutlery from another. She handed Alexis a spoon. "It's creamy potato soup. I hear your past few days have been ugly."

Alexis had learned to let topics of conversation come and go with Liz. She often changed the subject when she no longer felt comfortable. Alexis smiled and popped the lid on a container. "So, you brought me decadent, fattening comfort food. You're always sweet."

Liz settled into the chair across from Alexis with her own container and smiled. "I don't care what anyone says. A good, warm meal is the cure for almost everything."

"I don't disagree. Thank you," Alexis replied before she sampled the soup.

"You're welcome. How are you managing?"

"Alright," Alexis replied with a frown. "I don't think the police are close to finding the killer, though. That certainly makes me anxious."

"Do they have any leads yet?" Liz questioned.

"If they do, they haven't shared them. You need to keep being careful."

"You should be, too. You're not invincible."

The corners of Alexis' lips twitched in amusement, but Liz's gaze held genuine concern. Alexis put on a disarming expression. "I am taking every precaution I can. I promise."

Liz's eyes narrowed. "I will remember you promised."

"I've done everything the police suggested. I am suitably afraid of the creature, I assure you."

Liz held Alexis' gaze for one more piercing moment before she nodded. "Good. People would miss you. That's all I'm saying."

In need of a quick subject change herself, Alexis turned to a topic she knew would distract Liz. "How is Hope doing?"

Liz's face instantly brightened. "So adorable I think I'm going to die."

Alexis laughed and broke off a piece of bread from the loaf. "Is your phone full of pictures yet?"

"It's close. I'm not kidding," Liz replied with comical seriousness.

"How is she taking to training?" Alexis asked.

"Too smart for her own good. She does well in training, but the other day I watched her figure out how to get on the counter to the treat box." While Liz's expression held a stern frown, there was pride in her voice.

Alexis smirked. "I'm sure you put a stop to that."

"I did. It's just so hard to stay mad at her. You need a dog."

Alexis immediately shook her head. "No, no I do not."

"Why not?"

"I've had some negative experiences," Alexis answered.

Liz nodded. "I can understand, but you should at least think about a cat or something. Animals are the best early warning systems."

"If I didn't travel so much, I'd think on it. But I don't want to get an animal just because there is a psychotic creature on the loose. It wouldn't be fair to the animal."

"They bring a lot of happiness to an empty house."

Alexis knew exactly where the conversation was heading. With no desire to discuss her own love life, she changed the direction of the ship before it could set sail.

"Candice tells me a man has been texting you pretty consistently."

When Liz flushed and looked down at her soup, Alexis grinned.

"Candice is a traitor," Liz mumbled.

Alexis laughed. "You shouldn't tell her things you don't want the whole club to know."

"She is tight-lipped about her legal stuff, but she sure is good at pulling information out of us unsuspecting victims," Liz retorted.

"That's why she'll make a great lawyer. Is this man treating you well?"

"We've only gone on one date," Liz replied. "He was a gentleman. He always is when we talk." Liz's gaze stayed locked on what was left in her container.

"Are you comfortable with him? Does he make you laugh?"

"I am and he does. My therapist suggested I be honest up front. So, I told him why I'm in therapy before we even went to dinner," Liz said quietly.

"Well, you still went to dinner, so the conversation must have gone well."

"It did. I was surprised," Liz replied with a frown. "He told me he would like to see me again and didn't mind waiting. It's on me to ask him for a second date."

"Are you going to?"

"I want to. I think about it a fair bit, but I'm afraid."

"Of what?"

"Everything. Rejection. Poor judgment. Maybe I will really like him and fall into the same trap I was in a year ago."

"Only you will know when you're ready. You've learned quite a bit about behavior and relationships since then," Alexis said.

"I'd like to think I've grown. I still shy away from confrontation or situations where I should stand up for myself. But I don't want to let a good thing pass just because I'm too chicken to send a stupid text."

"Strength is rarely loud. It's the choice to get back up. It's the will to live your life as you see fit. You've never been weak, Liz. You chose a better life for yourself," Alexis replied gently.

"I'm not strong like you. You're so confident," Liz said, peeking up to search Alexis' face. "You fear nothing, not even some crazed, murdering creature."

Alexis sighed and set her own spoon down to give Liz her full attention. "We are different people, you and I. That's okay. You can't compare apples to oranges, hun."

"Maybe not. But it doesn't stop me from admiring the way you deal with things."

"I admire you for lots of reasons, Liz. You refuse to stay down. Strength isn't a lack of fear. It's taking action despite it."

Liz smiled and ran self-conscious fingers through her long, crimson locks. "You don't have to be my therapist, you know."

"I'm not your therapist. I'm your friend," Alexis replied. "I'm also your boss. I wouldn't lie to you on either front. You know you take care of yourself now. You don't need anyone else. Life is about what you want. If you want this man, send him a message. His rejection won't be anywhere near enough to break you."

"I'm supposed to be cheering you up. Way to be sneaky," Liz said.

A knowing smile touched Alexis' lips. "And so you have. I haven't thought about my dead employees or their families for a whole thirty minutes. You even fed me some of the best potato soup ever. You really should reconsider becoming my personal chef."

"I like it here. Maybe one day. You should take the rest home."

"Oh, I plan to."

"Good. I'm going to go help the guys get ready for tonight. You know how it can get."

"Thanks for lunch, then. Don't forget to be extra cautious. Keep Hope close," Alexis said.

Liz nodded. "You be careful, too. Remember what I said. You're not invincible."

Alexis leaned back in her chair and stared at the office door long after Liz had left. While she wasn't superstitious, Alexis recognized meaningful messages could find their way to a person through any medium. Liz might be human, but her insight was often profound.

Alexis knew she wasn't invincible. She had been injured often enough to prove it. But it was simple fact that she was more durable than most. Weapons of all kinds required more force to penetrate her skin, though magical beings often had such strength. Alexis' skill at shielding and combat outshined most others. This killer would find her significantly more challenging than the average humans he had picked off.

With a sigh, she tore her gaze from the door and packed up the leftovers from lunch, storing them in the mini-fridge in the corner of the room. She wasn't foolish enough to think she would walk away from this fight unscathed. Death was a possibility, though unlikely. But the oddity and timing of Liz's words picked at the back of her mind like a thorn.

Alexis also acknowledged she might have read too much into the statement. Liz saw her as a friend. She didn't have many, so it was more likely Liz's concern came from an observation uncomfortably close to the truth.

Begrudgingly, Alexis let the thoughts go. It was useless to ponder the motivations of the universe. There was practical work to be done before she could spend the evening focusing on the detectives and the killer. Alexis sat back at her desk and dove into work. She let stock reports, contracts, and emails bury any lingering thoughts of her vulnerability.

Hours later, the sound of a text message pulled her away from her computer. She blinked and checked the time. At seven in the evening, she should have quit hours ago. Annoyed with herself for losing track of time, Alexis snatched the phone from the desk. Surprise flashed across her features when Aiden's name displayed on her screen. He hadn't exactly been happy with her that morning.

Change in plans. Needed for an emergency vampire staking. Will meet you tomorrow evening.

Alexis raised an eyebrow. She could argue a demonic killer was more important than a rogue vampire. She and the detectives desperately needed to get on the same page as soon as possible. However, it was likely the FDPC Captain was unaware of their less formal relationship. At least, Alexis hoped so. Regardless, she doubted Aiden and Carley had any choice. She typed a quick response.

Tomorrow at eight, then. Moonlit vampire stakings are not ideal. Don't die.

Alexis locked her phone and stood up to stretch. Her evening suddenly opened up. Though she still had a late-night appointment, the rest could be spent scouring the city for signs of the killer's power. It wasn't the most efficient method of hunting, and though her previous attempts had failed, she wasn't afraid of doing things the hard way.

She slid into her leather coat and grabbed her briefcase. Alexis stopped by the fridge to retrieve her leftovers and slipped out of the club without saying goodbye to anyone. They were busy, and Alexis had her own preparations to attend to.

* * *

Two o'clock in the morning was a frustrating hour when there was nothing to show for a night's work. Weariness tugged at the edges of her consciousness. For an individual who claimed he wanted to be found, the killer was irritatingly elusive. But Alexis let go of her annoyance in favor of renewed focus. Her appointment promised to be short, but dangerous.

Alexis' body was nothing more than shadows in the darkness of the alley across from Dark Heart. Despite the uncertainty of the past twenty-four hours, she couldn't afford to ignore her responsibility to Carley. She hoped Belladona Le'Roe would decline her challenge. With a bit of tact and luck, Alexis could then disappear to her former solitude and Carley could live her life relatively unaffected. Alexis was a realist, though. Her hope was tempered by what she knew of Le'Roe's reputation. Plans for an unfavorable outcome were already formed.

Militar held his place as the lone bouncer in front of Dark Heart. He sat on a stool, his posture poor, with boredom etched into his porcelain features. Alexis saw through this ruse. She felt hints of his power in the space around her. He was vigilant, more so than he had been the previous night. After sensing the darkness around the club for hidden threats, Alexis saw no reason to disappoint him.

She consolidated her power and manifested in physical form. She slowly stepped out from the alley and leaned against the brick wall. With her power centralized, Militar's gaze easily found her through the continuous stream of people walking past. Alexis folded her arms and let him stare. She had no intention of crossing the street. Instead, she whispered in the darkness of his ears, "What says your Mistress?"

Militar didn't appear startled. He spoke instead as if she were right next to him. "She will meet you the night after next at the Chateaú Le'Roe when the moon is highest in the sky."

All hope for the quiet, peaceful ending to her time as Alexis Montral vanished. The path she had laid out for that identity was now permanently changed. She wasn't surprised, merely disappointed. None of her emotions seeped into her hushed tones. "So be it, son of House Le'Roe."

Having all she needed, Alexis didn't give Militar a chance to respond. She pushed off the wall and slid back into the darkness of the alley. After she made sure no one was following her, Alexis melted into the shadows.

She had the choice of continuing her search for the killer or returning home to rest. Finding the killer had to be her top priority. He was the largest threat to her way of life. But after days of searching, he still hadn't shown himself. With the next several nights promising to be long, Alexis saw little point in beating her head against the wall.

She traveled through the city's darkness. Within minutes, she was whole again in the comfort of her living room. Terry identified her presence and spoke quietly, "Welcome home, Alexis. You look too clean for your hunt to have been successful."

Alexis turned and headed down the hall to her bedroom. "Indeed. For all his bravado, the killer certainly hides like a coward."

"And Le'Roe?"

"She has accepted my request to meet." Alexis pushed through her bedroom door and sat on the edge of her bed to unlace her boots.

"Of course she did. I will double check the security software and hardware again. I have been keeping on top of it since this whole mess started, but there is no harm in making sure. I am sorry your night was long."

"Thank you. I really do appreciate your efforts. I know you work hard to keep this building ready for anything."

"It is my home, too. I will be more than happy to blast anyone dumb enough to challenge you in your own space. You should try to get some rest."

Alexis chuckled. "I entirely trust your judgment for blasting. Goodnight, Terry."

"Goodnight."

Alexis tugged her hair free and shrugged out of her clothing. Frustration still poured off her in waves. Alexis hated feeling powerless. She could handle playing a game with poor cards, but prided herself on being able to read other players. She also hated losing. With a shake of her head and more than a little disappointment in herself, she crawled into bed. Before she settled completely though, Alexis picked her phone up from its charger. There was one more ball to set in motion.

She selected the number from her ghost server and dialed. The phone rang twice before the person on the other end picked up.

"Yeah?"

Alexis smiled at the gruff tone. "Hey. I need you to do something for me."

CHAPTER SIXTEEN

Alexis looked up from her computer at the woman standing in her office door. In centuries past, she was labeled an Amazon by those who didn't know better. She was 6'11" and the body beneath the dark blue jeans and hooded leather jacket was rock solid. The oversized hood hid long strands of silvery tresses, the upper half of her face encased in shadows. Like Alexis, the woman had to hide much of her appearance to move around the world safely.

Alexis smiled warmly and gestured to the chair in front of her desk. "Welcome to my home, Krysta Nightsky. My hearth and hospitality are open to you."

The woman bowed low at the waist. Her light, melodious voice was as tempting as a siren's call. "I graciously accept your generosity, Alexis Montral. May your home be blessed by the spirits of friendship, wisdom, and all kinds of other mystical bullshit."

Alexis laughed as Krysta straightened and pulled her hood back. She was gorgeous, even by elven standards. Her eyes were clear blue seas that sparkled in the moonlight. Soft lines and strong bones blended together to form beautiful features. Her hair was pulled into a ponytail and did nothing to hide her ears, which were pointed and extended back six inches.

Krysta's ethereal beauty and musical voice fooled many, including Alexis when they had first met. She hadn't taken long to correct those assumptions. A savage brute of a woman, she had a natural talent for combat and war tactics, but her inability to follow orders along with a blatant distaste for authority had gotten her thrown out of the elven army. It was a shame, considering she had been their best warrior.

To top it all, elves were creatures of magic and Krysta had been born without. Instead, she drew empathic power from anger and aggression. She discovered a way to harness it and, when combined with her iron determination, she could use anger to boost her own physical prowess. She could push her body far beyond the natural grace and strength of her kin and even infect others into blind rages.

But Krysta's astute control over that particular emotion was not enough for her clan. With no apparent gift for magic as the elves defined it, she was considered a shame to her royal family and banished from the Court of the Moon. Most in the kingdom found her personality intolerable, so when it came to a community vote, the Queen's decision to disown her own daughter had little opposition. The Court of the Sun turned their backs to her, as well. From that day on, Krysta had been known as the Banished Princess. As far as Alexis knew, the title suited her just fine.

The warrior walked forward and lazily collapsed into the offered chair. "Why do you insist on greeting me that way? It's been a long time since I've sat in Navindi's court."

"True," Alexis replied, "but you are still Princess by birth of the largest elven clan in the world. I merely give you the respect you deserve."

"Bullshit. You use it as a polite way to remind me there are boundaries between us. You sure as hell didn't give me that respect when we were dating."

"You acted like a complete ass and didn't deserve it," Alexis answered playfully.

Krysta laughed. "It's good to see you."

"It's been too long. How have you been?"

"Bored, restless, itching for a good fight. Want to go up to your fitness floor? I'll let you make the rules," Krysta said with a grin.

"You just want to get your hands on me."

"Obviously. You've got a hot ass and you're one of the very few who can actually kick mine. You wouldn't have survived around me for as long as you have if it were otherwise."

"Your tendency to kill your lovers in the heat of the moment—and sometimes out of it—isn't always appealing, you know."

Krysta narrowed her gaze. "Hey. Everyone I've ever been with knew the risks. It's actually annoying most times. Not only does it become a complete sexual disappointment, but I also have a body to dispose of."

"A good lover is like a fine wine," Alexis countered. "They need time to age, to gain experience and power."

"Hence the reason I'm bored, restless, and wanting to beat someone. Bending you over this obscene desk is sounding more appealing by the second." Krysta had a dangerous gleam in her eyes.

"There is too much in this office that would be inconvenient to replace. Perhaps we can indulge another time. For now, I'm assuming you got the information I requested." Alexis enjoyed Krysta and the challenge she constantly presented, but needed to save energy for the killer.

Growling lightly, Krysta pulled a flash drive from her jacket pocket. "Fine, but I'm only giving it to you if you keep that promise."

"When have I ever broken my word?"

Krysta sighed and got up to walk around to Alexis' side of the desk. She leaned back against it and dangled the drive. "Everything you asked for is there. I'll admit, I'm surprised you are planning a trip into a council member's stronghold though. A bit political, isn't it?"

Alexis accepted the drive and immediately plugged it into her computer to browse its contents. "Circumstances have left me no choice. I'm not thrilled about it myself."

Krysta's tone turned serious. "You shouldn't be. That hotel is locked down tight and is crawling with bloodsuckers. Most of them are Children or Adolescents, but I spotted a significant number of Adults. Le'Roe also keeps an abnormally large amount of human servants. The numbers and potential powers against you will be staggering, even taking your skill into account. You should take me with you."

"The increase in the human servant population likely stems from having to feed such a large family. It's well known the World Council isn't happy with her about it," Alexis replied absently, distracted by the images on her screen.

"All the more reason to take me."

Alexis looked up into Krysta's eyes. "Is that concern for my well-being I detect?"

Krysta shrugged. "You're a big girl and can take care of yourself. But the fights you tend to get into are large and tempting. I usually find myself jealous upon hearing of them."

Alexis chuckled before turning back to the screen. "The best lies are always mixed with truth."

Krysta reached out and yanked the sunglasses off her face and threw them on the desk. She roughly cupped Alexis' cheek and turned her head so they were facing each other. Looking hard into Alexis' gaze she said, "You are one of the very, very few people who can tolerate me. More importantly, I can actually tolerate you. Finding your replacement would be a real bitch."

"How very affectionate," Alexis replied, the annoyance in her tone from being man-handled clear.

When Krysta roughly pushed away then folded her arms across her chest, Alexis let go of her irritation. She knew the offer was as close to sweet as Krysta would ever get. They were not lovers. They enjoyed each other, but it had stopped being more than that a long time ago. Yet Alexis still cared for Krysta and knew she felt the same… despite the elf's inability to express any emotion other than anger.

She sighed and stood to kiss Krysta's cheek. "I'm sorry. You would follow me into any situation, even if you knew we wouldn't win. You also know there is a good chance I would not do the same for you."

"You look out for yourself first," Krysta replied. "I've never held that against you. Besides, my reasons for wanting to help are selfish. Vampires would be good practice. Plus, you'd owe me. A debt from you would make it entirely worthwhile."

"Fine. We are both selfish bitches, but you can't help me with this. It's a territory and dominance dispute."

"Ah, so you did actually mark someone. I never thought I'd see the day."

Alexis rolled her eyes and collapsed into her chair. "I had no other choice. The woman is important, but has no experience and relies solely on a gun. I can't have someone like that walking around the streets unprotected. And don't yank my glasses off again. If you were anyone else, this discussion would have been over."

"A little defensive, aren't you? You know I hate when you wear them. There isn't a damn thing wrong with your eyes."

"There isn't a damn thing wrong with your ears or the color of your hair, yet you still wear hoods. The glasses are a habit I have to keep," Alexis replied irritably.

Alexis reached out to retrieve them from the desk, but Krysta was undeniably fast. She captured Alexis' wrist. "Fuck that. We are in your home. You don't get to hide from me."

Alexis looked up and met the sapphire gaze. Irritation pulsed through her. Krysta was an exceedingly arrogant and dominant individual who worked to conquer all aspects of her life and own the space around her. It was one of her most attractive and annoying traits. While it was always a gamble who would end up on top between them, she knew Krysta would never bow to anyone. Alexis could have all the power in the world and the way Krysta treated her would not change. Sometimes, it was nice. Others, it grated on her last nerve.

But the anger Alexis felt now was more than the situation called for. She yanked her hand free and the rage building inside her subsided. There was plenty of anger left, but it was solely hers and easier to reign in. "A fight with you is a luxury I can't afford right now. Stop picking one."

"This has something to do with those demonic murders happening around town, doesn't it? I've noticed they've all occurred in buildings I'm fairly certain you own," Krysta replied inquisitively.

"If I let this woman walk around the streets unprotected, the situation will only get more complicated. The last thing I need is another dead body associated with me."

"You're the hot gossip of the city right now; a brand new demon staking claim on fresh meat. There are plenty of tongues wagging. It's hard to throw a rock in this city and not hit something you own. So, it could be a coincidence, but I didn't think so."

"He's been leaving me messages."

Krysta's eyes widened as a realization dawned on her. "Holy shit. These murders are in the human news channels. You've been dancing with the FDPC. You marked a fucking cop, didn't you? Are you insane?"

"Who and what I mark, along with my reasons for it, are none of your business," Alexis replied coldly.

"For fuck's sake, Alexis! She'll turn on you the second you turn your back. Do you want to risk spending the rest of your existence rotting in some prison lab where they will strip you of everything you are?" Krysta leaned forward and placed her hands on the arms of Alexis' chair, caging her in.

Alexis felt Krysta's anger build all over again. It slid over her skin and pulled at her own temper. But years of practice had taught her to distinguish thoughts inspired by Krysta's anger that weren't hers. She called power over ice to cool the heat nudging against her mind.

"You're getting sloppy, Nightsky."

"Good! Maybe it'll show you how fucking stupid you're being."

The comment added just the little extra fuel Alexis' temper needed to spike. She was about to fire back with a sharp remark, but Terry's voice interrupted her.

"Excuse me, Alexis. Detectives Jameson and Thompson are here for their scheduled meeting. Shall I bring them up?"

Alexis took a calming breath and reminded herself Krysta's victories always came from lost tempers. She stared the other woman in the eyes and answered, "Yes, I do believe the Lady Nightsky and I are finished."

Krysta growled and jerked back to stalk around the desk. "Thanks for warning me the damned cops were stopping by for tea."

"Things are vastly more complicated than they appear, Krysta. If it wasn't safe for you here, I wouldn't have agreed to see you today."

"There is nothing safe about the FDPC, Alexis. Nothing. They don't discriminate between people who should be put to death or imprisoned and the people that do not."

"Technically speaking, you and I are in the first category," Alexis reminded her.

"True, and all the more reason!" Krysta barked back.

"Trust me," Alexis replied as she walked around to the front of the desk. "Think past your anger and remember I do nothing without reason. I'm a creature of self-preservation."

Krysta stopped and studied Alexis for several long moments. She finally stepped forward and shoved Alexis back against the desk hard enough to make it shift slightly, pressing flesh to flesh. "Fair enough, but you're walking a very dangerous line. Don't get caught with your guard down and fucking call me."

"Your services usually come with a price," Alexis replied in a teasing tone.

She wanted to ease the tension. It seemed to work as she felt the weight of Krysta's rage subside. She didn't expect it to go away entirely though. Krysta enjoyed the feeling far too much, but worked to control it. It was enough for Alexis.

"I'm sure I'd get my fee out of you somehow. Speaking of payment…" Krysta said, trailing off.

"Your fee is waiting for you in the armory. You can pick it up on your way out."

Alexis saw Krysta's ears twitch and her body tense a moment before she heard Carley's voice, "Whoa, there, giant woman. Why don't you take a few steps back and we can settle whatever problem you have like civilized savages."

Krysta chuckled and looked over her shoulder at Carley. The officer had her hand on the butt of the gun at her hip and was in a combat stance. "Is that cute little shrimp her? No wonder you marked her. She wouldn't last five minutes."

"Who the fuck are you calling 'shrimp', you oversized steroid addict?"

Aiden put his hand gently on Carley's shoulder. "Easy, Jameson. Use your eyes. She's elven. If the elves have a problem with Alexis, we can't help her."

"I don't give two shits about what she is," Carley replied stubbornly. "You can't tell me her stance isn't threatening. She's going to take a bullet if she doesn't back the fuck up."

Krysta calmly turned and walked to Carley. She stopped with just enough space for the detective to press the barrel of her gun against Krysta's chest if Carley chose to draw. Alexis made no move to stop them. The warrior was testing Carley. She had a soft spot for feisty individuals.

"You should listen to your partner, little girl. He seems to be the brains of the two of you," Krysta warned.

"He's actually an idiot who hopes you'll kill Alexis for him so he can stop contemplating how to do it himself."

"Detective Thompson is a demon hunting witch," Alexis chimed in.

"I see. The reason you are less concerned with ending up in a jail cell has become clear. If he decides to go after you when this whole ordeal is said and done, I won't lose any sleep over his death. What about you, little one? Do you like Alexis, despite what she is?" Krysta asked Carley.

"She saved my ass when she didn't have to and has put herself at great risk to help stop a monster. Who the fuck are you?"

"I am Krysta Nightsky," she answered with a savage grin.

Aiden's eyes widened, "Jesus, the Banished Princess. You laid waste to whole armies."

"Are you seriously chickening out on me right now?" Carley demanded.

"I'll stand up with you and protect you, but Montral is on her own with this elf. I won't fight a battle I can't win for a demon," Aiden said firmly.

Krysta studied Carley for a moment. "You would stand up to someone who is obviously your better to defend someone you consider to be a diseased freak?"

"Just because you apparently won a few wars doesn't make you my better," Carley replied, "but yes. I will defend her." The determination and sincerity in her voice caused Krysta to raise an interested eyebrow.

After several more moments she finally took two steps back. "Your partner is a spineless sack of shit, but you've got potential. If you ever want to learn how to swing a sword, give me a call."

Alexis walked up to Krysta's side. "Don't even think about it, Nightsky."

Krysta turned to pout. "But—"

Alexis cut her off. "Absolutely not. We just discussed allowing things to reach their full potential. This is one of those times."

Krysta sighed. "Fine. Call me when you have a plan. I can't go with you, but I can be around. If I'm lucky, you'll be followed by a few little shits on your way out. You better fucking come out though. I don't want to spend the rest of my days scouring the world for someone who can actually give me a good fight."

"I'm sure there are a plethora of creatures that would love the chance to kick your ass," Alexis replied.

"None as gorgeous as you. It takes away a quarter of the fun if they're ugly fucks. See you around."

Krysta pulled her hood over her ears and walked out of the office. There was an awkward silence before Alexis sighed and shook her head. She turned back to her desk and slipped her glasses back on her face.

Aiden's voice finally broke the silence. "So, the Banished Princess is your fuck buddy?"

Alexis chuckled. "I wouldn't call her 'buddy' to her face."

"Her temper is legendary. Why would you fuck something that would kill you the moment she got bored?" Aiden asked.

Alexis turned to face him. She leaned back against the desk and folded her arms across her chest, a knowing smile touching her lips. "You tell me, Detective."

An angry growl escaped Aiden as his gaze narrowed. She raised a hand to cut him off before he got a chance to reply. She had baited him but remembered she didn't have the time to let it play out. It was almost worth apologizing, but he'd tried to insult her in the first place. "My sex life is none of your business and completely irrelevant to the reason you're here."

"While that is true," Carley said, "I think Aiden and I deserve to know when she'll be around if she's as dangerous as the two of you seem to think."

"She is. Don't ever think Krysta Nightsky bluffs. It will be the last bet you ever lose. I have marked you. She won't hurt you. Aiden may be another matter, but he's a big boy and can handle himself. I asked her to do something for me. She was here to report back and collect her fee. There is no need to fear her until this mess is over."

"What did you ask her to do?" Carley questioned.

"Something neither one of you needs to concern yourselves with. Can we focus on catching a killer now?"

Carley grinned. "Hey, we are apparently linked for life. Forgive me if I'm a little curious."

"The time for curiosity is after the demon is dead," Alexis replied.

"I hate to agree with her, but she's right," Aiden said.

"Fine, but I have one really important question first."

Alexis sighed. "What is it, Detective Jameson?"

"Can we order take-out? I'm fucking starving."

CHAPTER SEVENTEEN

Aiden waited until Carley found her dinner before he dared reach for his own, preferring to keep his hands intact. He was sure she consumed as many daily calories as a competition athlete three times her size. He settled into a chair across the desk from Alexis with a beer and shrimp lo mein. Carley sat next to him with beef and broccoli.

As he ate, Aiden watched Alexis with renewed curiosity. He would never have guessed she had ties with elves. To know Krysta Nightsky meant she would be welcome in the Court of the Moon. The elves were a secretive people and though they had a deep love and respect for life and nature, they held no love for outsiders. Given Alexis' demonic heritage, Aiden was surprised any elf would tolerate her presence, even a banished one. Krysta Nightsky was known for her brutality in battle. Perhaps their skills had brought them together.

Despite her bloodline, Alexis was the most civil and cultured demon Aiden had ever encountered. She was also the most magically powerful. It was possible those traits had been enough to win attention from the Court. There were many stories of Krysta's banishment, ranging from murder to treason to misuse of magic. As far as Aiden knew, Krysta was the only elf to receive such a sentence. Death would have been considered kinder.

"Do you know Queen Nightsky?" he asked, unable to contain his curiosity.

Alexis looked up from her meal. Silence stretched between them for uncomfortably long moments. Alexis finally set her plate on the desk and leaned back with her glass of wine.

"I do."

Her flat tone and expression told him Alexis didn't want to discuss the topic. Her posture was slightly defensive. But her association with the elves added another layer to an already complex existence and Aiden wanted to know more.

"So, you knew Krysta before she was banished. You've been to the Court of the Moon."

"I spent time with Navindi prior to Krysta's banishment, yes," Alexis replied.

191

Aiden took a swig of beer as he studied her blank expression. He pondered the line of questioning that had the best chance to get him answers.

"Who is Queen Nightsky?" Carley asked before she took a bite.

"Navindi Nightsky rules over the elven Court of the Moon. She is also Krysta's mother," Alexis answered.

Aiden fought back a smile. He knew the topic would pique Carley's interest. The FDPC research database had almost no information on elves. He could just sit back and let Carley pepper Alexis with questions.

"So wait. That big brute back there is some kind of princess?" Carley asked as she reached for an egg roll.

"Technically, Krysta is elven royalty," Alexis paused and turned to look directly at Aiden, "and I will not discuss her story. It is not mine to tell. Nor will I discuss any aspect of the Court of the Moon or the Court of the Sun."

Alexis' direct rejection of the topic wasn't surprising, but Aiden was annoyed regardless. "Afraid of revealing too much about your own history?"

Alexis sighed. Aiden sensed her frustration. He didn't mind. Frustration led to mistakes.

"Believe it or not, the world doesn't revolve around me. The elves keep their kingdoms hidden and their citizens away for their own reasons. I won't ignore their wishes just to appease you."

Aiden set his meal on the desk and leaned back in his chair. He hadn't thought the privacy of another race would concern her. If Alexis was willing to protect the secrets of a race that wasn't her own, that meant she held some level of empathy toward others. He changed direction.

"Alright. But since we are discussing history, maybe you can elaborate on your connection with the killer."

Alexis shrugged and set her glass on the desk. She leaned forward to her computer. Aiden jumped and looked up as a large monitor lowered from a hidden opening in the ceiling. The screen dropped to visual height and filled with images of the two murder messages.

"Your wealth is almost disgusting, you know that right?" Carley said absently. "Do you have these in every room?"

"If I only had eighty to a hundred years of life, I might be sympathetic to that opinion. But I don't. So, I'm not," Alexis replied casually.

"This is a lot of extravagance for one lifetime, though," Carley said.

"I have a background and a persona to maintain," Alexis said before looking up at the screen. "To answer your question, Aiden, I haven't lied. I don't know the killer. But, somehow, he knows me."

"Yes, but how?" Aiden said.

"At this stage in the game, I have no reason to lie," Alexis said carefully.

"That isn't a very comforting way to start," Aiden replied with a frown.

Alexis sighed but let his comment stand. "My very first memory is waking in a small village in Spain during the Spanish Inquisition. Not a very nice time for someone like me. I was a fully grown adult. I remember nothing before the village."

She had a great deal of audacity to think he was that gullible. "You really aren't playing the amnesia card, are you? Because I will call bullshit."

"It's not amnesia. Someone I trust looked into the issue. The memories were magically ripped from my mind. There is scarring. I won't ever get those memories back," Alexis replied.

Aiden took another sip of beer and let the information roll around in his mind. He searched Alexis' face and body language for signs of deceit. As always, she was irritatingly difficult to read. He loathed the glasses covering her eyes. There was emotion in the dark, strangely beautiful depths.

It was too easy to blame lack of memory. Even officers fresh out of the academy knew memory loss was an attempt to escape conviction. Yet, there were implications in Alexis' claim that could explain much about her. Aiden found himself willing to hear her out.

"So, you were attacked."

"That is the conclusion my associate came to. In all of these years, I've not seen another demon like me. I've always known this wasn't where I was born, but I wouldn't know where or what to go back to."

"Sounds like you knew something someone really wished you didn't," Carley noted.

"I agree, but with no knowledge of my previous life, I have no idea what that 'something' could be. Their methods were nothing if not effective," Alexis replied.

"How does one remove memories?" Carley asked.

"Memory manipulation is a small niche in psychic magic," Alexis said. "It's difficult to isolate specific memories. They are often woven together in unpredictable ways."

"It's like discussing sports with the guys in a bar and suddenly remembering your departed Aunt Sally. Aunt Sally never did anything athletic or enjoyed sports, but she once knitted you a sweater in your team's colors," Aiden offered.

"I get that. So, was the asshole just not proficient enough to erase one memory?" Carley pondered.

"Either that or he intentionally removed all of it," Alexis said. "I'm more inclined to believe the latter."

"I agree, especially if he's anything like the killer," Aiden commented.

"If this individual was like the killer, he wouldn't have left it to chance by just stealing memories and dropping me in the middle of a village full of religious zealots."

"Perhaps your life means something to this thief, or he didn't think he was strong enough to kill you," Aiden suggested.

"I'm obviously in favor of still breathing," Alexis replied, "so I am not whining. It's possible the thief feared me, but that is all the more reason to kill me. There are only two reactions to fear—conquering or running."

"Not an entirely bad deal, considering," Carley said.

"For someone who has intact memories, that's easy to say. Not knowing who you are is its own form of torture. I don't agree with the thief's methods... or the killer's for that matter."

"You still end life and manipulate others," Aiden noted.

"So do you, little hunter. You also choose to put innocent people into research prisons where you know they'll be tortured and eventually die," Alexis said sharply. "You do it to save your own skin. Neither one of us is a saint, but when I find it necessary to kill, at least I don't condemn my prey to suffering."

Aiden took the blow to his chest. He lived with that guilt every day. While he did his best to keep innocents out of the FDPC's sight, he didn't always succeed.

"The research prisons don't torture. They're medical facilities designed to help the diseased," Carley said defensively.

"I'm sorry, but in this, you're wrong. First, humanity doesn't have the right to classify race as a disease," Alexis said. "Second, those prisons obtain knowledge through the blood and tears of inmates. I don't oppose punishing the guilty, but I do oppose the suffering of innocents."

Carley looked to Aiden for validation. It burned deep in his chest when he couldn't give it. He looked away in shame.

"She's right," he softly confirmed. "While we don't know exactly what goes on in the prisons, they are definitely not safe havens. Innocents are not treated differently than the guilty."

"How do you know that? No one has clearance to enter. I know you've never been to one," Carley replied.

The anger in her voice came from fear. Aiden understood the emotion.

"Innocents have families and loved ones. Guilty ones do, too," he said, looking up into Carley's face. "Many of them are marked or have marked others. Their suffering is often shared. If Alexis were to die in a prison…" he hesitated and looked away before adding, "you would die, too."

Aiden hated as he watched the implication manifest in Carley's features. The guilt would eat at her the same way it ate at him. Carley set her bowl of food on Alexis' desk.

"I don't think I'm hungry anymore."

"I know you notice odd behavior from me sometimes. Usually, I am trying to keep an innocent out of a case," Aiden said.

"Like Alexis? I figured out on my own you knew her," Carley said.

"Alexis may be innocent of these murders, but she's still a demon. You know our policy and now you are familiar with my second calling," Aiden replied carefully.

"I certainly appreciate your restraint," Alexis interjected.

"Don't be too appreciative," Aiden said. "You managed to outsmart the DNA test and the lab exam, so I had no proof to stand on. Plus, turning you in wouldn't have helped catch the killer. Devant would have been satisfied apprehending you. The killer would still be on the loose."

"Nevertheless," Alexis said, "my only conclusion has been the killer is from the past that was taken from me."

"If you can't remember anything, how can you translate the messages?" Carley asked.

"How does a person with Alzheimer's or dementia still speak English? When I look at the text, it's like looking at my native language," Alexis replied with a shrug.

"You've never seen it before?" Aiden asked.

"Not like that, no," Alexis said.

"In what way, then?" Carley pressed.

"On weaponry, but it was back in Spain," Alexis answered.

"We gave you time to think on the second message. Any thoughts?" Carley said.

Aiden frowned. He was interested in the weaponry, but had to admit it was another irrelevant side track. He listened to Alexis answer instead.

"The killer is a terrible poet. The first message assumes I know him through power and symbolism. I don't know if the seven seekers are real, but he is saying I am lost and he has found me."

"But you can't just go to him because you don't remember how?" Carley prompted.

"Correct. The second message is more inconclusive. 'Grains of sand fall in single file, eroding rock and reason all the while.' I think that's a reference to an hour glass, to time," Alexis said. "I've been here for centuries. Time has a way of eroding things."

Carley tilted her head while she studied the display screen. "Like memory. 'Has neglect been paid in blood, or has the desert finally swallowed the flood?' He's asking whether you are ignoring him or don't remember."

"I believe so. But he thinks time has caused me to forget, that I lost my rationality because I've been gone for so long," Alexis replied.

"He doesn't know your memory was taken from you," Aiden said.

"I don't think so, but it doesn't make sense," Alexis said.

"How so?"

"I've been out almost every night scouring the city for his power. I've had a taste from the crime scenes, so I know what he feels like. Yet I haven't found a single trace of him."

"So, he's hiding?" Carley asked.

"Yes. Why taunt me with 'come hither' messages and then run away when I try to do just that?" Alexis said with frustration.

"Because his motives are different than the messages imply. There is too much intent with his methods and he's too smart to have a debilitating mental illness like split personality. Maybe he's afraid of you," Carley theorized.

"I highly doubt that," Alexis replied. "He's a powerful and proficient assassin."

"Maybe not fear, but respect," Aiden said. "I'm betting he wants you to find him on his terms. Not yours. You're not doing something right."

Alexis raised an eyebrow at him. "That is certainly viable."

"Could he be the one that took your memory? Maybe he's toying with you," Carley wondered.

"I find it unlikely."

"Why?" Carley responded.

"Assuming we are the same race," Alexis said, "his physical and magical abilities are similar to mine. His strength and agility are superior to humans and he has innate proficiency with *two* schools of magic. We've seen his blood magic. I think his second is what keeps him from my senses and wards."

"What could that ability be?" Carley asked.

"True invisibility is a likely possibility, though not one I'd want to go up against. He could be very good with glamour. A skilled individual can use it like camouflage. He might also be able to project images or remove himself from history," Alexis said.

"What do you mean, remove himself from history?" Carley asked.

"He could erase his name, image, and involvement from all records of an event," Aiden offered.

"That would be impressive," Carley said.

"It would leave too many questions, though. I honestly think he has true invisibility or glamour," Alexis said.

Aiden agreed. But there was a detail he was immensely curious about. "If your race is innately skilled with two schools of magic, what is your second?"

Alexis turned her attention to him. Aiden felt the weight of her calculating gaze behind those reflective lenses. He was careful to keep his expression neutral.

"I'm not going to answer, little hunter," Alexis finally said.

"We are allies. Knowledge of all your skills would help us plan a better trap," Carley interjected.

Aiden gave Carley a mental high five.

"We are allies," Alexis replied coolly, "not *friends*. At the very core, Aiden is a demon hunter. I won't lay all my cards before a man who would like to see me dead." Her tone was factual, logical, and cold.

Aiden couldn't quite deny the truth, so he said nothing. Time spent in her company made it hard to wish her dead, but the hunter in him couldn't trust her. He refused to apologize for it.

"But you marked me. Aiden would have to be willing to kill me to end you. Where does that leave us with the killer?" Carley asked.

"I have no problem utilizing the full range of my capabilities to destroy our opponent," Alexis said. "But I've been overly generous with information that can be used against me tonight. I will not share this last bit unless the situation demands."

"Alright. We still know nothing that will help us hunt him, anyway. The messages are clues that aren't really clues if he just hides from you," Aiden summarized. He used the change of subject to take Alexis off the defensive. She had been more forthcoming when she was relaxed and in the flow of conversation. He was sure she hadn't meant to share she had a second magical affinity.

"Unfortunately," Alexis said. "The symbols he turned the body into mean nothing to me. They obviously mean something to him, though. Have the two of you had any luck there?"

"A crescent moon is connected with several types of magic, but not blood," Aiden said. "Though now that we can consider glamour or true invisibility, we can try and cross-reference it. I don't remember seeing it there, to be honest. Our archives didn't have a match for the first body."

"So, what is the FDPC's current plan of action?" Alexis asked.

"Right now, we have surveillance teams outside of buildings containing the largest number of potential targets from your list. The teams have tetrabind scanners and we have extermination units on standby," Carley answered.

"If he can hide from me, he can certainly hide from your scanners," Alexis said skeptically.

"He might not know he has to. He has no regard for human life, so maybe he's arrogant enough to think we can't detect him," Aiden proposed.

"He might just be," Alexis responded. "He targeted the buildings when I wasn't there. My wards work differently than your scanners."

"Exactly. If he continues his pattern, he might not think to shield himself as deeply or in a manner to avoid scanners," Aiden said.

"A viable plan, given the situation. I believe your scanners are more likely to catch him in the act and not the approach, though," Alexis said.

"I think so, too. I don't know much about the whole shielding thing, but if that's what got you through the lab cleaning, you should do more of it at work," Carley warned.

Alexis raised an eyebrow. "I'll keep that in mind. Are the scanners sensitive enough to pick up wards?"

"Depends," Aiden answered. "They didn't pick up any from the first scene, but it was also saturated with the killer's power. Your wards are very subtle, though. I have to work to sense them. You should be okay."

"Alright. I guess I'll keep doing my rounds at night. Maybe one of us will get lucky. It's late. You both are welcome to stay here tonight," Alexis offered.

Aiden was tempted. It was easy to lie to himself and say it was to learn more about her as a demon, but deep down, he found himself wanting to know the real Alexis. Her power had hummed quietly around him the entire night. Every time he was in her space, her energy rubbed against his. He wanted that connection—despite the dangers he knew it possessed.

"I think I'd rather go home tonight. I haven't seen much of it lately," Aiden finally said. He stood and shrugged into his jacket.

Carley nodded in agreement. "Yeah. Thanks, but no thanks."

Alexis rose to walk them to the door. "Alright. Thank you for tonight. Good luck."

"You, too. Thanks for dinner," Carley said before she walked out of the door.

Aiden nodded to Alexis as he followed his partner, then glanced over his shoulder when the office door closed behind them.

He waited until they were in his car and out of Alexis' garage to speak. He didn't want Terry listening in to the conversation.

"What do you think?"

"I don't know much about this mark she gave me yet, but I've learned I can sense her sincerity when I focus," Carley replied.

"You can tell when she's lying?" Aiden asked, surprised.

"It's more like I can sense how she feels about what she's saying. It isn't the same," Carley replied.

"So, what does that tell you? Does she really feel emotion or is she that good of an actress?" Aiden asked.

"The killer frustrates her. A lot. She's surprisingly patient when you press her, but I think that's because she likes proving you wrong. I can't fault her there," Carley replied with a playful smirk.

"Good thing I'm right more than I'm wrong," Aiden said.

"That's debatable. Anyway, I don't think she lied. There was only once I caught a bit of uncertainty in her response," Carley said.

"When was that?" Aiden asked as he came to a stop at a traffic light.

"The weapons she spoke of when we were discussing language. I really think there is more to that story."

"Alexis likely kept it brief for a reason, yeah," Aiden said.

"It makes me all the more curious," Carley admitted.

"Her story is puzzling, for sure. But it does help explain why she is different."

"True. Honestly, the killer's first message concerns me beyond the case," Carley said as she folded her arms across her chest.

"Why?"

"It blatantly states other people have been looking for her," Carley answered. "The killer is just the first to stumble upon her. What happens when we kill him? Others could follow in his footsteps."

Aiden frowned as the light changed and he urged the car on. "I hadn't thought of that."

"It isn't a positive potential future for the city. I don't want to imagine what dealing with multiple people with the killer's mentality would be like. We already know someone from her home doesn't like her and that person is powerful enough to subdue her."

As Aiden finished the drive to Carley's apartment, silence fell over them. The thought of more people like the killer running around the city terrified him. The FPDC wasn't prepared to handle it. He wasn't sure the full might of the demon hunter clans would be enough either, since the FDPC would see them as a threat, too.

Aiden pulled up to Carley's building and she stepped out of the car. He leaned over before she closed the door and said, "Hey, wait."

Carley bent down and looked inside at him.

"Start buying your own guns. Don't skimp on power. And spend the money on silver and iron ammunition," Aiden said. The seriousness in his tone hung heavy in the space between them.

Carley stared at him for a moment before she nodded and shut the car door.

Aiden waited until she disappeared into her building before he sank back into his seat. If it came to war, Aiden knew what side he would stand on. He didn't know what side Alexis would choose, but for the first time since meeting her, he acknowledged it could be his. Uncertain of how he felt about that, Aiden headed home. He had his own arsenal to inventory.

CHAPTER EIGHTEEN

Alexis came to an abrupt halt in front of the gilded doors of Chateaú Le'Roe. The sleek chrome of her Aston Martin reflected the antique street lamps adjoining the entrance. Thick, maroon curtains gently nestled against the bay windows lining the five-star hotel. Soft, genuine candlelight flickered intimately within thirty stories of bold, detailed architecture.

Alexis scrutinized its historic romanticism. She'd memorized every scrap of information the blueprints in Krysta's file provided, in case she found herself in need of a quick exit. She didn't expect it but preferred to be prepared. Her gaze roamed the front of the building as she counted the number of visible employees. Tapping into the shadows, she found eight vampires who could potentially block her leaving from the front. Krysta hadn't missed any—not that Alexis had expected her to. There was a reason she'd called Krysta for the job.

While she both admired and respected the appeal of the building, Alexis recognized it for the trap it was. The largest vampire family in the world rested within its walls. Walking into their hive with the sole purpose of aggravating the queen bee wasn't her idea of fun, but the choice had been removed the moment she'd marked Carley.

Sitting in the car mulling over her distaste for the task wasn't going to finish it any faster. Alexis pulled the key from the ignition and stepped out into the night. A chilly breeze toyed with the soft tresses she had left free around her bare shoulders. Le'Roe's power was known to be sexually based, so she had chosen her attire to cater.

Her dress was a bold scarlet. Thin straps held it to her shoulders. While the front had a tasteful cut, the back left much of her porcelain skin on display. Heels in black matched the darker jewelry adorning her wrists. She had left her pendant to stand alone against her chest. Le'Roe's lust was both her strongest asset and weakness. She could be manipulated, if one could keep a clear and clever head.

Alexis had every intention of forcing Le'Roe to lose control first.

A valet attendant scurried forward to greet her. He was short, skinny, and skittish. While his uniform was crisp and pressed, his tie was crooked and his left shoe was untied. He had obviously been young when he was turned. Alexis guessed nineteen or twenty. His features were a tad too sharp and a bit too thin, making him only mildly attractive. In this world, it made him expendable.

The expression on his face let Alexis know just how aware of his position he was. His face was flushed from a fresh feeding. His shy brown eyes lowered, his posture defeated. Smiling sheepishly, his thin lips accidentally flashed fangs. There was a touch of anxiety about him, and fear lingered in the air.

"Welcome, Lady Montral. Mother is eager to extend our highest hospitality and offers her deepest apologies. She desires nothing but your comfort tonight. Please, allow me to care for your car."

Despite the awkward mix of humanity and un-death all vampiric Children possessed, the valet's voice was smooth and well mannered. Alexis figured he had been a student of some kind caught in the wrong place at the wrong time.

She raised an eyebrow when he bowed low and raised a palm for her keys. She sympathized with his situation, but that wouldn't change how she treated him. He was the low man on the totem pole and would likely taste genuine death soon. Pity wouldn't change his fate.

Alexis tossed her keys carelessly into his hand. "Don't scratch it. It would be a shame if I had to seek restitution for two infractions in one night."

The stench of fear thickened as a shiver passed through the attendant. It pleased her, though not because she enjoyed terrorizing the weak. The boy would talk to others and start the ball rolling on the reputation she wanted to establish.

"Of course not, Lady Montral. I-I'll be careful. I promise. K-Kearney will escort you to our Elder. I hope you have a pleasant evening," he answered.

His fingers curled around the keys and he practically ran to the driver's side of the Aston Martin. He slipped his wiry frame inside and within seconds, the car's engine purred to life. Alexis shook her head as the car shot off in the direction of the parking garage.

She turned and walked toward the hotel. A man waited at the door with an amused smile across his lips. He was the polar opposite of the nervous Child who had taken her car. This man was at least four or five inches above six feet. Even Alexis had to look up to meet his sharp turquoise gaze. Immunity granted her freedom from fear of the power held there. He had shoulder-length blond hair pulled into a neat ponytail, which left his chiseled, Icelandic features uninhibited. A perfectly-tailored, charcoal Gucci suit stretched across broad shoulders. He was aristocratically handsome, but that didn't surprise her. Le'Roe wouldn't have allowed him to advance if he wasn't eye candy of some kind.

"Good evening, Lady Montral. We're honored to have you as a guest. Mother extends her deepest apologies and hopes you find me a suitable escort for the evening." His voice matched his looks, subtly laced with the accent of his heritage.

"You're wasting your breath. The only person I'm accepting the apology from is Le'Roe. An escort isn't necessary. This isn't a social visit," Alexis replied.

Kearney's charming smile never faltered, but there was a flash of curiosity in his eyes. With two attempts at an apology in less than five minutes, Le'Roe's minions must have been told to get an acceptance before she even made it to the Elder. Alexis knew better. It would defeat the entire purpose in coming.

She stepped around Kearney and headed through the double doors. Alexis didn't need him to find her way but knew he would follow regardless. He was likely assigned to engage, distract, and be the first temptation of a complicated trap. For a moment, she debated whether she was being paranoid, but dismissed the thought immediately. Paranoia was usually the right amount of caution for survival.

The inside of the hotel was a Renaissance painting come to life. Colorful murals decorated the walls with swirling images of life and landscape. The rose-hued marble floors shone with fresh wax and meticulous care. Over-stuffed antique chairs were arranged around the lobby, along with plush, red settees that rested snuggly against the walls.

Alexis didn't spare Kearney a glance when he came beside her. Her sharp heels clicked across the marble at a crisp pace. As she stopped in front of a pair of golden elevator doors, she felt a prickle of power dance along her skin and a quiet presence press against her mind. She called her power and shrouded her mind in darkness. Alexis pushed the presence away but it didn't resist.

"That was rather rude of you, Mr. Kearney," she said slowly, the warning clear in her voice.

Kearney stared at her. "Indeed. I'd apologize, but it wouldn't be genuine. You seem to know our home as if you visit frequently. I would have remembered a creature as beautiful as you. And, please, it's just Kearney."

Alexis reached out to press the "up" button. "Are you so sure of that?"

"Yes. You radiate both beauty and power. Neither goes unappreciated here."

Alexis smirked as the elevator doors opened and they stepped inside. She pressed the button for the twenty-fifth floor before Kearney even moved his hand. He raised an eyebrow at her as the doors slid shut.

"Flattery will get you nowhere. Spare yourself the energy and me the annoyance."

Kearney's deep laughter filled the cabin. "You're a hard woman to compliment, Ms. Montral."

"There is only one thing that appeals to me tonight and it's not companionship," Alexis answered flatly.

"Perhaps, but you may be surprised at what companionship can bring you within these walls. You should consider carefully before immediately dismissing the idea," Kearney answered.

There was something in the tone of his voice that made her turn to study him. It wasn't a threat, more like a warning. She didn't understand why he would warn her. He risked punishment and the loss of Le'Roe's favor. Perhaps the comment was meant to unsettle. It worked, but Alexis didn't have to let it show.

The elevator doors opened to a small hallway no more than twenty feet long. Lined with murals of Paris during the Renaissance, the floor was the same rose-colored marble. At the end of the corridor stood a pair of ivory doors guarded by two identical vampires appearing Asian in descent.

Black leather hugged their lean hips. Matching black silk shirts stretched across their chests. The vampires had done a good bit of weight training before they died. Despite heeled leather boots, their height wasn't impressive. Cocky smiles twisted their lips as Alexis and Kearney approached.

"Kearney, don't you know trash is supposed to go outside? She's too soft to be a demon. I'm not sure she deserves to bask in Mother's presence," the one on the left commented as his rich brown eyes roamed over Alexis' form.

"Perhaps we'll keep her for entertainment before tossing her back to the gutters she came from," the right one added. He licked his lips suggestively.

The guards folded their arms across their chests and leaned casually against the wall in perfect harmony. Kearney made no move to correct the twins' behavior.

Alexis sighed and shook her head. "Are you always this rude to your guests, gentlemen?"

"Not to the ones who deserve to be here. You're just a street rat with an inflamed sense of self-importance. We're going to send you right back, as soon as we're done making sure you get the point," the one on the left replied.

"Interesting, coming from men who will do nothing but guard a door for the rest of their existence," Alexis answered.

Both men glared at her as they pushed off the wall and advanced. Alexis hadn't wanted to make an example so early in the night. It would be a waste of much-needed energy, but the twins were not giving her much choice.

She called her power, and felt the darkness within the softly lit hall answer. The power quietly pulsed along her skin in subtle waves and spilled from her and into the corners. Small shadows came together in slender tendrils to creep into the light of the corridor. They slithered across the floor to wrap discreetly around the leg of each twin.

Neither vampire noticed as their bodies absorbed the darkness, too busy trying to invade Alexis' personal space and appear intimidating. It was going to take more than two egotistical vampires to get under her skin.

"We are Aki and Hiro, bitch. We do more than just guard doors. Now, get down on your knees and beg forgiveness. Maybe then we'll let you go," Hiro demanded.

Perhaps Alexis had nicked a sore spot.

"I bow to no one. Your place is still at the door while everyone else has a good time," Alexis replied. "I imagine you're good at kissing the floor. Let's test the theory."

It took less than a thought for Alexis to cause the shadow energy trapped in their bodies to grow at an exponential rate. The shadows shoved aside and damaged any soft tissue or organs in their path. Twin cries of anguish filled the hall as the guards dropped to the floor, writhing in agony. It wasn't long before the energy spread up through their chests and pleas for release filled the air.

Alexis purposefully didn't touch their lungs, needing their screams to be heard. She never moved but instead surrounded herself with an aura of power. She needed a defense in case Kearney decided to come to the rescue. Oddly, he stayed where he was, content to watch the events play out from a safe distance.

She felt the weight of his gaze just moments before she felt his presence, once again, press against her shield. She didn't look over at him. Instead, she shoved harshly back and expanded her aura until it pressed against his. Kearney's presence receded immediately, and his aura hardened. But he didn't lash back. He merely protected himself from the power swirling in the air.

Alexis let her lips curve in a sadistic smile. While she didn't enjoy the pain of others, it wouldn't hurt for Le'Roe's house to think she did. It would spare her energy later if the enemy knew she wouldn't hesitate to inflict it.

The suffering continued for several minutes before she finally gave them the key to their release. She raised her voice just enough to be heard over the screams.

"I don't see your lips on the floor."

The twins' eyes widened further as they began to understand what she demanded. Alexis knew how difficult it would be to even kneel in their current state. She didn't care.

"I don't think we can move, Miss…" Aki whimpered.

Alexis lifted a shoulder in a careless shrug. "That's not my problem."

The brothers looked at each other for a moment. Their breaths came in short, quick gasps. Each began to move agonizingly slow. Cries of pain escaped their lips as their attempts caused already displaced organs to shift even more. When the guards finally rolled over, their lips brushed the floor as they pleaded.

"Please…" Hiro said.

"We apologize," Aki followed.

"Please, please… release us…" the twins said in unison.

"I will not tolerate rudeness and petty insults. Next time you will remember your manners," Alexis said coldly.

She made them lay for several moments longer. Alexis heard Kearney cough slightly as his power continued to press defensively against hers. He hadn't made a single move, but she felt the simmering potential behind his shields. He was more than strong enough to make the final change from Adult to Elder.

Alexis wondered if Le'Roe would ever let him go.

Desperate cries pulled her attention back to the twins. They'd had enough. Alexis withdrew her power sharply. The shadows seeped out of their bodies in thick, swirling streaks and spilled back into the deep corners of the hallway. She let her aura of protection recede. She was safe for the moment and needed to conserve her strength. The guards' screams turned to whimpers. They would heal, provided they had a constant source of blood and their Elder's presence.

"Impressive," Kearney commented. A slight shiver ran through his voice from the power that still echoed in the hall.

"I only have so much patience. You didn't correct their behavior. You were either ordered not to or you wanted to see what would happen. Regardless, you're lucky you're not on the floor with them. Now, are you going to take me to the Elder or am I going to have to find my own way?"

"I'm not unaware of what goes on around me. Since I doubt Mother would be fond of having to repair the damage you would do to the doors, I'll show you in. But you should be careful what you wish for," Kearney answered carefully.

"It's not my desire to be here, I assure you," Alexis replied.

"If you didn't wish this, then why bother?" Kearney asked.

"One of your Children stole from me and damaged my property. To accept his pathetic and insincere method of compensation would make me stupid and weak..." Alexis replied, slowly turning her gaze to meet Kearney's, "...and I am neither."

"Then you are here out of duty. If Shawn hadn't taken a sip of your pet, you'd still be nothing more than a rumor," Kearney pressed, making it a statement more than a question.

"I enjoy my privacy. Now open the door."

Kearney sighed. It sounded almost regretful. "I've a feeling it's going to be a long night."

"So do I."

Kearney shook his head and stepped over the twins to the doors but paused to look down at them. They had slipped into unconsciousness. He reached down and took a wrist from each one and effortlessly dragged their limp bodies to the side. When he returned, the fingernails of his right hand extended into sharp claws. He raised his left hand and drew a nail across the skin, leaving a thin trail of crimson fluid in its wake. He pressed his bleeding palm to the door and, for a brief moment, the doors glowed with a subtle crimson hue. He removed his hand and both doors swung inward on their own.

Kearney stepped to the side and turned, offering Alexis his hand. She watched as the small cut sealed itself.

"Welcome to our home, Lady Montral. You honor us with your presence."

Alexis found Kearney's gaze. She doubted they were honored. She had no desire to step through the doors, but she'd come too far to turn back. She nodded once and slipped her hand into his.

CHAPTER NINETEEN

The doors closed with an ominous click as Alexis' heels sank into the plush, rose-colored carpet. She questioned the practicality of carpeting an entire room where blood was often spilt, but since she wasn't responsible for replacement costs, she refused to feel guilty about ruining it.

The room itself was large and spacious, more rectangular than square. The entrance Alexis had just come through was centered in the back. Directly opposite was a wall of white marble. Rose bushes had been carved into its stone; rubies set into the petals. Sculpted roses shimmered in the low lighting.

A four-foot high fireplace ran the base of the entire marble wall. Real flames danced behind a sheet of protective glass. Again, she pondered the Elder's wisdom. Flame was one of the most efficient ways to slay a vampire. Yet, Le'Roe kept a thirty-foot fire a few feet behind her throne. Alexis almost laughed. She was grateful for the woman's short-sightedness.

There were several other doors lining the left and right. Alexis recognized them as smaller bedrooms from the blueprints. The last room on the left had a set of double doors. Much like the other space, strands of ivy and roses were exquisitely carved into the wood. It was the master suite, Le'Roe's private chamber.

The room was filled with inviting sofas and chairs arranged in semi-circles that facilitated conversation. The corner to her left held a fully stocked bar. A middle-aged man in a black tuxedo tended it, filling martini glasses with blood from plastic storage bottles. Though his movements were smooth and practiced, his eyes were glazed and empty.

Alexis recognized him as a human servant, an individual who'd endured so many vampire bites without death or transition his mind had broken. The only differences between a human servant and a zombie were human servants still had living bodies. Their souls were trapped beyond even a necromancer's reach. As far as Alexis knew, the condition was irreversible.

The man would stay docile, serve drinks, and follow orders. If Le'Roe ordered him to attack, he wouldn't think of physical limitations or pain. He wouldn't fear death. He would fight regardless of loss of limb. While he was more predictable than the vampires, the servant's unwavering perseverance made him a threat she couldn't afford to ignore.

The centerpiece of the room was a large, ornate wooden throne lined with deep emerald cushions. It sat about ten feet in front of the fireplace. Alexis wondered if Le'Roe ever considered the chair's position could be used against her. The Elder's arrogance was astounding.

The substantial chatter in the room died the moment she walked in. There were twelve vampires scattered evenly around the space. Alexis didn't doubt there was a healthy range of age, but the mixture of power in the air was problematic. She was having trouble distinguishing between Adults and Children. When she tried to sense for others in adjoining rooms, she hit powerful wards. It was unusual for vampires to make use of wards. Their abilities were less like magic and more like talents. It meant Le'Roe must have a relationship with a powerful witch or other caster. Instead of tracking her opponents through their specific energies, Alexis was forced to match each face with a number and memorize them. It wasn't the most efficient method, but it would have to do.

The twelve men and women were from different regions around the world. All of them were stunningly attractive and had been turned before the age of thirty. It didn't surprise her. The whole magical community knew Le'Roe was a collector of youth and beauty. The attire was a mixture of sixteenth-century and modern formal wear. The dress Alexis had chosen fit perfectly.

She didn't fear the numbers against her, but she was a firm believer in the long-term benefits of caution. The fact the room seemed to be in a constant state of flux was unsettling. She was missing a key variable and began to worry whatever it was would get her killed.

Kearney led her to the center of the room. He stopped five feet from the throne and turned to face her. While his expression was completely formal and his eyes were blank, there was something about the way he looked at her that made Alexis believe there were things he wanted to say but couldn't. A sense of urgency seemed to pour off him and press against her shields.

"If you give me a moment, I'll inform the Elder of your arrival," he said, curtly.

Alexis felt a quick spike of power from him before a sharp, stabbing pain pierced her mind. It was gone as quickly as it had come, but she felt his presence inside her head. Alexis locked herself down and sealed her thoughts, feelings, and plans into a vault shrouded in her shadow energy and sealed it with frost. She threw Kearney into a small corner of her mind, not too dissimilar from a cage. He would have to fight to get anywhere else, but he was still inside.

Alexis cursed her carelessness. She would have to keep him from breeching her vault at the expense of all other things, which would leave her vulnerable to whatever happened in the room around her. She quickly began the process of casting him out.

"Wait! Please! I'm the only one in this room who doesn't mean you harm. I want to make a deal," Kearney said, his voice echoing in her mind.

Curious enough to pause, Alexis replied, *"Are you summoning your Mistress or speaking with me?"*

"I am doing both," he answered.

"Then you have until she gets here to convince me to trust you."

"That's more than fair. I first apologize for the pain. I've been trying to communicate since the elevator. Your shielding is substantial and I saw no gentle way to slip in."

"I don't have time or patience for an apology. All that matters is that you succeeded. Get to your point," Alexis replied coldly.

"Le'Roe is denying me the Ritual of Mastery. I no longer wish to be her pet. I will aid you in the coming battle if you aid me when I petition the World Council for my freedom. Make no mistake; there will be a battle if you choose not to bow to her."

As he spoke to her mind, Kearney also spoke to her physically. "Elder Le'Roe will be with you in a moment. May I offer you a drink?"

Slightly disoriented, Alexis had to work to keep her expression under control. She wasn't as skilled in mental communication as he, and it took her longer than she would have liked to sort through the blend of mental and physical voices.

"No. Thank you, Kearney," she replied before switching to the telepathic connection.

"I will not bow. Your reason for the deal is selfish enough to be valid. What are the terms?"

"I only ask that you not kill my brother. He will be escorting Le'Roe. He is addicted and doesn't share my wisdom or strength. He'll attack you if she bids it. As for your part, I will expect your aid when I address the World Council."

"So you've said. What exactly does that entail?" she asked.

"When the time comes, I will tell you," Kearney replied as he moved to stand beside her.

"I don't make open-ended deals," Alexis said, flatly.

"It's the best you'll get tonight, considering the time restraints. I can sense your power. I'm not foolish enough to think you can be a possession. My Elder does. I'd prefer you as an ally. As a gesture of good faith, I will not attack you. I won't help you, but I won't hinder you either. However, should you choose to accept my offer, I will give you the strengths and weaknesses of every vampire in this room and even slow their minds, should you need it."

Alexis loathed the idea of accepting a deal when she had no knowledge of what would be required of her. Kearney seemed to want nothing more than freedom. She sympathized but looks could be deceiving and his troubles were none of her concern. On the other hand, he could undoubtedly tell her what she wasn't seeing in the room. It was a dangerous piece of the puzzle to gamble on. Alexis watched the handle on Le'Roe's chamber begin to turn and knew she was running out of time.

"I will accept your offer, under the condition if what you demand of me risks more than you are risking tonight, I can decline and the offer is void."

"Agreed."

"Done," Alexis confirmed just as the door opened and the Elder emerged.

Le'Roe was a small woman. Even in six-inch heels, she didn't reach her escort's shoulders. Generous curves were wrapped in sky blue silk that clung in all the right places. Golden curls framed lush, exotic features and cascaded down her bare back. A heart-shaped, diamond pendant rested against her chest. Her remaining jewelry was simple, but tasteful. Le'Roe had no need to hide her flawless skin with lavish jewels. Her lips were painted with only a thin layer of gloss to accent their natural color. Alexis immediately understood why her beauty was deadly.

The man escorting Le'Roe was not exactly Kearney's identical twin, but he was close. Their facial features were almost the same, though Kearney's bone structure was sharper. His brother was shorter and broader, as if trying to make up the few inches in height with more muscle. Both brothers could turn heads, but Kearney had the better end of the genetic stick.

"That's my brother. Thanos. He has the ability to spell steal, so unless you want to arm him with your magic, you should refrain from casting against him. If you only attack physically, he can only respond in kind. He specializes in martial arts that are purely based on strength. Agility and speed are his weaknesses," Kearney whispered to her mind.

Alexis chose not to respond as Le'Roe practically glided across the room. She left the mental connection open so Kearney could speak but did nothing more than absorb the information. Le'Roe lowered herself into the throne and looked expectantly at Kearney. He bowed to her and gestured to Alexis.

"Elder Le'Roe, I present to you Lady Alexis Montral."

Alexis nodded once to Le'Roe as Kearney moved to take his position beside her, opposite Thanos. Alexis understood why Le'Roe wouldn't want to give Kearney up. His ability was extremely useful. The brothers gave Le'Roe a strong power structure.

She felt Le'Roe's lustful gaze slide over every inch of her body. She didn't squirm. The Elder wasn't flexing any power, but the hungry look told Alexis exactly why the vampire had allowed the meeting. A small knot of lust twisted her gut, but Alexis immediately squelched it. She knew the consequences of giving in to temptation.

"Good evening and welcome, Lady Montral. Crimson becomes you. Hiding your beauty behind false lenses does not," Le'Roe said, her voice as sweet as honey and laced with a deep French accent.

"Good evening, Lady Le'Roe, Elder of New York City. Thank you for the invitation to your home. The glasses, unfortunately, are mandatory for public travel." Alexis nodded to a third set of twins nearby. "Fond of sets, are you?"

The Elder's lips curved in an amused, wicked smile. "Why keep one of a delicious thing when I can have two?"

"Spoken like a true glutton."

The amused smile blossomed into laughter. "Lessons in gluttony from a woman who apparently owns half of Manhattan?"

Alexis lifted a bare shoulder in a casual shrug. "We all have our talents."

"I'm interested in hearing more about yours. Have a seat," Le'Roe said as her small hand gestured to the back of the room.

A vampire walked forward carrying a simple wooden chair. He set it down directly behind Alexis and returned to his position with the others. Alexis sat and confidently crossed her legs. "I'm afraid this isn't a social call and you've been borderline rude."

"Perhaps. Genuine beauty always captures my curiosity, especially when power is attached. Making my doormen scream was also rude, Ms. Montral. I'd call us even."

The bartender approached Le'Roe with his head bowed. He carried a tray laden with a single martini glass filled with blood. Le'Roe took it without so much as a glance. She took a slow sip as Alexis answered, "If your guards had been taught proper manners, I wouldn't have had to give them lessons."

Le'Roe raised an eyebrow. "Blunt, aren't you?"

"I didn't come here for booze and witty banter."

"Ah, a shrewd business woman. All work and no play makes a dull demoness," Le'Roe teased as she waved the bartender away.

"If I'm that dull, the pleasantries can be skipped and we can address the matter at hand."

Le'Roe stared blankly for a moment before she laughed. It was an intoxicatingly rich sound, capable of sinking straight into a person's core. Alexis wondered how long it had taken her to perfect it.

"I haven't had anyone play hard to get in a long time. I'd forgotten how entertaining it is."

Alexis almost rolled her eyes. "If that's what you think I'm doing, you're sorely mistaken. I've no interest in you or your family. You have nothing I want."

Le'Roe's smile turned sultry, confident. "I always have something to covet. If you really desire nothing of mine, then you won't mind playing a little game. If I win, you return to me once a week for a month to entertain me with these mysterious talents of yours. If you win, we shall skip further discussion and get to this ridiculous business you seem so intent on finishing."

"Don't accept. The bet will cater to her talents. Le'Roe has brought even the most asexual of individuals to their knees with just one kiss. It's not even her vampiric ability. She's had centuries of practice as a courtesan. Added to that, her lips are coated with a gloss containing a powerful aphrodisiac. The scent she wears and the lotion on her skin do, as well. I don't know if your body reacts to drugs, but it's not worth the risk. She means to have you by whatever means necessary," Kearney warned.

"If I choose not to participate?" Alexis asked.

"You don't seem like a cowardly woman, Lady Montral. Then again, you've hidden yourself for all this time. Perhaps appearances are deceiving," Le'Roe replied sweetly.

Alexis didn't take the bait. "I am not here to gain your favor or make alliances. I am here for you to answer for your house's disrespect. I won't leave without it."

"Behind every wall like the one you've built around yourself is a deep pool of burning passion. It's only a matter of time before I break through, Alexis. Once I tap into it, you won't even want to run from me. I always get what I want," Le'Roe said. Anger began to drip into her voice.

"I'll take great pleasure in being the first to deny you, Belladona," Alexis replied. The maintenance of her composure was much easier than anticipated.

"She is easily insulted. Prepare yourself for a fight. Le'Roe can enhance the power of any vampire. She can give Children the speed and strength of Adults, and boost an Adult's ability far beyond his base power level. Le'Roe doesn't fight her own battles. She empowers an army to do it for her."

Alexis inwardly sighed. Le'Roe's ability was the missing piece. She had done an amazing job of keeping it hidden from the public. Alexis would have been caught off guard, if not for her deal with Kearney. There would be no way to avoid injury. She accepted there would be pain and blood and began to adjust her strategy.

"You are gravely out-numbered, demoness. You are in no position to be cocky. I'll give you one more chance to consider my proposal," Le'Roe said.

"How sweet of you. You're nowhere near as confident as you profess. The numbers you have here are not enough," Alexis replied. She let her tone turn low and dangerous.

Le'Roe grinned and leaned back in her throne. "I approve your choice, pet. When you fall to your knees before me, everything you are and everything you have will be mine."

Alexis gave the smile she used against corporate executives from competing businesses when they believed they'd trapped her, a smile that said she knew something they didn't. A subtle, familiar tingling traveled down her forearms. The marks of her daggers had shown themselves on her skin. They would appear and disappear as she needed them.

"There are eight true Adults in this room, though there are more in the bedrooms. You will only need to directly worry about five. If you don't hit Thanos with spells, he can only harm you physically. I won't attack you, but I do ask you incapacitate me to remove suspicion. Anne can deprive you of your physical senses and her twin James can teleport. Hisae can make copies of herself. Baako wields lightning and Christine can control body temperature," Kearney said, flashing images of the different vampires in her mind as he went down the list.

"Once the fight starts, stay out of my head. You've given me enough to meet the requirements of the deal."

"I'm honored you find my voice distracting. Good luck, my lady. Try not to die."

During their conversation, Alexis felt the power level in the room shift. Le'Roe was empowering her army. Alexis called her own power and solidified her shielding.

Le'Roe's expression was self-satisfied and smug. "Bring her to me."

The instant the words were spoken, a man dove at Alexis. While he had the speed of an Adult, his dramatic leap screamed inexperience. Alexis jumped out of her chair and lifted it by the back. She brought the chair down with enough force to shatter it over her assailant's head before he even touched her.

He fell straight to the floor at her feet. Alexis drove the broken piece of wood in her hand straight through his back and into his heart. The destruction of the organ should have been more than enough to ensure he never rose again, but if she had to take the head later, she would.

Before anyone else could rush her, Alexis flexed her control over ice. She focused on each of the doors in the penthouse. A large shell of black ice formed around each one to seal them off. No one could get in or out of the room easily. Though Alexis cut off the possibility of help coming for her, the spell also ensured Le'Roe would not be able to get reinforcements from other rooms.

Alexis felt the ramifications of casting a slower spell when Thanos' fist slammed into her jaw. Pain blossomed across her face, but she could tell he'd pulled the punch. He didn't think she could take it and Le'Roe wanted her alive. His underestimation was her advantage. Alexis let the momentum of his strike spin her body in a full circle and she backhanded him with all her strength. There was a satisfying crunch of bone as the vampire went flying.

The weight of two vampiric energies assaulted her shielding. Alexis quickly scanned the room for the woman who could control body temperature. Her shielding would only last so long while distracted by combat. Alexis could be boiled from the inside out, which made Christine the largest threat.

Alexis found her at the edge of the room, intently focused. Three more vampires lunged. She let her body become the shadows and traveled through them to materialize behind Christine, the weight of both daggers comfortable in her hands. She slammed one through the woman's heart and twisted while she shoved the second through the back of Christine's neck to sever her spine. A thin layer of skin and muscle were all that kept the head to the body. Alexis yanked both blades free and kicked the corpse forward. It flew into another vampire as he ran at her.

A man cried out in anguish and rage a moment before Alexis felt the burn of electricity as it impacted her stomach. The searing pain was almost enough to make her cry out and Alexis dove behind a couch for cover. The skin along her abdomen was charred and some of the fabric of her dress had melted into the wound. A low growl of annoyance escaped her lips. She could do better.

Another man vaulted over the couch and swiped at her face with razor sharp nails. Alexis brought her arm up and blocked the attack. Her daggers faded from her grip, and she drove her stiletto up into the man's groin. When he doubled over, she sprung up and launched her fist into his chin in a fierce upper cut.

Just when Alexis thought she had steady footing, Thanos' body slammed into hers like a freight train. Thankfully, her head hit a carpeted floor, but she felt the skin on her bare back scrape along the rug. Thanos glared down at her with eyes expressing the fury his shattered jaw could not. Alexis felt more power grind against her shields. Thanos would have to wait his turn.

Just to irritate him, Alexis pressed a quick kiss to his bruised, bleeding jaw before she transformed into the shadows. She reappeared behind Kearney and slammed his head into Le'Roe's throne. A piece broke off the back, and Le'Roe growled as she was forced to duck beneath the falling wood. Alexis ignored Le'Roe and grabbed Kearney by the collar. Pain suddenly laced across her chest and she realized he had scratched her. Though the cuts were shallow, blood still dripped down her toned stomach.

Kearney was faster than she gave him credit for, so Alexis sped her own movements. Her elbow caught him in the throat a moment before she threw his body into the wall. His head connected first and when he hit the floor, he didn't move.

Another vampire was instantly in her face. He took a swing at her head and she ducked under and drove her fist into his rib cage. Alexis spun around behind him and kicked him in the back with as much force as she could muster. His body went flying through the glass of the fireplace. His tortured screams were the last thing she heard before her world went completely silent and black.

Alexis froze. Her shielding had been breached. She needed time to regain her bearings, so she faded into the shadows. The loss of her senses was inconvenient, but it wasn't a death sentence. She flexed her power and produced enough shadows to slither through the whole room. Though she wouldn't be able to get her standard vision back until she took out the vampire responsible for stealing it, Alexis could use the shadows to trace every movement within the room. She could sense things magically her eyes would never show her. Shadows always revealed a person's true form. With her mind adjusted, she went back on the offensive.

She rematerialized behind two vampires and rendered them unconscious with a series of quick, decisive strikes. But Alexis wasn't fast enough to react to the pool of energy at her back. Fingers threaded through her hair and yanked her head. Fangs sank deep into the muscle of her neck as an empty void came rushing at her. She assumed it was Thanos, as his ability demanded he be filled with someone else's power.

Something was headed straight for her face, so she yanked her head and shoulder down and to the side. Vampire fangs ripped the flesh of her neck, but whatever had been coming for her face slammed into the vampire behind her instead. Alexis was suddenly released and she dove to the side to give herself space.

As she stood, she felt a sizzle of energy racing through the shadows toward her. She threw up her arm and a wall of ice the size of her body shielded her. The lightning bolt chipped off a large portion, but it didn't destroy the wall entirely. Alexis kicked what was left of the shield and it shattered into ice spikes that flew directly into the man who had cast the lightning. Alexis wasn't sure where they struck, but she didn't particularly care. He went down and that was all that mattered.

Distracted by the spell, Alexis hadn't felt the other vampires' approach until it was too late. Four sets of hands grabbed at her arms, her waist, and her neck. Though she couldn't directly feel them, Alexis knew they were tugging at her. She lashed out with shadows in response. She gave them the same treatment she had given the twins at the door. Hands suddenly released her as their owners' organs began to take damage from foreign energy. Alexis let go of direct control over the spell and allowed the shadows to grow and destroy as they pleased.

She stumbled with her awkwardly gained freedom and barely had time to raise an arm to protect her face from a blow. The knee to her stomach was unavoidable and it knocked the wind from her. Alexis promised herself she'd breathe when the muscles stopped shaking. She almost blasted her attacker with ice until she realized she was facing the void. Having no desire to fill that darkness with her magic, Alexis became the shadows and took a much needed breath.

The vampire who could teleport had to go. He was the next largest variable and it was easier to track him in the darkness. Though her injuries were largely superficial, some were going to be difficult to heal. The fatigue of extensive power use began to creep in. With four still in fighting condition, the chess match wasn't over and Alexis needed to stay smart. Though her body had a higher durability than most, she was facing powerful enemies and all they needed was one lucky, crippling blow.

She rematerialized in the middle of the room and used herself as bait. Thanos reached her first. Instead of waiting for him to strike, Alexis kicked at the lower part of the void. She pulled the attack just enough to let him dodge. She continued to lure him in by slowing her attacks to give him confidence. Once Alexis had him where she wanted, she slammed her spiked heel hard and fast into the center of the black hole. Thanos flew back and was out of her scope of immediate concern.

Power pooled behind her and she knew the teleporter was an instant away from manifesting. She turned into the shadows and gave him a taste of his own medicine. He appeared and then paused in what Alexis assumed was confusion. Whatever the reaction, it suited her as she reappeared to drag her blade across his throat. She shoved him forward before too much of his blood had a chance to spill over her.

Alexis caught bits and pieces of a woman's grieving cry. The vampiress blocking her senses was distracted, her hold faltering. A figure rushed through the shadows to the body that had just fallen. Though the figure ignored her, Alexis refused to hesitate. She slammed her foot down into what she hoped was the woman's head. The figure twisted and fell over what must have been her brother.

In an instant, all of Alexis' senses returned. The room was deafeningly loud, filled with pained moans and cries of agony. Flashes of white light and blood spotted her vision. Her entire body tingled, and then hurt. She swayed and staggered as she suddenly felt the floor beneath her feet. Just as her vision began to clear, Alexis saw a large fist coming directly at her nose.

She had enough time to turn her face away, but the blow connected solidly with her temple. Her head snapped to the side with enough force to fling her sunglasses away. It knocked her whole body into another vampire and pain exploded just under her left shoulder. Alexis looked down to see she had been stabbed with an iron poker from the fire.

Alexis raised her obsidian gaze to the woman holding the iron as her flesh excruciatingly sizzled. Shadow energy danced around her eyes and she growled low in her throat. The fear in the vampire's eyes was worth the pain. Quick as a viper, she slammed her fist down on the woman's arm and the iron was yanked from her chest. Alexis swung her fist at the woman's face, but the vampire leapt back several feet in retreat. Alexis started to close the distance but paused when the woman opened her palms.

Mirror images of the vampiress began to fill the room as Alexis heard Thanos close the distance behind her. She dropped low to evade the arms attempting to grab her. She launched herself backward and up, slamming her back into his chest. They both tumbled onto the floor and Alexis slammed both elbows into his ribs. Thanos grunted and several bones cracked. She scrambled to her feet before he could recover.

Alexis found herself surrounded by copies of the female vampire. Not having the time to determine which one was real, she focused her energy and formed a large sphere of ice. It hovered in front of her as it grew. Alexis spared Le'Roe a glance and flashed a bloody smile from cracked lips. The Elder's gaze was pure, primal fury. But beneath all the anger was fear and exhaustion. It had taken her substantial effort to empower so many. Despite the pain, Alexis found immense satisfaction knowing Le'Roe realized she was beaten. With the spell complete, Alexis dove behind an upturned couch a moment before the ice started to rotate.

As the sphere picked up speed, ice shards began to fly from it, showering the room with dangerous spikes and forcing even Le'Roe to take cover. After a full minute, the spell was complete. Alexis rose to take in the destruction. There were no more clones. The original vampire had fallen to the floor with a shard of ice buried through her right eye. Le'Roe and Thanos emerged a moment later. He wasted no time and charged Alexis head on.

Alexis leapt over the couch and met him. He was a skilled fighter and caught her with several painful strikes, but Kearney's assessment had been accurate. Alexis' speed, agility, and broader range of martial arts beat him. He fell unconscious at her feet after several long minutes of intense combat. She looked to Le'Roe and met the Elder's eyes. They were carefully blank, her features guarded. Le'Roe had returned to what was left of her throne.

Alexis looked around the room. Furniture was toppled or destroyed. The carpet was, indeed, ruined. Bodies littered the floor. Some were unmoving while others whimpered and cringed as they sought comfort in each other. Alexis felt neither guilt nor remorse, only weariness and exhaustion. She would likely have to repeat the performance many more times before the magical community understood she was not a toy.

Alexis bit back a sigh as she moved to pick up an overturned coffee table. She placed it in front of Le'Roe's throne. She repeated the process with one of the few chairs that didn't appear to be damaged beyond the ability to support her weight. Alexis picked her sunglasses off the floor and walked back to the bar to find an unbroken bottle of champagne and a glass to go with it. The bartender stood docile and unmoving.

She let him be and returned to her chair to sit and put her feet up on the table. Blood dripped off her stilettos in slow, thick droplets. She almost moaned in relief when the adrenaline finally settled. There wasn't a spot on her body that wasn't in stabbing, sharp pain. Blood still flowed from her deeper wounds.

But none of that showed in her expression as she faced Le'Roe. The night wasn't over. Her goal had not yet been achieved. So, Alexis slipped her sunglasses back on and popped the cork. Champagne filled her glass and she set the bottle on the table between them. She took a long, slow drink before giving Le'Roe her best professional smile.

"So, Belladona. We were discussing submission."

CHAPTER TWENTY

"Seriously, Carley. Get down. You have no idea what you're doing," Aiden said as he watched her climb one of several fire escape ladders alongside Chateau Le'Roe.

She glanced down at him, unwavering determination in her harsh gaze. "We've been through this. Alexis is hurting and needs help. It's not like we can walk through the front door and ask what room they're torturing a demon in. For the last time, help me or get the fuck out of here."

"I am helping you," Aiden said. "You're just not thinking clearly enough to see it. That wall is likely covered with cameras and vampire guards. Getting captured or killed doesn't help Alexis. On top of that, just because she's hurting doesn't mean she needs help. Has she reached out to you?"

"I don't know. I have no idea what that would feel like. But I do know I can feel what she feels and it's not good."

"It would be like—" Aiden started before Carley was suddenly yanked off the fire escape.

Aiden spun around fast. Calm, cold instinct washed over him. His gun was aimed squarely at the attacker's chest, but what he saw surprised him enough his finger eased from the trigger. Krysta Nightsky held Carley two feet off the ground by the back of her coat with one arm. Carley wiggled and kicked, but Krysta didn't budge, even making it look easy.

He was grateful he had hesitated when Carley slid her arms out of the coat to free herself. It put her body right in his line of fire. She turned and tried to slam her fist into Krysta's stomach, but the elf easily caught and held it with an iron grip.

"Relax, shrimp. I'm not going to hurt you," Krysta said before turning her shimmering gaze to Aiden, "but I won't say the same for you. Put the toy away."

"Let her go and I will," Aiden countered.

Krysta growled and stepped forward. She obviously held no fear of the weapon. Her anger was so heavy in the air Aiden could have sworn it was tangible. He had no desire to make an enemy, but Krysta's reputation kept him from lowering his weapon.

"Are you implying my word has no value, hunter? Duels have been started over less. Put the fucking gun down," Krysta replied slowly, her tone low and dangerous.

Aiden watched a subtle, crimson hue hover around the edges of her sparkling sapphire irises. His frustration turned to irritation, which immediately grew to anger. Rage pulsed through him like a runner's heartbeat. He was about to slip his finger back on the trigger, but Carley's voice made him pause.

"She could have hurt me if she wanted to. She could be hurting me now, but she isn't."

With each passing moment, Aiden's anger grew. He knew Carley was right, but he didn't care. He wanted to watch his weapon blow a hole through Krysta's skull. The thought gave him pause. The viciousness of it felt foreign.

Aiden's anger was hot, but a solid reason always fueled it. It wasn't like him to throw aside concern for people in the crossfire. Aiden met Krysta's gaze and suddenly realized the anger was hers. Her rage was as real as any magic and it was infectious.

He glanced at Carley, and one look told him she wasn't affected by the anger pouring off Krysta. It didn't make sense, unless she had the ability to direct it. Aiden decided to ponder that at another time. The elf's anger had almost forced him to make a second huge mistake. His first had been treating her like a suspect and not a warrior. He fought the rage and lowered his weapon. The moment his barrel was pointed at the ground, Krysta released Carley.

The anger didn't dissipate. It washed over Aiden in waves. He closed his eyes, took a deep breath, and worked to find the quiet place in his mind where he went numb, the place he used to hunt and walk through gruesome crime scenes. It helped clear his thoughts. He considered calling to his power to burn out Krysta's influence, but ultimately, she had achieved his goal for him. Carley was off the fire escape. There was no need for anger.

"I apologize for insulting your honor," Aiden said carefully.

Krysta raised a curious eyebrow and studied him. The anger in the air slowly began to fade. "You surprise me, hunter. Maybe you're not as dumb as you seem."

"Great. The pissing contest is over and we're all nice and cozy," Carley said. "There are more important things to worry about than who has the biggest dick."

Krysta laughed and Aiden wondered how a sound so beautiful could come from someone like her. He wrote it off to heritage, then flicked the safety on his weapon and holstered it.

"You win, Carley," Aiden said. "Your cock's bigger than mine. Now, what are you doing here, Nightsky?"

Aiden caught both the amusement in Krysta's eyes and the scowl in Carley's.

"Must you say my name so loud?" Krysta said. "I don't think the vampire on the eleventh floor heard you. We're fortunate he's just a Child and his hearing still sucks. The real question is what are the two of you doing here? Your presence only weakens your mistress."

"She is not my mistress," Aiden said.

"She's injured. She needs help," Carley answered.

"Of course she's injured. What the fuck did you think would happen when she faced an army of blood suckers in their own nest?" Krysta seethed. "She's doing it to protect you, shrimp. The least you could do is have the decency to stay where she left you."

"What are you talking about?" Carley asked.

"The demon doesn't give two shits about Carley," Aiden said, though his conviction seemed to shrink daily. "She's just going to use her and then toss her corpse aside like yesterday's trash. The only person Alexis cares about is herself."

"Alexis is a self-serving bitch, but she's not beyond affections and she takes her responsibilities seriously. If I ever needed her, she would come. Walking into a Council member's home is an exceedingly atypical move for her. If she didn't want to make the point that attacking the shrimp will cost lives, why the fuck would she walk into Le'Roe's center of power? She has nothing to gain and everything to lose."

"Damn it, I have a fucking name," Carley said irritably.

Aiden set his jaw and momentarily ignored his partner. Alexis had displayed no signs of being power hungry or political. Making an enemy of House Le'Roe was definitely not a wise decision. Nothing about Alexis ever seemed to add up. He wanted to believe in her but couldn't stop the fear of the day she would turn on them.

"I don't know," he finally answered.

"That's what I thought," Krysta replied. "The next time you're considering spewing ignorance in my presence, think twice. I'll take great pleasure in removing your tongue."

"Stop it, both of you," Carley said. "This isn't helping. I assume, since you're here, you know what's going on and have some kind of plan."

Krysta turned her gaze to Carley and shrugged. "Certainly. I plan to wait."

Carley's expression flattened and she fell silent. Aiden inwardly winced. He wanted to be able to back her, but he agreed with Krysta. He couldn't deny her logic simply because she was irritating and Carley didn't like the answer.

"That's your brilliant fucking plan," Carley scoffed. "To sit and do nothing while she bleeds?"

"There is no circumstance where Alexis would accept appearing weak. Until she walks out that door, she's on her own," Krysta said.

"Yet, you are here. Why?" Aiden asked.

"I believe there is more to Le'Roe than the rumor mill states," Krysta replied. "She may not have created the circumstances for this trap, but she won't turn away the benefits."

"We didn't even know Alexis had to face this battle," Aiden said.

"How do you know she'll win?" Carley asked.

"Alexis is one of the most resourceful people I've ever met. She is an intelligent and proficient combatant who shouldn't be underestimated." Her gaze locked with Aiden's.

He understood what she hadn't said. She believed Alexis would kill him if he hunted her. He had known he would need assistance to battle this demon, but in reality, it no longer mattered. She was bound to Carley and he refused to risk Carley's life.

"So, we're going to stand out here like a bunch of fucking idiots until she walks out?" Carley asked as she folded her arms across her chest.

Krysta flashed a beautifully deadly grin. "Since your foolishness has gotten us seen, yes. We are. However, I was thinking of having a bit of fun. Interested, shrimp?"

Carley narrowed her gaze suspiciously. "What's your definition of fun?"

Krysta laughed. "I was thinking of trouncing the scrawny valet and liberating Alexis' car."

"Beating people is fun for you?" Aiden asked.

"Hell, yes. Get off your high horse and stop pretending the pain of a vampire offends your pristine moral compass. Beating the shit out of some demon satisfies and entertains you just as much as beating anything at all entertains me. You may have become a hunter for moral reasons, but no hunter stays a hunter unless he enjoys it."

Aiden narrowed his gaze and set his jaw. Krysta's insight to his nature was as annoying as Alexis'. He once believed he wasn't easy to read, but lately he was beginning to wonder. On the other hand, it was likely both Krysta and Alexis had encountered other hunters over the years. Perhaps he'd done nothing to make himself stand out from his brethren. That thought wasn't particularly pleasant, either.

"I hunt because I'm good at it and I do find satisfaction in destroying something that thrives on human pain and suffering," Aiden replied.

Krysta considered him for a moment and then nodded. "You know humans would cage or kill both you and Carley if they knew. Neither you, nor the shrimp, are *human*."

Aiden set his jaw. "Some things are worth the risk."

Krysta studied him closely before she shrugged. "Regardless, taking out a scrawny vampire with one punch holds only mild appeal to me. But watching Carley do it sounds highly entertaining. Up for it, shrimp?"

Fear for Carley's safety moved through Aiden's veins like ice. He grabbed her arm. "Don't do it. You don't know this woman and you know nothing about the vampire. You need to get it into your head that you're not invincible."

Aiden watched as Carley looked between him and Krysta, debating which path to go down. He swore sharply when he recognized the expression in her features. She never backed down from a challenge, even if she knew she had no chance. In the office, with a bunch of cops where the only thing she would suffer was bruised pride, it was okay. But out in the world, losing meant death. He wanted to strangle her himself.

"Damn it, Carley! You don't survive in this world by taking every piece of bait. We are at an Elder vampire's nest. You know what's creeping around. We are likely already on surveillance cameras."

"I won't hide behind other people's skirts, Aiden. I need to start showing I can handle myself." Carley's tone was calm, but serious.

"Then learn how first," Aiden said. "Don't go gallivanting off just because some butch, egotistical sociopath thinks it would be entertaining to watch you die."

"Oh, for fuck's sake, little witch. Stop your whining. Alexis would have my hide if anything happened to Carley. Even worse, she'd kick me out of her bed permanently," Krysta said dryly. "Since you both pine after her, you understand it isn't a position to give up lightly. Nothing will happen to Carley. I give my word."

"I don't pine for her," Carley and Aiden said together.

Krysta smirked knowingly. "Well, then, you are both blind and stupid."

When they glared at her, Krysta laughed and tossed Carley's coat back at her. "Coming or not?"

"Going," Carley answered as she slipped into the jacket.

"Excellent," Krysta replied before shrugging out of a backpack Aiden hadn't noticed she was wearing. "Take this and wait out front. If we're not there in ten minutes, you can come down with guns blazing and play the white knight."

Aiden fought for patience as he took the bag. She had given her word and Carley hadn't given him a choice but to trust it. She slung an arm around Carley's shoulders and guided her to the garage. The night had quickly gotten out of control, not that anything lately had gone the way he planned. They would all be lucky if they didn't end up dead or in prison before dawn.

He sighed and walked to the front of the hotel. Guilt for Carley's situation ate at his chest. He knew she'd spent her entire life doing nothing but proving herself. Aiden didn't know what more he could do to show her that being alive was the best evidence of strength and wisdom.

He found a bench and sat down. Krysta's bag dropped between his feet and he opened it to pull out a folded wool cloak. After finding nothing special about it, he set it on the bench. The remains of the bag were a disposable cell phone, a military grade survival knife, three bottles of water and eight protein bars.

Aiden took out the cell phone to check the contact list, as well as both the outgoing and incoming call lists. All were empty, but he expected that. He dropped the phone back into the bag and placed the cloak on top before closing it. Just as he checked his watch, Aiden heard the low purr of the Aston Martin's engine.

The car slid up to the hotel entrance and idled a bit before turning off. Krysta stepped out of the driver's side and slipped the keys into her coat pocket. Carley wasn't far behind and they made their way to him.

Krysta sat beside him and reached between his legs to get her bag. "See? Back all safe and sound."

He looked over at Carley and studied her. "You okay?"

She nodded once. "Fine."

Aiden let his gaze linger. She didn't appear injured and her expression was solid. There was more to worry about at the moment though, and he could ask her later when they were alone.

"Find anything interesting in my pack?" Krysta asked as she pulled out a protein bar.

Aiden turned his gaze and studied Krysta's face closely. She didn't appear upset. She just leaned back and took a bite of the bar. Instead of committing to an answer, Aiden tilted his head. A lie could make her angry, but so could the truth.

Krysta chuckled lightly and shrugged. "I'd have done the same thing."

"You wouldn't have given it to me if there was something worth finding," Aiden answered. "I was tempted to take a protein bar, though."

"Hmm. That would have pissed me off. I don't share food," Krysta replied flatly.

"Despite the circumstances, I really have no desire to piss you off," Aiden said.

Krysta grinned and took another large bite. He saw her smile fade as she looked to the front of the hotel. His hand moved to the butt of his gun. When he saw nothing out of the ordinary, he turned back to her. Carley beat him to his question.

"What is it?"

Krysta reached into her backpack and pulled out the cloak. "She's there."

"How do you know?" Aiden asked.

"See those small spots of shadow beneath the street lights? There's a path of them. She's bleeding."

"Those spots could be dead bugs in the light bulbs or something," he countered.

"I've made her bleed enough to know what it looks like in shadow form. Those spots weren't there before."

"She's right," Carley added, "I can feel her."

Several long, twisting tendrils of shadow formed in the light of the lamps. They grew and spun along each other until the silhouette of a woman appeared. The shadow faded and Alexis stepped forward.

Aiden wasn't prepared for the visceral, protective anger that slid through him. Her dress was in tatters, clinging desperately from her shoulders. There were bruises, burns, and lacerations all over her. Blood trailed down pale, bare skin.

His response confused him. It was as if it were okay for him to plot her death, but anyone else needed to be brought to justice. It made no sense, but he couldn't deny the feeling, so he kept his mouth shut.

"What are you three doing here?" Alexis asked coldly, no hint of discomfort in her voice.

Krysta moved forward and wrapped the cloak around her shoulders, hiding her wounds from any potential people walking on the street. "You didn't call."

"Because I neither wanted nor needed you," Alexis replied.

Krysta stepped back and anger flooded the air. It tugged at Aiden's own, but he felt the difference now that he understood what to look for. He worked to shield, but it seemed the rage could pass through magical defenses. That alone was irritating. He sighed and went back to the tactic of trying to stay numb.

Krysta opened her mouth to reply, but no words came out. Carley came up next to Krysta and glared. Aiden wondered if Carley felt Krysta's influence. Her temper was as bad as his.

"You didn't call us, either," Carley accused.

"You and your carelessness are the reason I'm here. This is no place for you, or this discussion. I suppose all of you drove separately?" Alexis asked. The chill in her tone was enough to make even Aiden shiver.

"I took a cab," Krysta answered shortly.

"I drove. We parked three blocks down," Aiden said.

"Fine. You may as well be useful. I'll ride with Aiden. Krysta and Carley will drive the Aston back to my apartment. End of story. No protests. No discussion."

Carley opened her mouth, but Alexis silenced her with a single glare. Both Carley and Krysta turned and walked to the Aston Martin. It wasn't long before it shot out of the hotel entrance. Once Krysta was gone, Aiden felt better. It was easier to think when he didn't have to work at maintaining his control over his temper. He came to stand beside Alexis.

"Those two are going to get along fabulously," Aiden commented.

The corners of Alexis' mouth twitched slightly. "After they butt heads for a while. Lead on, then."

Aiden nodded and started down the path to where he'd parked. They walked in silence. He didn't ask if she felt well enough to make the trip. He didn't doubt they were being watched and he wasn't entirely sure she even felt her wounds. There were some schools of thought that believed demons didn't feel pain. Alexis gave no indication either way. It only made him more curious. He had never been in a position to learn demonic anatomy from casual conversation.

When they got to the car, he opened the passenger door for her. She wrapped the cloak tighter and carefully got into the seat. Aiden was unsure what to make of her respect. Her attempt to not drip was obvious, but she was covered in blood. There was no stopping some of it from pooling on the seat.

Aiden closed her door and got in through his own and began the trip back toward Manhattan. After several minutes of silence, he glanced at her, catching only her profile. Even bruised and bleeding, she was beautiful. Her face was a blank mask. Aiden wanted to peel it back and see what was underneath.

"I'll see to it that your car is detailed," she said, quietly to break the silence.

"Unnecessary but appreciated," Aiden replied. "I'm sure I'd be screwed if someone got this car to a lab for testing."

They drifted back into silence. It wasn't exactly awkward, but it wasn't easy, either. There was tension in the air. Aiden finally glanced over again. "Do you feel pain?"

"Are you asking as a hunter or a man?"

Aiden turned back to the road and considered his response. He could lie, but it didn't feel right and he believed she would know. If he was going to pry, he could at least be fair about it.

"I'm asking as a man, but the hunter will always listen."

Alexis was silent for so long he thought she wouldn't answer. But she turned her head to look out the window. "Yes, I feel pain. Exhaustion, weariness."

Aiden smiled, surprised. If she was willing to be honest, there was much more he was curious about. But he had a feeling flooding her with questions would only make her shut down. He sighed and shook his head. "I've never encountered another of your kind who showed signs of it."

"I think it's been well established you've never encountered anyone like me."

Aiden smirked. "You're not wrong. You shouldn't have let Carley ride with Nightsky though. That elf is a time bomb."

Alexis sighed and took off her glasses to rub her eyes. "First of all, you're going to have to get it through your head Carley is mine. I take that seriously. I wouldn't have done what I did tonight if her safety wasn't one of my top priorities. I've made an enemy of House Le'Roe. They fear me. That will keep them away for now, but to say Le'Roe isn't happy is a gross understatement. She had the largest House in the United States, possibly the world. Her feelings regarding an individual don't go unnoticed by the Councils and I don't shed my blood for just anyone."

When Aiden didn't respond, Alexis continued.

"Second, I wouldn't have just gone through all of that to send Carley off with a mindless barbarian. There is no one I trust more with Carley's safety than Krysta, even when she's pissed. Most times, her fury sharpens her focus. As it is, Krysta isn't all that angry tonight. She is upset with me, but this is her relatively calm irritation. She won't let anything happen to Carley."

Aiden took several minutes to consider Alexis' words. As much as he hated thinking about it, Carley was bound to Alexis. Even if Aiden chose to believe Alexis was nothing but a predator, her concern for Carley's safety still made sense. Their bond was locked in. Carley's death would now be exceedingly painful for Alexis.

"I don't seem to have much choice but to trust your judgment," he said.

"I know what I'm doing, Aiden."

He started to reply in protest but realized he couldn't. Instead, he changed the topic. "How many more times will you have to do what you did tonight?"

"You know the routine. There are some who will favor my actions with Le'Roe and seek me as an ally. Others believe they are stronger and can take what she sought. It's going to take time and death for leaders of the community to understand I want no part of their squabbles," Alexis replied as she pushed her glasses back on her face.

"So, we're going to have to haul you out of situations like this often, huh?" he teased.

"Tonight was unacceptable for everyone involved, including myself. It won't happen again." Alexis apparently didn't see the humor.

He was surprised she included herself in the blame. "I was kidding. I know you can't afford to show weakness. You are one woman against entire clans."

"Hopefully, in the future, my fights will be solely with leaders. Vampires don't work the way other species do. Elders don't have to prove their strength to their own house. To other Elders, yes, but not to their own people. There are not many races that work that way."

"I suppose you needed to make a statement, but I won't lie, Alexis. Numbers are hard to beat. I'm glad Krysta was lurking," Aiden said.

Alexis raised a curious eyebrow and turned to study him. "Are you?"

"Yes," Aiden said. He meant it.

She turned back to the window. "If I choose to trust you with some responsibility, would you run from it?"

"Depends on what you're willing to trust me with," Aiden replied carefully.

"Carley is loyal and self-sacrificing to a fault. I'd like to be able to tell you when I'm going to these meetings and know you'll keep her from following me."

"Have you met Carley Jameson? No one 'keeps' her from going where she wants to be."

"You're a resourceful man and she trusts you. She's hot-headed and needs to learn the rules of the game sooner rather than later."

The offer to trust was unexpected. It would mean once the case was over, he couldn't pretend to forget she existed.

"If I say no?"

"I'll chain her to my walls, if I run out of options. But it would be nice to have your support there. Carley cares about you and values your opinion."

Aiden shook his head. "Not lately."

"That's partially because you're angry, and your prejudices shine through. She has done the best she can, given her circumstances. She listens to all the information presented and makes choices that are best for her. You and I won't be able to protect her from every hurt."

"I'll keep that in mind."

The silence returned. Aiden didn't agree that he'd voiced his opinions with anger. Perhaps with desperation and concern, even exasperation, but not anger. He wondered if he was frightening Carley. She should be afraid, but not of him. Maybe the only reason she accepted the mark was because Alexis appeared calm, reasonable, and in control; whereas he came off an unstable idiot. Aiden inwardly cursed himself. He had done nothing but drop the ball with this case. He needed to be better.

"You can trust me with this," he finally said as he pulled into the underground garage beneath Alexis' building.

He maneuvered the car into an open space next to the Aston Martin. Krysta and Carley had made it back safely. Aiden turned the engine off and twisted to find Alexis looking right at him. The weight of her gaze was always heavy.

"Don't say it unless you mean it. If you were just hunting me, Aiden, I'd kill you. No fuss. No suffering. Nothing more than self-defense. If you betray or manipulate this trust, it won't be just self-defense. You understand?"

Aiden raised an eyebrow. "So, a part of your true nature finally shows its ugly head."

For a moment, Alexis looked offended. She chuckled, but it was the bitter chuckle of frustration and disbelief. "If my true nature is protective, then yes."

Alexis opened the door and had one leg out before Aiden gently touched her shoulder. She turned her head back to him.

"I'm sorry. I don't like threats any more than you. You can trust me. You have my word," Aiden said as he met her gaze.

Alexis stared at him. Aiden meant what he said, so there was nothing but sincerity in his features. They needed to be able to work together to keep Carley safe. One day, she would be able to protect herself, but she would be vulnerable for some time yet. Alexis needed all the help she could get. He had become painfully aware his knowledge of demons wasn't as vast as he thought. He could do this one thing without guilt or fear.

Alexis finally nodded. "We are in agreement, then. I won't apologize for the threat because I meant it. But I will apologize for the situation that made me feel compelled to make it."

With that, she pulled her shoulder free and got out of the car. For a moment, Aiden watched her walk to the elevator and wondered if he would always find himself watching her walk away.

CHAPTER TWENTY-ONE

Carley stepped off the elevator to follow Krysta down yet another blank hallway with unlabeled doors. She was quickly becoming frustrated with never knowing where she was in Alexis' home. Krysta pushed through the fourth door on the left. As she trailed behind, Carley thought about memorizing the door number. But she soon realized it was futile without knowing the floor number as well. She took a seat on a bench by the wall and sat on her hands.

Her feet tapped against the white, marble floor as her gaze traveled around the room. Krysta had called it 'The Medical Wing.' While it was certainly designed for treating injuries, Carley wasn't convinced it was large enough to be classified as a wing. She was impressed with its contents but curious as to why Alexis needed the room at all. The curiosity reminded her of the hints of phantom pain in her body. Her concern for Alexis returned and her feet tapped faster.

Four stretchers lined against the wall across from Carley. Carts and cabinets filled with medical supplies were scattered around the room. The lighting was soft, but several hospital-grade, mobile exam lights were attached to the ceiling above each stretcher. The large drain in the middle of the floor was almost ominous. Images of bloody rivers dripping down the drain flooded her mind. She quickly looked away.

"Will you cease that incessant tapping? Alexis is alive and on her way. You have nothing to worry about."

Carley looked up to see Krysta positioning two of the exam lights over the second stretcher, having shed her leather jacket. Carley had never seen the elf without it and wasn't afraid to admit she was staring.

Krysta wore a fitted black tank top and a pair of black, straight-legged jeans. While Carley was certain the outfit wasn't meant to draw attention, it accented Krysta's physical power. She had the type of large, shredded muscles Carley only saw in air-brushed fitness magazines. Strangely, her size didn't rob her of grace. Her movements were naturally fluid and agile. Krysta was a predator, born and bred for the hunt.

The rest of her was equally distracting, with skin cream-colored and flawless. Her hair was long and pulled back, the color of sparkling snow. Carley's eye gravitated to those pointed ears. The shape was completely foreign but not unpleasant. It only added to the ethereal beauty.

The irritation in Krysta's sapphire eyes melted into amusement. "Like what you see, shrimp?"

Carley couldn't stop the light flush that burned her cheeks, but she lifted a shoulder in a shrug. She wasn't going to deny it. "Yes. You've always had your jacket on."

"Well, feel free to stare if it will keep you from that fucking tapping," Krysta replied as she dragged a cart of supplies to the stretcher.

Carley smirked and set her feet flat against the ground. "Do all elves look like you?"

"If you're talking about my majestic good looks, then yes. If you're referring to my muscle structure, then no."

Carley's brow furrowed. "I'm confused."

"By human standards, all elves are inherently beautiful. Agility and dexterity come naturally, but we lack the physical prowess of other races like were-animals. Elves are stronger with magic," Krysta replied.

"Doesn't that leave your race at a disadvantage?" Carley asked.

"Hardly. Many would rather have magic than physical strength. A vast majority of our warriors are battle mages. Those unfortunate enough to be born with only small gifts in magic tend to become the front line of our armies. It's a pathetically small front line. Magically weak elves are rare," Krysta replied.

Carley tilted her head. "You're a magically weak elf."

Krysta nodded and something flashed in her eyes Carley couldn't quite read. "I am, and I was banished for it."

There was more to the story, but she wasn't sure how much prying Krysta would tolerate. "So, you compensate by being super jacked?"

"It's more like surviving. Magic is fast, shrimp. Blink once and you're fucked. To beat a caster, you need the right equipment, strength enough to wield it as though it weighs nothing, and you must be smarter."

"What about people like Alexis? She has magic yet I've seen her train without it. She is kind of a physical bad ass," Carley said.

"One of the reasons I like training with her is because she's a challenge. A fight is like a chess match. The more steps ahead of your opponent you are, the better your chances of victory. You set traps and make sacrifices to kill that fucking queen. Alexis is a queen, shrimp. She is dangerous and exposes the areas where I've been slacking."

"For all your brawn, you advocate for brains."

"Without brains, there is nothing. A good warrior and survivor has ample amounts of both. Your body needs to be able to execute the maneuvers your mind plots. So, what about you? I don't see a whole lot of brawn on you, but you're a cop, so you should have some."

Carley lifted a shoulder in a shrug. She quickly learned during training, terminations of the diseased required intense fitness. She kept up with it. But Carley knew her athleticism didn't compare to that of Krysta or Alexis. The term 'diseased' was also slowly becoming inaccurate in her mind. Krysta certainly didn't look sickly. She just wasn't human.

"I've got a gun and special bullets," Carley replied when she could come up with no other viable advantage.

"That's a pretty shitty start."

"I am acutely aware of that, thanks."

"Well, you're a fast learner and have a nimble mind. That puts you ahead of the game. You're brave, too. You just need some education and training. You'll get plenty of both as Alexis' mark," Krysta said.

Carley started to reply, but the dull ache of Alexis' wounds grew more intense. The mark fascinated her. She focused on the sensation and felt Alexis drawing closer. She looked to the door moments before it opened. Alexis walked in and silently crossed the room to the stretcher Krysta had prepared. With the echoes of what Alexis felt banging around inside her body, Carley wondered how she could even walk. Aiden followed and it dawned on her Alexis likely didn't want to show pain in front of Aiden.

She stood and walked to the stretcher as Krysta put on a pair of exam gloves. As Carley helped Alexis out of the cloak, she found herself conflicted. On the one hand, she firmly believed Aiden's anger and mistrust was completely unfounded. On the other, she acknowledged he had more experience with demons. She knew she would sacrifice herself to end Alexis if she was as bad as Aiden believed.

She tossed the cloak on the floor while Aiden leaned against the stretcher across from Alexis. He folded his arms across his chest and seemed content to remain silent. But he watched Alexis closely. Curiously, his gaze wasn't cold or angry. It was almost concerned. His demeanor had shifted since they left the hotel. She wondered what was discussed during the ride over.

Krysta looked Alexis over and shook her head. "That dress is fucked. There's nothing to save. Cutting it off will be less uncomfortable."

Alexis stared at Krysta for a moment before she sighed and nodded. Blood-crusted heels were kicked to the side and she pulled her glasses from her face to set them on the stretcher. Carley was caught off guard by the darkness in those eyes. Alexis hid them so frequently it was easy to forget why. The emotion and expression within was still surprising, though now those shadow-filled eyes were tightly guarded.

What Carley could see was annoyance and acceptance, but not a drop of modesty. Alexis wasn't afraid of being naked before practical strangers, yet she refused to show pain. Distracted by her thoughts, Carley almost missed the safety shears tossed in her direction.

"You're up," Krysta said before turning to pick through the supply cart.

Carley stepped in front of Alexis to survey the state of the dress for herself. There were large tears at the midsection, almost like claw marks. The material was melted not far below the rips and there were numerous holes and torn straps.

Carley frowned. "Sorry, but try to stay still. You stomach looks like the dress burned into your skin," she said softly. "It will hurt when I start to pull at it."

"Just do what you have to. I'm more interested in efficiency," Alexis replied curtly.

The tone hadn't been exactly sharp, but it was expectant. Carley met Alexis' gaze and studied her for a moment. She was uncertain what she wanted to see but searched anyway. She found herself hoping Alexis wasn't too annoyed with her. Alexis angled her head to better hold Carley's gaze. Her expression softened slightly. "I'm alright, I promise. I'm sorry you feel some of it, but I've told you before I'm more durable than you. I heal faster and I've lived through worse."

"I know. It's just… weird. I don't know enough about you or the mark to gauge the severity of the situation. I'm sorry I overreacted," Carley replied before she began to cut through the frail strips of fabric.

"And I apologize for my callousness. I am used to being alone. I should have told you so you would have an idea of what to expect. All of us made mistakes tonight."

Silence fell across the room as Carley began to rip the scorched dress from Alexis' skin. Her own stomach tightened as the pain trickled down through the mark. She gritted her teeth and tugged until the dress came away in scraps she tossed on the floor. When she had gotten as much as she could, Carley set the shears down and looked at her hands. They were covered in blood. The fact that it was Alexis' made it all the more unsettling.

She stepped to one of the industrial sinks and scrubbed her hands. Fresh blood always came off easier than dried. She patted her hands on a towel and sat on the stretcher Aiden leaned against. Krysta set a tray loaded with supplies next to Alexis.

"What caused the burn?" Aiden asked.

To his credit, Aiden's gaze stayed above Alexis' chest. Stylish red panties had somehow survived destruction but didn't hide much. Carley regained some of the respect she had for him.

"A lightning bolt, actually," Alexis answered.

"For you to take hits like this, how many of the blood suckers were there?" Krysta asked as she placed a gloved hand on Alexis' chest and shoved her back onto the stretcher.

Alexis glared and Krysta rolled her eyes. "It will be easier for both of us if you're laying down."

"A simple 'please' would have sufficed."

Krysta shrugged and began to clean Alexis' wounds. "My way worked just fine. Are you going to answer my question?"

"I'm tempted not to. We need to revisit your lessons in manners," Alexis said.

Krysta growled with annoyance. "It's not my fault you're just fun to push around."

Alexis sighed and closed her eyes while Krysta worked. Carley could sense her fight for patience. Expressions skittered quickly across her face, too quickly for Carley to identify. But when she spoke again, Alexis seemed to have regained her composure. "There were twelve in the room, thirteen if you count Le'Roe."

"You and I have beaten more than twelve before and walked away with less injury," Krysta noted as she began to wash the blood from Alexis' body and clean her wounds.

Carley winced and tried to separate herself from the sensations pouring off Alexis. It was hard. Their proximity amplified the mark, but she hadn't gotten much practice differentiating between her own body, Alexis', and the connection between them. The pain was distracting. She tried to focus more on the talk around her than the discomfort.

"This was different," Alexis said.

"Why?" Aiden asked.

"Le'Roe's abilities blindsided me."

"She's not just a giant whore with irresistible vampire sex talents?" Krysta asked as she began to probe the stab wound in Alexis' chest. "You have bits of black shit in here. You're healing around it. I'm going to have to cut to make sure it's out. Irrigation isn't going to work."

Alexis shrugged. "Whatever is necessary. Le'Roe is, actually, a giant whore. She owned a brothel when her vampiric life began. She uses it to her advantage. I won't begrudge a woman owning and claiming that power. However, that has nothing to do with her ability. She can augment the power of any vampire, or multiple vampires, she chooses."

"Augment them how?" Krysta asked.

"She can turn Children into Adults temporarily. She can raise the natural strength of an Adult's ability beyond anything they could achieve on their own," Alexis replied.

"Holy fuck," Aiden said quickly.

"Precisely. I couldn't tell any of them apart or how many there were. She kept power levels fluctuating until conversation degraded to violence. I had to change my plan significantly," Alexis said.

Krysta paused and looked up at Alexis. "That's how Le'Roe gained a seat on the Council. The little bitch bribed her way up the chain."

"I would assume, yes. She could easily be their drug dealer. Le'Roe might keep them drunk on false power, and in return, they grant her some say in what goes on in the area," Alexis said.

"I know I'm ignorant of a lot of this, but what do you mean by Council?" Carley asked.

Aiden looked over at her. "Councils are how vampires choose to govern themselves. You know they live in smaller groups with one Elder. Those Elders answer to the Council of their region. There is a Council for each continent and one for the world. Le'Roe is a member of the North American Council."

"Does everyone just know everyone else's business in the magical community?" Carley asked.

"It's like how you know about the political systems of other countries. You know of their leaders, for the most part. You might not know intricacies, but you know enough to understand the general concepts," Alexis offered.

"Okay, that makes sense. So, you fought a leader of some kind," Carley replied thoughtfully.

"In a manner of speaking. Le'Roe is the Elder of her line and she had the largest line in North America. She isn't popular among vampires because of it. But given the nature of her ability, I understand why she relies on numbers. She needs an army," Alexis said.

"Most vampire lines are small but strong, shrimp," Krysta added. "They ruthlessly weed out the weak."

Carley sucked in a sharp breath as Krysta slid a scalpel through Alexis' chest and began to cut flesh stained with black ash. She resisted the urge to rub her own in the same spot, still amazed Alexis didn't flinch. She remembered Alexis noting that the mark could be closed off or opened with skill and experience. With the interest of answering her curiosity, Carley stopped trying to fight or block the connection. Instead, she made her first attempt to reach down into it to look.

The echoes of pain in her body multiplied tenfold. Her face scrunched in a wince. Exhaustion made her bones ache. Emotions filtered through the tangle of sensations. There was regret, not for the actions or lives taken, but that the evening's events had been necessary at all. There was sadness from a loss Carley couldn't identify. Affection for Krysta snuck through just before everything suddenly shut down. Even the pain subsided. She looked up to find Alexis' gaze boring into her. Her heart jumped as if she had gotten her hand trapped in the cookie jar. She tried to read Alexis' response, but those obsidian depths were frustratingly restrained.

"Alexis," Aiden said sharply.

The sound of his voice startled Carley. She broke eye contact to glance at Aiden. A moment later, Alexis turned her attention to him, as well.

"I'm sorry. What did you say?"

Aiden narrowed his gaze and glanced between Alexis and Carley. "I asked how much damage you did to Le'Roe's power base."

"Of the twelve in the room, four survived. Her two strongest are alive, but one has no desire to protect her interests. He surprised me by taking himself out of the game early. Le'Roe's house wasn't completely in order before tonight. It's in shambles now."

"So, Le'Roe isn't going to like you for a long time," Aiden replied.

"I doubt she'll ever be fond of me. I turned her down sexually and forced an apology she didn't want to give. She is a spiteful woman who holds grudges."

"I take it she didn't leave you much choice? Pissing her off definitely has its negatives," Krysta replied as she began to bandage Alexis' wounds.

"Le'Roe came into the meeting with the intent of subjugating me," Alexis answered.

Krysta laughed. "While I can't blame her for trying, it was a very stupid move."

"Why does it matter whether or not she likes you?" Carley asked.

"Almost all the vampires in the city belong to Le'Roe, which means they're now unfriendly at best. At worst, they're hostile, but I don't think Le'Roe will be in a hurry to pick another fight with me," Alexis replied.

"So, vampires are going to be more willing to attack us. Wasn't the point of you going through all this, marking me included, to keep vampires away?" Carley asked.

"Belladona is known to be a sore loser. In theory, Alexis' victory should have done just that. Other leaders would give Alexis respect after being beaten and remain neutral, but not the vampire queen. She's a bit of a bitch," Krysta said before she stepped back from Alexis and stripped off her gloves. "You're as pretty as I can make you."

Alexis nodded and slid off the stretcher. She walked to a cabinet and pulled out a fresh pair of dark jeans and a blue sweater. As she dressed, Carley looked away. Alexis had apologized for sharing power in Dark Heart. She said it had been rude of her. Carley imagined taking a peek at someone's emotions without consent was wrong. Carley sighed as guilt began to make her skin itch.

Alexis stepped into a pair of black boots and returned to the stretcher with a new pair of sunglasses. "This won't be an isolated incident, Carley. Other groups will offer similar challenges. When I don't bring you to something, it's for a reason. As you see, I've made it through just fine."

"I understand you might not be able to take me, but I need to know when it's happening. And you're not fine. I felt how much you hurt before you cut me off, which I'm sorry for. I think I was rude," Carley said as she shoved her hands in her pockets.

"Yes, but I forgive you. You're curious and exploring. A mark usually comes after two people know each other substantially better. I didn't expect you to learn how to open it on your own. You seem to have a natural knack," Alexis said as she slipped the sunglasses on her face.

"Can't you leave those off for now?" Aiden asked.

"See? I'm not the only one," Krysta added.

"Like I tell her," Alexis pointed to Krysta though she looked directly at Aiden, "the glasses must be habit, second nature. If they're anything less, there's a risk I'll forget them. It needs to feel strange for them to not be on my face. You've seen why."

"And maybe the glasses make you seem more foreign. When I can see your eyes, it's almost like you're a person. I can almost believe you have a heart," Aiden replied.

"Your inability to see me as I am is your problem, not mine," Alexis said coldly.

Carley didn't blame her. She could count the number of times similar words left her own mouth with the same venomous tone when she defended her sexuality. Carley shouldn't have to justify her lifestyle and neither should Alexis.

"Cut the crap, Aiden. If that's what she needs to survive, let her have them."

Aiden shrugged and stayed silent. Carley was glad he didn't push the subject. She wasn't in the mood to pull out her soapbox.

"Son of a bitch," Alexis said quietly.

The tone in her voice immediately worried Carley. She looked to Alexis and the expression on her face wasn't reassuring.

"What?" Carley asked.

"The killer is at Power," Alexis said.

"You're sure? Right now?" Aiden said, the urgency in his tone matching Alexis'.

"I'm positive. I don't think triggering my wards was a mistake. He's evaded others. He wants me to know he's there. I have to go. Now," Alexis replied.

"You can't go out in public looking like you were in a fight. As cops, Carley and I will have to ask you about it," Aiden said.

"Here. Take my necklace," Krysta said. "My mother filled it with glamour charms. It will project the appearance you think of." The elf unclasped the simple chain around her neck. An emerald stone hung from it.

Krysta transferred the necklace and a cold stab of fear cinched Carley's stomach. "Are you going to be able to fight in your condition? You just took on a hotel full of vampires."

Carley felt the weight of Alexis' gaze. "There isn't a choice."

Before Carley could reply, Alexis dissolved into shadows. It was strange to see in a fully lit room. Alexis was a wispy cloud of darkness that vanished entirely a moment later.

"Fuck," Carley muttered.

"She'll beat him, shrimp. She's got a will of iron," Krysta said.

"I wouldn't be so sure," Aiden said quietly.

"You still underestimate her, hunter," Krysta countered.

"You underestimate what she's up against. Alexis is at a strong disadvantage. She's tired from a previous fight and this killer wields blood magic."

"Oh shit. Even if I had stitched the wounds, it wouldn't matter. He can pull from her," Krysta said.

"Yes, and he will have the same physical attributes as she does," Aiden said.

"Well, then we should get our asses in gear," Carley said as she pushed off the stretcher.

Aiden put a hand on her shoulder. "We should wait twenty minutes. We'll have to explain to Devant how we knew to go there. We will give Alexis that long. After that, we'll get in the car and call Devant on the way over. Then we'll be able to say Alexis called us. There will be more back-up and a cover story."

"She could be dead in twenty minutes," Carley argued. "That asshole creates entire staged murder scenes in less than three."

"Alexis isn't human. He'll have a harder time with her, even injured," Aiden replied.

"I'll take one of her cars and go now. You two cover her from the FDPC end. Your line of work is just as threatening to her as the killer," Krysta said. She grabbed her leather jacket off the bench and ran out of the room.

Carley balled her fists at her sides. "I hate being powerless."

"You just have to be smart with how you use your particular skills. Right now, our strength is steering the FDPC away from her as a suspect," Aiden said gently.

"I feel pretty damn powerless when other people are doing my fighting for me."

"You think this is our fight? This killer wants Alexis. From the beginning, it's been her fight. Humans have just been caught in the crossfire," Aiden countered.

Carley didn't bother to point out if Alexis died, so did she. Aiden would only give her a lecture on how she should have thought of that before accepting a mark, followed by a larger rant about how Alexis was as dangerous as the killer. She wasn't in the mood. His words wouldn't change the situation and she didn't regret the mark.

She conceded Alexis was dangerous, but the demon wasn't a threat to humanity. Carley felt enough of Alexis' emotions to believe she wasn't evil. Evil didn't regret, and it wasn't sad. In a world she was only beginning to understand,

Alexis seemed to maintain her independence with little loss of human lives. Carley refused to condemn the woman just because of her race.

So, to vent her anxiety, she paced and tried to reach down the mark again. But Alexis was either too far away or blocking her. Carley could only feel she was still alive with her injuries. The hands on her watch seemed stationary. Twenty minutes was a long time to sit with the knowledge they might be the last minutes of her life.

CHAPTER TWENTY-TWO

Alexis rematerialized in the darkness of an alley a block away from Power. She tried to force patience into her steps, but her feet hurried despite restraint. She kept a steady image in her mind of what she looked like without bruises and stab wounds. Krysta's pendant quietly resonated as it projected the image onto her skin. As the bouncers let her past the front doors, her heart plummeted. The killer's presence vanished from her senses, and her wards no longer tracked him. In that moment, Alexis knew she was no longer looking for a fight... but rather a corpse.

She would have preferred the fight, despite her current condition. In the foyer, she began to silently account for her employees. The two responsible for ticketing and entry were at their stations. Rose covered the coat check, which meant Liz was on break. Alexis pushed through the line into the main dance room. Nothing seemed out of place, which made her all the more apprehensive. The dance floor was loud and full. The correct number of bouncers and bartenders circulated and served drinks, but a dark feeling twisted in Alexis' mind.

She wove through the crowd to the lounge and scanned the area. Candice manned the bar and the bouncer assigned to the room roamed properly. Genuine concern crept into the corners of her heart. Aiden said the killer would escalate and take someone closer to home. Liz wasn't at the bar chatting with Candice, which was how she typically spent her breaks.

With a frown, Alexis turned and checked the bathrooms. They were filled with patrons using them for their intended purpose. She received dirty looks and a few obscene comments in the men's room, but she ignored them. Worry had grown to a pulsing throb in her body. Liz wasn't there.

Alexis checked both offices and the storage room only to come up empty handed. She hoped for an innocent reason for Liz's absence but knew hope would only make it worse later. She returned to the coat check and Rose smiled at her.

"Hi there, Ms. Montral."

"Hey, Rose. Have you seen Liz?"

"Yeah. She went on break a few minutes ago. She said she was going to make a call out back. I hear she might have a new boy. After what the poor thing has been through, she deserves someone who will treat her right," Rose replied.

Alexis' frown deepened. She had warned Liz and the entire staff not to go anywhere alone.

"Thanks," Alexis replied.

She cut through the crowd again to the back door beside the bar. As always, there was a bouncer guarding it. She had to lean into his ear so he could hear her over the music.

"Rick, did Liz go out there?"

"Yeah," he replied.

"She went out alone?" Alexis said. She didn't bother to hide her irritated disbelief.

Rick narrowed his gaze. "Yeah, why? You know that alley is closed off at both ends. It's safe."

Any hope Alexis had for Liz's life was extinguished. She closed her eyes for a moment to prepare herself for what would be on the other side of the door.

"I gave you the safety briefing from the FDPC for a reason. It's the bloody FPDC. Whatever is out there doesn't bow to the laws of physics the way us mere mortals do. Step aside, please. I need to check on her," Alexis replied.

Rick's face paled. "If that's what you're worried about, you stay here. I'll go get her."

"I don't plan on going out there. You aren't, either. The FPDC was clear this creature can't be stopped by any one man. You're bigger than me. I need you to block the club's view of the doors. I don't want panicked guests. If Liz is out there, I will call her back."

Understanding flashed in Rick's features and he positioned his body to block the view of the alley Alexis would create when she cracked the door. She wanted to hesitate, as if time could ensure Liz would be smiling on the other side. But she forced herself to open the door just wide enough to see.

The view twisted her stomach painfully. There was blood everywhere. It splattered the walls and formed large puddles on the ground. The killer hadn't solidified any of it. It fell in rivers. Mangled organs and body parts littered the ground aimlessly. If she stepped into the alley, her boots would be covered in meat. The killer had left only one recognizable piece of Liz. Her severed head sat neatly on the floor. Lifeless eyes stared directly at Alexis.

She'd handled her share of gruesome deaths, even committed them herself earlier that night. But it was always different when the bits and pieces left used to belong to a friend. Alexis had chosen to protect Liz. Those empty eyes rightfully accused her of abandonment. The killer's symbolism was not lost.

Alexis didn't have to worry about committing the scene to memory. The image was already burned into her mind. It wasn't something she would ever forget. This time, he hadn't left a written message. As she stared at Liz's empty face, anger for the killer was almost as potent as the guilt. Liz would be the last. She promised herself this killer would share the same fate he'd condemned someone so innocent to. Alexis closed the door softly and locked it.

She turned to Rick and he glanced over his shoulder at her. "What's back there, Alexis?"

Alexis let the grief show in her face. "What's left of Liz. I need you to get Dan and Brian over here with you. This door is not to open for any reason. None. Then, I need you to get on the radio and get our exits secured. I'll call the FDPC and address the club."

Rick nodded grimly. "I should have…"

Alexis didn't let him finish. She needed him to hold together. He was one of her strongest bouncers. "Don't do that. We still need to help her by preserving what happened and protecting the rest of the people here. The FDPC said the killer won't attack groups, so we have to stick together. Two people doesn't define a group and he could have slaughtered you just as easily. Keep what you know to yourself. We can't let panic swarm the club. Liz still needs you."

Rick frowned but nodded again and got on the radio. Alexis stepped away from him and into a corner behind the bar. She grabbed the wireless phone that was kept by the register and dialed Aiden's number, silently grateful to her past self for committing it to memory. He picked up on the first ring. Alexis pressed one hand to her opposite ear to try and drown out the music of the club.

"Thompson."

"It's Alexis," she replied.

"Are you okay?" he asked immediately.

It surprised Alexis that he asked the question at all. "I'm fine, thank you. But there is a body. I am locking down the club."

"If the body is inside, you need to evacuate," Aiden replied.

"The body is in an alley behind the club. The killer isn't inside. I've searched and I don't feel him, but I don't know if he is outside lurking," Alexis replied.

"Alright. Keep everyone inside until we can get our armed units there. Shouldn't be more than twenty minutes," Aiden said before he disconnected.

Alexis put the phone back into the charging station and went to her office to pick up a radio. She slipped an earpiece on and listened to the chatter for a moment and absorbed the general state of emotion in her employees. She then chimed in and began to issue orders, keeping her tone compassionate but firm and authoritative. Scared individuals enjoyed having others in charge. They liked having assigned tasks to keep them busy. Hard decisions were not up to them, and it often gave comfort.

She filled the role easily. No more customers were to be admitted and every exit was to be guarded by two staff members. Those who remained were assigned to positions that would help serve and calm irritated or frightened guests. There would be lots to handle when she finished speaking to them.

Alexis waded through the crowd again to the music booth. The DJ handed her a microphone before he turned off the music and raised the house lights. There was a roar of disapproval from the crowd. Alexis switched on the microphone.

"Ladies and gentleman, I need your full attention, please. If you will settle down." Alexis paused to let silence fall over the crowd. "My name is Alexis Montral and I am the owner of Power. A crime has been committed on the property. The police will be here shortly and they have asked for your patience and cooperation. You are safe, but the police have requested no one enter or leave the building. No more alcohol will be served, but water, juice, and any food you require are on the house. My staff is in place to help you. Thank you for your understanding and your cooperation."

Alexis turned off the microphone and handed it back to the DJ even as the patrons began to call out questions. Answering them wouldn't help ensure peace and stability. As it was, there were already a few deviants headed toward her bouncers. Rumors began to spread like wildfire between both the staff and guests. The radio was filled with them. Alexis tuned them out and spent the endless minutes waiting for the FDPC by helping to manage the more difficult customers and running for supplies from the storage rooms.

A tap on her shoulder pushed Alexis to quickly distribute the sodas she had been carrying. She turned to find Candice standing before her.

"Hey. Can I talk to you for a minute?"

"My office. We can't take long, though. We are both needed out here."

She led Candice to her office and opened the door. When she stepped inside, Alexis followed and closed the door behind them. Alexis leaned back against it and folded her arms across her chest. She knew what was coming. Candice and Liz had been close. She'd no doubt noticed Liz's absence. Alexis tried to make herself feel marginally better by telling herself it would be best if she heard it from her and not the FDPC.

"I can't find Liz. I've looked everywhere. She was here earlier," Candice said as she slipped her hands in her pockets.

Guilt pulsed in Alexis' chest. She replied softly. "Liz is gone. She was murdered in the back alley."

She watched the mix of emotions play across the bartender's features as they paled. Candice brought a shaky hand to cover her mouth and she pushed off the door to guide her to a seat in front of the desk. Alexis crouched in front of her and offered a box of tissues from the desk. The tears had started, though Alexis wasn't sure Candice was aware of them.

"Are you sure it's her?" Candice asked as she looked down.

"I really wish I wasn't. I'm sorry," Alexis replied morosely.

She drew a deep, sniffling breath and let it out slowly before accepting the box of tissues. Her makeup began to run with her tears. "I'm sorry, too. I know you did things for her no one here knows about. She told me."

Alexis sighed and sat back on her heels. There was no way to explain her guilt to Candice. "I was as close as she would let me be. Liz needed patience."

Candice dabbed her eyes and shook her head. "Ain't that the truth. You're a stronger woman than I am. I'm going to need this whole box."

Alexis winced. "I'm not stronger. I've just seen death often in my life, enough to know there is only one thing I can do to help her now."

"What's that?"

"Protect her body for the police so they can find the thing doing this. I can make sure no one else gets hurt. Then, when I am home, I can ruin my makeup, too."

Candice looked up at Alexis. A false smile touched her lips. "You don't wear makeup."

Alexis smiled sadly. "A lady never tells."

Candice nodded and looked down at the tissues in her lap. "I guess it's just easy to forget the dead need help when you're thinking of your own pain."

"I suppose. I'm also the manager, so the safety of everyone else here is my responsibility. I've found responsibility often silences emotion."

"I don't envy you that."

"I'll get my time later, and I like it that way."

"Just don't forget you're allowed to be human, too. You're not a machine, Alexis," Candice said as she lifted a tissue to carefully dab around her eye.

The irony almost made Alexis laugh bitterly. Instead, she merely nodded and leaned back against the desk. "I know."

The radio chirped in Alexis' ear. Aiden had arrived. Alexis patted Candice's knee before rising.

"The FDPC is here. We need to go make appearances."

"This is related to the safety briefing you gave us?" Candice asked, the first hints of fear fluttering in her gaze as she quickly looked up.

"Unfortunately. Don't go anywhere alone. I mean it. That's why Liz died. She went into the back alley by herself," Alexis replied.

Candice swallowed once. "I won't. I promise."

With a satisfied nod, Alexis turned and opened the door. There was no point in sharing her belief Liz would have died whether she was alone or not. Anyone who went with her only would have made a bigger mess.

Alexis walked with Candice back to the main dance room. She went to assist customers and Alexis went in search of Aiden and Carley. The FDPC had begun to systematically remove everyone from the club. Lines were forming and armed officers had replaced her bouncers at all the exits. Alexis found the detectives near the front supervising the evacuation.

"Good evening, Detectives. Thank you for coming so quickly," Alexis said.

"Hello, Ms. Montral. We are going to have to ask you to fall in line with everyone else. Once we secure the scene and get a look at the body, we will start interviews," Carley replied.

Carley's tone was professional but she saw the worry in her eyes, felt the concern pulsing through her. Alexis began to heavily shield against everything, including her mark. The technicians would bring in their machines soon. Alexis hoped Aiden knew to keep Carley away from them. There hadn't been time to explore whatever power she had, let alone teach her how to shield.

Alexis nodded to them both. "Of course."

With the scene officially out of her hands, she fell in line. Outside, the club was just as loud as the inside. The FDPC blocked off the street. There were heavily armed officers up and down the road. Several ambulances and trucks of FDPC technicians were spread out in front. Medical personnel handed out blankets and water. Alexis was grateful she didn't spot any treating serious injuries. The murder alone would bring negative press.

With nothing to do but wait, she leaned her back against the brick wall of the club and watched the FDPC usher equipment inside. Movement caught her attention and Alexis turned to see Krysta walking on the sidewalk toward her. She had her hood up and head down, but Krysta was hard to miss regardless of the effort she put into blending in.

Alexis frowned. It was risky for her to be at Power without the glamour pendant. There were a significant number of police trained to pick anything out of the ordinary from a crowd. Krysta's size alone drew attention.

The woman was entirely too stubborn for her own good. Whatever she wanted to pass on could easily have waited until later. In an effort to help her get off the street faster, Alexis looked beyond her for a reason to walk in that direction. Candice sat alone on the curb with a blanket draped over her shoulders. Alexis pushed off the wall and started to cover the distance.

She and Krysta had worked together often enough that much of their communication was non-verbal. As they passed each other, Alexis slightly turned her hips to bring her pockets closer to Krysta's hand. The object slid into her back pocket effortlessly as they continued in opposite directions. Alexis didn't look back and knew Krysta wouldn't, either.

She stopped near Candice and sat down beside her. "How are you holding up?"

"Alright. The police have been nice. An officer brought me a blanket and took my statement. He said he didn't think it would be too much longer before the detectives would let us go home."

"The detectives are kind and efficient. When they release us, I want you to find others who live near you and go home in groups. Don't worry about who stays behind to lock up. The club will be in police custody for a while."

"Okay. I'll start spreading the word."

"Thanks. Everyone's paycheck will stay the same while Power is closed. I'll make sure the bartenders are compensated for the loss of tips," Alexis said.

Candice hugged the blanket closer to her chest. "I know all of us appreciate that. I am going to try to organize something for Liz. I don't think she had any family here. I've no idea who will take care of her funeral."

"I've been wondering the same. The police may be able to find any family in Scotland she had. We won't know anything until they are done. If there is no one, I will take care of the arrangements," Alexis replied softly.

"I am sure there are lots of us who want to help. You wouldn't have to do it alone," Candice said.

Alexis smiled sadly. "We will cross that bridge if we get to it."

"What about you? Are you going home alone?" Candice asked with a knowing gaze.

The lie slid effortlessly off Alexis' tongue. "No. I have friends who have been staying with me and the police will escort me home."

Candice's eyes shifted to something behind Alexis. They widened with recognition just before Alexis felt Carley's presence close in.

"Excuse me, Ms. Montral."

Alexis glanced over her shoulder to see Aiden and Carley waiting. Candice had recognized Aiden. One of the reasons she was a good bartender was she remembered names and faces. Alexis wasn't sure whether the recognition was a good or bad thing, but it was certainly something she would have to deal with later. Candice would ask her about it. She looked back and gave Candice a sad smile.

"I have to go."

When Candice disappeared into the crowd, Alexis turned to face Aiden and Carley. "I wish we could stop meeting like this."

"So do I. At this point, we know his methodology. We just have a few questions and everyone can go home," Aiden said.

"Whatever I can do to help," Alexis replied.

"About what time did you get to the club?" Aiden asked.

"I think it was around two-thirty. I could be wrong, though. I wasn't looking at the time."

"Do you personally manage the club?" Carley asked.

"I have my hands in quite a bit of it. I enjoy it. I'm involved in the hiring, human resources, and even inventory. But I also have three managers I work closely with. They handle the brunt of operations," Alexis answered.

"Were you the one to find the victim?" Aiden asked.

"I was, yes."

"How did you know to look for her? Several of your employees said you went on a search for her almost as soon as you entered the club," Carley said.

"Since this began, I have gotten into the habit of accounting for my people when I visit a business. I noticed Liz was out of her station immediately," Alexis replied.

"By 'Liz,' you mean Elizabeth Camshire?" Aiden asked.

"Correct," Alexis said.

"Were you close to her?" Carley asked.

"As close as she would let me. When she first came to work here, she was in a severely abusive marriage. I have been trying to help her find her feet ever since."

"So, you knew her on a more personal level," Aiden inquired.

"Yes. We shared meals and conversation frequently," Alexis answered.

Carley flipped through her notebook. "Her name is on the list you gave us."

Alexis nodded solemnly. "It was. I even spoke with her personally about it. I thought to offer her my home to stay in for a while, but knowing you believed I was his actual target, I thought that would be just as dangerous for her. I spoke with her at length about the precautions you gave me."

Carley's knowing gaze bore into Alexis. "The killer found a way even among a busy crowd. There wasn't anything you could have done."

Alexis understood what Carley was trying to convey, but she rarely indulged in comforting lies. There was more she could have done.

"He is escalating. It is likely you or someone just as close to you is the next target. Can you reprioritize the list you gave us?" Aiden asked.

"Candice Brown. She is a bartender here. I was just speaking with her. Mark Harrison. He is my secretary. Lydia Cardone. I have business dinners with her on a regular basis and enjoy her company. Those are the top three that come to mind. I will go back through the list and email it to you," Alexis replied.

Carley scribbled the names down in her notepad. "Alright. That will help us focus our targets and try to lay traps for this thing. I think that's all we need from you tonight. I'm sorry for your loss."

Alexis nodded and lowered her gaze. "Would you guys find out if Liz had any family? She never spoke of any, but I've seen a picture here and there in her apartment. I think they still live in Scotland. It's important to me and the other people who work here."

"We will see what we can find and let you know," Aiden replied, studying Alexis carefully.

"I appreciate that, thank you."

"Do you need an escort home?" Carley asked.

"No, I'll be fine. A friend is waiting for me. Goodnight, Detectives," Alexis said.

They both nodded and Alexis left them to walk down the sidewalk that led to the garage where she typically parked. Her response to Aiden brought Krysta to mind. She reached into her back pocket for the object Krysta had passed to her. It was the key to her Lamborghini. Krysta must have put the car in the garage. That one move made up for her behavior in the medical room, though Alexis was still irritated she'd taken the risk to pass the key when she could have sat in the car and called. On the other hand, there was still one thing that needed doing and Alexis wanted to do it alone.

She found the Lamborghini in a reserved spot on the first floor of the garage. She slipped inside and as she drove to Liz's apartment, the rush of the events at Power began to fade. Alexis felt the weight of her injuries, the drain on her power, and the guilt that twisted her heart. She'd scored no victories that night, only forged new enemies and lost innocent friends.

She pulled into the drop-off lane in front of the apartment building. Edward was at his post at the door. Alexis had worn through her patience for social interactions. Edward didn't deserve rudeness, though. She stepped out of the car, but left it running.

"Hey, Edward. Do you mind keeping an eye on that for me? I'll only be a few minutes."

"Not a problem, Ms. Montral. Long night?"

Alexis nodded and replied softly. "Yeah."

"Miss Camshire isn't home right now, if you're looking for her," he replied.

Alexis lowered her gaze and paused. "She's gone, Edward. She won't be coming home anymore."

Surprised understanding flashed in his features, followed by sympathy and sadness. "I'm so very sorry. She was a beautiful person."

Alexis merely nodded and headed inside. She didn't want to answer any questions, despite her belief Edward would be kind. She had a feeling Edward knew more of grief than most people.

She took the stairs to the sixth floor, needing time to prepare herself for Liz's apartment. The space would forever be a reminder of her failure. If she couldn't keep Liz safe, it was almost comical to believe she could protect Carley. Self-pity was unproductive, but she intended to wallow in it for a night.

The climb made her body ache all the more, but Alexis finished it anyway. She knew some of the dressings on her injuries would need changing when she got home. Exhaustion tugged at every corner of her being. She pulled herself up the last stair and pushed through the door. At the end of the hallway was a potted plant where Liz hid a key. Alexis had warned her against it, but at the moment, she was grateful. She didn't want to have to break into the apartment by shadow melding. What she wanted couldn't meld back out with her.

Alexis pushed the key into the lock and stepped inside. The door softly shut behind her. She left the lights off. She didn't need them to navigate and the darkness was comforting. She made her way to the living room and looked around. The silence was profound, as if the space knew Liz would not return.

Alexis sat down on the couch and let her gaze roam over the canvases on the walls, the furniture that still carried Liz's scent, and the mug full of cold, forgotten tea. Surrounded by Liz's belongings, Alexis reminded herself why she never took in strays, especially humans. They were always broken and fragile. Their deaths always hurt.

She turned her attention to the pair of soft, dark eyes watching her quietly. Hope's nose nudged the door of her crate gently. Alexis loathed dogs. Her first encounter with the species hadn't been pleasant. Ever since, dogs had seemed like inconvenient, slobbering disasters waiting to happen. But she reached out and opened the crate door.

Hope yawned and padded clumsily out and flopped down at Alexis' feet, tail slowly swishing across the carpet. Alexis could take Hope to a shelter, but the dog would likely share Liz's fate. She owed Liz's memory. The least she could do was make sure something that had given Liz so much happiness had a good life. Alexis reached down and ran her fingers through Hope's fur. The puppy wiggled onto her back and exposed her belly. Despite her mood, Alexis smiled and indulged the puppy.

"You're going to have a new home. It's not going to be as nice as this one, but we will make it work."

Alexis stood and ushered the puppy back into the crate. Hope expressed her displeasure with a quiet, pouty whimper. She closed the door and lifted the crate by the handle on top. It was small enough to manage without being awkward, but Hope would quickly grow out of it.

Alexis carried the dog to the door and set the crate out in the hall. She held the door open as she looked back into the haunting silence one last time.

"I'm sorry, Elizabeth. For everything," she whispered.

The door fell softly shut, ending Liz's chapter in Alexis' life.

CHAPTER TWENTY-THREE

Alexis sighed as her gaze shifted between three different displays projecting images of the crime scenes. She'd been staring at them for hours in search of anything that tied them together. There were bits and pieces linking the first two, but the third made no sense. If her wards hadn't assured it was the same killer, she would have believed there was a copycat. As it stood, the only thing connecting all three was her. And yet, she knew everything needed to find the killer was right in front of her. She just couldn't make sense of it.

Alexis shook her head and removed her glasses to rub her eyes. "I'm missing something. He's here but I can't see him."

"Welcome to detective work," Carley replied miserably as she threw her pen on an open file folder.

"I certainly don't envy your profession," Alexis said.

"You're sure there isn't anything else in the messages? Could you have made a mistake translating?" Aiden asked.

She slipped her glasses back on and pulled the page containing the messages from the file in her lap. Alexis read through them again. It wasn't like there was a way to confirm it. They couldn't exactly go to a library and pick up a Demonic to English dictionary.

"It's possible, I suppose, but I don't think so. The messages are cryptic, but not difficult. I don't find myself second guessing when reading."

"And you're positive you don't know the killer?" Aiden pressed, leaning back against the couch to study her closer.

"I'm positive I don't know him *now*," Alexis replied. "I have no memory of this person, so I've not encountered him in, at least, several hundred years. I've mentioned before there is a point where my memory just stops."

"So, all we're missing is what you can't remember," Carley said miserably.

"Unfortunately. Before you ask, there is no spontaneous chance I'll remember. It also can't be retrieved by other means," Alexis said.

"How do you know for sure?" Carley asked, curiously.

"I told you I had someone who specializes in psychic magic look into it. The memories literally don't exist anymore. There is a vacancy, a scar."

"And you're just... okay with that?" Aiden said in a critical tone.

"I've had to learn to be okay with it," Alexis replied. "There is no getting it back, and this is the first time in more than five hundred years there has been any sign I have a history further back than the Spanish Inquisition. I've worked very hard to accept something I can't change and move on."

Aiden raised an eyebrow. Alexis was in no mood to be studied and there was an intensity to his gaze she couldn't quite read. Her wounds from the battle with Le'Roe had healed, but emotional wounds, like Liz's death, always lingered.

She returned her attention to the screens. Something soft and warm brushed against her leg and she glanced down to find Hope, tail swishing back and forth with poorly contained happiness. Sweet, pleading chocolate eyes looked up as the puppy set a rather slimy looking tennis ball at her feet.

"Why do you insist on bringing me that? It's your toy. I said you could keep it," Alexis asked the dog.

Carley laughed. "Aww, come on. She's a puppy. She just wants you to play with her."

"It's covered in slobber," Alexis replied with disgust. Hope whined softly and nudged the ball with her nose.

"Just throw the damned thing," Aiden said before returning his attention to the file in his lap. "A little dog slobber never hurt anyone. You're going to make a terrible owner. Why did you even take her?"

Alexis let the question hang in the air. She'd let her distaste for dogs as a species affect how she treated Hope. The puppy hadn't proven to be a large inconvenience, nor was she an ill-behaved terror. There were certainly areas for improvement, but she was young and Alexis hadn't bothered to take time to train her. She had to do better, to remember the reason she'd taken the dog to begin with.

Alexis reached down to pick up the ball. The puppy's entire body wiggled with excitement and, when she whimpered, Alexis was forced to admit Hope was adorable. She threw the ball down the hallway and watched as the dog scampered after it as fast as her inexperienced, awkward legs could carry her.

With the puppy momentarily occupied, Alexis wiped her hand on her pants and returned her attention to the display screens. She leaned back in her chair and studied the images for the second scene. Absently, she took her pendant from her chest and spun it slowly between her fingertips, an old and unconscious habit.

The crescent moons had to mean something if the killer had taken the time to paint the elevator with them. Perhaps his magic was tied to the moon. She shook her head and tossed the idea to the side. He had committed murder in broad daylight, and it was a full moon on the horizon, not a crescent. Aiden and Carley hadn't had luck linking blood magic to moons, though they'd found evidence in their database for moons and invisibility.

Alexis returned to the idea of moons and the shape of the body in the first scene. Something told her they were the key. The messages were taunts and hints to something the shapes of the two scenes were supposed to reveal.

She used the tablet in her lap to switch the images on the screen to the first murder. The body was in a distinct shape, but it matched nothing familiar. She supposed it could be a symbolic representation of the sun or a star, but neither she nor the killer had power born from the star.

Alexis sighed again and went back to the messages themselves. Dead bodies shouldn't have been required for a conversation. She possessed several phones, offices, and a front door. She continued to twist her pendant between her fingertips and the texture finally drew her gaze to it. As she studied the pendant, an idea formed. Alexis pulled a hard copy of a photograph of the arrangement of limbs in the first scene. The body could be a crude, primitive copy of her pendant. Her stone was blue, but human blood couldn't match that color. The killer had done his best with his chosen materials. He'd made a flesh snowflake.

Assuming they were the same race, it was possible the killer possessed a necklace like hers. Perhaps his pendant was in the shape of the crescent moon. The theory didn't change much. Alexis had no idea how the pendants were linked. Hers was bound to her magic, but she had never been able to figure out its purpose. As she pondered the theory further, Alexis studied the jewelry and brushed her thumb across the stone.

Her vision wavered. The room around her became blurry just before it disappeared entirely. Alexis froze as she felt the killer's power link with hers. It wasn't a deep connection, but strong enough to make her nervous. He didn't share her uncertainty. He pushed himself further into the link, and her vision bloomed to life. It wasn't her living room she saw, but a dark warehouse. Storage containers and file cabinets were neatly stacked in rows, which created a small network of hallways. When deep, smooth laughter filled her ears, Alexis realized she was seeing through the killer's eyes.

There you are. Finally.

He spoke in the language of the messages. Alexis understood him effortlessly but was still caught off guard. She had never heard it spoken before. It occurred to her he probably didn't speak English. The killer had demonstrated no respect for humanity, so there was no reason for him to learn.

She was about to reply before a thought stopped her. If she could see through his eyes, then it was probable he could see through hers. She didn't like the idea of giving him a prime view of her living space. It put her security and Aiden and Carley at risk. She knew where he was, and felt it pleased him. Further conversation would only tempt her curiosity and put herself and others at risk. Without a solid understanding of how the spell worked, Alexis fell back on the method that severed almost all connections. Shielding.

Wait! Don't! Please!

She paid him no mind. Alexis yanked her power back and threw up her strongest shields. She squeezed his power off hers, inch by frustrating inch. He struggled and dug claws of his own power into her walls as he tried to climb his way back in. Alexis didn't panic at his resistance. She merely added layer after layer of power until she overwhelmed him and he lost his grip. She instantly sealed the final gap so he couldn't slip back in. The killer's power retreated and so did the image of the warehouse.

For several moments, Alexis' vision swam. Colors, shapes, and depths weaved in and out of one another. It left her mildly disoriented. But it wasn't long until her living room reformed and she saw Carley and Aiden kneeling beside her. Only then did she register the detectives calling her name.

"I'm here," Alexis said, slightly breathless.

"What just happened? You were fine and then all of a sudden you zoned out and shielded like you expected to get hit by a tank," Aiden replied.

Alexis sighed and nodded. "I'm okay. I think I just accidentally made a connection with the killer. I know where he is."

"What? How?" Carley asked.

"I think it was through my pendant," Alexis answered as she looked down to study the piece. It was warm and shadows swirled through the cerulean stone.

Carley raised a skeptical eyebrow. "The necklace. You talked to our guy through a piece of jewelry?"

"Don't look so surprised," Alexis replied and let the pendant drop against her chest. "I'm sure you've come across objects of power in your work. My pendant is such an object. I've just never known what it does. All I knew was that I can't take it off."

"What happens if you try?" Aiden asked quietly.

Alexis gave him a demonstration. "This is the first time I've seen it do anything other than that. It leads me to believe it's a tool for communication, but I'm still not entirely sure how it works. I must have activated it by accident. I think the killer has been using these murders as a way to ask me to call him."

"Couldn't he have looked you up in the fucking phone book?" Carley said.

"I'm not condoning. I'm theorizing. Right before the connection was made, I was wondering why he didn't just call me with technology. I would have much preferred it," Alexis replied.

"So, what makes you think that's what he's doing and it's the pendant he wanted you to use?" Aiden asked as he studied the necklace against her chest.

Alexis pointed to a display screen depicting the first murder victim. "To start, I was thinking of him, the pendant, and communication when the connection triggered. Look at the arrangement of the body in that scene. It's the shape of my pendant. We are the same race, so I thought he might have a pendant, too. Perhaps his is in the shape of the crescent moon from the second murder. Even the messages he left behind fit if you think about it this way."

"Perhaps, but that doesn't explain the third. There was no message. Just a mess," Carley observed.

Alexis sighed and leaned back in her chair. "True. The third doesn't fit, but we know it wasn't a copycat. Aiden, you felt it. I know you have no experience with what power feels like, Carley, but it's a very individualized and unique thing. As unreliable as your police machines are, they picked up the same signal at all three scenes. Do we really need to explain the third murder?"

"A very valid point. Even if there was a copycat, he still committed the first two murders. That's enough to warrant his death. I hate to break it to you, partner, but your life is about to become very outside the book," Aiden said.

Carley lowered her gaze for a moment as she pondered the information. "Alright. We go kill him, then. You said you know where he is?"

"He's in one of my storage warehouses downtown," Alexis answered. "It doesn't contain anything of value, just old tax information and other business documents I can't throw away for however many years. The building isn't worth the energy to ward and has minimal security. It's a good place to hide."

"Do you keep staff there?" Aiden asked immediately.

Alexis shook her head. "The only ones who have access are those who deal with those documents in accounting. They only stop by to deposit paperwork. He is alone, but that doesn't mean he will stay there. If we delay too long, we could lose him."

"Agreed, but we can't go without a plan," Carley said.

"We know almost nothing about him," Aiden observed. "We are nowhere near prepared for a hunt."

"We don't have much choice. The addition of my skills boosts your normal arsenal. We know he has blood magic, so we need to avoid bleeding at all costs. His weapon of choice is a blade," Alexis replied.

"I'm open to suggestions," Aiden said. "Assuming he has your superior strength, speed, and durability, I don't see how Carley and I can avoid being cut."

"I'm hoping most of the fighting will be left to me. I'm the one he wants and I'm the one best equipped to handle him. I should be able to keep him busy enough that the two of you can remain on the outskirts for support. But if he does come at you, stay away from the blade," Alexis said. "If you have to take a blunt force hit to avoid being cut, do it. I do have access to armor that protects against some blade strikes, but it won't protect your face and it won't stop a powerful, penetrating blow."

"So, if we were slashed, it's likely we would be okay. But if the asshole stabs us, we're fucked?" Carley said.

"Essentially. Military technology has come a long way, but developing strong, lightweight armor is still challenging."

"I'm not going to ask how you have access to military grade armor," Aiden said. "I'm just going to be grateful. But it's still not a solid plan."

Alexis raised an eyebrow. "Did you think killing this demon was going to go smoothly?"

"No, but I thought I might have a cavalry of officers at my back. Our lack of numbers could hurt us. If you are involved, our department can't be. Unless you'd like to surrender yourself to them," Aiden replied.

"I'm not that noble or self-sacrificing. But I can work from the shadows. How fast can an extermination team be mobilized to the warehouse?" Alexis asked.

"Twenty to thirty minutes, depending on traffic," Carley answered. "Fifteen if they bust their ass and get a NYPD escort."

"If we haven't killed him in fifteen minutes, one or all of us will likely be dead. I travel much faster than you. I'll get there and get started. You guys will have to drive. Call your back-up as you're pulling in. The timer starts then. With any luck, he'll be dead before you get there. If he isn't by the time the cavalry comes, I'll improvise," Alexis said.

Aiden sat back on his heels and looked at Carley. She raised a shoulder in a shrug and nodded. Aiden sighed and looked back to Alexis. "You know if the officers come, they will target you, too. You can't kill them, Alexis. You know this." Aiden's tone took on weight.

Alexis understood his desire to protect his comrades, but she had no reason to care about their well-being. They still hindered her daily life, even if she now found herself in the company of two unique officers. But she also knew she wouldn't be able to get either one of them moving unless she promised something.

"I have no intention of ever being seen by your officers. Should the need arise, I'll use non-lethal force and fear tactics. But I won't stand there and let them kill me."

"That's the best I'm going to get, isn't it?" Aiden asked.

"I refuse to die for someone who hates me. They're not the noble, selfless creatures you believe them to be and I don't share your misplaced loyalty or lack of self-preservation."

Aiden frowned for a moment but eventually nodded. "Alright. Let's see this armor, then."

Alexis rose from her chair. "Shut everything down and close the file, Terry."

"Certainly," the computer replied. The display screens turned black and receded into the ceiling.

Alexis walked to the large crate in the corner and called to Hope. The puppy came running, slobbery tennis ball in tow. Alexis opened the crate door. "In you go."

The puppy's tail lowered, her expression full of pout, but she trotted into the crate. Alexis shook her head and walked to the elevator.

"You'd think it was the end of the world."

Carley smirked. "Get used to it. Those sad, puppy dog eyes are going to plague you every time you shut a door."

"Thankfully, I'm immune to most guilt trips," Alexis said dryly.

The elevator doors opened, and everyone stepped inside. Alexis manually entered the floor. She still didn't trust either of them with the details of her building. It would take more than surviving one hunt together for her to share her personal life.

Thoughts of Carley made her aware of their bond. As the elevator moved, Carley's heart rate slowly rose. Alexis knew it was anxiety. Fear before a fight was a good, natural thing. It would keep her sharp and alert. Alexis had every intention of using that connection to keep a close eye on her.

Alexis had anticipated having to face her opponent alone. If everything went according to plan, she still would, but uncertainty skittered inside her mind. The demon knew things about her, things she was supposed to know. She had convinced herself the past didn't matter. But, after hundreds of years, it was finally within her grasp. This killer knew who she really was. He knew where she came from.

Despite being happy with her existence, Alexis struggled to contain her curiosity. She needed to resist the temptation. The killer had to die. He was perilously close to destroying all she had worked for. All that really mattered was her life now. She could do nothing about the past, but the desire persisted, despite her attempts to rationalize it away.

The elevator doors opened and Alexis stepped out into the floor that held her armory. She had no intention of showing Aiden the full extent of her arsenal, but she did want him to see enough to show she wasn't above fighting with technology.

Alexis faced a demon who potentially possessed intimate knowledge of her strengths, weaknesses, and fighting style. Aiden was a wild card and she wished she could trust his priorities. The uncertainty reinforced her need to have the killer dead before the detectives got there.

Once everyone was out of the elevator, Alexis led them down a white, sterile hallway with harsh, fluorescent lighting. It wasn't a floor she lived on. There was no need for decoration or comforts. She turned to the first room on the right. Its door was as plain as the hallway but had both a hand and ocular scanner for security. She removed her glasses long enough for the scanners to register both her eye and her hand. With a loud tone, the door unlocked, and she pushed inside.

The back wall was lined with massive cabinets designed to store clothing, but they rested behind a wall made of chain-link extending from floor to ceiling. The only break was a padlocked door. The left and right walls held sets of black lockers. A wooden bench rested in front of each set.

"Is this your version of a panic room?" Carley asked as she studied the area.

"That's next door," Alexis replied and pulled a key from her pocket to unlock the cage door.

She stepped inside and opened the second cabinet on the left. The top half contained several racks of hangers holding black long-sleeved shirts of different sizes. The bottom was a series of drawers containing pants of the same color. The garments were an experiment in textile technology, but she had put them to the test enough times to be confident.

Alexis pulled the top drawer open and selected a pair of pants and a shirt. "Take one of each in your size. They're supposed to be tight and worn under your clothing." She stepped out of the way to let Aiden and Carley pass.

Carley picked out a pair of pants and studied them with obvious skepticism. "Great. We're going to fight demons in yoga pants."

Alexis rolled her eyes and opened the locker. She kept some of her own things there for situations like the present. A pair of black military combat pants, a black turtleneck, and a pair of combat boots lived inside. She quickly slipped out of her clothing and into the armor. The combat pants were next, followed by the sweater. Aiden and Carley found their own spots on the bench and began to dress in the armor.

"So, for real, this feels flimsy as shit. Like those moisture-wicking shirts I wear to the gym," Carley said.

Alexis smirked and finished tying the laces on her boots. Without warning, she turned into Carley and shoved her back against the lockers, forearm pressed into her chest to keep her still. At the same time, one of her daggers materialized into her second hand and she slashed Carley's midsection before Aiden ever heard Carley's body hit the lockers. She didn't add much strength to the slash, only enough to make her point. The shirt didn't tear.

Carley's pulse pounded in her ears. Alexis kept her gaze locked and watched as the detective processed that she couldn't move but wasn't hurt. Her eyes were wide and her chest rose and fell rapidly beneath Alexis' arm. The intensity of her gaze trapped Alexis. In less than a heartbeat, the connection between them flared to life. At first, there was fear. But as Carley noticed the feel of Alexis' body, their eye contact lingered, and fear melted into need.

Alexis immediately lowered her arm and stepped back. The blade in her hand disappeared into shadows absorbed by her skin. The last thing she wanted was affection before a fight.

"Holy shit," Carley said breathlessly.

"You could have fucking killed her! What the fuck were you thinking?" Aiden exclaimed.

"The point, Detectives, is that I didn't. The fabric works," Alexis replied calmly.

Carley drew a slow breath and let it out before she looked down at her stomach where the blade had crossed. "Alright. What is this stuff?"

"An experimental synthetic blend. There're some long, scientific names in a report upstairs, but I'm mostly a business woman. What matters is the fabric stops slashing blades and you now have faith in it."

Carley shook her head. "Could have given a girl a little warning."

Alexis shrugged. "Drama is an effective tool."

"No shit," Carley replied.

"Did that dagger just appear and disappear from shadow magic?" Aiden asked carefully.

Alexis turned her gaze to him. His tone had gone flat. It dawned on her he hadn't seen her weapons before. His expression was calculating. Once again, she pondered whether he'd stab her in the back. They'd made progress in understanding each other, and the strange connection between them persisted despite their best efforts. But the look in his eyes reminded her he was a hunter first and an individual second.

"It did, yes," Alexis answered.

"So, you can never truly be disarmed," Aiden persisted as he folded his arms across his chest.

"Not in the sense you are implying."

"What is that supposed to mean?" Aiden asked.

"It means what it means, Detective."

Aiden set his jaw and turned away to finish getting dressed. Alexis closed her locker and locked the cage containing the cabinets. When she turned back around, Aiden and Carley were mostly finished.

"Ready, then?"

"What? No watches with lasers or motorcycles with bombs hardwired into the frame?" Carley joked.

"Maybe next time," Alexis said. "Stick to the plan. Call your back-up. We finish before they get there and you make up whatever story you like."

"Watch yourself. He's already proved cunning," Aiden said.

Alexis smirked. "Your concern is touching, little hunter."

Her body became the shadows and vanished before Aiden could respond. The entire situation left a bad taste in her mouth. There were too many variables, too many unknowns. As she moved through the city unseen, a sense of dread sunk into her stomach. There were very few scenarios where everyone came out intact. Either the killer would die that night, or they all would.

CHAPTER TWENTY-FOUR

Darkness consumed the warehouse. Security lighting was minimal and mostly outside. Small rays from the city wiggled through windows but were quickly swallowed by shadows. Like any other night, the warehouse was empty, but Alexis was well versed in the deception of appearance.

There wasn't an inch of space she couldn't sense. Nothing moved. No traces of power, no unique signatures of energy pulsing in the night. Yet, she knew the killer was there. He stalked her.

With her body as shadows, Alexis gave him no physical target. He had no way of knowing her exact location. But that also meant small fractions of her power were everywhere. She couldn't camouflage it. The killer could sense her. The fact Alexis couldn't sense him in return was troubling.

The only feasible explanation was true invisibility. Neither his body nor his power would leave a trace unless he wished it. The ability perfectly countered any advantage darkness gave her. If she showed herself, she would never sense him coming. But she couldn't wait him out, either. The clock was ticking.

The killer's refusal to step forward was confusing. Alexis had contacted him in the method he wanted and come on his terms. She had a hard time believing he was suddenly shy or didn't sense her presence. Something was off.

Acutely aware of the passing seconds, Alexis pondered how to proceed. She could use herself as bait, manifest in the center of the room and take the chance she was a better fighter than him. But if she died, Carley would die with her and Aiden would walk straight to his death. After weighing the possibilities, Alexis wasn't confident the fight would go in her favor. The smallest nick could be a death sentence.

If she wanted any tactical advantage, she needed to draw him out. That left her using Aiden and Carley as bait instead. There had never been witnesses to his crimes before. It was possible he would move against them. They were armed and posed a threat, even if it was small. But if Alexis was the killer's intended target, he might just sit back and let them roam.

She loathed the idea, either way. One of the detectives would die before she could make her move. If it was Carley, Alexis would be substantially weaker, assuming she survived the breaking of the mark. But she would have Aiden as back-up. It wasn't ideal, but he had more experience, at least. If Aiden died, Alexis would be fully functional but on her own. Carley was better than the average human, but that wasn't saying much.

Alexis knew she had no right to gamble with other people's lives, but if she died, everyone would die. The killer had laid his trap well, and as much as she hated it, using the detectives was the best option. Guilt stabbed at her heart.

The sound of Aiden's car pulled her from her thoughts. Time was up. She stayed in the shadows and traveled outside. Their only advantage was for her to remain hidden. Both detectives stepped out of Aiden's car and Alexis took the opportunity to whisper through the shadows to their ears.

"The plan went south. He possesses genuine invisibility. The only option that doesn't end in all three of us dying is the two of you enter to draw him out. I'll cover your backs. He can't see me either and that is the only break we have. The door code is 102874."

Aiden and Carley glanced at each other. Aiden didn't like it. No doubt, in his mind, the potential for her betrayal was larger than he wanted to risk. But there were no words of reassurance he would believe. After a moment, he nodded once to Carley and drew a lighter from his pocket.

"Alright, this is going to be different than any training simulations or exterminations you've ever been on. Back-up is on the way, but we want him dead before they get here. We don't know what power you have yet, so your gun will be your only defense. Shoot to kill. However, your power could still manifest if you're in danger. So, take a deep breath and remember that it could save your life."

As he spoke, Carley drew her gun and checked the magazine before sliding a bullet into the chamber. She looked back at Aiden and did as he asked, but Alexis felt the anxiety driving her racing pulse.

"How will I know?" Carley asked.

"Right now, you probably won't. But trust yourself. Don't be afraid of something rising up inside of you. If something seems wrong, if your stomach tightens and your skin tingles, don't brush it off. Say something or act," Aiden answered.

"You don't have your gun out," Carley noted.

"My other talents are stronger. The gun is my back-up. Let's get moving. We stay together. Splitting up is death."

Carley nodded and they both advanced to the building with practiced, well-trained movements. Alexis' stomach churned with worry for them, especially Carley. But there wasn't time for sentimentalities. Emotion would only make her falter.

Once Aiden and Carley were inside, she assumed the shadows in the rafters of the warehouse. If the killer really was of her race, then blood manipulation and invisibility were his only two magical talents. He was confined to the ground and whatever he could access by climbing. She could see the entire warehouse. Once he made his move, there would be no hiding from her.

* * *

Carley kept close to Aiden's flank, gun at the ready. The warehouse was, predictably, dark. Even though she knew it would be that way, part of her cursed the narrow visual field of her flashlight. She kept it and her gun together, sweeping from side to side as they navigated the spiraling halls of filing cabinets. Carley wouldn't have believed Alexis needed an entire warehouse for Internal Revenue documents if she hadn't been walking through a library of them.

It took genuine effort for her to keep her breathing slow and controlled. Fear was a centipede crawling through her veins. She understood what Alexis hadn't said. The killer could end either one of them with one shot. The old saying of death and taxes resonated in her mind, but she couldn't bring herself to smile at the irony.

Despite her thoughts, Carley's hands were steady as she searched row by row with Aiden. Training kept her weight balanced, but the silence of the warehouse made her steps sound thunderous and clumsy. She pondered why Aiden put more faith in a lighter than a gun.

Her inquisitiveness was quickly buried beneath self-doubt. It wasn't just the demon she feared. Carley didn't know how to direct power or use it in a helpful manner. She was painfully aware she was the weakest link. While she feared death as much as any rational person, the fear of being responsible for Aiden or Alexis' death was greater.

The rows of cabinets and storage containers were endless. They all looked the same, save for identification numbers printed on the front. With the limited light, Carley felt like a rat in a maze. Maintaining her sense of orientation was difficult. The further into the warehouse they advanced, the tighter the noose became. She had walked into traps before, but none had the sense of finality of the current one. If she got out alive, she would count herself lucky. Skill would have nothing to do with it.

They approached an opening to what appeared to be a center point for the warehouse. She estimated the space was fifty feet in diameter. A desk toward the northern side held a closed laptop. There was too much open space, no cover of any kind. A burning in her stomach flared and spread through her body. Her skin tingled, and her heart raced. She stopped advancing and whispered to Aiden, "Something is wrong."

Aiden stopped as well but kept his eyes on the circle. "I know. We'll be sitting ducks."

"You said speak up. I am. If we go in there, it won't end well. I'm sure of it," Carley said.

She believed it. Her instinct had never felt so strong. The thought of stepping forward made her physically queasy and her body felt alive in ways she had never experienced. The killer would make his move there.

"You're probably right, but what choice do we have? Devant is on his way," Aiden replied.

Carley swore softly. She wouldn't make good bait if she refused to wiggle on the hook. She nodded once and advanced a step to signal to Aiden she was begrudgingly ready. He joined her, and they stepped into the clearing together, their pace slow and steady.

Her spine began to itch, a scorpion skittering up her muscles to dig pincers into the base of her skull. She tried to push the sensation aside. Alexis had their backs. She couldn't think of better protection, but the sensation continued to squirm inside her brain. Her eyes began to feel pressure, but she kept both her flashlight and her gun moving. As they got closer to the center, the itching and pressure turned into pain.

Her eyes throbbed and, suddenly, her vision went hazy. She froze. Carley was able to see, but there was a layer of gray fog that dulled the color and sharpness. Time slowed. Aiden turned and spoke, but his words were swallowed by mist. He was both miles away and five feet from her at the same time.

A tall man with moonlit skin appeared behind Aiden. Short locks of rust-colored hair spilled around the twin pools of blood that were his eyes. A red crescent pendant hung from his neck. Carley tried to call out a warning, but she was horrifyingly paralyzed.

The killer's grin was as savage as it was breathtaking, his motions fluid and fast. He slashed across Aiden's neck with a short sword glowing with crimson runes. Aiden's head slipped from his shoulders while Carley could do nothing but watch.

Her heart lurched, but just as rapidly as it had clouded, Carley's vision cleared. The pulse in her throat hammered as her mind tried to process Aiden's death. And yet, he stood looking back at her, alive and whispering her name. Confusion washed through her, but she didn't stop to ponder it.

She ran forward and shoved Aiden to the side just as the man with crimson eyes appeared. Carley's gaze locked with his. She could see his surprise, but his hesitation was no more than a moment. His arm began the swing of his sword. Carley did the first thing that came to mind. She drove her knee into his groin with all the strength she could muster.

* * *

Alexis didn't debate how Carley had seen their prey. She manifested behind the killer just as Carley's knee caught him. He grunted, the direction of his swing altered, but not stopped. She sacrificed a killing blow to catch the elbow of his sword arm to protect Carley. She grabbed the killer's short, red hair as Aiden yanked Carley away. Alexis threw the demon's head toward the ground. Her daggers appeared in her hands as she went in for the kill. He rolled over, raising an arm in defense. "Wait, Commander! Please!"

Though tempted to pause, Alexis followed through. The killer yanked his head to the side, but Alexis' blade still caught him. Blood trickled down his face from a gash in his forehead.

"Please! Do you really not know me?" he pleaded.

The language rolled off her tongue as easily as if she had spoken it the day before. "I don't need to remember you. You are destroying everything I've worked hard to build. It ends now."

"I was sent here to bring you home, Commander. We've been searching for you for so long," the killer replied, desperation in his voice.

"I lead no armies," Alexis growled.

"Oh, but you do. You can't remember anything at all?" the killer asked.

Alexis inwardly cursed. She had given him too much time to talk. After more than five hundred years of wanting, Alexis had to know.

"I remember nothing. Not you, these armies, or this home you speak of. My home is here, and you've almost ruined it."

"Calm down. Everything is going to be okay now. This isn't your home. Just… let me stand up," the killer said as he slowly started to rise.

Alexis kicked him square in the chest to put him flat on his back. "I don't think so. Say your piece from the ground."

"Alright. Alright. My name is Tyrlik. I am your second in command," he replied, glancing at Aiden and Carley.

Alexis formed a ball of ice around her fist and shot it at the ground an inch from his head. "They're not your concern. I am. If you've been searching for me for so long, why have I not encountered more of you? It's not like I'm hiding."

Tyrlik didn't jump when the ice hit the floor beside him. Instead, he calmly returned his attention to her. He was regaining his composure. Alexis didn't like it. She needed him nervous. He was taller than her by several inches. Black armor that looked like leather stretched across broad shoulders and a wide chest. She had a feeling the material was harder than any leather she had encountered. His breast plate was decorated with the head of the same creature that formed the hilt of her daggers. If she really had led armies, perhaps the beast was her crest.

His arms were bare and corded with hard muscle that outmatched her own. Armored leggings protected powerful thighs. Assuming their metaphysical speed and strength were equal, Tyrlik's physical attributes and size would best her. Alexis had to be smarter.

Logic told her to end him now, but her heart pleaded for his knowledge. The desperation to finally know who she was burned in her throat. She looked into his eyes and, for the first time, knew what it was to look on another like her. The last thing she expected to feel was a longing to belong.

"It's very difficult to get here. This realm is hidden from our Seekers. Sending a platoon is not currently possible. We had to wait for a path to open. I was chosen to come because we spent a great deal of time together. You should know me," the killer said.

"Well, I don't. You could have easily approached me in a variety of other ways. Soldiers don't slaughter needlessly."

Tyrlik studied her for an endless moment. "There is a saying that no one is innocent. Everyone commits some act of wickedness and deserves their fate."

"The saying exists, but it doesn't mean it's right. Answer my question. I'm growing impatient."

Tyrlik laughed and shook his head. "You used to make decisions that led to the deaths of innocents every day. Now, you cater to these pitiful creatures when you could rule them. You hide in their world like a coward. You have grown weak without your memory. Soft. Your mother and our Emperor will be disgusted."

Alexis stiffened just slightly. He saw it and grinned. She wasn't sure why his words stung. She had no reason to care what he or her supposed family thought and she couldn't think of a way to validate his words. Yet, the knowledge she would be found lacking made her chest heavy.

"So, what? These murders were some kind of test?" Alexis asked.

His lips curved in a sneer. "In a manner of speaking. I have proved the basic individual you are is flawed. Without your upbringing and centuries of training from the best masters, you are nothing more than a half-breed mongrel. You were never worthy of leadership. Despite all of that, the Emperor would still be displeased if I left you here."

Alexis let the anger of her lost memory harden her heart. He wasn't going to tell her anything of value. He wanted to distract while he gained the upper hand. "Then why even play the game? Go back to where you came from and say I wasn't found. You get your obvious desire to lead and I go back to my own existence."

Tyrlik chuckled at her, eyes alight with jealous malice. "My dear Commander, the Emperor has a weakness for you. He would endlessly search for you..." his toned dropped low, "...unless I brought him evidence of your death."

It was all Alexis needed. He had come to kill her and take whatever position she once held. A bolt of ice flew from her dagger toward his face, but only drove into the concrete where Tyrlik once laid. He had vanished in the blink of an eye.

"Fuck," Alexis muttered.

* * *

It took everything Aiden had not to open fire on both demons. He wanted to trust Alexis, but instead of killing their target, she chose to have a nice, cozy conversation. Worse, he couldn't understand what they were saying. There was no way to determine if she was turning on them. Granted, the tone of her voice held anger and confusion, and she kept her opponent pinned down, but none of it really mattered. Alexis made her choice when she hadn't taken the kill shot while she had the opportunity.

Even given his anger at her betrayal, the thought of scorching her along with her buddy made his skin crawl. He wasn't even sure it would work. She had been cunning to hide the ice from him, but Aiden understood. That was the core problem. He was starting to understand her, and it left him conflicted. Letting a dangerous opponent live didn't seem like her. Yet, she just put a monster's words above his and Carley's safety.

The risk of Alexis changing sides was too great. Killing her would kill Carley, but she was likely better off dead than bound to the life Alexis would give her. The guilt Aiden would carry for the rest of his life would be a fitting punishment for his failures. But Aiden didn't want either Carley or Alexis to die. The battle between logic and emotion left his thumb twitching across the spark of his lighter and he cursed himself for letting Alexis worm her way through his defenses.

When she cursed in English and the frosty mist from her ice bolt cleared, Aiden saw their target was gone. They were back to square one, open and vulnerable. Out of options, he ran to Alexis and put his back to hers. Carley was right on his heels.

"God damn it, Alexis! You had one fucking job. Why couldn't you just waste him?" Aiden demanded.

"Fuck off. You have no idea. I'm still here with you," Alexis replied angrily.

"Stop it, both of you. We still need to live! What do we do?" Carley said.

With their backs together, the enemy was forced to come at their front. It wasn't particularly advantageous. Alexis could vanish again, but Aiden no longer trusted her. Yet, her power still might be all that could save them. He didn't think Carley would get lucky enough to see the killer a second time. Aiden had no choice but to gamble on Alexis.

"I don't know," Aiden admitted.

"He won't run. He needs me dead…" Alexis trailed off for a moment before her tone grew deathly serious. "Aiden, light this whole place on fire."

"Are you fucking nuts?" Aiden asked with disbelief.

"With us inside?" Carley said, her tone as astonished as Aiden's.

"He can't hide. The flames will burn him if he gets too close, the same as it will for us. It will force him to act. We're out of time. Light it up. I can hear the sirens of your back-up."

"It will burn us, too, in case you've forgotten! How do we stop that?" Carley asked, unconvinced.

"Aiden can control the fire and I can shield us with ice if need be."

Understanding her plan, Aiden swore when he could come up with nothing better. "Fine, but your ice better be strong enough to stand the heat."

Aiden sparked his lighter and felt the flame take shape. Fire leaped into his palm and power poured through him. The fire grew until all it demanded was food and freedom. Aiden began to launch streams all around the warehouse.

He encouraged the heat with his energy until it melted the metal cases and began to consume their contents. Aiden released his control, but kept the flames pushed back just far enough to protect his team from severe burns. The warehouse's fire alarm triggered. The sprinkler system activated, but the pipes froze beneath Alexis' power.

"Alexis!" Carley screamed.

Aiden turned in time to watch Carley jump in front of her and take a sword straight through the stomach. Aiden's heart sank like a lead weight.

* * *

Phantom pain exploded through Alexis' core as the sword shoved through Carley. She swore sharply and wrapped one arm around the girl's shoulders. She yanked Carley off the blade and winced when Carley cried out, her blood warm against Alexis' skin.

With a wound as large as Carley's, Tyrlik could kill her with a thought, despite the added durability she possessed from the mark. Once again, Alexis was stuck. She could save Carley and take a potentially deadly blow from Tyrlik or defend herself and have a fighting chance on an even playing field. The decision was automatic.

Alexis spun and took Carley with her, giving her back to Tyrlik. She called to her power over ice and formed a large, hollow sphere in the middle of the clearing. She shoved Carley into it. As she worked to seal Carley inside, she felt Tyrlik step close. Her muscle braced for a blow as she worked to finish the spell.

Out of the corner of her eye, she saw Aiden's fist come straight for her. It was covered in fire, and for a brief moment, she thought she was his intended target. But his gaze was beyond her, so she ducked low and finished the spell to shield Carley. Aiden's fist traveled over her and slammed into Tyrlik's jaw. He grunted and the blow to her back never came.

Aiden's punch wouldn't have done more than superficial damage. If she was lucky, Tyrlik had gotten burned. She didn't want to see Aiden dead and he needed to be alive to finish the job in case she fell. She would protect him for as long as possible.

She stayed low but put a hand to Aiden's chest and shoved him hard enough to send him flying from danger. While crouched, Tyrlik drove his knee toward her head. A frozen mist began to swirl around her body and she blocked the strike with her arm. Frost clung to Tyrlik's armor and she smirked. Even if he vanished now, the frost forged from her power marked him to her sight. He couldn't hide anymore.

She spun her body underneath the elbow he tried to slam into her back and felt the wind from the narrowly evaded attempt. With Aiden and Carley as safe as she could make them, Alexis stood to properly engage.

He wasted no time. His sword came at her face in a vicious backhanded strike. Alexis leaned away to dodge it but wasn't quite fast enough. The tip caught her cheek and pale flesh parted in a small, but gaping wound. It hadn't hurt, but any bleeding injury gave Tyrlik a terrible advantage. Already, the wound bled more than it should. Thick crimson lines poured down Alexis' cheek as if he'd sliced to the bone.

Instead of falling back to defend, Alexis lunged forward into Tyrlik's exposed chest, a strategy forming rapidly in her mind. Her proximity limited his ability to swing the sword at full strength. Shadows joined the swirling sapphire mist, probing Tyrlik's magical defenses for weaknesses.

Her elbow connected solidly with his nose and frost sprayed across his face. He twisted his hips and blocked her attempt to kick his knee, but his thigh became encased in ice. Every time their bodies collided, frost exploded between them. The cold magic slowed Tyrlik's movements and reaction speed.

Immediately capitalizing on the advantage, Alexis sacrificed power in her blows in favor of speed. She moved around Tyrlik's body and peppered him with lightning fast strikes to any opening he gave her. Even blows he parried worked in her favor.

In attempt to strike at Tyrlik's exposed face, Alexis caught his boot to her chest and was knocked back several feet. The blow didn't hurt, but the distance put between them gave him more use of his sword. He flexed his muscles in an attempt to shake off the frost, but her focus was stronger, and the magic clung.

"That bitch of a mother trained you well. Her conniving and manipulative ways taught you cunning," he snarled.

Alexis knew anything he said was meant to bait her. She wanted the information but learned lessons well. She didn't validate him with a response. Her daggers appeared in her hands as he lunged and swung. Their blades sang as they collided in a quick dance of blows. His longer reach gave him an edge, but she was patient. Her ice continued to slow him. She just had to wait for an opening.

It came when she parried an oncoming swing. She turned her dagger to lock her hilt into his sword and she lunged forward into his open chest. Sparks flew as her dagger slid down the length of his blade and she slammed her off-hand weapon underneath his leather spaulder. Alexis brought her face close to his and twisted her blade. Blood poured across her hand as he cried out.

"What's my name?!" she demanded.

When he only laughed, Alexis shoved the blade hilt deep. He grunted, but his malicious grin remained. "How adorable. Of all the things you could ask, you want to know your name. You weren't worthy of it then and you most certainly aren't worthy now."

He drove his head forward in a violent head butt. Alexis saw stars as she fell back a step but maintained enough of her composure to rip her dagger from his shoulder and unlock her other blade from his. He quickly followed with a cross slash, the tip of which sliced her chin before she could dodge.

Alexis saw the back swing coming. She jumped forward and caught the surprise on his face as she shoved her dagger into his wrist with all the force she could muster. Ice encased his entire arm and he dropped the sword. Only his armor saved him from a severed hand.

The disarm left her vulnerable. Tyrlik's hand shot to her face and he cupped the slash on her cheek. She hissed as both wounds widened until they became one gash that followed the line of her jaw. In little more than a second, Alexis was so light-headed she fell to her knees. Blood from his shattered nose stained his teeth as he grinned.

A sizeable portion of her blood solidified in a ball that hovered beside his head. Tyrlik continued to siphon from her, crimson streams dancing up his arm to feed the ever-growing sphere. Alexis' blood pressure plummeted, and weakness overcame her. She heard Carley's voice in her head but couldn't make sense of it.

"The fire was brilliant, and the little Seer was a neat trick. But it still wasn't enough because you just lack what it takes..."

Even as Tyrlik's words echoed in her ears, a single piercing gunshot brought her attention to focus. Tyrlik's hand shook over her wound and gave Alexis a small reprieve from his power. She looked up to find him staring at a gunshot wound to his chest in disbelieving annoyance. She had no strength left to fight him physically. Half her blood was in his possession. But her power hadn't abandoned her.

Her daggers formed from the swirling shadows behind her opponent. With just a thought, Alexis drove the blades straight through his neck. His head fell and bounced off her shoulder to the floor. His power over her faded and the sphere melted and rained blood over her and the ground. Tyrlik's body fell a moment later.

Alexis shivered despite the heat and looked back at Aiden. The barrel of his gun still smoked. She nodded to him. "Thanks for choosing me."

Aiden shrugged and holstered his weapon. "You pushed me and Carley out of danger."

She fought for the energy to stand. He stepped forward, but she waved him away. "Don't. You can't have any of my blood on you when you see your Captain. The fire can burn it away in here, but not off clothes you wear outside. Go help Carley."

He hesitated long enough to make her smile. When he finally turned, Alexis let the sphere of ice around Carley turn to mist. She sat in an expanding puddle of blood, hands pressed to her stomach.

"Fuck, are you okay?" Aiden asked before he took a deep inhale of smoke and had to cough it back out.

"I'm peachy. What the fuck do you think?" Carley managed. The weakness in her voice stole any humor. She was deathly pale. Alexis opened the mark wide and sent down as much energy as she could while still leaving enough for the escape.

"Shit. Alright. I'm going to have to carry you. It's going to suck," Aiden replied.

Carley only groaned in response. Alexis slowly got to her feet just as Aiden lifted Carley. Twin cries of pain caught her attention.

"Aiden, are you alright?" Alexis asked.

"I think you broke some ribs with that shove. I know you didn't mean to, but we need to get out of here. I can't hold the fire back much longer and Carley is heavy when it hurts to stand up straight," he replied.

"One last thing," Alexis said.

Tyrlik's weapon and pendant were not artifacts she wanted to leave behind. They might survive the fire. She bent and retrieved the necklace from the stump of the demon's throat. She held the pendant at eye level and frowned as blood dripped from the crescent.

"Blood on the moon," Aiden said from beside her.

Alexis' frown deepened. "Indeed..."

"What does that mean?" Carley asked. Her head rested against Aiden's shoulder.

"It's an omen many witches, and most other races, believe in," Aiden replied.

"An omen for what?"

"Trouble," Alexis answered. "Blood on the moon is trouble on the horizon."

"I think we've had enough for one night," Carley said softly.

As if the words themselves were an omen, a loud explosion from the warehouse door drew their attention. Alexis sensed the shadows and swore. "It's a fire rescue team with some FDPC. I have to go and you two need to let yourselves be found."

"You'll be okay getting out on your own?" Aiden asked.

"I'll manage. Just try to keep them away from the body and scorch my blood if you have any energy left," she replied.

"Good idea," Aiden said.

"Be careful," Carley said. Her voice was getting weaker.

Alexis merely nodded and faded into the shadows. She lingered only long enough to watch Aiden ignite both the body and any blood in sight before stumbling into the arms of the search and rescue team. Tyrlik's artifacts couldn't follow her into the shadows so she would stick out like a sore thumb if she didn't take the back alleys. Floating swords tended to draw attention.

She glanced one last time at Tyrlik's smoldering corpse. Disappointment washed through her. She had learned just enough to reawaken her bitter lust for the past. It hurt all over again. For that, Alexis hated him. With no real sense of victory, she fled into the night, leaving his body to burn with the rest of the evidence.

EPILOGUE

Alexis hit the end button to terminate the call and tossed her phone on the couch beside her. She took a sip of bourbon and relaxed as she stared at the fire in her hearth. Three days had passed since the warehouse burned to the ground. Alexis was fully healed, but it was the first chance she'd gotten to relax since the battle. The lights were off in the living room and she had left her glasses in her bedroom. The low, flickering firelight suited her mood.

Hope was pressed against her thigh, head in Alexis' lap, snoring softly. She let her fingers slide through the soft fur. Next Monday evening, a dog trainer would be visiting. She and Hope were going to learn to work together. Liz's memory deserved no less. She found herself smiling down at the puppy. Perhaps, when it hurt a little less to look at her, she would grow fond of the dog.

Alexis glanced over at her phone and sighed. Aiden had called to inform her both he and Carley were being released from the hospital. Aiden said there wasn't much the medical professionals could do for his ribs. They were not badly broken. Time and rest would give a full recovery. Carley, on the other hand, recovered faster than anyone anticipated. The surgery to treat her wound had gone well. The stitches would be removed in another day or two.

The news hadn't surprised Alexis, though she expressed concern that Carley's spontaneous healing abilities would attract the wrong kind of attention. Possessing demonic endurance would be frowned upon. Aiden assured her he'd covered it. When brought to his attention, Aiden told his Captain that Carley had been stabbed by a sword enchanted with blood magic. Not all blood magic had negative effects. Some was used for healing. Remnants of the missing blade's power aided Carley's recovery. It wasn't a complete lie and it protected both Carley's newly discovered seer abilities and Alexis' mark.

The record for the warehouse had also been set. Aiden and Carley had been scouting buildings owned by Alexis hoping for some blind luck and found it. They got caught in a battle between two different demons. Both detectives sustained injuries. Once the building caught fire from the power of the unknown opponent, the suspect was slain. The victor neither helped nor hurt them. He took the suspect's weapon and vanished.

Aiden and Carley had barely escaped the flames. Captain Devant apologized for not sending in back-up, but he couldn't justify the lives of a whole task force for two unresponsive officers. Devant's crew wasn't trained for burning buildings. He'd waited for the fire department to send his team in with them. Naturally, Aiden and Carley understood. What little ashes remained of the suspect were secured. The case was considered closed.

Except, for Alexis, it wasn't. If anything, Tyrlik's death brought more questions than it answered. It brought back anger and frustration she'd put to rest centuries ago. She couldn't imagine herself leading an army. She was capable but lacked the desire. Alexis wasn't a solider.

She still didn't know where she'd come from, or even her name. The longing to know who she was and where she belonged ripped through the old scar and burned fresh in her chest.

Alexis looked down at the coffee table where Tyrlik's pendant and sword rested. His first message implied others were looking for her, but they couldn't see into the world where she lived. Despite learning her pendant was a tool of communication, it still wasn't useful to her. She had to know the individual she was attempting to contact, or at the very least, know something about them. Yet she didn't know anyone. Her connection with Tyrlik had been blind luck. Even with the feeble bits of knowledge she obtained, she was no better off than when she'd started.

Alexis sighed and set her glass on a coaster. In all reality, her situation had not changed. She resided in the only home she had. Who she was now and what she had built were all that mattered. The past was just as unobtainable as before. Alexis liked who and where she was. She had no choice but to stitch up the old scar and move on.

She stood to pick up the sword and the crescent pendant. As she started to head to the bedroom, Hope yawned and scrambled off the couch to follow her on sleepy, unsteady paws. Alexis turned into her room and waited for the dog to pass before closing the door. She had Terry lower the weapons safe from the ceiling.

Alexis set the sword in a rack and hung the pendant from it. Both items would be secure and out of the wrong hands. She sent the safe back up and turned off any thoughts of the past.

Her present and her future were heading in new, unplanned directions. Alexis turned to the window and parted the curtain to look out over the city. Already, a local werewolf pack had contacted her for a meeting. Alexis had no doubt more requests would come. She had no need or desire to grant their wishes. Alexis planned to send her refusal soon. The wolves wouldn't like her answer. She didn't care. Alexis refused to cater to the petty politics of the different factions, even if that made her more enemies than friends.

She didn't know what to do with Aiden. Their powers had mixed and blended. There was chemistry between them. But the only thing they had in common was Carley. Aiden didn't fit her life. While she was intrigued by their connection, it wasn't enough to push for more. He was the image of the fire he tried to bend to his will. Wild. Unpredictable. All-consuming. Aiden had his uses, and that is where Alexis planned to keep him.

Carley was a separate problem entirely. Her power as a seer had manifested in the warehouse. No one would have survived without her. But now that Carley's power was active, visions would become more frequent. And more vivid. She needed to learn control, otherwise she would succumb to one at a crime scene and be identified. Neither she nor Alexis needed more trouble from the FDPC. Alexis had more than her fill of the authorities. Carley's training needed to begin sooner rather than later.

There was also the matter of the mysterious individual who had bound Carley's power. There must be a story behind that. Someone would come for Carley… and Alexis had no intention of letting the detective fall.

She glanced up at the skyline above the city. The moon peeked out above the tallest buildings. City lights colored the wispy clouds with rust. She shook her head. Blood on the moon, indeed. Trouble was coming. Alexis would be ready for it.

ABOUT THE AUTHOR

Courtney lives in Phoenix, Arizona, with her dog Ellie. She works as a surgical neurophysiologist and enjoys a career that allows her to help others. She's been writing as a hobby since she was old enough to understand how words form sentences.

Outside of work and writing, Courtney loves to explore the world around her, whether it's through hiking, camping, or snowboarding. Fitness of almost any kind motivates her, and archery steals her heart. The world inspires her, and she hopes to share that inspiration through the written word.